EVERY MOTHER'S NIGHTMARE

BOOKS BY S.E. LYNES

Mother

The Pact

Valentina

The Proposal

The Women

The Lies We Hide

Can You See Her?

The Housewarming

Her Sister's Secret

The Baby Shower

The Ex

The Summer Holiday

The Split

The Perfect Boyfriend

EVERY MOTHER'S NIGHTMARE

S. E. LYNES

bookouture

Published by Bookouture in 2025

An imprint of Storyfire Ltd.
Carmelite House
50 Victoria Embankment
London EC4Y 0DZ

www.bookouture.com

The authorised representative in the EEA is Hachette Ireland
8 Castlecourt Centre
Dublin 15 D15 XTP3
Ireland
(email: info@hbgi.ie)

Copyright © S.E. Lynes, 2025

S.E. Lynes has asserted her right to be identified as the author of this work.

All rights reserved. No part of this publication may be reproduced, stored in any retrieval system, or transmitted, in any form or by any means, electronic, mechanical, photocopying, recording or otherwise, without the prior written permission of the publishers.

ISBN: 978-1-83618-652-6
eBook ISBN: 978-1-83618-651-9

This book is a work of fiction. Names, characters, businesses, organizations, places and events other than those clearly in the public domain, are either the product of the author's imagination or are used fictitiously. Any resemblance to actual persons, living or dead, events or locales is entirely coincidental.

For Kim Nash, Sue Watson and Emma Robinson, my same-time-next-year therapists, WhatsApp cheerleaders, champion cheese consumers and all-round fabulous author pals, with love.

PART I

ONE

MELISSA

The day after

The call comes in at four. It is the call Melissa Connor has been expecting, the one she has been dreading.

It is a humid late-June afternoon. The staff office at Arlington Road Primary hums with the smell of stale coffee and struggling perfume. Apart from extreme tiredness and the bone-softening heat of the poorly air-conditioned space, there is nothing particularly unusual about this fuggy summer Monday at the fag-end of the school year, save for the fact that both Melissa's kids, Dan and Casey, are away from home.

Melissa is typing up a parents' letter. It is from the head and concerns a bullying incident in which the notorious Jamie Fisher punched three Year 5 girls in the chest, apparently *to see if their boobs had come in*. Ten years old. Ten. The head wishes politely to encourage parents to talk to their boys about respect and to ensure that internet access is supervised.

Melissa is doing her best to avoid typos, acknowledging office manager Alice Brierley's monologue on her marital problems with occasional nods and hmms while simultaneously ignoring the dark thoughts swirling in her head.

Her phone is in her bag. She can almost feel it pulsating, waiting. Her kids are too old for this kind of vigilance, she knows that, of course she does, but frankly she wishes she could keep the damn thing on her desk where she can see it.

As it is, all she can do is pretend to listen to Alice and try not to think about Summer Camp, the traditional weekend when the local teenagers trek to somewhere near Weymouth, pilgrim-like, to celebrate the end of their A levels. After all the hard work and stress, it's only right that they should be... *letting their hair down* is the phrase Melissa has been using, although she's aware it makes her sound ancient. *Losing their virginity* is the pithier version her friend Sarah chose on Friday evening over too many Proseccos and a Chinese takeaway. *Two hundred inebriated eighteen-year-olds and a bonfire party by the sea. What could possibly go wrong?* Sarah had meant to be reassuring; Melissa had laughed along. The beach party was last night. Melissa hasn't slept a wink.

The moment she hears the buzzing, her senses prick. Here it comes, she thinks. Here it is.

Bzz. Bzz. Bzz.

'Sorry,' she says to Alice, diving into the mess of her handbag. 'Better get this.'

Thankfully, Alice backs away, waving her hand. *Of course; go ahead.*

Melissa pulls out the phone and stares at it. Tension rises like mercury. An unknown number. This is how it happens.

Her breath hitches.

'Hello?'

'Melissa Connor?' It is a woman's voice: young, earnest, West Country accent.

'Speaking,' Melissa manages.

'Mrs Connor, I'm PC Belinda Riley. I'm a family liaison officer with Weymouth Police. I—'

'Police?' Melissa's voice sounds like someone has her by the throat. Sweat pricks at her hairline, rolls from her armpits. But this is the script. This is what she'd known she would say, almost from the day her daughter was born. 'Is everything OK? Has something happened?' *Something bad. Something bad has happened.*

'Mrs Connor, if I could ask you to just—'

'Sorry. Sorry.' Melissa's elbows hit the desk; her clammy hand closes over her mouth.

'I'm calling regarding your daughter, Casey.'

'Casey,' she whispers. In her peripheral vision, Alice frowns and mouths, *Everything all right?* Melissa dips her head, fingers now shielding her eyes, the wood veneer of her desk misting.

'Firstly, your daughter's all right. OK?' The cop's voice is kind. 'There's nothing life-threatening or life-changing.'

'Nothing life... What? Oh my God.' Melissa makes herself breathe.

'She's not seriously injured, but she's sustained a fair bit of bruising and was found in a state of some confusion earlier this afternoon by a member of staff at Heaven View campsite—'

'Found? What do you mean, *found*? Sorry, I... Sorry.'

'I know this is difficult, but stay calm for me. She's been taken to Dorset County Hospital. They're checking her over as we speak.'

Nausea rolls in. Grabbing her bag from the back of her chair, Melissa stands. Vaguely, she is aware of the dull hubbub of the office falling into silence. 'Do you know... do you know what happened?'

'She can't remember much at the moment, but I'm afraid she was found in a state of undress by one of the site staff.'

'Undress?' Melissa's throat strangles a sob.

The cop hesitates a moment before continuing. 'She didn't

know where she was or how she got there. Apparently, the staff member was clearing the site when he found her. The kids come with their pop-up tents, you see, and they just leave them behind with the rest of their rubbish when they go.'

'Y-Yes. So, Casey... was she found in her tent? In... in the staff quarters?'

'I don't think so, no. She was in general camping, I believe.'

'But she was staff. She was working there.'

'Mrs Connor,' the cop cuts in. 'Are you able to get here?'

'Of course, yes. I'm packing up now.' Holding the phone to her ear with her shoulder, Melissa glances at Alice, whose forehead furrows with concern. Melissa turns away. This is all too painful, too private to be happening here; she feels like she's being watched by a thousand eyes. 'So,' she says, voice low, 'do you know whose tent she was in?'

'I'm afraid I don't have all the information at this time. As I say, she didn't know where she was or how she'd got there or why her clothes were missing.'

'Her clothes were... Wait a second. Sorry, I... Can you give me a second?'

'Sure.'

Cradling the phone to her chest, Melissa closes her eyes. Nightmare, she thinks. This whole situation is every mother's nightmare. But today she's not every mother, she's *that* mother, the one on the news, the one you look at and think: *Thank God that isn't me*.

She opens her eyes and turns back to Alice.

'Everything OK?' Alice asks.

'It's Casey. There's been... She's in hospital.'

'Oh my God. Over in Dorset?'

'Can you finish the bullying awareness letter? It has to go out tonight.'

Alice nods, eyes wide. 'Of course. Off you go.'

Melissa gives a brief smile of thanks. Without a backwards

glance, she hurries out of the office, as if by pretending to be invisible, she will somehow make it happen.

In the entrance hall, she returns to the phone, to Riley. 'Sorry. I'm just leaving. It's a three-hour drive, give or take. I should be there by seven, seven thirty.' She places her hand over the exit button, waits for the click and pushes open the heavy door, wonders if she sounds normal, if she sounds too together or too freaked out. 'Can you tell me... Was she... I mean, she hasn't been...'

'As I said, that's all I can tell you at the moment. She's in good hands, and they're checking her over and taking her bloods.'

'Bloods? You mean testing? What for?'

There's a pause. 'Why don't we talk when you get here? I won't be leaving your daughter's side, don't you worry. If you make your way to A and E and give her name at reception, they'll point you in the right direction. Oh, and you might want to bring a change of clothes for her. Drive safe.'

'Wait.' Melissa takes a shallow breath. 'Hello?'

But the line is dead.

TWO
CASEY

The day after

'Casey. Mate. Wake up. Wake up. Can you open your eyes?'
What? Hot. It's so hot.
'Casey? CC? Can you hear me, matey?'
Spider? Is that you? She's not sure she's said it out loud. Her eyes are closed, but she can't figure out how to open them. Swirling echoes of light on her eyelids. It's so hot. She's boiling.
'Casey? Casey?'
Spider is calling her by her name. He never calls her by her name.
'Spider?' Her voice is a croak.
'Mate.' The word is long and full of relief. 'Oh, matey. You gave me a fair old cardiac attack there.' His educated accent, an accent you don't expect when you first see him, an accent at odds with his funny way of talking. 'Can you get those peepers open for me? You don't have to if you don't want to. Everything's tickety-boo. Just take it slow. Easy does it. Spider's right here. You're all right.'
Why is he telling her she's all right?

A jarring rasp. She flinches, screws her eyes tighter.

Spider's voice comes again, louder this time. 'Miss London, can you come in ASAP, please. Spider here. Come in ASAP, please. It's urgent, over.'

Urgent. Casey shifts. Her body hurts. Her neck, her arms. Her throat is dry, so dry. 'Spider?'

'I'm right here. Can you open your eyes? Don't worry if you can't.'

She is trembling suddenly. Her whole body is juddering from head to toe. Spider has his arm round her. His hand tightens on her shoulder.

'Hey, hey,' he says softly. 'Easy does it. You're all right.'

'Spider?' She sounds so small. Like she's speaking from far away. 'Where am I?'

'You're at Heaven View. You're in a tent.'

'I'm too hot.'

His arm is thin but heavy, his warm, rough fingertips on the top of her arm. The smell of woodsmoke and patchouli, roll-ups, green.

'Spider.' The shaking is in her voice too. She sounds like a frog with a sore throat. Water. She needs water.

'I'm right here, matey. Can you open your eyes? Slowly. It's OK. You're OK. Let's get the old peepers open and we can get you out into the air.'

'I need water.'

'Gotcha. I'll get you some water, don't worry.'

Another spark, like a cough, a tinny voice over a walkie-talkie. 'Spider, this is Candy. What's happening? Over.'

Casey squeezes her eyes tight. The light mutates to purples, muddy greens, yellow flashes. Sweat runs down the side of her face.

Spark. 'We have a situation. I've just found Casey Connor in one of the abandoned tents in general camping. She's disorientated, and she has bruising to the neck and arms. She's conscious, but we need an ambulance and police pronto. Over.'

Spark. 'Bloody hell. Is she OK? Over.'

Spark. 'Nothing broken, I don't think. Can you call emergency services? Police and ambulance. Over.'

Bruises. Bruises on her neck and arms. Something is about to land. A rock, a meteor above her head, falling towards her. It's coming for her. She can feel the cool of its shadow spreading around her. She forces her eyelids apart, strains against the rushing light. Too much light. Too bright. She closes her eyes again. Tears run out, trickle down her cheeks.

Spark. 'Will do.' Miss London's voice. 'Where are you? Over.'

Casey tries again. Filters the light through her eyelashes this time, opens slowly, slowly halfway. Green. Everything is green. She's so hot. She's burning up.

Spark. 'Pale green two-man Decathlon.' Spider's voice. Beside her. 'Two thirds down the field, about two metres from the pathway. Over.'

Spark. 'Roger that.' Miss London. 'Stay there. Over.'

Spark. 'I'm gonna have to move her out of the tent. She's dehydrated and it's too hot in here. We need water and shade, over.'

Spark. 'OK. Over.'

Casey blinks her sticky eyes. Spider is bathed in green. He is smiling at her with his funny teeth, his funny wispy beard, his eyes all the colours of ferns in autumn.

'You had me going there, Coppadin,' he says.

At the sound of her nickname, more tears fall. She sniffs.

'Hey. It's OK. I've got you.'

'I...' She becomes aware of her belly, air on the skin. She looks down. Her stomach is bare. She can see her pants, her legs, filthy feet, her flip-flops just beyond. She's wearing a high-vis waistcoat. There's a fleecy top on the floor beside her hand. It's not hers. 'Oh my God,' she says. 'Where are my clothes?'

'It's OK,' Spider says gently. 'I found you. Only me. I covered you up straight away. I didn't look. I promise I didn't look.'

She starts to cry hard now. Spider's arm tightens around her shoulders. He's seen her like this. How mortifying. But also, somewhere, she's glad it was him. She leans into him, her friend. Her funny, weird pal. Her hands float up to her chest; she glances down at the neon yellow, the hard nylon of Spider's staff jacket. Spider has seen her naked but for her pants. Her face burns. All of her feels like she's on fire.

'Don't worry about it,' he says simply. 'Can you remember what happened? Who you were with? Did you partake of something illegal by any chance? I won't tell anyone. I'm not judging.'

'Nothing. Honest.' She shakes her head; feels Spider tense against her.

'The emergency services are on their way,' he says. 'They'll need to check you out.'

Darkness pools inside her. Soft ground. The rustle of leaves. The roar of the sea. The burnt smell of bonfire. What is in the darkness? Who? What can't she remember?

THREE

DAN

The day after

Dan wakes with a thumping headache and a sandpaper mouth.

'Oh, man.' Blinking open crusty eyes, tongue churning, trying to work up saliva. Above him, a passing breeze rattles the thick white canopy of the teepee. He is on top of his sleeping bag. He is fully dressed. He shifts onto his side, groaning. Sees the others, caterpillars in their quilted cocoons.

The floor is a mess of crushed cans, bottles, cold leftover noodles stinking in half-collapsed cartons, socks, trainers, sliders, rumpled clothes, an empty baggie. A packet of condoms, unopened. By his feet, a crushed Evian bottle.

'Gross.' Grimacing with disgust, he sits up and scratches his head.

The stifling air in the tent is a miasma of stale alcohol, feet, grease, garlic, BO. He wonders if air can have an alcohol percentage; if what he's breathing is, like, thirty per cent proof. He closes his eyes. He needs a bacon roll. A bacon roll and some water. A bacon roll, some water and some serious painkillers. Coffee. No. The thought of coffee makes him feel sick.

One of the guys farts – long and loud, like a sigh.

'Jesus,' he mutters, feeling around for his Nikes. He has to get out of here. Get some fresh air.

He finds his trainers and pulls them on; notices as he does so that his knuckles are burgundy. It's blood. Dried blood.

His vision clouds. He pushes his hands through his hair. What the hell happened? Why are... why *were* his hands bleeding? Just how wasted was he last night?

Instinctively, he looks over at Byrne's bunk. In contrast to the rest of the tent, Byrne's sleeping bag is rolled up like an army pack, the zip of his leather monogrammed travel bag a toothy brass line running parallel. Beneath, his trainer heels press together: brilliant, immaculate white.

'Shit,' Dan whispers, rubbing his thumb lightly over the grazes, which have not yet scabbed hard and are still a bit sticky. He feels for his phone. Finds it in his shorts pocket. Checks it.

Dead.

Plugging it into his portable charger, he glances again at Byrne's empty bedding, a pit forming in his stomach. Where is he? He's obviously not been back all night. If he'd seen the tent in this state, he'd have lost it.

Outside, the grass is dry, the sun high, beating down. Gulping at the fresh air, Dan straightens the rumpled roll of himself and almost blacks out. He leans forward, presses his hands to his knees, waits for the dizziness to pass before stretching, slowly this time. The sky is blue. It's hot. Another hot day. Must be after midday. He has no idea where the hours have gone, what time he got to bed. It will come to him. He just needs to wake up, get his shit together.

Casey appears in his mind's eye: her angry scowl.

'Shit,' he whispers to himself. The pit in his stomach tightens. There was an argument. They never argue, but last night they did. Yes, definitely, that definitely happened. Nausea rolls in, causing him to heave. Another memory – drinking warm cider, the feeling that this was one drink of many. Someone offering to put a splash of vodka in the can, him holding it out – *Cheers, mate. Go for it.* Jesus, the drinks must've gone straight to his head. His new-found fitness has turned him into a lightweight.

The thought of falling out with his sister is horrible. He should check on her. He has the feeling he needs to apologise. Did he see her after they argued? What were they arguing about? Another wave of nausea, the popping black spots of low blood sugar. He can remember looking for her, his trainers bright flashes on the dark tarmac path, the smooth rhythm of them hypnotic. God, he must have been flying. That must have been afterwards. He can't remember finding her.

He swallows hard, his throat dry. Casey had a shift today, he's pretty sure, up at the clubhouse. He sets off, squinting against the sun, wishing he'd grabbed his shades, his baseball cap. Chill, he tells himself. Casey's fine. She'll be at work. There's no way she'd flake. Neither would he. Reliability, responsibility, respect... drummed into them both since birth: his dad, all but absent through their teenage years, held up as a shining example of what happens when you adhere to none of the above. Dad is a strained weekly phone catch-up, twice-yearly beers in front of the social crutch of a football match, a collection of photos long deleted from Mum's phone. It's been the three of them for so long, looking out for each other. Mum thinks Dan didn't catch the suppressed delight on her face when he told her he and the lads from the pub were going to Summer Camp.

'You'll look after her, won't you?' Pretty much the last words she said.

'Of course I will.'

But he wasn't going to watch his sister every second, was

he? She's eighteen. And besides, she didn't want him to. She made that crystal clear. He stops in his tracks.

That's what the argument was about.

His sister had been talking to Byrne by the bonfire. When they saw him, they sprang away from each other like they'd been caught doing something they shouldn't.

'Hey, bro.' Byrne's eyes jumping from her to Dan as he stepped away, the palms of his hands flashing pink in the hazy dark. 'Catcha later, yeah.'

Dan mumbling something like, 'Yeah, sweet. No worries.'

Once Byrne was far enough away not to hear, Dan saw red. 'What the hell?'

Did he grab Casey's arm? Did he do that? Did he speak to her like that, grab her arm like that? He thinks so. Can sort of feel himself doing it.

Oh God.

His sister. Saucers for eyes. He could tell she'd been drinking, maybe even taken something. 'What d'you mean, what the hell?'

'He's twenty-fucking-six,' Dan hissed. 'Way too old for you. And he's not... he's not nice, all right? He's not a nice guy.'

'Why are you friends with him then?' She shook his hand off, fury in her face. 'You can't tell me who to talk to. What are you even doing here anyway? It's like you're spying on me or something. Get a life, will you? God, you're pathetic.'

Pathetic. That pissed him off. In the cold light of the day after, he can see it was because it was true. But what he said was true too: Byrne Sharp is not a nice guy. It's taken this weekend for him to truly realise that.

Dan's head spins. Park that thought. Deal with it later. First, he needs something to eat and to lay eyes on his kid sister, even if she doesn't want to lay eyes on him. God, how he wishes he hadn't grabbed her arm like that. Hadn't walked off in a rage.

Despite the heat, he shivers. The sun is blazing down now.

He should go back and get his cap, but he can't be arsed. The air smells of burnt wood. He suspects the bonfire's embers are still glowing down at the beach, floating up to the campsite in little black flakes. Maybe Casey's on the sand, crashed out. Maybe she found her toxic mates. Whatever, she'd better be up at the bar.

His phone buzzes into life. He checks the time: 1.30 p.m. Later than he thought. All those hours, fallen away. In the top field, the luxury chalets look dead. Thin music trickles from somewhere. In the teepee field, a dozy body is shambling towards the shower block, hair sticking up at the back, towel over one arm. The lower field is about a third empty already. Anyone staying past midday has to pay for another night, so those on a budget will have moved on an hour or two ago. If it's anything like it was back in 2018, any tents left now will be mostly abandoned.

He wishes he'd never come back. He's too old.

As he nears the top of the rise, where the so-called clubhouse stands sentinel over the site, his texts load. A long line of messages from last night, all from him to his sister.

Where are you?

Case? You OK?

Call me when you get this.

I'm going to bed, but call me or text and let me know you're OK, yeah?

Case. I'm sorry. Text me.

On the far side of the site, creamy sunlight winks on the sea. Dan stares at it a moment. Somewhere in his brain, a distant alarm bell sounds.

Five texts he sent.

Why didn't she text back?

FOUR
DAN

The day after

He calls his sister, but she doesn't pick up. Minutes later, he's at the clubhouse, scanning for her. At the outdoor tables, kids are drinking lattes, puffing on vapes. They look like children acting in a play about grown-ups. A young girl eyes him shyly, and he feels himself blush. He's had a lot more attention since he started working out, but this girl looks no older than seventeen. He doesn't want that kind of attention. When he met Livvy in halls, they were friends for ages before they even kissed. It hurts to think of Livvy. It all hurts so much, and right now it feels like he's been hurting for a long, long time.

Why the hell did he come here? Why did he even give Byrne and his stupid knuckle-dragger mates the time of day?

'Hi,' the girl says and smiles as he passes by.

He returns her smile so she doesn't feel bad, but doesn't stop, heading instead for the bar. There's no sign of his sister, only a dude with a bum-fluff beard, hooded eyes and a resort shirt that's seen better days, wiping glasses with a tea towel.

Dan raises a hand. The dude tips his chin.

'Yo,' Dan says, resolving in that moment never to say that stupid word again. 'Is Casey here? Casey Connor?'

The dude shakes his head. 'She didn't show.'

'Seriously?' Dan's chest hurts like someone's just kicked him there. 'Did she text? Did she call in sick? I mean, have you heard from her?'

'Nah, mate. She ain't here.'

A burning feeling in his gut. In the distance, he thinks he hears sirens. Trying not to panic, not to put those sirens and his sister together, he speed-walks back the way he came, legs pumping as he passes the chalets, eyes flitting as he searches for a messy shock of pink hair. At the teepees, he sees only three nerdy kids with Mohicans and fake tattoos passing a joint between them, then down to the mess of general camping, what Byrne calls the losers' enclosure. There is litter everywhere, like, seriously, everywhere. Rumpled clothes, cans, camping chairs, bags of food, shoes, sliders. At the far side, a super-skinny guy in a high-vis waistcoat, a walkie-talkie in his hand, is standing by one of the tents. It looks like the guy he's seen with Casey a few times picking up litter – Spud or Spade or Spider or something. Nearer to the tarmac track, two girls in bikini tops and cut-off shorts are chatting, one holding a tiny mirror while the other applies make-up. As he passes, one of them wolf-whistles. When he turns, they both collapse in hysterics. But he's not in the mood. He needs to find his sister.

Mouth filling with bitter saliva, he breaks into a jog. Seconds later, he's racing down the sandy track that leads through the dunes to the beach. The bonfire is a blackened circle of embers, still smouldering with the last of their heat. Around it, a handful of kids are asleep under blankets. The sea is almost flat, glittering in the early-afternoon sun. If he wasn't so stressed, he'd wade in and go for a long swim. But he has to find Casey.

He climbs back over the dunes to the site, his belly churning with a fear that intensifies by the minute. Should he dial 999? No, that's too intense.

Staff camping.

'Idiot,' he sighs. Why didn't he think of the most logical place? She's slept in, that's all.

Yes. In her tent. That's where she'll be. He'll go there now.

FIVE
CASEY

The day after

Casey is sitting on a camping chair on the grass outside the pale green tent. A paramedic is shining a thin torch into her left eye. Now into her right. She has already asked Casey what her name is, how many fingers she was holding up. Spider said she should've stayed in the tent, really, for evidence, but she was burning up, claustrophobia making her hyperventilate. It's such a relief to be out, but the sun is high and it feels like it's burning her.

The tiniest breeze whispers through the tall trees on the far side of the path. She lifts her face while the woman takes her pulse; feels the sweat cool on her forehead. Her face is sticky and gross. There is something rotten inside her; she can feel it. She breathes in deeply. Tries not to freak out. Her exhale shudders out like rocks. Her heart keeps doing little runs, like an engine being revved. She wonders if the paramedic is picking it up, but her face is unreadable. Spider shouted for a chair, before. There was a crowd of people, but the policeman moved them back. She saw Olive and Ethan. Olive's face crumpled up. *Oh my God, are you OK?* Then she turned to one of the police officers. *Is she OK? What happened?* The police told everyone to stay right back. She's not sure now how long they've been here. They came before the ambulance, she thinks. It's all a jumble.

A guy she doesn't recognise appears with a big parasol. 'Give her some shade, yeah?'

Spider is back too, loping a little way behind. 'Cheers, my friend,' he says. 'Much obliged to you, sir.'

Spider pushes the parasol through the gap in the camping chair and stakes it into the ground. The shade is bliss. The water he hands her is liquid coolness, literally. She gulps it. Someone is radioing for a SOCO, but she doesn't know what that is. Miss London was here too, before. Casey's pretty sure she heard her voice. Someone else, a policewoman, she thinks, asked Miss London if there was CCTV.

'Only up at the clubhouse,' Miss London said. 'I can get the tape to you.'

Casey drifts. Time has passed – seconds or minutes, she can't say. She drinks more water. The flask is a pale blue thermal one with H_2O on the front in a gold handwritten font. The water is so cool and she is so thirsty, she feels like she could drink forever, like if she drinks enough she'll be able to close her eyes and let herself float away, away, out to sea, away from all this. Her neck hurts. Her arms are smudged with bruises. The back of her head hurts too. The paramedic put a dressing on it. She feels like she's full of darkness, like the darkness inside her is solid, like if she peeled off her skin, there would be just a black statue: no bones, no blood, no heart.

'I put my jacket on her to preserve her modesty,' Spider is saying now to a female police officer, who is writing everything down on a notepad. There are three officers, she thinks. Spider's voice cuts through the background hubbub, teenagers rubbernecking, gossiping. 'And I put my arm round her, but only because she was shaking. That was it. I thought we should stay in the tent, but it was too hot. I was worried about dehydration.'

'Don't worry,' the cop says, and, 'You did your best.'

The crackle of a radio. The tent is being cordoned off, a ribbon of tape rolling out. Another police officer, a man, emerges from the tent with transparent plastic bags. In one is an empty water bottle; in another her phone, then her flip-flops; in another what looks like baby wipes or tissues; the last bigger – a navy-blue fleece. The bags are labelled, but she can't see what they say. Jesus, what the hell happened?

'Great,' a female police officer says. She's the same one who was talking to Spider just now. 'And we'll need the tent and the victim's clothing.'

Clothing? What clothing?
Victim? Of what?

'I can take the tent down for you,' Spider says. 'Whatever you need.'

'It's OK. We'll do it. And we'll need you to come to the station later and make a formal witness statement.'

'Course.' Spider nods. Casey can tell by the way he's digging into his jeans pockets that he's dying for a roll-up. Not talking in riddles will have been a strain.

Her heart revs again. She closes her eyes. But her breath shortens and her mind fills with leaves fluttering black against bright moonlight. She can hear their rustle and hiss, sense something, something bad. She gasps, opens her eyes to the paramedic.

'Are you OK?' the woman asks.

'Yeah. Yeah, fine. I'm fine.'

'Breathe,' she says, crouching in front of her, her irises dark and round against the whites, tiny red scribbles of veins. She holds Casey's wrists lightly, her thumbs brown against the pale underside of Casey's arms, her nails short and clean. The bruises look as if someone has grabbed her with sooty hands. The ambulance lady breathes deeply to show her what she means. 'In through your nose, out through your mouth,' she says and repeats it like a poem. 'Breathe with me. That's it. Breathe in. And breathe out. You're doing great. You're going to be OK.'

Casey matches her breath for breath until she starts to feel self-conscious. The woman feels suddenly too close.

'I'm OK,' she says, withdrawing her wrists from the woman's grip but attempting a smile, worried about offending her. 'Can I call my mum? Or my brother? My brother's on the site somewhere.'

'Do you have your phone?'

She casts about her, as if the ground will offer up her iPhone. But no, she doesn't have her phone or her Havaianas – they're in evidence bags. God knows where her clothes are. 'No,' she says. 'I don't.'

'We'll get in touch with them, don't worry.'

'I don't know their numbers off by heart. Can you find my brother? His name is Daniel Connor. And I need my mum. Melissa Connor. She'll be at work. She works at Arlington—'

'Try not to worry about any of that now.' The paramedic stands up. 'The FLO will get all that from you. That's the family liaison officer, all right? OK, lovely, let's get you into the ambulance.'

Beyond the cordon, another police officer is moving people along with lazy sways of his hand. *Keep walking. What's happened? You'll find out soon enough. Can you tell us what's happened? Move along. Oh my God, has someone been hurt?*

'Hey, matey.' It's Spider. The sight of his kind eyes makes her own fill. 'Can you walk?'

Behind him is a stretcher-type thing on wheels.

'I don't need that,' she says. 'I can walk. I want to walk.'

The policewoman takes her arm. It's more difficult than she thought it would be to stand. She is so stiff, all over, and her legs are shaking. Slowly, she is led up the hill. A stone of dread lodges in her belly. It's like she's done something wrong. Like she's being arrested. Like she's in deep trouble.

SIX

DAN

The day after

At the bottom of general camping, tarmac turns to dried mud as it passes under a five-bar gate. On the gate is a handwritten sign: *Staff Camping. Keep Out.* A rough daub of a skull and crossbones in white paint. Casey will be crashed out, hung-over. She'll be mortified to have slept through her shift, even more furious with him for checking on her. But he'll take whatever she wants to throw at him; the only thing he cares about right now is that she's OK. Maybe she got with Byrne when she was a bit out of it, but she'll have come to her senses and told him where to go by now, seen him for the creep he is. Hopefully. Hopefully she never got with him at all. Hopefully he won't be in her tent with her, oh God, please, no. But even that he can take as long as she's there.

At the gate, he stops. He's already been here. The memory is certain and hazy all at once. He remembers this skull and crossbones. Yes. He was here. That skinny dude with the neck tattoo, the one who was up at the tents just now, asked what the hell he was doing. It was only when Dan said he was looking for

Casey, that Casey was his sister, that the guy seemed to change his mind.

'You can check her tent,' he said through peg teeth. 'But I ain't seen her.'

The tattoo was a web. Spider. His name must be Spider.

Now, heart in his mouth, Dan pushes open the gate, the memory lodged in his muscles: pushing this gate, the damp darkness, the smells – woodsmoke and something else, maybe patchouli or some herb or other – a woman with a long blonde plait feeding a baby by the fire, himself looking for his sister, his belly a fist. Now, again, looking for her a second time, the same fingers of angst curled and tight inside him, the same rising dread.

It's like time is repeating itself.

He walks further in, eyes darting about in case someone spots him and shouts at him to go away. The fire pit is low, a burnt kettle hanging over it from a makeshift tripod. There's no sign of the hippy woman, no sign of anyone. Last night, Spider showed him to the two-man tent Dan himself had slept in when he came to Summer Camp the first time, the one he'd used a few years later to go Interrailing with Rory. Now, he kicks himself. If he hadn't spaffed all his money up the wall, he'd have been able to lend Casey enough to rent the chalet with her friends and she would never have had to get a job here.

He kneels in front of her tent. Please God, let Byrne not be in it. He unzips the door, but before he even pulls it open, he knows it's empty.

Last night, her tent was empty. Now, today, it is still empty. Time repeating, taunting him.

'Oi!' A woman is striding towards him. 'What the hell do you think you're doing? This is a private area.'

'Sorry!' He throws up his hands. 'I'm looking for my sister. She hasn't been in touch since last night and she didn't turn up for her shift. The guy said it was OK. Spider. He said I could look.'

At the white lie, the woman visibly softens. She's the one who was feeding her baby last night, but she looks different with her hair tucked in a hat, a bit too old to have such a tiny baby. 'Casey, you mean? I'm sure she'll be fine.'

'It's not like her to not show for a shift.'

The woman takes in the information with a slow, considered nod. Improbably, she lifts a walkie-talkie from her faded red cloth bag and speaks into it. 'Spider? Spider, it's Ness, come in, over.'

Fixing Dan with her pale blue eyes, crow's feet white against her suntanned skin, she speaks into the radio again: 'Spider? Can you hear me? Casey's brother's here lookin' for her. Says she didn't show for her shift this morning. Can you keep an eye out for her? Cheers, over.'

They wait. There is no reply.

With a frown, the woman drops the radio back into the pouch. 'Not like him not to answer. But he should be in general camping because they were clearing leftover tents from midday. Why don't you try there?'

'Thank you,' Dan says. 'I think I saw him there actually.'

Ness nods. 'If I see her, I'll tell her you're looking for her. You got a mobile she can call?'

'Yeah. Cheers.' He pulls out his phone, raising it above his head by way of goodbye.

The woman returns to where the kettle puffs above the fire pit. He wonders how she came to be here, what her life is, what any of these lives are, so different from his own. They are nomads, he guesses, though how anyone ends up like them is a mystery to him.

Beyond the gate, the site rises ahead, the sea to his back. He's about to check his phone again, but there's crowd of kids on the path and two... Wait, are they police officers? The air is electric. Something has happened. Something bad. Pocketing his phone, Dan quickens his pace. At the top of the rise, in front of reception, an ambulance is pulling away. With a forlorn wail, it disappears.

Dan breaks into a run.

'Excuse me,' he mutters, pushing through the kids to the police. ''Scuse me, sorry, I...'

At the front of the crowd is a line of incident tape. A police officer holds up a hand. 'Stay back, please.'

'I...'

He sees Spider heading back down the hill. He's not wearing his high vis anymore, just a ratty T-shirt that's coming away at the neck. Kids are holding up their phones, talking in scandalised whispers. He hears the word *unconscious*, the word *girl*, the word *rape*. Spider's head dips as he approaches. For some reason, he is allowed on the other side of the tape. When he reaches the cop, he says, 'Excuse me, Officer. This chap is the victim's brother.'

'Victim?' Dan's body flushes with heat.

From the road, another siren screams.

'Spider?' Dan stops, temples throbbing. 'What the hell's going on?'

'Oh, man.' Spider shakes his head, digging in the back pocket of his jeans, pulling out a pouch of tobacco. 'We found Casey in one of the tents.'

'What? What do you mean, found her?'

'She didn't know where she was.' He drops dense clumps of tobacco into a Rizla and rolls. 'She's all right, don't worry. But they've taken her to A and E.' He lights the roll-up; pulls a strand from his teeth.

'What for? What happened?'

A tall female police officer looms over them.

'This is the victim's brother, ma'am,' Spider says, his bony hand landing on Dan's shoulder.

'I've been looking everywhere for her.' Dan feels the prick of tears at the back of his eyes. 'She didn't reply to my texts last night. She didn't turn up for her shift this morning. I was worried about her. I... I have to get to the hospital.'

The cop nods, letting him into the cordoned-off area. 'Of course. I need a quick word before you go, OK? Don't worry, it's just procedure. Then I'll see if I can get someone to take you. Your sister's going to be all right, but we need you to stay right where you are. I'll be back in a tick.' She turns and walks away; black shoes covered in blue bags place themselves with precision on the grass. In a wide square around a cheap green pop-up tent, incident tape vibrates.

Dan points at the tent. 'Is that where she was found? Who found her?'

'Yes,' Spider says. 'And I did. I put my jacket over her. I closed my eyes. I didn't...'

'What do you mean? What? Why would you...?'

Spider looks pained. 'She didn't have any... I mean, she wasn't dressed.'

'She was naked? Oh my God.' Dan bends and spits onto the tarmac. He blinks over and over; wipes at his face. His face feels dirty, his hands.

Byrne was talking to Casey last night at the bonfire. He didn't sleep in the teepee.

And now Casey's been taken away in an ambulance.

SEVEN
DAN

Five months before

The Coach and Horses is dead. Again. Dan is bored shitless. He's done all the cleaning he can think of, even removed the gunge from the dishwasher rim with a flathead screwdriver wrapped in a dishcloth. There was so much gunk he wondered briefly if it could have some secondary use, like excluding draughts or waterproofing jackets. He wipes down the bar for the billionth time, straightens the crisp packets in the snack display basket and tries not to admit to himself that he is, privately, wondering if that guy Byrne Sharp and his friends will come to the pub like they did last week.

    He stares at the door, which remains in its default position of shut. Last week, at around nine, Byrne and his two sidekicks swaggered through that shabby portal to the dead zone like actors who'd stumbled onto the wrong film set. Tanned and buff, with laser-precision haircuts, geezer energy like the kind you'd normally find down at the Shire Horse or the Bell or one of the gastro pubs in Kew, all too-tight clothes, loafers, no socks – in January. Players. What his sister would call *fuckboys*.

At first, Dan assumed they'd come in for a joke – *Let's go down the old man's boozer, take the piss out of the geriatrics and their games of dominoes.* When they first walked in, he felt his body bristle with fear. Guys like that asked you questions you couldn't answer, got lairy over nothing, perceived slights, *disrespect*. If they caused trouble, there was only him here, and he knew he would not be able to handle any form of conflict. The punters, when there were any, were mostly in their seventies, so it wasn't like they could back him up if things took a turn.

Funny, Dan thinks now, looking about him at the empty chairs, the silent piano, the old Wurlitzer gathering dust in the far corner, he kind of hopes they do come back. Which is weird, but at least they were lively. And they didn't cause trouble actually. They were a bit noisy, sure, and they referred to themselves as *the boys* in a way that suggested a club rather than a noun, one with a selection process, an elite membership, initiation rituals. But at least they were a change from the decrepit regulars who make their pints last three hours, and at least they invited him to play pool, which was pretty friendly. Dan actually managed to have a few laughs while he earned his minimum wage. It's been a long time since he's laughed, he thinks now. So long since he's had any banter, he worries he's lost his edge. He jokes about with Mum and Casey, but it's not the same kind of laughs as you have with lads.

In the howling emptiness of the deserted pub, the thought that he doesn't laugh much any more makes him feel heavy. He misses Rory and his mates from school. He misses his uni friends. This can't be his life. How is this his life?

The door bursts open. Dan feels his chest expand. It is them. It is actually them.

The boys.

All three of them are wearing police-style shades. At seven in the evening, it's dark out. But Dan has to admit, they look like celebrities. Gym guns bulge in tight stretchy fabric jackets the likes of which he's never seen before. White T-shirts shrink-wrap six-packs, flab-free waists. Dan sucks in his non-existent stomach. He's lost weight these last few months. Hasn't felt like eating. It's ages since he's been for a few too many beers, but all he's got to show for it are sticky-out ribs, a face as pale as milk and a girlish little pot belly that makes him look like a snake that's swallowed a tennis ball. He glances down at his thrift-store shirt, which he used to like but which right now looks proper shabby.

'Yo, my brother.' Byrne Sharp raises his hand in salute and grins widely.

The warmth of the greeting is a surprise. Dan feels his shoulders straighten.

'Er, hi. You came back.'

Byrne's black hair has been shaved around the sides since last week, the longer bit slicked and shiny on top. 'The usual, please,' he says and grins again.

'Same as last week? Guinness, you mean?'

When Byrne doesn't answer, Dan fills three pint glasses to two-thirds, trying not to notice his complete lack of bicep as he does so, and how sad that is – both the lack and the noticing. How lame. He is also trying to ignore the slightly tense feeling he remembers from last week. It's not their fault; it's his own lack of confidence. He wouldn't be like this if his friends hadn't all buggered off around the world or gone into graduate training schemes.

He fills the first pint to the top. The other two lads, whose names he has forgotten, saunter over to the pool table in a cloud of what they seem to think is banter.

'You ready to have your ass whipped, bruh?'

'I'm ready for you to be my bitch.'

'Yeah, right. Gonna humiliate you big style.'

'I'll humiliate your mum.'

'Hey, you got a pound coin?'

A moment later, the harrumph of fifteen pool balls dropping into the tray. It reminds Dan of the documentary on prisons he saw last week, which he wishes he'd never watched. One of the inmates had loaded a bunch of snooker balls into his sock and used it to batter a man to death. He wonders if the show has given him an irrational fear of prison. There was this other guy who got life for punching his mate in a drunken fight. One punch to the head. The mate died. Dan had never seen anyone look so sad and sorry in his life.

He puts three pints of Guinness on the bar. It'd be cool if he knew how to do a shamrock in the foam, but no: another thing he can't manage.

'Thank you, my good man.' Byrne gives a brief nod, the old-school manners very much part of his schtick.

'At your service,' Dan counters with a small, ironic bow.

Byrne scrutinises him. 'You been hitting the weights, my friend?'

Dan nods, loathing the glow he feels at the attention, the word *friend*.

'A bit,' he replies. He does not admit that the day after these guys came in last week, he went to the gym for the first time in his life. He has been every day since but so far hasn't noticed any real difference. But Byrne has.

Byrne presses his phone to the reader. 'Told you you'd feel better, didn't I?' He nods over to the pool table before returning his mirrored sunglasses to Dan, who sees only himself, smaller and stranger. 'Robbo and Jay first. Winner plays me. Winner of that plays you. I guess that means me against you.' He grins again, teeth white and even.

It takes Dan a moment to catch on. 'Oh,' he says. 'You're saying you'll be the winner.'

'Always.' Byrne points at him, rewarding him with yet another Hollywood smile before lifting the three pints and going to join the others.

Dan watches him a moment – the dancer-precision of his movements, the way he puts one forefinger to the tabletop before jumping up effortlessly, so that one moment he is standing, the next sitting on the table having turned a slick one-eighty, the pool cue lolling against his shoulder. If Dan tried that, he'd end up on the floor in a heap with a broken cue and his pint spilled all over him.

Scared of being caught staring, he sets about emptying one of the fridges so he can clean it and restock it. It isn't dirty. It isn't empty either. But it's too embarrassing to stand here scrolling through his phone, which has nothing on it anyway except for evidence of all his friends living a better life than him.

George, a regular with a nose like a bruised and misshapen strawberry, shuffles in and orders a pint of London Pride and a packet of pork scratchings. Thankful for something to do, Dan pulls a glass from the overhead rack. The guys are laughing, trading loud insults that make his insides tighten. George throws them a withering glance before returning his near-white irises to Dan, who smiles an apology as he sets the pint down on the bar. George picks it up as if it were a Ming vase and carries it pointedly to the furthest corner, where he sits down so slowly it hurts to watch.

'No way,' one of the boys yells. 'You fucking cheat!'

'Robbo.' Byrne doesn't shout, but his deep voice cuts through all the same. 'Language. Show some respect.'

Avoiding looking anywhere near them, Dan searches for another meaningless task. Jesus, there's no point even slicing up a lemon; the chances of having to make a gin and tonic are vanishingly small. He begins to empty out the second fridge. At his back, comes the smack of cue ball against colour, then the throaty rattle as one falls into a pocket, a victory cry from either Robbo or Jay. Dan feels the pull to go over and maybe watch a few shots – but these men are not his friends.

'You ready?'

He looks up. Byrne is at the bar, a pool cue in each hand.

'Um.' Dan stands up; wipes his hands on his jeans.

Byrne smirks and leans towards him. 'It's OK, we won't tell the boss.'

Dan laughs, a hollow sound even to his own ears, and lets himself through the gate at the end of the bar. Across the dark red multitude-of-stains-hiding paisley carpet, he walks to where Robbo is lining up the triangle, tongue poking out the side of his mouth with concentration. Jay is standing in the shadows, draining what's left of his stout.

Byrne breaks strongly, sending the green stripe into the middle pocket. He pots two more stripes before fluffing a more complicated shot off the cushion. Dan manages to pot one and feels relief course through him. He narrowly misses sinking a second. All the while, Byrne asks him questions. 'Where you from?' 'How come you working here?' and 'What d'you wanna do long-term?'

'Not far,' Dan replies, and, 'Just temporary,' and, 'Graphic design.'

'And what've you done to make that happen, my friend?'

'Um...' Dan's face flames. He lowers himself to the cue, lines up the shot. It is at least easy to avoid direct eye contact – not that there's any to be had, since Byrne has kept his shades on. He waffles on about how hard it is to get into artistic jobs at the moment, how nepotism is rife, how it's all about contacts. The green spot bounces off the pocket.

Crap.

'Sounds desperate.' Byrne makes a face. 'Next you'll be telling me you live with your mum.'

To Dan's horror, the others, who he didn't think were listening, collapse against the backs of the leather armchairs, clutching at their stomachs, helpless with laughter at Dan's hilarious life. Dan laughs along, to show he can take it, though heat climbs up his neck.

'It's just until I find something,' he says. 'I help out with the rent and stuff. She's a single parent, so...' At this completely dishonest reframing of his situation, Dan feels the heat deepen.

Byrne slaps him on the back. 'You're a good man. We'll soon have you up and running, won't we, boys? You won't be chipping in on the rent; you'll be buying your mum a house. Start visualising it, my brother. And never, ever blame the world for your problems.'

The game continues. So does Dan's excruciating self-consciousness. A few seconds later, Byrne looms behind him, causing him to fluff yet another shot.

'So, what do you do?' Dan brings himself to ask while Byrne chalks his cue. For some reason, he feels like he's talking to someone much older, though he suspects that is not the case.

'I'm a businessman,' Byrne replies, repositioning his feet, bending low, chin almost touching the cushion.

Dan suppresses a snigger. Who the hell describes themselves as a businessman in their twenties? But there is no trace of irony, no hint that he is anything other than deadly serious.

Byrne sinks his last stripe and moves on the black. 'Top left,' he says, tapping the pocket with the tip of the cue with almost feminine delicacy. A moment later, the black drops into it. He stands up straight then leans forward a fraction, the slightest bow.

Dan nods. 'Well played.'

Byrne turns his attention to Robbo and Jay. 'You guys go again, otherwise I'll be on all night. I'll get more drinks.'

Dan makes his way back to the bar. From the corner of his eye, he sees George raise his empty glass.

He nods. 'I'll bring it over.'

'Good man,' George replies and returns to his paper.

Dan pours another pint of Pride for George, who will drink

it while he finishes his crossword. At around 9.30 p.m., he will fold up his paper, leave the pub and shuffle slowly home to his ancient Border terrier, Scruff, for whom, in the last year, the walk has got too far.

Byrne is waiting at the bar.

'Same again?' Dan asks.

'Zero,' Byrne replies. 'Only ever one alcoholic drink, my friend.'

'I noticed that last week. Three Guinness Zeroes then?'

Byrne nods. 'Let me tell you something. Two pints is four units, and four units is for losers.'

'Right.' Dan hears the nerves in his voice. He glances around the bar, searching for something to say. Something that doesn't make *him* sound like a loser.

'Four units and your decision-making starts to fail,' Byrne goes on. 'Six and it leaves you altogether. Eight and you're a mess.' The word *mess* is infused with disdain. 'That's why we stick to two.'

'That's very... disciplined.'

'Exactly. Look at you. Looking better in just one week. That's discipline, friend. It's powerful, very powerful. You've gotta get up early, hit the gym, take care of business.'

Dan nods in agreement, as if Byrne is describing his life, as if he is even talking the same language. But he makes a mental note to wash his sheets in the morning. The thought of Mum doing them, that he has let her do that for nearly two years, is suddenly beyond embarrassing. He'll tidy and clean his room too. And tomorrow he'll relaunch his attempts to find a job, maybe even finish creating that schedule he started eighteen months ago, the one where he was going to get up at eight, do two hours' job-seeking, then two hours of his own designs before a healthy lunch and training for a 10K in the afternoon.

Yeah, that schedule.

'So, what kind of business are you in?' he asks, since Byrne is still at the bar and seems happy to chat rather than watching the others scrap over who is or is not getting his ass whooped, who is a pussy, whose mother is... Dan doesn't know what, since that particular slur seems to be one they never finish.

'I have several income streams,' Byrne says after a moment. 'I was a fencer in my youth.' *Youth.* He says it like he's old.

'What, like, a landscaping business?'

Byrne laughs. 'The sport. Fencing the sport.'

'Oh! You mean like *en garde* and all that?'

'All that. I was excellent with a rapier, you might say. I trialled for the Olympics.'

'You're *joking*?'

Byrne shakes his head, as if joking about such a thing would be out of the question, and takes a sip of his alcohol-free stout. 'I could've won gold, but...' He gestures towards his head with a loose wave. 'I have this annoying vertigo thing. I was quite brilliant, but unfortunately my... medical situation was unpredictable and there were too many bullshit hoops to jump through, so alas, it was not to be.'

Dan frowns in genuine sympathy. 'That must've been really shit. I'm sorry.'

Byrne shrugs. 'I could've turned my face to the wall. I could have sunk to my knees and blamed everyone else for my problems. But that's not how you win in this life. Winning always means triumphing over some form of adversity. I was a brilliant fencer. I'm still a brilliant fencer, not to mention most forms of combat. In fact, fencing was the first thing I monetised.'

'Monetised.' Dan is about to ask Byrne what he means, but a call comes from the pool table. 'Yo. Byrne. It's you and Jay.' It is Robbo, whose heavy face, short sandy hair and stocky build make Dan think of an ape.

Byrne raises his glass at Dan. 'That's why I have my own apartment and a great car. I monetise.' With that, he heads towards his friends, leaving Dan open-mouthed, breath stolen by the mic-drop there at the end. Dan wishes some of his old mates were here. Maybe as flies on the wall. They would laugh at Byrne Sharp, call him a dick. But what then? Then they'd catch a bus and go back to their parents' houses – a nice car and an apartment no more than a dream. Byrne has these things already, and he can't be older than late twenties, thirty tops. There is something exhilarating about his zero-irony, zero-negativity approach to life, something thrilling.

Dan puts the empty glasses into the dishwasher. Raises a hand to George as the old man shuffles out, tells him he'll see him tomorrow. From the pool table, the clack of balls, the rolling rumble of another potted colour returning to the tray. These guys have jobs. They make enough to stand on their own two feet. It would be easy to joke about their smooth-boy style, their overly curated appearance. But what has he, Dan, got to show for himself? What have his friends got, really? If they're travelling, it's on money saved from free accommodation at a cost to parents who have already put them through expensive degrees. And earlier, when he tried to pass off living with his mum as a favour to her and not the reverse, he felt more ashamed than he can ever remember feeling in his whole life.

EIGHT

MELISSA

The day after

Finally the M27 ends and the A31 to Dorchester begins. Melissa is aware of the fizz of stress in her blood. The nearer she gets, the worse she feels. The traffic coming out of London was murder, the roadworks a nervous breakdown; by the time she got to Winchester, she had to pop a propranolol just to carry on driving.

Casey, she thinks. It is all she can think. *Casey, Casey, Casey*.

The thought of Casey is visceral. The physical feeling of her drum-tight teenage body in Melissa's maternal embrace: a muscle memory and a longing all at once. Her cool, independent, hard-working girl. Her feisty, stubborn, funny, fair, kind, clever daughter.

'Oh, love,' she whispers, tears in free fall, knuckles white on the steering wheel. 'Hang on, baby. Hang on.'

She pushes away the tears, the ends of her fingers rough, scratchy. There is no time for crying. She has to get to that hospital and, short of a helicopter, driving is the quickest way, even in this rust bucket.

About half an hour ago, stuck in a jam at the roadworks, she left a message on her friend Sarah's voicemail.

'It's me. Listen, something terrible's happened. Casey's been... They found her in a tent. The police called me at work. I think she might have been sexually assaulted. They've taken her to Dorset County Hospital. I'm on my way there now.'

So far, there's been no reply. Now, as if by telepathy, her phone lights up. Sarah's face flashes, grinning on the screen. How often that happens, she thinks. That kind of psychic connection. Enough to make you believe in a higher force. She shouldn't answer it. She's driving. She'll get her licence taken off her.

Fuck it.

She answers. 'Sarah? Hold on – let me put you on speaker.'

'Mel?' Sarah sounds fraught.

'I'm driving.'

'You on hands-free?'

'My car doesn't have it. You're on speaker. It's OK. I won't take my eyes off the road.'

'I could've driven you.'

'I couldn't wait, love.'

'I know, I know. Oh my God. It's absolutely... Are you OK? Silly question, sorry.'

'I just have to get there.'

'Of course. Of course you do. So she was found in her tent? Any updates?'

'Not her tent, no. Someone else's. Didn't know where she was or how she'd got there.'

'Oh God. Oh my God.'

'I just have to get to the hospital and they'll tell me what they know. She'll be completely traumatised.' Melissa stifles a sob.

'Do you know whose tent it was?'

She shakes her head, despite the fact that Sarah cannot see her. 'All I know is she was found by someone. I think she must have been given something, or she took something, and... God knows. Actually, I don't even know that. My mind's racing all over the place. The police are checking her bloods apparently, so they must think... My mind's racing... Sorry, I already said that. Sorry. I can't think straight.'

'Are you OK to drive? I can pay for a cab. If you need to stop, just order an Uber – I'll pay.'

'You're so lovely. But I'm OK, honestly. I'd prefer to be doing something. I don't think I could sit in a cab. I'd chew my own arm off.'

'OK.'

'I'm going to go, babe,' Melissa says. 'I shouldn't be on the phone.'

'OK. Which hospital is it?'

'Dorset County. It's Dorchester.'

'OK. Drive safe. Love you. Keep in touch.'

'Will do. Love you. Bye.'

'Let me know when—'

Melissa cuts the call. Then she straightens her arms against the guilt and shame flushing through her. Everything she just said to Sarah was the truth.

So why did it all feel like lies?

NINE
CASEY

The day after

Casey opens her eyes. For a moment, she has no idea where she is – until it hits her. Spider found her in a tent. In her pants. And now she's in hospital and everything is horrible.

She blinks, vision sharpening, sense of smell attuning to what she thinks must be some sort of disinfectant. She hurts all over; the back of her head feels tight. The woman she met before is sitting in the chair by the bed. She's reading *Grazia*. She's called an SO something. It means an officer trained in sexual offences. Sexual offence... investigation techniques. An SOIT, that's it. She was the one who said she didn't have to have the physical examination if she didn't want to.

Casey didn't want to, no way. It was the last thing she wanted. But she knew she had to be mature about it. She could hear Mum telling her to let the professionals do their thing, her voice so strong in her head, like she was there. *Just agree to everything. You have nothing to hide, OK?*

So she agreed.

Everyone has been so kind, but it still feels weird – like she's being looked after and spied on all at once. She scrambles for the SOIT's name, but it's gone, like so much else, like her head is full of holes. The empty space where the previous night should be is frightening, the idea that it's so bad her mind has blocked it out. The SOIT said something about a court case. That she'd be with her for that or for any ensuing investigation.

Court case, she thinks. Actual court. Like something off Netflix. A bad dream, with a bad dream's weird, mixed-up timeline. She closes her eyes to a vision of herself in the dock, hands clasped in front of her, head bowed. In response, her entire body flushes hot, an echo of the burning humiliation she felt less than an hour ago. And sure enough, her mind strays to that mortifying ordeal. As if being found in her pants by Spider wasn't bad enough. Private parts of her stripped bare, not just to be viewed but probed, prodded, scraped at. The posh woman with the glasses, smiling but cold. *Casey, I'm what's called a forensic medical examiner. There's nothing to be frightened of – we just need to make sure we collect any evidence as soon as we can as a precaution. It might feel a bit strange, but I assure you it's just procedure, OK? It's nothing to worry about. I promise.*

Swabs. Samples. Blood, hair, skin cells. Crumpled pink cotton in a clear plastic bag – her own knickers some alien thing she couldn't even recognise. Spider's high-vis neon yellow in another, bigger bag. They put her in a hospital gown, but it gapes open at the back, showing her arse to the world in the gross paper pants they gave her. Paper sliders on her feet, like she's in a mental hospital. Everyone was so calm and quiet, but even so, thank God for the nurse, so nice, her kind voice, her warm, dry hand. *Now, you will feel some discomfort, my lovely. Try and breathe deeply. I know it's yucky, but you're doing great. Remember, these doctors do this all the time, OK? I think you're very brave, I really do.*

That helped. Afterwards, the nurse squeezed her hand,

smiling down at her in silent communication, like they were a team: *We've done brilliantly.*

If only Mum could've been there. But when you're eighteen, you're legally an adult. She *is* an adult. But she didn't feel like one then. Doesn't feel like one now. Nothing can change the fact that she wanted her mum so badly she had to bite down hard on her lip to stop herself from crying. It didn't change the fact that afterwards, when they left her behind the curtain, she couldn't keep it together any longer and wept like a child. The long paper sheath covering the bed wrinkled up as she swung her legs over the edge. Spots of red blood on the white. She fought the urge to screw it up and run away with it, find an incinerator to throw it in.

'There's no evidence of sexual assault,' came the medical examiner's voice.

Casey gripped the edge of the bed and breathed out long and hard. Tears were trailing down her face, hot shame persisting despite the huge wash of relief. She was so desperate for her mother she thought she might choke.

'Come on, lovely,' the nurse said when Casey pulled back the curtain. 'All over now. Let's get you back to the ward. See if we can find you something to eat, eh?'

That nurse made it bearable. Casey thinks she'd like to be a nurse one day, or at least someone like that. Someone good who makes other people feel better.

She tries opening her eyes again to the bright overhead lights of the hospital ward. She feels old, like she imagines being old is like – aching all over, fighting to stay awake but far from sleep. There is a wad of cotton wool in the crook of her elbow held in place by a strip of white surgical tape. That's from where they took her blood. *Bloods*, they said. She wonders what they'll find. Roofie, she thinks. What else could it have been?

The SOIT hasn't noticed she's awake. Casey stays as still as she can, just to be alone for a bit longer. The woman said she was like a family liaison officer. When she introduced herself, she said it like Casey would know what she meant by that, but Casey didn't have a clue. She's never had any dealings with the police, ever. Her idea of rebellion is a Jägerbomb and one of Immy's Marlboros, nicking a pint glass once from the Old Swan in Richmond. The woman said a family liaison officer is police but more of a caring role, most often called a FLO, which sounded like someone from the past. Or maybe Casey only thought that because it's like Florence Nightingale. Anyway, she was like a FLO only more specially trained. Maybe she won't be around for much longer if there's no evidence of sexual assault. Who knows? If Casey doesn't know what went down, they sure as hell don't.

Would there have been more blood on the paper sheet if she'd been...

She can't even think about it. She wonders if there'll be a detective, later, asking her questions. Maybe there won't be. Hopefully there won't be. Casey just wants Mum to come and take her home. She wants to be at home right now, in her room, in her bed, under the duvet, curled up in a ball. She feels dirty, even though they let her have a shower. She wants another shower. She wants to scrub herself raw.

Another flash: dancing near the bonfire, sipping from Immy's can of mojito. She shivers; presses her eyes tight shut again. A noise like a trapped animal escapes her.

'How are you feeling?'

She opens her eyes to see the cop leaning forward, her shelf of bosom pressing against the side of the bed. Belinda? Or Brenda.? Something beginning with B. She's gentle actually. Chubby cheeks and freckles that remind Casey of a kid she knew in primary who smelt of Dettol. She is smiling at her, eyebrows all wonky with sympathy.

'I'm OK, thanks,' Casey says shakily. 'Is my mum coming?'

The cop's eyes flutter briefly as if she has an eyelash stuck in one. 'Mum's on her way, don't you worry.' Her accent is soft Dorset.

'Does she know?' Casey asks.

The SOIT frowns. 'Know what, love?'

'That I was found... y'know... like that?' Casey closes her eyes. To flames leaping on the beach. The flat sea, the moon fragmented on the dark surface. Dan shouting at her, grabbing her arm. Her friends dancing without her, not even looking for her, not even checking their phones. Darkness filling her, solid and thick. Is her memory coming back, or was it always there? Is it hiding from her, or is she hiding from it?

She opens her eyes. Better to keep them open, keep them on Belinda-maybe-Brenda. Like she's a lighthouse or something.

The cop smiles kindly. 'Your mum knows you were found in a confused state, but we've told her you're all right, and she's on her way. All she's worried about is that you're OK. You've got nothing to worry about and nothing to be ashamed of, all right, my love? And at least we know your injuries are only where we can see them.' She offers another smile, as if not being sexually assaulted is great news, which, Casey supposes, it is.

Maybe-Belinda cocks her head, her eyes lowering to the bruises on Casey's neck. 'Is anything coming back at all?'

'It's all a blank,' Casey replies. 'I'm so sorry.'

TEN

DAN

The day after

Once he's given his statement to the SOCO, a cop gives him a lift to the hospital. He enquires at reception, then runs to the ward, where a nurse tells him to wait in the corridor. They're checking his sister over, she tells him. He'll be able to see her shortly.

Dan takes a seat. His foot taps against the vinyl floor of the corridor. The smell of hospital cleaner takes him back to having his appendix removed when he was twelve. Minutes pass. Half an hour. How long does it take to check a person out? It feels like he's been waiting hours. He needs to see Casey and make it OK again. The jigsaw of last night is coming together and the picture is not pretty.

Casey was at the bonfire with Byrne. That he remembers clearly. Casey laughing like she thought Byrne was hilarious; Byrne, with his stupid white teeth, grinning like gaining the admiration of a girl eight years younger than him was some sort of achievement. Dan remembers the hot rage passing through him, the same heat that fills him now as he sits in this damn place waiting, waiting, waiting for his sister to be poked and prodded and God knows what. Spider said it wasn't serious, but what does that even mean? How would Spider know about other, hidden damage, damage Dan heard in whispers as he pushed through the crowd, damage he won't name now, even in his own head?

Could Byrne and Casey have got together later? Could Byrne have forced her to do stuff she didn't want to do? Could Byrne be capable of *that*?

Byrne is not a nice guy. He told Casey that. He bloody well *told* her. Did she ignore him? Very possible. He didn't exactly make a great job of warning her. She was so angry, she might even have got with Byrne to spite him. Maybe. Maybe if she was drunk. But it was only the truth. It has taken Dan a stupid kids' camp to look this truth in the eye and accept what it says about him, falling for Byrne's slick and easy ways. It will take him a long time to wash off the stain of ever having become so-called friends with Byrne Sharp. He feels so bloody grim, his own failure to see what he knew deep down clinging to his skin like grease.

But at the bonfire, Byrne backed off. Yes, he did, hands thrown up as if to say, *whoa, dude, chill*, as if Casey were Dan's property, a possession to be surrendered from one man to another. Which would be in keeping. Dan and his sister argued. A drunk, stupid argument. His fingers tight around her arm. He remembers the pit in his stomach when he walked away. The same pit hardens again now. *People know when they're in the wrong*, Mum always says. And he knew; even drunk, he knew he was so, so wrong to grab his sister like that.

If only he hadn't got so wrecked afterwards – sharing cans with randoms, doing shots – he'd be able to hold on to his thoughts now: the events, the sequence. They would not be slipping about like a new pack of cards. He warned Casey off Byrne – that's what the argument was about. But the defiance in her eyes comes back to him now. As he walked away from her, he told himself he was leaving her alone because she'd told him to... but now, sitting here while she is lying on a gurney somewhere, with all that that might mean, he knows he left her to prove a point. He left her because of his own dumb pride.

He looks down at his bloody hands.

So how did he skin his knuckles? Can he trust the memory of falling over? Maybe. But when did that happen?

His phone buzzes in his pocket. He takes it out. There's a new message on the Boiz thread. It's from Robbo.

Anyone seen Byrne?

The icon is a raised white fist, the sight of which makes him cringe in a way it didn't a few months ago but should have. He opens the thread. Scrolls back through *Where the f are you/I'm down by the fire/near the DJ/at the beach bar* to the first unread message, sent at 11.33 p.m. It's from Byrne. Our leader, Dan thinks, with a lacing of bitter, silent irony. The big man. The message is a photograph. The image is slow to load.

When its outline finally clarifies, Dan sees and doesn't see it. He sees it and can't comprehend it.

Casey. Is it? Yes. Yes, it is. It's Casey. It's his kid sister. Her eyes are half closed, her mouth slack. Her shoulders are bare. Her hands are crossed over her chest. She looks naked, but then he sees that her hands are clutching at the straps of her top, which is undone. Behind her, a rough texture that looks like bark. She looks completely out of it.

His blood slows.

He reads the caption.

Dan, bro, your sister is fit. Full picture tomorrow mofos.

'Case,' he whispers, tears pricking. 'Oh my God. Oh my God.'

He sits back, head hitting the corridor wall. He closes his eyes, but all he can see is his sister, half naked and... was she unconscious? *Full picture tomorrow*. He's going to be sick. He can feel it, the heaving, the need. Casey. Oh God.

He makes himself breathe deeply while he gets himself together. He can't cry. He cannot cry.

Casey. His sister. Byrne. What the hell? Should he tell the police?

Quickly, he thumbs a separate message to Byrne.

Delete that photograph of my sister now or I'll fucking end you.

'Daniel?'

He startles; looks up to see a pretty blonde nurse. Despite everything, he smiles, his best effort to appear normal. 'Yes?'

'You can see your sister now. Not for long, OK?'

At last.

He sends the message.

ELEVEN
DAN

The day after

Casey is on the far side of the ward. She looks so small, her hair mussed up like candyfloss, black around her eyes, pale under her tan. From this distance, he thinks she looks like a punk doll, and in that moment, she must sense him because she glances towards the door. Their eyes meet. Her face lights up, a wide grin. She's not mad at him.

'Dan.' Her voice is croaky, her eyes shiny. She reaches out to him.

'Case.' He rushes to her, takes her hand and holds it tight. She bursts into tears, and then his eyes are filling too and he's blinking like mad. He wants to hug her, but there are bruises all up her arms, a bandage at the crook of her elbow, and he worries he'll hurt her. 'Case,' he says again. 'Are you OK?' A stupid, stupid question. He didn't bruise her like that, did he? Jesus, there are bruises on her neck too. He can't have grabbed her by the neck, can he? No, no, he didn't. No way. 'Who did this?'

'I don't know.' Casey takes a tissue from a little packet and presses it against her eyes.

'Case.' Dan sighs, still holding his sister's hand, his mind returning to the photograph. Byrne sent it. But he wouldn't hit a woman. Would he? Would he be capable of *this*?

'Hello,' comes a voice.

He startles. A policewoman is sitting in a chair by the bed.

'Belinda,' Casey says, gesturing to the cop. 'Belinda, this is my brother, Dan.'

'Hi,' he says, attempting to smile before turning back to Casey. There is so much more he wants to say – mainly he wants to apologise for grabbing her, for shouting at her – but the cop is right there, and even though she's pretending to read a magazine, he knows she's listening, just fixed onto her chair like a... like a bloody barnacle. 'I wish I'd been here,' he adds and wonders if he's ever felt more helpless in his life.

'You couldn't have come in with me anyway,' Casey says, her voice wobbly. 'Headline is: no sexual assault, OK?'

He breaks, covering his eyes with his free hand, the other squeezing his sister's.

'Hey,' comes Casey's voice, soft, like she's the one comforting him. 'It's good news.'

'I know that. I know.' He sniffs; knuckles away his tears. The cop hands him a tissue. He thanks her without looking at her. 'I thought...' he manages. 'I don't know what I...' He wants to show her the photograph. Tell her about it at least. But how can he, when she's in this state? She's too fragile. It would destroy her. Maybe there's a way he can find Byrne and get the thing deleted. Then she won't ever have to know.

'Softy.' Casey's face is a mask of sympathy. It should be him in that bed, he thinks, covered in bruises. He should never have left her, never have stormed off. He glances at the black clouds on her arms, on her neck.

'Who did this to you, Case?' he asks again.

She shakes her head. 'I can't remember.' But she is staring at the scabs on his knuckles. 'What happened to you? Did you hurt yourself?'

He sniffs; wipes at his eyes. 'Must've fallen over,' he says. 'I got pretty wasted. I shouldn't have had a go at you like that.' He side-eyes the barnacle, returning his gaze to Casey's. With a pang, he realises he didn't mention to the SOCO back at the campsite that he'd argued with his sister. He just said he'd seen her by the bonfire last night, woke up late and realised she hadn't replied to his messages. He'd been worried, he said, had started looking, and then he saw the police and that was the first he knew of it.

But the police won't think he attacked his own sister, will they? He's pretty sure all he did was grip her arm. No, no, he'd never, *ever*...

'I don't take any notice of you anyway.' Casey is smiling, which makes him want to cry again. 'It's not your fault. Honestly. You didn't do this.'

Her faith in him is almost more than he can bear. *But I grabbed your arm*, he wants to say. *I shouted at you, right in your face.*

He looks into her eyes. 'You really don't remember anything? Do you remember chatting to Byrne?'

She shakes her head, as if to clear it. 'It's weird. I do remember chatting and us arguing, and then I think I saw Immy and those guys. Immy gave me a can of mojito and then... it all goes a bit blurry. I can remember trees. Like, treetops?'

'Treetops,' Dan says. Thinks: bark, the bark against her back in the photo.

'Were you with someone by some trees?'

She shrugs. 'Maybe. I keep remembering random stuff. Like childhood stuff. Like my short-term memory has gone or something. Like, do you remember that time Dad kicked off about the broken window in my bedroom?'

He smiles. 'That was a long time ago.'

'We were trying so hard not to laugh, and I looked at you and...'

'You said it must've been the window cleaner. But I knew you'd done it because...' Because he could see it in her face. Is she telling him to read her face? Does that mean she knows more than she's letting on?

The policewoman turns the page of her magazine: a soft shush, the quiet clearing of her throat. Casey's gaze is still fixed on his. Her hair moves back a fraction, wig-like, but her eyes do not budge. 'You knew it was me,' she says.

His eyes flick towards the policewoman, who is either oblivious or pretending to be. Is Casey signalling something to him, or is he being paranoid? Is she telling him she's done something? Or is she literally only talking about a childhood memory to keep their minds off things? He gives a glacier-slow nod.

'It was an accident,' he says.

Slowly, his sister raises her forefinger to her lips, as if in thought. Is she telling him she won't tell? Or is she telling him: *Don't tell*? Don't tell what? She hasn't done anything.

Has she?

For Christ's sake, he wishes he could just ask her. Doesn't this policewoman ever need a pee break? A coffee? The best thing – the only thing – he can do now is find Byrne and sort this out. If Byrne did inflict those bruises, he's a dead man.

Dan raises his own forefinger to his lips, his eyes moving back to his sister's now. But whether he means *I won't tell* or *You won't*, or whether he's seeing shapes in the clouds, he hasn't the slightest clue.

'Listen, I've got to go back to the site, but I'll be back.' He stands up; his sister's face falls. But how can he tell her about the photo? How can he share that he's thinking about the blood on his knuckles, wondering how the hell it got there, about what he will say if the cops want to speak to him again? He has to get to Byrne right now and make sure he doesn't send that photo anywhere else. That photo needs to be deleted, deleted, deleted.

Yes. He can make this one thing right.

TWELVE

MELISSA

The day after

Melissa reaches the hospital at 7.25 p.m., blood racing, hairline damp. She grabs her phone from the passenger seat. Two messages: one from Dan, one from Sarah.

Dan: *Mum, can you call me when you get this?*

She closes her eyes. He obviously knows about Casey. Was he there when they found her? Are they together? Hopefully he was able to get to the hospital. Hopefully he'll be with her. She starts a text but hesitates. What if he doesn't know? He could be in a state of blissful ignorance, chilling out with his friends at the campsite. But no. He will know. Even without a call from the police, it will be all over the place by now. At the thought of her daughter's trauma reduced to hot rumour, Melissa shudders.

I'm sure you know, she types, just in case. *Casey has been taken to Dorset County Hospital. Are you here?*

She checks Sarah's message.

Have booked 2 nights in Dorchester Premier Inn in your

name. Is near hospital. Double room no twins soz. Let me know if I can do anything else. Love you. S xx

Her eyes fill. 'Oh, Sarah,' she whispers. Types: *Thank you*. Adds a heart.

As she gets out of the car, she composes a third text, this time to Casey.

Am here baby. I'll be five mins xx

If it takes away even one gram of her daughter's anxiety for the few minutes it will take to get to her, it's worth sending.

There is no reply. Of course, she thinks. Casey won't have her phone.

At reception, a guy in a pale blue uniform directs her to Purbeck Ward. There, a nurse gestures in the direction of a bed against the far wall. Though every cell of her being is screaming at her to run, Melissa forces herself to walk, giving herself time to take in the scene. Her eyes are dry. The skin on her face feels heavy, like it's trying to slide away. Her heart thumps.

Casey is sitting up in bed, dressed in a hospital gown. There is a plump female police officer at her side, leaning towards her, rosy complexion, thin brown hair tied in a ponytail. They are chatting. The woman is smiling, something tender in her expression, her pink cheeks. The simple sight of her daughter safe and clean and propped up against the white pillow is a relief so huge Melissa has to fight not to fall to her knees and wail. Her daughter looks ashen, small and oh so young. A child. No more than a child. How can this have happened to her girl? To anyone's girl?

'Casey.' Her voice is hoarse, but her daughter's head twitches.

'Mum!' Casey bursts into tears. They both do.

Melissa runs the last few metres to her daughter's bedside and opens her arms. Her daughter's shoulders rise, bracing.

'Oh God,' Melissa chokes. 'Can I hug you? Will it hurt?'

Casey holds her arms wide. Gingerly, Melissa leans in,

barely daring to touch her. Casey lays her head on Melissa's chest, a sob breaking from her. Her hair smells clean but faintly of woodsmoke. Melissa kisses her over and over.

I will hold on to this girl for the rest of my life, she thinks. I will never, ever let her go.

'Oh, my love,' she whispers. 'It's OK. It's OK, it's OK, it's OK.'

'I'm so sorry.' Casey cries into Melissa's chest. 'I'm so sorry.'

'Oh, darling. Don't say that. You've nothing to be sorry about, nothing at all. You're safe now – that's all that matters. It's all going to be OK.'

Questions teem in Melissa's brain, fried from stress, too little sleep and the hair-raising drive. Nothing matters right now, nothing except this: her daughter, safe, in her arms. Alive. Alive, alive, alive.

Finally, they part, settling for holding on to each other's hands. Melissa glimpses the surgical dressing on the back of her daughter's head.

'It's just a graze,' Casey says. 'And a few cuts on my back. Bruises look worse than they are.'

'Where's your brother?' Melissa says when she is able. There are other, urgent questions, but she cannot bring herself to ask them.

'He went back to the site. He said he had to pick up some stuff. I told him to go. It's fine. I was pretty sleepy.'

Melissa tries not to feel disappointed in Dan for leaving his sister, tries then not to let her eyes rest on the small grey marks on her daughter's forearms. Fuzzy fingerprints. The same prints dapple Casey's neck. Dear God.

'Can you remember much?' she asks.

Casey shakes her head. 'Treetops. Bits and pieces from earlier on.'

Melissa studies her. Her daughter appears to have no memory at all of last night. Is it some sort of trauma reaction?

'Hello there,' says a voice.

Remembering the police officer, Melissa turns to see her standing with her hands clasped across her round belly with the air of someone waiting their turn.

'I'm PC Belinda Riley,' she says. 'We spoke on the phone.' She offers her hand to shake.

'Melissa Connor,' Melissa says, the other woman's palm warm and a little damp against her own. 'Pleased to meet you. Thanks for... you know – looking after her.'

The woman withdraws her hand and waves away the thanks. 'I'm here for Casey, and I'll be her point of contact if it turns out there's to be an investigation.'

'An investigation? Have you had the results of the examination?'

'Let's sit, shall we?' Riley shifts to take the seat furthest from the bed, gesturing to the one she has vacated so that Melissa can be closer to her daughter.

'Thank you,' Melissa says, meaning it. She hooks her bag over the back of the chair and sits down before leaning forward to take Casey's hand. Their gazes meet, but no matter how hard she looks, she can't see any hint that her daughter knows what happened.

'So,' she says, initiating the calm conversation she has rehearsed over and over in the car, 'what do we know?'

'Well, I *can* tell you there's no evidence of sexual assault,' Riley says. 'So that's something.'

Melissa exhales heavily and glances back to Casey, whose eyes swim with anxiety. Melissa squeezes her hand. *It's OK. It's all going to be OK*. 'Thank God for that at least, I suppose. And do we know who did this to her?'

PC Riley shakes her head. 'Not at the moment. The scene-of-crime officers have been interviewing people at the site; the bloods should be back soon, so that'll tell us what was in her system, and the forensic medical officer has swabbed her for any evidence. They're keeping her in overnight as a precaution. Bit of a bump on the head, so...' Her eyes flutter, as if bothered by a piece of grit. She blinks, whatever it was apparently cleared, and goes on: 'Can we... can we step outside a moment?'

She eyes Melissa meaningfully. So much is being said without words, Melissa thinks. But she cannot read any of it.

'Back in a tick, love.' She gives Casey's hand another squeeze as she stands, strokes her hair back from her face and kisses her on the forehead. 'Do you want anything? Hot chocolate or something?'

For the first time in these fraught few minutes, Casey's face relaxes. 'Actually, hot chocolate would be amazing. And maybe a sandwich, if they have any? I haven't really... I didn't eat the meal they brought; it was disgusting.'

In the smile they share, Melissa glimpses her daughter, the one who left home little more than a week ago: determined, forthright, the barest lacing of the humour they have always shared. She is in there still. This thing will not define her. Melissa will make damn sure of it.

'If you want to go and get her some treats, there's a Costa,' Riley interjects. 'I'm not going anywhere for the moment.'

Her smile is warm and cheerful. She has joined the police to try and make a difference, to make the world a better place. Melissa knows this instinctively. She follows her out into the corridor. Behind them, the door closes with a hushing sound.

Riley stops, places her hands on her hips and meets Melissa's eye. 'How's Mum?' Her head tilts to one side in concern.

For a moment, Melissa has no idea who she's talking about. 'Me? Oh. Yes, I'm... Just keen to get her home. Has she remembered anything yet?'

'It's coming back slowly, I think. She remembers talking to someone called Byrne at the bonfire, which is more than she had back at the site, but after that it drops out. It can take a while, especially if she took something or someone gave her something. She might get flashbacks. Hopefully, it'll come back and she'll be able to identify who did this to her.'

'Is there anything I need to do?' The calm question belies the buzz of nerves in Melissa's belly.

Riley presses her mouth tight, that strange eye flutter again, before she says, 'The old TLC works wonders. Apart from a few bruises and the graze on the back of her head, there's minimal physical damage.'

She does not say anything about mental damage, but Melissa hears the words even so.

'Do you think she was attacked? I mean, it's obvious, isn't it? Those bruises.'

'It's best not to jump to conclusions. She could've fallen.'

'What, into someone's fingers?' Melissa feels heat flash in her face, sees a blush blooming on the other woman's. Guilt stalks in. This woman is doing her best.

'She could have been dancing,' the cop says, her voice lacking the confidence of a moment ago. 'You know what teenagers are like. And it's not just alcohol any more, is it? They get so wrecked these days.'

'I guess we all did.' As the words leave her, Melissa imagines Belinda Riley as a young woman, at home with elderly parents, perhaps, who doted on her. She was not invited to parties, Melissa thinks. She did not get wrecked and find herself in dubious situations with boys who knew no better. Or men who did.

'It's different now though,' Riley adds. Another tight press of her lips, a shake of her head. 'Anyway, I just wanted to talk to you privately. Casey's memory most probably will come back, but we don't want it influenced by people giving her information or telling her things that may or may not be true. We're waiting until she's had a chance to recover, hoping she'll remember who assaulted her in her own time.'

Nerves flare in Melissa's stomach. Irritation, too, at this

woman weaving some sort of mystery, withholding information for her own glorification. 'So *is* there something you haven't told her?'

Riley fixes her with her round blue eyes. 'A female witness has come forward and told us she was attacked during the weekend. She was able to name her attacker.'

Melissa's hair follicles itch. This was not something she'd considered on the way here, and she thought she'd considered everything. She clears her throat before asking: 'Do you have a name?'

'I can't tell you that at the moment.'

'But do you think it's the same boy?'

Riley's eyes do that fluttering thing again. 'Let's just say,' she says once she's got it under control, 'he's helping us with our enquiries.'

Melissa covers her mouth with her hand, her shock genuine. She doesn't trust herself to speak – couldn't speak even if she did.

THIRTEEN
MELISSA

Four months before

Melissa is in the kitchen trying to defrost a block of beef mince by flipping it and scraping off the browned bits in order to make spaghetti bolognese for dinner. The block of meat is like an iceberg, she thinks, slowly melting in a translucent sea of onions.

'Mum.'

She turns to see Casey hovering at the door in a Fontaines D.C. T-shirt and balloon-baggy jeans. Her bleached hair is dyed lilac this week and is held back from dark brown roots with what look like tiny bulldog clips. Melissa thinks she looks cool. She also looks preoccupied, her forehead creasing between her eyebrows in the way it does when she's worried. Her face is a little flushed.

'Casey.' Melissa matches her daughter's serious tone and adds a questioning smile.

Casey returns the smile, but hers is troubled, and her eyes lower as she edges past the fridge to sit down at the small IKEA table wedged up against the window. She opens the little cutlery drawer hidden beneath the tabletop – these Swedish designers really do think of everything – and takes out three knives and three forks before opening the other drawer and pulling out some table mats that have gone fluffy at the corners. Outside, pigeons roost under the eaves of the house behind, their throaty corr-corr soothing. The smell of cigarette smoke drifts through the open fanlight. That'll be Sandra on the fire escape, back on the fags.

'Can I talk to you about something?' Casey asks.

'Sure. Anything.'

'So, you know Summer Camp?'

It is an odd question; they both know she knows Summer Camp. Every single parent in a five-mile radius knows. Most will already be wondering whether their kids will make it through the weekend without alcohol poisoning, a drug overdose or that all-encompassing umbrella term of horrors: *worse*.

'Sure.' Melissa turns back to the stove and sloughs off more browned bits from the mince. It is oddly satisfying, like collecting fluff from the dryer. She flips the meat-berg and refocuses on her daughter.

'Well, so yeah,' Casey says. 'Right, so, the guys are booking, like, a chalet?'

Silent alarm bells are already ringing at the word *chalet*. Melissa knows she should turn off the gas and sit down, meet Casey eye to eye, but at this precise moment, it's easier not to.

'So, I was thinking,' Casey continues. 'If I, like, do more hours at Luigi's, maybe—'

'Let me stop you right there.' Melissa makes herself turn to face her daughter. 'I know you mean well, love, but I really don't think it's a good idea to be taking on another shift when your A levels are only a few months away. It's not long now, and you can work all summer if you need more money.'

'But that would be after Summer Camp. And if we go for a chalet, there's a deposit.'

Melissa returns to the mince, no more than a medallion now. She bashes it with the spatula to break the rest up. And braces herself. 'How much is a chalet?'

'They're, like, two thousand for a week? But you have to take them for the whole week.'

'Two thousand pounds?' Melissa's hand flattens itself to her forehead. She sighs. Ye gods.

'Not each!'

'Oh, that's all right then. Cheap as chips.'

'Mum, please. Don't go off on one. We only have to pay the deposit now.'

Melissa closes her eyes. Of course. Of course Casey's friends are going for the top accommodation money can buy. Of course, at barely eighteen, they can't possibly stay in anything so basic as a tent. On a campsite. But it's not her daughter's fault, is it? Her daughter isn't even asking her for the money, God bless her. It's Melissa who moved them from their lovely little end-of-terrace in a cooler but scruffier area once Richard left. All for the school. Ofsted Outstanding. Great sixth form. It's not Casey who chose to live in a flat above a bookie's with three flights of stairs and no lift and not really enough room for a table in the kitchen. The school is good, sure, but sometimes Melissa thinks she's traded knife amnesties and posters advising her not to carry a piece for a friend for a whole different set of problems altogether. She wouldn't mind, but the kids round here do drugs just the same. God knows, they have much more money to buy the damn things.

'Sorry,' she says, summoning an attitude of calm and facing her daughter once again. 'How much is the deposit?'

'Two hundred and fifty. It's, like, half.'

'So five hundred pounds each total?'

Casey reddens; dips her head. Even her parting is deep pink. 'I... I just thought...'

Melissa feels the nausea she has felt so often since living

here, the gut-rot of never being able to keep up, the endless sickening grind of other people's ridiculous budgets.

'I can give you a hundred,' she says. 'I've been putting a tenner away each month. I've already got it.'

Casey looks up. 'Honestly, that's really nice, but I can pay. But maybe I could borrow it and pay you back?'

'No need. I did the same for your brother when he went. I wasn't going to give it to you until after the exams, but if you need it now... How much have you got saved?'

'Maybe fifty? I had more, but I...' Casey's eyes fill. 'I thought we'd be camping. I didn't know they'd—'

'Hey. Don't get upset. You bought your phone last month, didn't you? How many kids round here buy their own phones? Like you say, you thought you'd be camping. We've got all the gear, haven't we? Sleeping bags and all that.'

'I'd prefer to camp, but Immy... The thing is, I'd need two hundred, but I can pay you back and I can save the rest by the time we have to pay the balance.' Casey knuckles away tears.

'Hey.' Melissa crosses over to her daughter and throws her arms around her. Her lilac head presses against her ribs. 'Don't worry. We'll think of something.'

'Immy says we have to pay the deposit next week or we'll lose it. There's teepees, which are a bit cheaper. I tried to suggest—'

'I suppose a normal tent is out of the question?'

Casey shrugs. 'They're really not into it.' Her voice rises, indignant. 'They're just sucking all the fun out of it. Making it about something they can put on Instagram. I don't even want to go any more. Maybe I won't go.'

Feeling herself overheating, Melissa lets go of her daughter and steps back. Casey sniffs; looks down at the floor. Poor kid. She *does* want to go; they both know that. Melissa suspects it's not just the phone that has left her daughter low on funds. Her friends have started going out to local pubs recently, and the price of drinks is hair-raising, not to mention the social-media-friendly outfits required, the make-up, the hair, the brows, oh, and the goddam nails.

'I get it,' she says to the top of her daughter's head. 'I do, honestly.' And she does. Every time she thinks she's got her head above water, there's some new request from the school for something she cannot remember her own school ever having: new iPads, an organic catering company to save the poor darlings from the horrors of a carrot not teased from the ground by someone whose Christian name you know... The demands are constant. They are relentless.

Casey is still looking at the floor.

'How many in a chalet?' Melissa asks.

'Four.' Her daughter raises her head, but her eyes are still downcast. 'I mean, they sleep eight, but the guys said it's better if everyone has their own room?'

Melissa takes a breath. *Don't shout. Do not shout. It isn't Casey's fault.*

'I think it's stupid,' Casey blurts. 'We could easily share and then it would be literally half.'

'Don't most of the kids take tents? It's called Summer Camp. Clue in the title. Dan and his mates all took tents.' Melissa can still picture Dan and Rory, Sarah's son, bucket hats, shorts, rucksacks on their backs. On the railway platform, all ready for fun, grinning like two Cheshire cats.

'My friends don't have tents,' Casey says miserably.

'Of course they don't.'

'Immy says—'

'Immy.'

'Don't, Mum. She's nice really.'

Spoilt is what she is, Melissa only just stops herself from saying. *Eighteen and already totally out of touch.*

'Don't we always find a way?' she asks instead, after a moment.

'I could borrow some from Dan,' Casey says quietly. 'He's been doing loads of shifts lately. Then pay you both back over the summer?'

Melissa bites her lip. The fact is, she doesn't have two hundred pounds spare and Dan is to money as a sieve is to water. She opens her mouth but, as is so often the case, doesn't really know what to say.

A smell reaches her, cinder-toffee-ish, sweet but singed.

'Shit,' she says. 'The mince.'

FOURTEEN
CASEY

Four months before

Casey throws herself onto her bed and groans. Why the hell did she even mention the chalet? The look on Mum's face, oh my God. She went bright red and her eyes went all shiny, and Casey could totally tell she was pretending not to be upset. And now she can't take it back, and she can't pretend she isn't desperate to be with the others, and if she doesn't get a place in the chalet, she'll be on her own like an absolute Billy-no-mates. She should have asked Dan first. He's crap with cash, but surely he's saved something since he left uni? Mum only charges him for food. And Mum's under enough pressure as it is without paying for a stupid luxury chalet for Casey and her stupid friends who can't even sleep in a stupid tent.

Casey stifles another long moan against her arm.

Maybe all she wanted was confirmation that the chalet thing is actually madness. Because it is. Immy is mad. Her friends are mad. Why does she have the maddest friendship group in the whole entire school? Why can't she be friends with more normal kids, like Olive and Ethan and those guys? She bets they're going with tents. It's so unfair. Casey doesn't even want to be in a chalet anyway.

She rolls over and pulls the pillow over her head; pushes her nose into the mattress until she can barely breathe. Mum saving up a tenner a month makes Casey's heart hurt. A hundred quid means she must have been saving for nearly a year. No one else's mum is doing that. No one else's mum is sleeping on the sofa bed so her kids can have their own rooms. She never complains, even says she prefers it because she likes to watch *Newsnight* in bed. Casey wants to cry. She wishes she could reverse time and not say anything at all. Because now Mum'll feel bad if Casey ends up in a tent just because they can't afford to spend ridiculous amounts on a stupid luxury chalet just so Imogen *Beyoncé* Croft can have a hairdryer point.

'ARGH.'

The smell of spaghetti sauce drifts through the flat, but she's not ready to go back into the kitchen. She hears the key in the door, her brother call out: 'Yo, bitches.'

He's started saying that recently. She *thinks* he's joking, but it's a bit cringe. He's joined a gym too, and his arms are inflating day on day. The other morning, he was making an omelette – he's obsessed with omelettes these days – and Casey looked at him and thought, does he even have a brain any more? He looks like someone who makes speaker calls so they can hold their phone coming out of their chin like a weirdo. And last week, when she suggested going round the charity shops, which he would usually, he said no, he was going for a workout. He said it like it was what he always did, like it was normal. She wants her old brother back, eating Maltesers and laughing at stupid shit on YouTube.

He's moving about in his room. She listens. He sniffs. Clears his throat. The first notes of Fontaines D.C. leak through the thin wall.

At least he still has good taste in music.

With a sigh, she heaves herself up and goes and knocks on his door.

'Yo,' he says.

She rolls her eyes and pushes open the door. 'He-ey.'

Her brother is sitting on the end of his bed, hooked over his phone like a prawn. He is pink-skinned, also like a prawn, his damp brown hair shining. The smell of soap or aftershave or whatever is overpowering; it's gone straight to the back of her throat. She tries not to cough. But it's better than the eau de stinky sock this room used to smell of. Even the bedding looks freshly washed.

He glances up at her over his bulging thighs. 'You OK?' he says. 'You look like you've been crying.'

'Just tired. A levels suck. Have you been to the gym?'

He smiles. 'Fit body, fit mind. Lying in bed is for losers.'

'Wow.' She throws up her hands. 'Thought we didn't use that word.'

'What, fit?'

She rolls her eyes and grins at him. 'You know which one I meant.'

'Don't tell Mum.' He grins back. 'I'd never actually call anyone that. Guess who fired off three internship applications this morning as well?'

She raises her eyebrows in approval. 'Amazing.'

'And one job application, not that I'll get it.' He frowns. 'Actually, no, maybe I will!' He throws out his arms and pulls in his fists, making his new biceps bulge. 'Manifest!'

'That's so great.' She smiles warily, not wanting to pee on his bonfire. A month or two ago, she was low-key worried about him. He'd been getting up later and later, and his room was gross. He said he was getting up late because he didn't get home from his shift till midnight, but no one needs to get up at four in the afternoon. She'd started to think he was becoming depressed. Leaving uni seems really hard. Dan said it's like you spend your life with everyone telling you what to do and where to be, and then suddenly you have to figure it all out by yourself and there's no work because graphic design jobs are rarer than hens' teeth and now it's all going to be done by AI anyway.

Casey thinks this change in him has come since he met that guy at the pub. Byrne something. He's started making these smoothies now with spinach in them – yuck. He and Mum had a big row about housekeeping last week because he made an omelette with, like, six eggs. Lunatic. It's like he's gone from one extreme to the other, bedbug to... whatever this is... and there's a glint in his eye sometimes, and she thinks he might have gone a bit manic.

'Dan,' she says, sitting next to him.

'Case,' he says, putting his arm round her. 'S'up, sis?'

Her heart warms. She rests her head on his shoulder and tells him about the conversation with Mum. He listens without interrupting, and she loves him just for that even though she loves him for lots of other stuff too, like how he looks out for her, how her friends think he's cool, how he makes her laugh, especially when they have dinner with Mum. Dan is hilarious.

'I can lend you some,' he says when she's finished. 'I mean, not this month, but next?'

'It's OK, I'm having a rethink,' she says, knowing this means he's broke.

'I could—'

She lays a hand on his leg. 'Seriously. Love you, dude, but we both know you spend it like Beckham.'

'I'm getting better at saving. Byrne says—'

'Byrne says,' she mimics, and he mock-punches her on the arm. 'Seriously. How can you be saving if you've got a gym membership? And the new threads. Superdry?'

'I got it on Vinted.'

'What about the shoes then?' The pervert shoes, she doesn't add, because he was so gassed about them.

Her brother reddens. 'You haven't told Mum about them, have you?'

'Course not. You said not to. Where are they? I haven't seen you wear them.'

'Under the wardrobe. I'm going to pretend I bought them next month.'

'Tricksy!'

He laughs. 'I could borrow some cash from Byrne. He's always saying if I need a loan...'

'That's not a good idea. I don't even know him.'

They sit with that for a second, until Dan pulls his shirt over his head, making the T-shirt underneath ride up his belly. OMG, she thinks. He has actual abs.

'That T-shirt's as white as a toothpaste ad,' she says as he hangs his shirt in the wardrobe. 'What are the square creases on it?'

'You don't iron them out. Otherwise people can't tell it's new.'

'It's very... clean. Like, *fuckboy* clean.' She laughs – laughs more when he pulls an offended face and pushes her backwards onto the bed.

'It's fresh,' he says after a moment, smoothing down the T with his hands. 'Byrne reckons girls like the clean look.'

'Thought you were more... I dunno, low-key?'

'I am.' He looks around the room; seems to be struggling to find a way to say something. 'I just don't want to look like a loser, that's all.'

'Oh my God, stop saying that word.' She mimics their mother: 'There's no such thing as winners and losers...'

'Only human beings,' he chimes, in chorus.

She gives him a side hug. 'You could never be a loser.'

. . .

Later, in bed, she's almost asleep when it comes to her, proper lights up in her head like a... well, like a light bulb.

She kicks off her duvet and opens her laptop, brings up the Heaven View website and finds the email address. If Dan can get a grip on job applications, so can she. Before she can overthink it, she types.

> To whom it may concern,
>
> My name is Casey Connor. I am currently studying for my A levels and am looking for work over the summer. I am outgoing, polite and have a lot of experience working in the service sector...

When she's finished, she revises it a few times, reads it back and fires it off. Hopefully Heaven View will give her a summer job. That way, she won't need any money at all – from anyone.

FIFTEEN
MELISSA

The day after

In Costa, Melissa picks up an egg-and-cress sandwich. She orders a large hot chocolate and a flat white for herself. When the barista asks for her name, she gives it through thin lips. Not his fault some pillock in PR has decided that this is what constitutes personalised customer service. Not his fault she feels like grabbing one of those trays and banging it over and over on one of these awful cheap plastic tables.

Breathe. The only way to get through this is to stay calm. Casey needs you. She needs you more than she ever has. You need to keep your shit together.

Melissa breathes deeply. Waits calmly for her order without so much as touching a tray. She's so exhausted she can barely stand, but the ordeal is over; that is how she must try and see it. What has happened has happened. The only way now is forward.

PC Riley has gone back to sit with Casey – not before laying a hand on Melissa's forearm and telling her to take all the time she needs, and to call her Belinda. Melissa felt herself bristle, a lifelong aversion to sympathy made manifest. Belinda means well, she can see that now, but the fact is, Melissa doesn't need or want *time*; she doesn't want sympathy either; she wants Belinda to leave them the hell alone for two sodding minutes so she can have a private conversation with her own daughter. She wants to set up a cordon, hold up a flaming torch and shout at everyone, including the police: *Stay back. Keep away.* The poor girl has been through too much already, and that's without having to undergo a forensic examination on her own. At eighteen, they're adults, yes, but they're not. They're so not.

At the thought of her daughter, scared and alone in the dehumanising space of a medical room somewhere in this sterile white labyrinth, tears prick. Her baby. Her baby girl. Alone and afraid, no one to hold her hand, being brave, trying her best to manage the shock and shame Melissa knows she must have felt. Christ, she's not even had a smear test yet. Not suffered the 101 indignities most women face for whatever reason at some point in their lives. If only Melissa could have been there.

She pushes the watery brim from her eyes. Move forward, keep calm and carry the fuck on. Casey hasn't been sexually assaulted. That's a good thing, a very good thing under any circumstances. Best not to think about what has happened, better to focus on how best to protect her precious girl from what comes next. Casey can't remember who attacked her. If she could, she would have found some way to indicate that to Melissa, even if she didn't want to tell the police. And now the police are interviewing someone. They won't say who.

Melissa looks about her, half expecting to find herself being watched. Belinda's confidential tone circles around and around: *A female witness has come forward... was able to name her attacker... he's helping us with our enquiries.*

It is all so surreal. She wonders how the hell they'll get through this, what shape they will all be now. Dan will be devastated. He will feel responsible. Why didn't he stay by his sister's bedside? What was so important that he had to go back to the site?

If only she'd had the cash to pay for the chalet. If she hadn't been so skint – or so damn proud – Casey would not have...

Did it start there? That first conversation? When her daughter knew she could not ask for that kind of money, the kind every single other parent she knows would be able to hand over without blinking? Because the fact is, Casey never did ask, did she? She only wanted a loan. Because she's a good kid, the best, and she would rather remove a limb than put her mum in any kind of difficulty. Empathy beyond her years, that girl. And it was, what, maybe a week or so later when she'd waltzed into the kitchen.

'Oh my God, Mum, guess what?' she said in a merry, tinkling voice while Melissa was putting out the breakfast things, a silly-me smirk playing across her mouth. 'My wages have just dropped in my account. I forgot I was owed them.' A laugh, cheeks pinking. 'So I *can* pay the deposit.'

'Wow,' Melissa heard herself say, nowhere near knowing how she felt about the humongous waste of money but understanding that she'd have to keep it to herself. 'I can still give you the hundred for spending.'

'It's OK! I'll get, like, two more wages before we go, so it's all good.' Casey was smiling so very brightly Melissa should have known right there and then it was a lie. But she was too busy fighting her own hurt. She'd saved ten pounds a month. She'd put an actual ten-pound note in a jar every time she got her pay cheque and only once had to dip into it for groceries.

'And I won't be going out now until after exams,' Casey went on, oblivious, 'so I'll have plenty to take to camp.' A soft kiss on her cheek. 'Why don't you get a mani or a pedi for yourself? Or a massage? You're always saying your shoulders are like rocks.'

Melissa stared at her daughter and wondered what the hell she'd done in a past life to deserve this girl.

'That's so kind, but I gave your brother the same. And it'll make me happy if you take it.'

Casey rolled her eyes, her grin widening. 'Well, all right then. That's super generous.'

'You can give me a shoulder rub later.'

'Deal.'

'Deal.'

They worked it out, like they always did. At least that was what she thought. But now, *secrets and lies*, is all she can think. *Secrets and lies, secrets and lies, secrets and lies.*

Casey's lies, yes. But her own, too. She's up to her bloody eyes in them.

'No,' she whispers, to no one, feeling herself pitch forward, righting herself just as the barista calls her name. *Don't think about that now. Do not think about that now.*

SIXTEEN
CASEY

The day after

A woman appears at the door to the ward just as Casey's drinking the last of the hot chocolate. She is smart, tall, thin; a big nose, brown hair and eyes a bit too far apart, but her features work somehow. She's wearing a pale grey trench, black leather cross-body bag, high heels. She mutters something to the nurse at the desk before heading over to Casey's bed.

Belinda stands up and places her magazine on the chair. The woman's eyes flick over to Casey. Mum is standing up too now. She gives a wobbly smile.

'DI Chambers,' the smart woman says, shaking Mum's hand. 'You must be Casey's mum. I just need a quick word with Casey in private, if that's OK?'

'Of course.' Mum locks eyes again with Casey.

Casey tries to read what she's trying to communicate but can't. A flash of moonlight in trees, herself running, her flip-flops slipping on mossy ground. Her heart quickens. It's like her body is remembering before her mind.

Mum is leaning over. She kisses her on the cheek. 'I'll be

right back,' she says softly. 'You'll be fine. Just tell the lady what you can remember, OK?'

Casey grabs her mother's hand, panic rising. 'Can't you stay?' she says, a sob catching in her throat.

'You'll be fine,' Mum repeats.

Their eyes meet again in the silent communication they have always shared but that for some reason today Casey cannot fathom. Something intense, something urgent, but what?

'They said it might come back in flashes,' Mum says. 'You've done nothing wrong, OK?'

Casey holds on to her mother's hand a second more, convinced there's something she's not getting, before reluctantly letting her fingers slide away. She watches Mum and Belinda walk towards the exit and feels her stomach drop.

The woman sits down.

'I'm Detective Inspector Jackie Chambers,' she says and somehow manages to smile seriously.

'Hello,' Casey says quietly. DI. Detective Inspector, of course. She knew it. The woman looks like she's come to a fancy dress as a TV detective, after all.

Chambers tilts her head to one side in a gesture of sympathy. 'How're you feeling?'

'I'm OK, thanks. Bit achy, but OK.'

Chambers looks about her. The ward is hushed now all the visitors have had to go. Casey wonders where Dan is. He said he'd be back soon, but it's after eight and there's no sign of him. The detective turns her attention back to Casey. Her thin smile does not reach her eyes, and this makes Casey feel even more nervous.

'I've asked your Mum and PC Riley to grab a break so we could have a little chat. I know you're tired and you've been through a lot, and I'll need you to give a formal statement tomorrow down at the station, but the sooner we can get some information, the better.' She reaches into her bag and pulls out a notepad and a silver pen. She meets Casey's eye and pushes the end of the pen: *click*.

Casey frowns. 'But they said I wasn't assaulted...'

Chambers gives a slow nod. 'There was no evidence of a serious sexual assault, so that's a good thing obviously. But you were assaulted. You have a nasty graze on the back of your head and extensive bruising. Do you have any idea who might have inflicted these injuries?'

'No.' Casey shakes her head, her throat all but closed. Byrne's face comes to her, by the bonfire, smiling, tender. Then Dan shouting at her. Immy giving her a cocktail in a can – *You're playing catch-up, babe*. The smell of the fire. The crash of the sea. Music.

'Do you know who might have wanted to do something like this to you?'

She shakes her head again. 'No.'

'We have your blood results,' Chambers says, glancing at her notepad. 'I can tell you you've tested positive for flunitrazepam. It's a sedative. You might know it as Rohypnol or by some other name. Do you know what that is?'

'I didn't take anything.' Casey can feel the detective watching her. 'So... wait. Does that mean I was roofied?'

Chambers presses her mouth closed and gives the smallest of nods. 'It would appear that way. You told attending officers and paramedics at the scene you couldn't remember anything. Is that still the case?'

'I've remembered a few bits from earlier. I remember doing my shift at the clubhouse and that I went back to my tent to get changed, then I headed down to the beach. I remember the bonfire. I remember talking to people there.'

'Anyone specific?'

'A guy called Byrne Sharp.' She feels herself blush. But something else too. A hot, stressy feeling. 'I saw my brother,

Dan,' she goes on, flustered. 'And Immy and Charlotte, my friends from school.'

'Would that be Imogen Croft and Charlotte Green?'

She nods.

'That's good. Would you know what time that was?'

'Maybe nine or so.'

'And you have no idea how you came to be in the tent, how you came to be without your clothes or how your injuries were sustained?'

Casey shrugs. 'Not at the moment, sorry.'

Chambers gives an encouraging smile. 'You've already remembered more than you were able to at first. Have you had anything more like flashes at all? Flashing images? A face perhaps, or a place? An impression of a place? Can you remember going anywhere with anyone? Anything really, even if it doesn't seem relevant.'

Dread rises. Casey closes her eyes. 'I'm so sorry. I'm really trying. I keep seeing trees, like the tops of trees with moonlight coming through. And it comes with a horrible feeling, like a dark feeling. I feel scared.'

Chambers makes another note. She frowns then, as if something has just occurred to her. 'I need to tell you there's been a development,' she says, and it seems to Casey she is watching her like something out of a nature documentary: a predator, specifically, waiting to pounce. 'A woman has come forward to make a complaint, and we're trying to get hold of a second woman who witnesses say left the site on Friday after being assaulted.'

Casey's heart has begun to thump, but she's not sure why. 'Who? I mean, who are they complaining about?'

'One of them is a man called Jacob Crossley, and one is the man you mentioned. Byrne Sharp. Mr Crossley was over the age limit for the weekend event. He's helping us with our enquiries. We haven't managed to locate Mr Sharp yet, but we're keen to speak to him.'

'Complaints,' Casey says. 'What kind of complaints?'

DI Chambers is still looking at her intently. Casey can feel the prick of sweat at her hairline, the woman's stare like a drill. 'Aggressive behaviour and attempted spiking, by which I mean administering a sedative without consent. The taking of photographs without consent. And choking.'

Casey reaches for the plastic water glass; takes a sip, another. The trees, the leaves, the moon. Fingers around her neck, squeezing. The air cold on her belly.

'Oh God,' she says, tears spilling, throat almost closing. 'I think...'

'Yes?'

'I think... Wait...'

'You think?'

'When you said choking... We were in some woods. I can remember hands round my neck.' Her heart hammers. She begins to cry. 'I can't pin it down. But I can feel hands round my neck.' She is sobbing too much to carry on.

The detective pulls a tissue from the box beside the bed and hands it to her. 'I know this is hard, but you're safe now and you're doing really well.'

When Casey looks up, Chambers is digging in her bag as if looking for something.

'Now,' she says, pulling out a phone. 'I need to tell you that a photograph of you was sent from Byrne Sharp's phone to Jacob Crossley's phone, and to the phones of two other men: Robert Baker and your brother, Daniel Connor.'

'A photograph?' Casey feels like she's going to cry. 'Of me? Dan didn't...'

'I'm sorry, but you might find the image upsetting. I'm only showing it to you to help you remember, OK? Are you ready?'

Casey nods. She feels sick, so sick. The detective holds up the phone. Casey finds herself staring at a photograph of herself. She is standing with her back against a tree, apparently naked, arms crossed over her chest, mouth open, head to one side. She looks drunk. A mess.

'Oh my God.' She claps her hand over her mouth. Tears roll out and down her cheeks. 'Oh my God.'

'Do you have any recollection of this photograph being taken?'

She can't tear her eyes away from the image, even as she wants to grab the phone from the detective's hand and throw it across the room. 'Is it... Are there more?'

The detective shakes her head. 'There are no more images on Mr Crossley's phone. It was sent to a WhatsApp group, of which your brother was a member, along with a kind of taunt.' Chambers stares at her, right into her eyes.

Casey looks down into the bedclothes wrinkled up on her lap.

'Have you any idea why he might have done that?'

'What did it say? The taunt?'

Chambers thumbs the phone and, holding it at arm's length, reads stiffly: '"Dan, bro, your sister is fit. Full picture tomorrow mofos."' She looks up, her expression neutral.

And then it comes again: the patchy light, the bark against her back, his hands. His face in shadow. The change in his expression from tender to hard, the blackening of his eyes against the whispering trees. So sudden, so shocking.

Him. It was him.

'Casey?'

'It was him,' she whispers.

'Who? Can you tell me?'

'Byrne. Byrne Sharp. I can see him.'

'Well done. That's incredibly helpful.'

Casey feels hot. She pushes the bedclothes back a little. 'He's a friend of my brother's,' she says, after a moment. Like that would explain anything. 'Dan knew him from the pub; he hasn't known him long.' Tears fall thickly. She wipes them away with the back of her hand. 'You just don't think something like this will happen, like, in real life...'

'Do you know Mr Sharp well?'

'No!' She shakes her head, more tears spilling. 'I think Byrne and his mates came into my brother's pub one night. I think he won an Olympic medal, or he could have, and now he's, like, an influencer? He does self-defence videos and lifestyle stuff. Dan said they come here every year. I don't know why because I think they're twenty-six. It's a bit...' She stops. She's gabbling. 'Sorry,' she adds. 'It's just... I can't get my head around it. I can't remember going to the woods with him, but I know it was him. There was light in the leaves, like moonlight. Did you say you're looking for him? What about Dan? Have you spoken to Dan?'

The detective puts her phone back into her bag. 'The SOCO spoke briefly to your brother at the site, but he didn't mention the photograph.'

Casey shakes her head. Something else is coming back – the argument with Dan by the bonfire.

'Casey?'

'Sorry, I just remembered a bit more. Dan and me had an argument.'

The detective appears to consider this. 'What about?'

'About Byrne.'

'Why would you argue about Mr Sharp if you hardly knew him?'

Her cheeks blaze. 'Byrne and me were getting on well. Dan didn't want me to, you know... He said he was too old for me and that he wasn't a nice person.' She sniffs, wiping tears into her hair. 'Not a nice guy, he said. I should've listened.'

'Does your brother know or suspect Byrne Sharp did this to you?'

'I don't know. He didn't say anything.' *Why not? Why didn't he mention the photo?*

'We're interviewing everyone who was at the site over the weekend. Sometimes an incident like this is actually the tip of the iceberg.' Chambers stands up and readjusts her bag so that it sits on the back of her hip. 'You can come in tomorrow morning and we'll take a formal statement, OK? Hopefully some more will have come back to you by then. But you've done really well. Really. Now, try and rest.'

She turns away but then stops, as if she's forgotten something. She turns back, standing now at the end of Casey's bed. She is so tall.

'Your brother's very protective of you, isn't he?' she asks.

Casey is aware of her pulse throbbing in her ears. 'I mean,' she says, 'he's my brother, so... but he'd never hurt anyone.' She thinks of his expression earlier. The intense look in his eyes, the scabs on his knuckles, the message he was trying to communicate while Belinda read her magazine, ears flapping. She thinks of him last night, snarling at her. His fingers tight around her arm. She knows he wouldn't have done that unless... unless what? Did he know something about Byrne even then?

'Well, I'll see you tomorrow at the station.' With the briefest smile, Chambers twirls once again on her heel and walks slowly out of the ward. Her head is high, shoulders square. The click-clack of her footsteps fades until, with a swing of the door, she is gone.

Byrne took a nude picture of her while she was out of it and sent it to Dan. Now Byrne is missing and Dan had blood on his knuckles.

Dan, she thinks. What the hell have you done?

SEVENTEEN
DAN

Three months before

'Let me show you something.' Byrne rests his cue against the pool table and strides towards the door. 'Come on,' he adds, beckoning without turning around.

Obediently, Dan follows him outside. Only as the door shuts behind him does it occurs to him that this could be a scam, that the others are right now emptying the cash register. But that doesn't make sense. There's barely a penny in there. No one pays cash these days, not even George, and the boys won't be nicking the booze because... because more than two units is for losers.

Dan makes his way down the pub steps and follows Byrne around the corner to the car park, where a beautiful sky-blue vintage sports car is parked next to a scruffy black Transit van, as if the van has been put there to show the car to best possible effect.

'Check this out.' Still wearing sunglasses, Byrne leans against the car and crosses one loafer across the other, revealing his tanned ankle. The car – and Byrne for that matter – looks like something from an old cop series. Except those guys were never as dench as Greek gods.

'Is that actually your car?' Dan asks.

Byrne presses his mouth closed tight and gives a slow nod.

'It's so cool,' Dan says. 'I love anything vintage.'

'Vintage cars, yes. Clothes, maybe not.'

In all their chats, this is the first jagged thing Byrne has said. Dan fights not to feel the sting of it. Byrne has given him so much advice these last few months, often sitting up at the bar while the others play pool and just chatting about life and stuff. Through him, Dan has learned tons, like the fact that eighty per cent of women are only dating the top twenty per cent of men. Byrne is helping him get into that top twenty, and already Dan can feel girls looking at him in a way they never have before. Byrne's right – Dan needs to lose the second-hand clothes. He needs to dress for success.

Byrne unlocks the passenger door, gets in and winds down the window.

'Come on,' he says, gesturing towards the driver's side with his head.

Dan walks around the pristine vehicle and slides himself onto the flawless tan leather seat. The dashboard is matt black with cool old-fashioned dials. Even the steering wheel is class, braided with more toasted leather. He really should get back to the pub. The door isn't visible from here; a customer might have come in, even the landlady, though she is too lazy to check on him more than once a month.

'It's a 1974 Mercury Capri,' Byrne says. 'A classic. Four cylinders, one hundred horsepower, Europe's answer to the Mustang back in the day. Forty grand, one of these would set you back.'

Dan fights to conceal his shock. How can *anyone* pay forty thousand pounds for a car, let alone someone in their twenties?

'If you close the pub, we could go for a drive.' Byrne eyes Dan like a lizard. 'Not like there's anyone in there.'

Dan checks his watch. It's only half past ten.

'I don't close up till eleven,' he says with a sinking feeling. Rules aside, there's no way he'd let Byrne and his boys see him mopping the pub floor and cleaning the loos.

'Up to you, bro,' Byrne says in a tone of solemn respect. 'Up to you.'

They bump fists. Dan feels himself blush. Byrne respects him.

That's because he's starting to respect himself.

Two weeks later, a little after eleven, Dan is locking up the pub while round the corner, Byrne, Robbo and Jay wait in the Capri for that promised drive – and a visit to Byrne's riverside apartment. Dan has told them he'll only be a few minutes and has done what his mum would call a spit-and-polish job on the cleaning. But what the hell, right? No one comes in, and anyway, he never agreed to cleaning toilets when he took the job, just as he never agreed to share tips with the landlady or work without food for eight solid hours at a time or ruin his trainers with spilt beer and bleach.

He pulls his phone from his jeans. A flutter of nerves rises in his belly. Still hidden behind the damp brick wall, he sends a quick text to his mother.

Going to Byrne's place. Have key. See you tomo. Xx

He pockets his phone, relieved to have got the communication with Mum out of the way. From all the banter during their many games of pool over the last two months, he knows that if they caught him texting his mum, they would call him a douche, a wet wipe, a pussy.

He heads for the car park, nerves sharpening now. Being invited to Byrne's gaff feels like a big step, like he's won something. Until now, he's only seen these boys in the pub. Even though it's only for a few games of Xbox, it feels like some sort of bridge he's crossing. To what, he's not sure.

He rounds the corner, catching the low rolling tones of R&B blasting from the open window of the sleek blue vehicle. Vape smoke floats towards him; disintegrates into the night. He climbs into the back, where Robbo is drumming the back of the passenger seat headrest in time with the music. R. Kelly. Dan says nothing, of course, doesn't want to come off as some judgy nerd. The car smells strongly of synthetic vanilla, leather, and the woody, spicy scent Dan has come to associate with Byrne Sharp.

Byrne revs the engine before Dan has even got the door shut. The others laugh, are still laughing as the Capri screeches out of the car park onto the road, Dan scrabbling to do up his seat belt. Jay and Robbo laugh at everything, Dan has noticed. At least everything Byrne says or does, provided the intention is comedic. When they attempt to joke around in return, there is something desperate in their tone, as if they are primary school kids trying to earn a smile from the teacher. Last week, when Robbo laughed at something Byrne hadn't intended to be funny, the air in the pub had thinned. Dan had felt it in his gut, wondered what it would be like to have that kind of authority.

Byrne drives like a Formula 1 racer. Glad of the empty streets, Dan doesn't speak for fear his voice will come out high like a girl's. Jay and Robbo are all *whoa*s and f-bombs as Byrne flies through an amber-to-red near St Margarets. Not for the first time, Dan wishes he was travelling with Rory, or that Rory was back here; it wouldn't matter which. They could play a bit of Xbox, talk shit as they made their way through a twelve-pack of Bud and a cheeky Domino's.

His phone pings. Mum. Shit, he thinks.

'That your girlfriend?' Byrne asks from the driver's seat. 'Tell her you're with the boys, yeah?'

'It's... it's no one,' Dan says, his voice a croaky whisper.

Robbo laughs. 'Does no one wear a bra?'

'Or is it your boyfriend?' Jay cackles at his own so-called joke, and before Dan can comprehend what is happening, Robbo has grabbed his phone from the back pocket of his jeans.

'Hey.' Dan grasps for it, hating himself and everything about this. 'Give it back.'

'What is this piece of shit?' Robbo asks. 'This is prehistoric, man. What's your password?'

'None of your business.'

'Burn!' Jay throws out his fingers with a flourish. '*Feisty* man.'

'Give it back,' Dan says, aiming for lightness in his tone. 'Come on. Don't be a dick.'

Robbo holds the phone out of reach. On the screen, the sight of his mother's reply makes Dan's throat close. He should've set the messages to private. He unclips his seat belt and lunges, but he's already guessed what happens now.

And sure enough...

'OK, love,' Robbo reads out in a mumsy voice. 'Thanks for letting me know. Don't forget to double-lock when you get in. Have a good time. Love you.' The last two words he imbues with mocking incredulity. 'Love you,' he repeats, fluttering his eyelids and making a kiss-kiss mouth.

'That your mummy?' Jay crows from the passenger seat. 'You tell mummy-wums you're going out to play with your friendy-wends, did you? Awwww.'

'I...' Dan begins, but he has no idea what to say. He should've waited until his mother had replied before getting in the car. Shit, shit, shit. 'It's not about her being my mum,' he tries, but his words sound pathetic even to his own ears. 'It's about respect, that's all.'

'Respect yourself first,' Byrne chimes in, overtaking an Uber as the 33 bus comes straight for them in the opposite direction.

Dan inhales. With a hair-raisingly slim margin for error, Byrne pulls in. The bus blasts its horn. Dan tries not to exhale audibly. His heart is battering so hard he's scared they'll hear it. Holy shit.

'Yeah, bro,' Jay crows, quashing any hope that this conversation is over. 'Respect your*self*, innit, not your mommy.' This last is delivered in a bad American accent.

'Mummy's boy,' Robbo sneers.

Ahead, the bridge rises towards the Georgian riverfront of Richmond upon Thames. Yellow street lights droop in the dark water.

'It's calm,' Byrne says. 'You're your own man. You can do what you want, when you want, with whoever you want.'

'As long as it's OK by Mumsy,' Jay quips, causing another explosion of sniggers from Robbo.

'As long as you're back before it gets dark,' Robbo just about manages, pinching an imaginary handbag at his chest.

Dan says nothing. He wants desperately to explain that it's not like that. He's not on a curfew and he's not a mummy's boy. But if he doesn't let Mum know he's going to be late, she'll worry, and if she worries, she won't sleep, and then she'll be tired for work. And that's not OK.

'You treat your ma with respect.' Byrne is slowing now into the line of traffic. 'I like that, bruh. How you treat your women is important. She's a woman in your home, under your protection. It's called consideration.'

Robbo and Jay fall silent. The air shifts.

'Th-That's exactly it,' Dan says, glancing at Robbo, whose hilarity is freeze-framed in his idiotic grin, his fading euphoria a reflection of Dan's own bewilderment.

'We don't want to be weak,' Byrne goes on. 'But it's OK to be considerate to our women. Especially our mums, yeah?'

'Y-Yeah,' Dan manages. 'She doesn't sleep if she worries. She's got a right to know.'

'Self-respect is about decency. A good man takes care of his mum. He takes care of his women.'

'Yes,' Dan says again, grateful but with no clear idea what he means.

At that moment, Byrne swings the car hard left. Dan is thrown on top of Robbo.

'Whoa, man,' Robbo protests. 'You trying to get with me? You fancy me or something?'

Jay sniggers into his hand.

Dan rights himself, pushing back his hair, and, perhaps a bit stoked by Byrne's surprise support, says, 'Mate. I'm not that desperate.'

In the rear-view, Byrne grins from behind his gold-framed police shades. Dan feels warm delight expand in his chest.

'Bu-u-urn,' Jay jeers, shaking his hand so hard his fingers click.

They are all laughing now, tension bursting like a thousand fragile soap bubbles, though Robbo looks like he's bitten into a lemon. As he tentatively allows himself to laugh along, Dan thinks about Rory, about how when they used to crack up together, no one had to get burned or owned or beaten in any way. They found silly things the funniest: off-the-wall memes, animals doing batshit stuff, jokes about vacuum cleaners and light bulbs.

With these guys, humour is a test, something to withstand in order to prove yourself. It is loaded. Like a gun.

EIGHTEEN
DAN

Three months before

The car almost skids to a halt. Dan is thrown forward. But they have stopped finally. The ordeal is over. They are in a car park somewhere beyond Kew, he thinks, though he has had his eyes closed for much of the last few minutes. Relief at making it here alive drains through him. He can almost feel it seeping out like liquid through the soles of his trainers. He needs to get a grip, he thinks. He needs to man up.

Byrne turns off the engine. 'Home sweet home, boys.'

'Sick,' Robbo says, already fidgeting to get out.

'I'll just text my mum and let her know,' Byrne adds.

There is a beat before the others fall about in noisy hysterics. Dan fights a feeling of betrayal. It is as if Byrne has built him up only to knock him down. But he's only joking. This is just their humour. With guys like these, it's important to show you can take a joke, otherwise they'll really roast you. Byrne's probably just guarding against Robbo and Jay turning against him. Yeah, that's what that was. In a way, he was protecting Dan.

Robbo throws open the car door. 'Oh, my days.' He is

shaking his head now, as if he can barely recover from so much laughing. 'Oh, my word.'

'Just let my mum know,' Jay manages, wiping at his eyes. 'Classic.'

Dan takes a beat. Robbo and Jay are scuffling outside, trading insults, slurs on each other's mothers, threats to whoop each other's ass at *Call of Duty*. With a sinking feeling, he hauls himself out of the car. The urge to go home is strong. He could feign a stomach bug or a headache, but no, he'd never live it down, not after the mum stuff.

'Come on,' Byrne says, throwing a brotherly arm around his shoulder. 'Let's have some fun.'

Minutes later, Dan is letting his dazzled eyes wander around Byrne Sharp's swanky flat, his belly flipping with a mix of jealousy and awe. It is not a flat, it is an *apartment* – open-plan, wide windows, balcony with a view up the river. One of the walls is entirely given over to dark-blue-painted kitchen units. Classy antique-effect brass handles match the brass mixer tap on a white porcelain sink. Shiny marble worktops are spotlit by hidden downlighters. There is a juicer, a chrome coffee machine, a space-age stove. He's used to his mates' houses being much higher spec than the flat he shares with Mum and Casey, but this kitchen, this whole place, looks more expensive than anything he's ever seen in his life. How can this be Byrne's actual home?

Opposite the kitchen area, a sixties-style mushroom corner lamp casts an orange glow over a low charcoal-grey velvet corner sofa. There are framed pop art images; on the back wall hangs a screen at least two metres across.

Byrne has achieved all this on his own – with discipline, hard work, dedication. It is awe-inspiring. The guy is actually a bit of a legend.

'This is...' Dan begins. 'I mean, you actually... You're not, like, renting?'

Byrne slaps him on the shoulder, a fraction too hard. 'All bought and paid for, bruh, all bought and paid for. Jay's about to purchase his first place, and my man Robbo ain't far behind. They've been helping me with my business ventures, haven't you, boys?'

'We're Byrne's associates,' Robbo says, randomly performing a kung-fu kick.

'Get us some cans, Robs,' Byrne says.

Robbo opens a huge American fridge at the far side of the units and pulls out four cans of Guinness Zero, which he places on the bar with the concentration of a monkey doing long division.

'But how?' Dan asks. 'I mean, how do you afford it?'

'Glad you asked. Let me show you something.'

Byrne leads him to the corner sofa; picks up a remote from a smoked-glass coffee table. A moment later, the huge screen blooms into a dizzying array of smart TV choices. He brings up YouTube and types *Stay Sharp* into the search engine. The channel appears. On it, there is a circular photo of Byrne in white fencing kit but without the helmet. Two narrow swords are crossed in front of him in a way that reminds Dan of a superhero. Byrne's expression is serious, his beady brown eyes staring straight out as if to lock with an invisible enemy. A short paragraph reads: *I'm Byrne and I'm here to tell you how to stay sharp. It's kill or be killed out there, people, so subscribe here for the hottest tips on how to uncover your power and be the best possible version of yourself.*

Byrne is grinning, an expression that says, *Check me out*.

'See there,' he says, pointing to the thumbs-up icon. 'Two hundred thousand followers and counting.'

'Wow,' is all that Dan can think to say. He feels as if, with one breath, Byrne Sharp could blow him into floating wisps like a dandelion in a stiff breeze.

Byrne clicks through some of the short videos, showing a

few seconds of each. Dan is vaguely aware of the others settling themselves on the sofa, of the cans being placed on the table, though he cannot sit down, cannot give Byrne anything less than his full attention. There are clips of Byrne fencing, Byrne shirtless, boxing a punchbag, lifting weights, doing sit-ups. The standard of the clips is high – no shaky cameras, no inaudible speech, no poor lighting. Professionally made then, high quality, like everything Byrne does.

In some, Byrne demonstrates fencing moves – the lunge, the parry, the riposte. Then there are more clips, this time Byrne in his blue kitchen making a smoothie, or frying eggs, or assembling robust-looking salads with all kinds of seeds on top. Another account is called Sharp Style. Here, Byrne is pictured outside a country house somewhere showing off yet another vintage car. There are clips of him clay pigeon shooting, driving, going for dinner with various glamorous women, always in shades, always tanned, always in his uniform of tightly fitting clothes, always clean-shaven, hair freshly cut.

Glamorous, Dan thinks. The man is so damn glamorous. Dan has always thought of guys like Byrne as posers – materialistic and shallow, vain, preening – but maybe there are such things as winners and losers. And maybe Dan is the loser.

'Sponsors,' Byrne says. 'If you get enough followers, companies will pay good money to advertise on your account. All I have to do is live my best life and the money keeps rolling in. Free clothes. Free hotels. Free restaurants, products, supplements, you name it. Round the clock.' With impeccable timing, he turns to catch the can that Robbo throws to him. 'There's a self-defence course on there too. For women. I made it with one of my female associates.'

He brings up a third account: Stay Sharper, the art of self-defence with Byrne Sharp. There is a description below, but Dan doesn't have time to read it because Byrne chooses a video at random and presses play. In it, he has an attractive blonde woman pinned to the wall by the neck. Dan feels himself flush with stress.

'It only takes six seconds to lose consciousness once an attacker has cut your air supply,' the voiceover says. It is Byrne, of course, serious and punchy, the same way he speaks in real life.

'Remember your first rule. Stay sharp. Stay calm. Make your neck short, widen your stance so you drop down a little.' As Byrne narrates, the woman moves. 'Now rotate your torso slightly. Punch the attacker's arm at the wrist like so. Then elbow hard to the head.' The woman pushes out. His arm is knocked away. She elbows Byrne in the head, causing him to fall. A second later, he is up again and the manoeuvre is repeated, Byrne's voice continuing the narration. 'If your attacker falls forward, wrap your arm around the head like so. The other arm comes up under the armpit to stop him grabbing your legs. Spin and push. Push him against the wall in the guillotine lock. Then both arms around the neck and pull.'

Dan watches the woman turn Byrne around in a kind of headlock. It is impressive, him helpless in her grip with just a couple of deft moves.

'There's loads more where that came from,' Byrne says. 'Show your sister, your mum too. Get them to subscribe. It's not just women who can learn from this, but I earn more with Tisha because people like to watch a beautiful girl being strangled.'

'Right.' Dan swallows.

'You got to learn to monetise your life,' Byrne adds.

'Right. Sweet, yeah. Absolutely.' Dan cannot think of a single thing about his life that would be of interest to anyone beyond his mum, his sister and a few of his friends, let alone of enough interest for anyone to subscribe or for investors and advertisers to come knocking on his virtual door. He doesn't even have a car, let alone a fast one. And he could never carry off mirrored sunglasses.

He could buy a dog, he thinks. Teach it to do tricks. But he can't afford one. A cute rescue? Girls love dogs, don't they? They love men who love dogs – Casey has told him that, he's pretty sure. But it's no pets in the flat.

In his mother's flat.

Byrne has sat down. Dan is the only one still standing. He takes off his shoes as the others have done before lowering himself, lowering himself further, and further again, to the point of falling, before his arse finally connects with the cushions. Still, he feels like he's falling backwards, somehow caught in the momentum, his limbs lifting involuntarily like a dying fly. It is like trying to sit in an upholstered bucket.

'It will come to you soon enough, bro,' Byrne says, handing him a can of the non-alcoholic stout and a glass. For a second, Dan thinks he means the art of sitting on the lowest sofa in the world before he realises he means money.

How? he wants to say. *When?* It occurs to him that he craves it. For the first time in his life, he craves money. He wants confidence, style, success. He wants to be... not Byrne exactly but like him. In his own way.

The huge TV screen is flickering, the remote in the grip of Robbo, who is setting up the Xbox.

'You've found your discipline,' Byrne says, as if continuing his lesson. 'You're hitting the gym, yeah? You're buying decent clothes. That's step one. Taking back control. Doing what makes you feel good. Turning from boy to man, am I right?' He gestures with his hand to indicate Dan's new-found physique. 'Looking good, my friend. Bitches gonna be forming an orderly queue.'

'Forming an orderly queue.' Robbo places his can on the coffee table and, inexplicably, laughs. 'Mate, you swallowed a dictionary or something?'

'Don't say that,' Byrne replies with a curtness that puts

Dan's teeth on edge. 'You make yourself sound stupid when you disrespect yourself like that, you feel me?'

'Sure.' Robbo's face falls.

Dan has no idea what just happened. The only offensive thing he heard in the exchange was the word *bitches*, which he's pretty sure was a joke, and Byrne said that, his posh pronunciation flashing with street slang as it sometimes does.

'So,' Byrne says, turning his attention back to Dan. 'You getting any?'

'Any?'

He raises his eyebrows, gathers his lips in a pout and makes a fist.

Dan feels himself blush. 'Er... well, I... I actually broke up with my girlfriend last summer.'

'Wait, when?' Byrne takes off his sunglasses. His eyes are beady and small, which Dan suspects is why he never takes off his shades. 'Last summer? And no bitches sniffing about since then?'

Dan closes his eyes at the language but says nothing. It's just the way Byrne speaks, the way these boys speak. Just words. They don't mean it. Byrne loves women. He respects them. Why else would he do those amazing self-defence videos, unless he saw himself as a protector? Which sounds a bit outdated, but not if it comes from a good place and when, actually, most men are physically stronger than most women. Wouldn't he, Dan, be ready to kill anyone who tried to hurt Casey or Mum?

'Bro?' Byrne is still waiting for an answer.

'I've not met anyone else I really like yet,' Dan offers, hoping this will get him off the hook whilst somehow making it seem like he's in a position to choose. The truth is, he has precisely no options and doesn't feel comfortable admitting that he is still not over Livvy. After almost a year, he can't stop thinking about her, and when he does, he feels himself fill with regret. Maybe if Byrne could help him get a job and a flat while she's away, if he could get himself into shape, he might be in with a chance of winning her back. He imagines meeting her off the plane from India – her all tanned and travel-cool, him all handsome, square-shouldered and successful. Her eyes lighting up. *Dan! You've changed.* Him: *I've got wheels. Come on.*

'Staying picky is good,' Byrne is saying. 'Once you get into that twenty per cent, you can make chicks earn your attention. They want real men. They don't want boys wearing their skinny little shoulders as earrings, trust me.'

Dan straightens his neck, lengthens his spine.

'You have to show up. You have to pick up the tab, know what I'm saying? You need this.' Byrne rubs his thumbs against his fingers, the international sign language for money. 'If you have that, you get to choose. And then you make *them* work for *you*, know what I'm saying?'

'Sure.' Dan nods wisely and sips his Guinness Zero, wondering if these are the only twenty-something guys he's ever met who don't drink a few too many beers when they get together. Maybe only losers do that. Maybe Byrne's right about what women want. Livvy said she needed freedom and travel. She said she wanted to find herself. But maybe she needed to find someone else. Maybe she wanted the kind of freedom only a man with cash can bring.

'I'm going for a smoke. Come with.' With the silky stealth of a panther, Byrne rises from the sofa and heads for the balcony.

Dan hesitates. The others are lost in *Call of Duty: Modern Warfare III*, thumbs twitching, marbles for eyes, bright white towelling socks making bulldog paws of their feet.

He follows Byrne outside, where tall street lamps glimmer in the dark water of the river. From behind the muscular triangle of Byrne's back, vape clouds puff, disperse, releasing the aroma of black-market cannabis. He persuaded Dan to try it last week outside the pub. It made him cough, made him feel sick.

Dan tunes out the rat-a-tat-tat of gunfire behind him, the swearing and shouts of exasperation. Jay and Robbo are not at all like his other friends. Neither is Byrne, in a different way. Dan's friendship groups have always been shifting, amorphous things; shambolic, with no clear leader. Byrne is the clear leader here. For all the banter, Robbo and Jay seem at times frightened of or at least intimidated by him. And where Byrne's nicknames for them are many, they never call him anything other than his name; they don't even shorten it. Dan knows that everything Byrne says is aimed at building his confidence so that he can *actualise his potential*. Already he can feel himself improving. He just needs to stop overthinking and be less of a boy and more of a man.

Because the sad truth is, even Rory's Instagram makes him feel like a loser these days. He should've borrowed the money and gone with him and the lads. He had saved almost enough from the pub to fly and out and join them, but he's blown it all now on box-fresh T-shirts, a gym membership and new shoes. It's hard to know which path to take; for every message from Rory, there are three from Byrne, links to flats there's no way he can afford, even to rent. He has to start earning decent money, get a deposit together. He can't take the shame of living with his mum for much longer.

'I'm thinking of bringing you in,' Byrne says.

Dan takes a sip of his Guinness Zero. 'To... to the business?'

'Not yet,' Byrne adds. 'But soon. I have more lucrative strands. You're smart. A smart guy. I could use a smart guy like you.'

Dan cannot think how to reply. A thrill passes through him. A more lucrative strand. Himself in an apartment like this. Well, maybe not like this, but something, something that would be his, something impressive to people his age.

'Yo,' Byrne says, and Dan sees he has walked off and is

disappearing back inside. The conversation is apparently over. For now.

Dan steps back through the French windows.

'Robbo,' Byrne says. 'Turn that off.'

Robbo's eyes swivel with panic. He looks like a kid who's had an ice cream wrenched from his hands, but incredibly, he obeys. The screen goes black.

Byrne sits, his magnificent quads enabling him to lower himself into the sofa with apparently no effort whatsoever. Dan tries but can't do it without leaning on one hand. When he hits the seat, he still feels like he's been folded in half.

'S'up?' Jay asks, ripping a sliver of nail from his thumb with his teeth.

'Two words,' Byrne says, steepling his hands. He waits a beat before adding, 'Heaven. View.'

'Result,' Robbo says. He makes a fist and cackles.

Dan's stomach clenches.

'We doing it again?' Jay asks at exactly the same time as Dan says, 'Do you mean the one in Weymouth?'

'I do indeed.' Byrne eyes Dan, giving his trademark grin. 'Summer Camp, my man. Sweet, sweet Summer Camp.' He turns to his boys, who are one step away from rubbing their hands.

'You guys go to *Summer Camp*?' Dan's voice sounds like it did when he was fourteen and it started breaking.

'Three years now, bruh.'

'But that's for kids.' Dan feels the crease of a frown on his forehead. 'Aren't you guys a lot older?'

'We are indeed.' Byrne stretches back, cradles his head in his fingers. 'And the older we get, the younger they get, know what I'm saying?'

As Jay and Robbo burst into the manic laughter of acolytes, Dan feels a dark and creeping chill. Summer Camp is for teenagers who've finished their exams, not fully grown men with careers and apartments.

But maybe he's being too serious. Isn't this part of his problem, this overthinking, this hesitancy? Byrne was clearly joking. It's just a bit of fun, and it's not like they're *old* old, like in their thirties or something.

Byrne slaps him on the shoulder, his fingers squeezing into Dan's flesh. 'It'll do you good to have some fun for a change. You can buy the girls a drink or two, build some of that confidence we've talked about. Practice makes perfect.'

'Right,' Dan says, without knowing what he means. But he's second-guessing again. It's really not that deep. It's a chance to get to know Byrne better, find out more about the business, what opportunities there might be. Maybe, maybe when they get back, Byrne will trust him enough to let him in. He can finally stop working in the pub with its rubbish conditions and shitty wages. Who knows? In a year or two, he might even have enough for a deposit.

'Are you in?' Byrne is grinning at him, reaching now for the Xbox controls.

Dan nods; returns his smile. 'Sure,' he says. 'Sounds good.'

NINETEEN
MELISSA

The day after

Detective Chambers emerges from Purbeck Ward, her face unreadable.

'Ms Connor,' she says. 'I've had a quick chat with Casey. She's starting to remember, but I'll need to see her in the morning so she can make a formal statement.'

Melissa bristles. 'Even though she's the victim?'

'I'm afraid so. The situation has developed. If you can bring her in once she's been discharged, that would be ideal. I can tell you she's remembered the person who attacked her.'

'She has?' Heat flushes through her. 'And who was it?'

A perfunctory smile flashes on the detective's lips. 'I'll let her tell you that herself. Let's hope she can remember a fuller picture tomorrow.' She turns on her perfect burgundy kitten heel.

Rattled, Melissa watches her go, her stride smooth and confident, head and neck Pilates-straight. Melissa doesn't like this woman. It is a gut feeling, something animal, chemical, unexplainable. Maybe she's overthinking, but to her ears, that sounded like a veiled warning, like she thinks Casey is stringing them along or something. For God's sake, is that how they treat a poor girl who's been drugged and stripped and left in a tent all night long? There are bruises all over her! She's been poked and probed and jabbed and all she gets is some snarky cop raising an eyebrow? What the hell? Melissa wonders if Detective Chambers is heading back to the station now, if she'll have to work late, whether her dinner will be waiting in the oven in some glossy kitchen somewhere. She hopes it dries out.

She needs to see Casey alone. If only she could get rid of Belinda bloody Riley. Is a private chat with her own child too much to ask?

She makes her way back to Casey's bedside, Riley trotting beside her. Her daughter is as pale as the proverbial ghost, her eyes even rounder, even more haunted than before.

'Hey.' Melissa takes her hand, hyper-aware of Belinda earwigging behind her. 'The detective said you'd remembered who did this?'

Casey nods, her eyes flicking briefly to Belinda. 'It was Byrne Sharp.'

'Byrne Sharp,' Melissa repeats. It is all she can think to say. Her eyes search her daughter's, but all she can see is honesty.

'He's one of Dan's mates,' Casey says, as if Melissa doesn't know that. 'He's that guy from the pub, you know, the one Dan keeps going on about. I can't believe he did this to me, but he did. He sent a photograph of me to… to his mates. It was horrible.' She starts to cry. 'I could see his face. I could feel his hands on my neck.'

'Hey, hey,' Melissa says, shushing her, reaching for her hand. 'Don't upset yourself. It's over. Tomorrow you can give your statement, and then I'll take you home and we'll watch all the Harry Potters back-to-back with a tub of ice cream bigger than our heads, OK?'

Casey sniffs. 'The detective said they're still looking for

him. They need him to help them with their enquiries, but they've been talking to one of his friends. Jacob something. I guess that's where she got the photo.'

Melissa does her best to stay composed. 'You don't need to worry about any of that now,' she manages after a moment. 'All you need to do is sleep and then tell them everything you can tomorrow. OK?'

If Melissa could do it all for her, she would, in a heartbeat. Write her a script and read it for her. But she can't.

There is only so much a mother can do.

TWENTY

CASEY

Two and a half months before

On Friday after school, Casey knocks on Dan's bedroom door.

'Come in.'

She pushes open the door in time to see Dan jump up from the floor. He is wearing a gym vest and shorts and he's panting like he's been doing exercise. He looks less pale than normal, but that might just be because he's sweating so much. His arms seem a bit bigger now she looks at him, more toned.

'Were you doing, like, press-ups or something? I thought you did all that at the gym?'

'I was just doing a quick routine before work.' He says it like he's defending himself against criticism, but his face glows an even deeper pink. 'It's about using your time efficiently, that's all.'

'You a fitness freak now?'

He frowns. 'I'm just... I'm just trying to change my life, bruh.'

Casey is not sure how to respond. It feels mean to argue, and she decides to let the *bruh* go.

'I was coming to see if you wanted to watch a movie later,' she says. 'Mum's going to Sarah's straight from work and I'm going to chill for a change. I got a box of Maltesers from the Co-op.' She grins.

'I can't, sorry.'

'That's OK,' she says, too quickly, too cheerfully, which makes her feel like a saddo. 'I was supposed to be going out with Immy and them, but—'

'You remembered she's a bitch?'

'Wow. Really?' Casey scowls at him. 'Your vocabulary's really expanding.'

'Sorry,' he says.

'That's OK. They're going to this restaurant in Richmond, but it's really expensive.'

Dan makes an *I told you so* face, but this time she can't be bothered to take him on, even though, grim word choice aside, her gut tells her there's some truth in what he's saying. 'Would've been good to chill,' he adds with a note of apology, 'but I'm working seven till close, then I'm going back to Byrne's for a bit.'

Casey feels herself sink. She really wanted to tell him she's been looking at old photos of herself and Liam from their holiday last year. But it's too embarrassing to say it out loud just like that. It would've been easier while they were watching crap on TV.

'So are you, like, friends with this Byrne guy now?' she asks instead as Dan lifts another brand-new white T-shirt with the label still on out of his drawer. It looks like there's a pile of them in there.

He shrugs, folding the T back into its square like they do in shops. 'No one else around, is there?'

'Thanks.'

He laughs. They both do.

'You know what I mean,' he says, the pristine Fruit of the

Loom sliding into his rucksack alongside his new perv shoes and what looks like a pair of black jeans – since when did he have black jeans? 'You're working really hard,' he says, 'and that's good. Do you need cash? For the restaurant? I can give you, like, twenty?'

'That's nice, but I don't want to go anyway.' Casey sits on the bed. 'Just need you to stop me from calling Liam.'

Dan smiles and sits beside her. '*That* bored, eh?' He switches to his American-woman-on-a-talk-show voice: 'Don't do it, gurrrl.'

She laughs. 'Maybe I should give him another chance?'

Dan shakes his head. 'It'll be the same. Trust me. And he's got to be the one to...'

'Take the initiative, yeah, I get that.' Liam's dopey face comes to mind. He was sweet, so sweet, but yeah, Dan's right; boredom is messing with her mind. Loneliness too maybe. She exhales; shrugs. 'My life is literally so dead right now.'

'I remember that,' Dan says, leaning into her a second. 'But it's not your life; it's a stepping stone to your life, that's all. Honestly, this summer will be lit.'

Casey bites her lip, wishing Dan could stay home. 'So what's this Byrne guy like?'

'He's good. I mean, he's not... he's not like Rory or anything, he's more... clean? I dunno. Like laundered? He's sharp, like his name.'

'Nominative determinism.'

'Wow. Revision's going well.'

'I am a walking dictionary right now. So, what, he doesn't dig his clothes out of a skip and he washes at least once a week?'

Dan laughs. 'No. I mean, yeah. Of course. But he, like, it's hard to explain. He wears a lot of white.'

They both giggle. Dan's T-shirts come to mind. The last time she put them in the wash, she counted five.

'I'm picturing an angel,' Casey says. 'Like a saint with a halo and wings.' She presses her palms together as if in prayer.

'But at the same time,' her brother goes on, ignoring her, 'he's super switched on. He's making me think about things. Like, you saying about Liam, I'm thinking how I should've taken control a bit more with Livvy, you know? I should've booked more things. I should've gone travelling instead of staying here. I can't even remember why I stayed now. I mean, I wanted to get a job. I didn't want to rinse Mum for free rent and then spend it on flights. But it's not like I've even got a real job, is it? And I'm still living here.' He claps his hands on his knees. 'Anyway, this is all negative talk, and negative talk means negative thought. Byrne's teaching me how not to be a loser.'

'That word!' She wags her finger.

'I know! I know. Chill. You know what I mean. He doesn't mean half of what he says. He uses different words to us, that's all. He's got this YouTube channel. It's called Stay Sharp.'

'I see what he did there.'

'I mean, yeah. There's a lot to take the piss out of, but he does workouts for different levels of fitness, and lifestyle videos where he makes nutritious food and drinks, and cool fencing moves, *and* he does a self-defence channel for women. That's called Stay Sharper. You should check it out. It's actually quite cool.'

'Wait. He does self-defence? For real? Let's see.'

Dan grabs his laptop and brings up the account. Casey refrains from slating the thumbnail with the dude staring out intensely with swords crossed across his chest like some sort of Marvel character. He's even dressed in white – fencing whites, she guesses. What macho BS is this?

'Wow,' she says, not really hiding the sarcasm.

'I know, I know, but... check this out.'

He presses play and together they watch a clip of an attractive young blonde woman being held in a neck lock by the guy from the photo ident.

'Is that him?'

Dan nods.

Byrne Sharp is dressed in white shorts and a white vest that shows his massive shoulders, round arm muscles and shiny, tanned skin. As the video plays out like some sort of dance choreography, the urge to giggle comes to her. But she's not sure how much her brother likes this guy, so she keeps it together for his sake. And as the short clip plays, her mouth falls open.

'Wow,' she says, this time without the sarcasm.

'Cool, right?' Dan says before bringing up another one. Together, they watch the slim blonde overthrow Byrne, who must be tens of pounds heavier than her and all of him solid muscle. He is much more handsome than he seemed in the photo.

'Play another,' she says. 'Is that his voice, by the way? It's very... assertive.'

Dan nods and plays another clip. In it, Byrne has the same woman on the floor, her arms pinned above her head. While he narrates, the pair move in graceful slow motion – almost like dancers. The woman brings up her legs and immobilises him before pushing him away from her and somehow managing to roll him onto his front. They do the whole thing again at full speed.

'That's absolutely amazing,' Casey says. 'Oh my God, let's go try it.'

Giggling, they make their way into the living room. For the next half an hour, with the furniture pushed back, they practise three of the moves until Casey manages to pull her brother over her shoulder and they both collapse in hysterical giggles.

Panting, she pulls him up.

'That was awesome,' she says. 'Absolutely awesome.'

'I told you,' Dan says, clearly pleased. 'He's hard to describe and he's not everyone's vibe, but he's a good guy. We're thinking of coming to Summer Camp.'

'Really? Don't you have to be under twenty?'

'He's got a mate does fake IDs. It's just a laugh, that's all.'

'Sure.' Casey isn't sure, not really.

'You don't mind, do you? I won't come if it's not cool with you.'

'No, no. It's fine. Actually, I need to tell you something. Don't tell Mum though, OK? It's about Heaven View.'

TWENTY-ONE
MELISSA

Two months before

Melissa is attempting to complete the grocery shop, a weekly endeavour that always reminds her of *Supermarket Sweep*, the game show she watched as a teenager. She is exactly like those contestants, running round the aisles trying to shove as much stuff as she can into the trolley before the buzzer goes. The difference, alas, is that none of it is free, and in this case the buzzer is the time limit on her half-hour parking slot.

She lifts some value bran flakes off the shelf, a bulk bag of porridge oats and pushes on, ignoring the granolas, the mueslis and the luxury cereals with the lovely crunchy bits of dried banana.

'Melissa?'

She freezes. It is too late to duck behind the sliced loaves. Too late to run screaming into the car park for that matter. She turns, pretends to register only now the presence of the woman she already knew was there, lets her mouth break into a smile of feigned surprise. 'Sylvia! How on earth are *you*? Haven't seen you in ages.'

Immy's mother rolls her eyes. The only part of her face capable of movement, Melissa thinks, and feels immediately like a bad feminist.

'Oh, you know.' Sylvia almost yawns. 'Apart from Imogen driving me mad as usual, we're all fine. How are you? Casey's working *very* hard apparently.'

'She is.' For some inexplicable reason, Melissa feels her hackles rise. 'She really wants to get into York, so...'

Another eye roll. 'I don't know how you do it. Dan was a hard worker too, wasn't he? You're obviously running a little hothouse there.'

The hackles are standing rod-straight now, bristling. 'I don't think so. I don't force them to work or anything.'

Sylvia laughs. 'I wish I could force mine. I've had to ground Immy, but judging by the music coming out of her room, I don't think it's done much good. Put it this way, I'm crossing my fingers Cambridge needs more class-A rowers.'

'I'm sure she'll do brilliantly,' Melissa replies with a jolly chuckle forced from somewhere deep. 'She'll probably cram it all in at the last minute.'

'I'm sure she will. Immy's lucky; she's never had to work too hard. I think she's just naturally bright, you know, which makes her sooo lazy.'

Melissa opens her mouth to reply, but Sylvia interrupts her before she can get the words out.

'Listen,' she says, laying a hand briefly on Melissa's arm. 'I was so sorry to hear about Casey not being able to join them in the chalet.' She pulls a pained expression.

'O-Oh,' Melissa stutters. She has no idea what Sylvia is talking about and it is hard in the heat of the moment to scan her mind for clues. Didn't Casey tell her she'd managed to pay the deposit? Yes, she did. Melissa had to push her to take the hundred for spending money. Angel, Melissa had thought. Saint.

'I told Immy to tell Casey there was no rush,' Sylvia adds, her head tipping to one side in sympathy. 'I would've covered it until you got the cash together.' She offers a beneficent smile Melissa wishes to God she could drive her fist through without incurring a GBH charge.

'I... I think Casey preferred to camp in the end.' Melissa tips her chin, recovering, improvising. Lying. 'That's what her brother did, and I think he must've told her that's what the cool kids did.' She feels her blush deepen, burn. Shame on me, she thinks. 'You know how she idolises Dan,' she adds. Immy and her brother famously hate one another. Really, this is all so beneath her; it's pathetic, but she's enjoying it too much to stop. 'I swear, if Dan told her to wear an old shoe on her head, she would,' she trills, the train to hell going full steam ahead now. 'Girls and their older brothers, eh?' She laughs, steps back, shaking Sylvia's condescending hand from her arm. The break gives her a beat, allows her to get a hold of herself before this thing descends into a full-on Bette Davis/Joan Crawford scenario.

Sylvia is still smiling, though her jaw looks a little tight. We are idiots, Melissa thinks. This woman, this town, turns me into someone I don't want to be.

'Well, I'm sure they'll all have the most amazing time,' Sylvia says after a moment. 'Wherever they're sleeping. And they'll be together at the beach, won't they? Makes no difference where you stay; it's what you bring to the party that counts, eh? Dancing round the bonfire! Sand between their toes! Oh, to be young!'

'Were you ever young, Sylvia?' Melissa's hand flies to her mouth. But Sylvia is saying goodbye now and somehow still smiling, and Melissa realises she can't have spoken aloud. Thank God.

'Sorry to rush off,' Sylvia mutters, leaning in and lowering her voice conspiratorially. 'I've got ten coming for dinner. I must be mad! I only really come here for the emergency bits and pieces I've forgotten in the Ocado order.'

Wow. Melissa almost applauds.

'Yeah,' she manages instead. 'Menopause brain, eh?'

In no way acknowledging the M word for fear of succumbing to a sudden attack of involuntary ageing, Sylvia waves with the ends of her fingers and struts away towards the cleaning products. I should follow her there, Melissa thinks. Grab some bleach to douse myself with after that grimy exchange. She checks her watch to see the parking ticket has only three minutes left.

'Shit,' she mutters and legs it for the till.

TWENTY-TWO
MELISSA

Two months before

Back home, Melissa tries not to wait for Casey to come back from school. But Casey is all she can think about, and every chore she tackles feels like a diversion. Casey told her she'd paid that deposit. She did, definitely. It was about a week after they discussed it. She definitely said her wages had come in, that it was all good, all paid up.

Casey lied. And Casey never lies to her, never.

Does she?

Or is Melissa like so many parents, thinking her daughter is a paragon of virtue when in fact she's nothing of the sort?

No. Melissa doesn't think Casey is a paragon, nor would she want her to be; she's just a great kid. The best. She is. And they trust one another. There are without doubt things Casey gets up to that she doesn't share, but that's her business and everyone has a right to privacy; Melissa's always been strong on that, never checked her kids' phones, never gone into their rooms without knocking, never looked in or even opened drawers when she's been delivering clean clothes onto their beds.

There must have been some sort of misunderstanding.

The intercom buzzer goes. With a flash of nerves, Melissa makes her way to the door of the flat and pushes the button.

'Hello?'

'Forgot my key, soz,' comes her daughter's voice through the little speaker. 'Can you let me in? I'm dying for a wee.'

Melissa buzzes her in and opens the door to the shared stairwell. Hand still on the catch, she listens to Casey's rapid thudding footsteps, her quickening breath, her weary sigh as she hits the first landing two floors down. These sounds, she thinks. These little sounds. Come September, they will be gone. This stairwell will be silent. There will be no buzzer at 4.30, no *soz I forgot my key*. Only silence.

Casey appears, pushing past, bobbing comedically as she dashes to the loo.

How could she not love this girl? How could anyone not love this girl? She and her brother are the loves of Melissa's life. Richard, her ex, was only ever a passenger who turned into an annoyance. She needs to stay calm and give her a chance to explain.

Two minutes later, Casey is sitting at the kitchen table while Melissa fixes her some hazelnut spread on toast.

'I saw Immy's mum today,' Melissa says, placing the toast and a glass of milk in front of her daughter.

'Oh yeah.' Casey breaks eye contact immediately, which Melissa tries not to read as proof of dishonesty. She picks up her toast and takes a huge bite, possibly to stop herself from saying any more.

'Yeah,' Melissa says carefully. 'I was doing the supermarket shop and she collared me.' She waits, but her daughter says nothing, so she carries on. 'She said you weren't staying in the chalet with the others after all. I thought you said you'd paid up?'

'Erm. Yeah. Uh.' Casey frowns as if she needs to think. She is still chewing. After a few interminable seconds, she takes a large slug of milk. With excessive care, she replaces the glass, wipes her mouth with the back of her hand and sighs. 'I decided not to in the end. Sorry, I thought I'd told you.' She looks up, and in that moment Melissa knows she has taken the time to chew over not just the snack but her story. It's so unsettling. Dan is the fibber; Casey has always been straight up. 'A tent is way cooler.'

'So why say you'd paid the deposit?'

'I said I was *gonna* pay it.' Casey's face matches her new hair dye: deep pink. 'I thought I'd told you I was camping?'

She takes another bite of toast. She's a bright kid, but like most kids, she has no idea how transparent she is.

'Casey, love,' Melissa says, her voice firming. 'I want you to tell me the truth. We can't have trust if you don't tell me the truth. I told you we'd find a way. I said that, didn't I? Today I had to stand there listening to Sylvia bloody Croft giving me her insincere condolences that our poor family couldn't afford a chalet. But much worse was having to pretend it wasn't the first I'd heard about it. Do you get how that might have been... unpleasant?'

Casey's eyes fill. Her toast remains on the plate, a jagged arc bitten out of each corner.

'I was just trying to save you money,' she says quietly. Miserably.

'I get that. And that's kind. I love that you're kind, but that sort of thing is for me to decide. I'm the grown-up, OK? And for the record, I told Sylvia you thought it was cooler to camp. I assume that's what you told Immy?'

Casey looks so uncomfortable that for a moment Melissa thinks she might be sick.

'Case?'

Her daughter's bottom lip trembles.

'Is there something else? The truth, please. Now.'

Two tears roll fat as raindrops down Casey's cheeks. She sniffs. More than anything, Melissa wants to cross the small space between them and throw her arms around her, but she can't. She can't move.

'I'm sorry,' Casey whispers. 'I was trying to do the right thing.'

'The right thing is to tell the truth. You know that.'

She nods, miserably. 'I got a job.'

'A *job*? What? Where?'

'At the campsite. For the summer.'

'*What?*'

'I was going to tell you.'

'What do you mean? What? When?' Melissa shakes her head, as if to clear it.

'I kept meaning to tell you, but...'

Melissa waits, confusion filling her. 'But what? And why, love? Why get a job there?'

'Because then it's free to go to Summer Camp. Even the camping is free. All summer. They have a staff bit where you can pitch your tent. All I have to do is work my shifts, then I can meet the others later. That way I can save for uni. I thought it was a good idea. I thought you'd be pleased.'

'Hang on. You're not working the whole summer, are you?'

No last girly day trips. No Harry Potter movie nights. No footsteps on the stairs.

Casey stares down at her plate. When she speaks, she is barely audible. 'Well, till the end of August. Maybe a bit of September.'

'That's the entire summer. You've taken a job for the entire summer away from home without talking to me first?' Melissa hears the screeching tone in her voice. 'You're going to be away for the best part of three months and then you're off to uni and you didn't think to tell me?'

Casey's shoulders heave. Melissa cannot find it in herself to go to her. Her heart feels like it's breaking in half.

'I can't believe it,' she says eventually, already aware she's made a mess of this. 'I told you I'd find a way. Haven't we always found a way? Haven't I always, always got us what we need? And pretty much most of what we want?'

'Yes! It's not about that. I... You've been amazing. You are amazing. I just thought—'

'You just thought, but you didn't think.' Her voice is rising; she cannot stop it even as she feels herself unspooling. 'I'm the head of this household – do you hear me? I make the decisions. Not you. It's not for you to decide. You're a child. And you've acted like one.'

Casey stands. Her hands press down on the tabletop, fingertips white. 'Now you're just being horrible about it. You're always going on about responsibility, and that's what I did; I took responsibility. I thought that was a good thing.'

'Of course it is! Of course it's a good thing, but lying isn't!'

'I wasn't lying; I just hadn't—'

'Leaving me to be humiliated in front of Sylvia isn't—'

'I'm sorry, I—'

'I nearly died of shame, love.'

'I'm not going into the stupid chalet! I thought you'd be pleased.'

'No, you didn't. If you'd thought I'd be pleased, you would've told me straight away. You thought I'd say no, that's why, but you didn't give me a chance to say anything at all, did you? You knew what you were doing was underhand. And you knew I'd be upset. That was sneaky, love. That's not like you.'

Casey's eyes are narrow; her jaw sets. 'I'm eighteen! I'm legally an adult! I can do what I want!'

'Not while you're still living under my roof, you can't.' Melissa's voice trembles with the effort it takes her not to shout. Even in the white heat of it, she knows she is having the type of argument she never thought she'd have, the type she's been arrogant enough to think was for other mothers, other daughters. And worse, she sounds like Richard when he used to go on at the kids.

'Listen to me,' she says, unstoppable as a glass falling to the floor. 'While I'm paying the bills and doing the supermarket shop and washing your clothes and cleaning up after you, you're a kid, OK? You're not an adult until you're standing on your own two feet. You're not an adult. Nowhere near.'

'See? You're always making it about money!'

'No, I'm not!'

'You are! Oh my God. I was *trying* to stand on my own two feet. Maybe I'll just leave. Then I won't be such a big financial pressure.'

'Casey!' Melissa's heart thuds; her brain scrambles. But her daughter has already left the room in tears, unable even to slam the door because the door sticks and is wedged open with a rock, a rock they stole from a beach in Dorset when Casey was a little girl and holidays were camping and fish and chips and building sandcastles and picnics and dodging rain showers in café awnings and all Casey wanted was a rock to paint a heart on and be allowed to take it home and keep it and everything was so much clearer.

Melissa sits down shakily at the kitchen table. She has never argued like that with her daughter, not even when Casey was thirteen and fizzing with rage and pimples. She feels terrible, will feel ill until she's put it right. They both will, she knows that, even in the immediate aftermath. They never, ever fall out like that. That was a disaster. She's so damn cross with herself.

And the worst of it is, she's a hypocrite. Because she's just railroaded her daughter for lying and keeping secrets, all the while knowing she's been keeping a secret of her own. And now Casey's leaving home so much sooner than planned.

A punishment, she thinks. One she deserves.

TWENTY-THREE

DAN

One month before

Byrne and the boys pick him up at eleven. He is careful to meet them in the car park. He's got used to the piss-taking and the bad jokes, but he will never let them watch him clean up the pub. He's not sure he could stand it, like one more push and he'd crack and they'd all start laughing at him and never stop until...

Until what? He imagines himself in the back seat of Byrne's speeding Capri, Robbo lunging over him and opening the door, pushing him out onto the road, himself rolling into the gutter as their cackling laughter fades over putrid clouds of exhaust. No sooner has he shaken that little mental reel away when another follows: this time it's him pushing Robbo out, him closing the door to Robbo's anguished cries.

No. He would never do something like that. *But they would*, comes his own voice in his ear. Robbo and Jay would definitely. It is totally their humour. And still, lying there in the wet leaves at the side of the road, bloodied, broken, half dead, he'd have to laugh along, have to eat shit until they drove back around to pick him up. Really, it would be better without them. Dan and Byrne could have sensible conversations without childish interruptions all the time. They could talk business. Dan has been working on a few ideas for a new logo for Byrne's Stay Sharper account. But there's no way he's going to show Byrne with those guys around.

'Yo. Wet wipe,' Robbo is calling through the open window of the back seat, Jay in shadow next to him. Beyond them, the industrial units, closed up like cells for the night. The air is clean after the heavy shower that drummed down on the pub roof at around ten, the tarmac still black and shining.

'The fuck you been doin'?' Robbo shouts. 'We growin' beards here, mate.'

Dan crosses the car park towards them, taking his time, betraying nothing. With these guys, indifference is the best defence, he's found. But it's OK anyway because Jay answers for him: 'Shaggin' your mum.'

Witty, Dan thinks with a sarcasm that feels heavy and sad as the two apes begin to wrestle, hurling insults at each other's mothers and sisters over the thrum of the car engine until Byrne shouts at them like a dad at the end of his rope to pack it in.

Dan gets in beside Byrne. The passenger seat is a kind of status in itself, he thinks, like being added to the Boiz WhatsApp group after their evening at Byrne's apartment the other month. As he clips in his seat belt, Dan is aware of a weird kind of promotion, can practically feel Robbo and Jay's jealousy pulsating from the back seat. Something else now. Byrne's eyes on him. He turns to find himself being appraised.

'Nice T,' Byrne says. 'White as snow. Jeans true black. Sharp.'

Dan looks down at the T-shirt he has just pulled on in the pub loo, tries not to blush at the whiff of bleach coming from his hands. 'I got the ones you said.'

'Wear it no more than three times, yeah? After that, the

lights don't pick it up. You give your threads to the charity now, yeah? You don't buy them there. Self-respect, my brother.'

'Safe.' Dan presses his mouth tight shut, fighting the blush of pleasure he can feel rising up his neck. Ignore the others, that's all he has to do. Ignore them and talk to Byrne as he drives them into town. It's not that deep. And Byrne doesn't need to know he bought the jeans from Oxfam for two quid and dyed them in Mum's washing machine.

Byrne screeches out of the car park. Dan lets the autotuned R&B drown out the bickering from the back seat while the Victorian terraces of St Margarets and Richmond flit past the windows of the sky-blue vintage Ford Capri.

The cannabis vape is passed around, making a tin hotbox of the car. Dan doesn't ask about the congestion charge or where they're going or how much it costs to get in, understanding on an instinctive level that none of these questions would be cool. It feels weird to be going into a club stone-cold sober save for the last-second shot of brandy he stole from the optic. It feels weird to go along with a plan the details of which are a mystery to him. But he goes along with it anyway, wishing he'd downed a double.

Forty minutes of white-knuckle ride later, Byrne swings into an underground car park near Hyde Park Corner. He parks up and with astonishing slickness produces a baggie, a credit card and a small tray before placing the tray on his knee and setting about chopping four lines of what Dan presumes is coke. When the lines are offered to him first, Dan declines.

'I would normally,' he says, 'but I'm pretty wired. Too much coffee on shift.'

'Safe,' Byrne says with a nod while the others bow their heads and sniff like dogs. 'I've got ket if you prefer? Slow it down a bit?'

Again, Dan shakes his head, even as nerves rise through him. It is strange to him that Byrne is so judgemental about alcohol yet they're all prepared to put Class A drugs up their noses. Dan tries not to think about the trail of devastation that lies behind even one gram of this stuff. But who's the one being judgemental now?

'Sure?' Byrne asks.

'Nah,' he says. 'I'm good, thanks.'

'Respect.'

He follows Byrne and the boys to a doorway somewhere near Selfridges, where a long line of people snakes down the wide pavement – girls in miniskirts and tops that look like hankies, gym-ripped guys in tight clothes, sharp haircuts, tans.

With his usual air of importance, Byrne walks directly to the front of the queue. There are pink neon lights around the entrance. It's not the kind of place Dan would even dream of coming to – he knows that without going inside. Sticky music venues at the back of old pubs are more his thing, but as Byrne has said to him a few times in their chats at the bar, it's good to try new things, expand your horizons.

They are let in, leaving a cacophony of protest from the queue behind them. Inside, Byrne muscles into the crowd, his tight white T-shirt glowing neon in the lights. Dan looks down at his own new Fruit of the Loom T. It is not the brand Byrne suggested – that was a lie – but it was the most expensive he could afford. Like Byrne's, it is glowing. His arms look darker in comparison, darker too after the three sunbed sessions he has kept secret even from Casey. When he looks up, he catches the eye of an attractive girl with long blonde hair and black eye make-up. She smiles and looks down at her feet. Assuming the smile is for someone near or behind him, he looks about before glancing back at her. She is looking at him again, her smile wider now, as if amused. This literally never happens. Awkwardly, he raises a hand to his chest and waves before pushing on towards the bar.

At the bar, Byrne buys them all a Guinness – their two allocated units, Dan supposes. For some reason, he thinks of the last time he saw his dad, a year ago maybe; Dad buying him pints all evening with a slight air of desperation, as if it was the only way to make him stay.

He thanks Byrne, lifting his glass before taking a long pull of the stout. He likes Guinness, he does, but he would have preferred something lighter: a lager, something to quench his thirst. He wonders if the others like Guinness or if they drink it to please Byrne, if it is part of being in the Boiz clique. It occurs to him that the drink is black like the jeans Byrne told them to wear, the head white like their T-shirts. It is this eye for detail, this ability to get others to follow and create a brand, that makes Byrne so successful, he thinks. He gives no reason; he just says do it.

Half an hour passes. Robbo and Jay shout idiocies into each other's ears, occasionally passing on the joke to Dan, who laughs politely. Byrne says little. He is watchful, as if on security detail or undercover cop work. Dan is desperate for a pint of lager, but they are drinking lime and sodas now apparently. He speaks to two girls, who are nice enough, but he doesn't dare make any kind of move. He thinks of Livvy, wonders what she's doing now, where she is, whether she misses him even a little bit. He was weak, he has been thinking ever since that conversation with Casey. He let her fill in for his passivity, let her organise their social life, remember their one-year anniversary, her own birthday. He shouldn't have let her do that. He should have taken charge, showed some leadership. Been a man. Sipping his drink, he wonders what Livvy would think of him if she saw him here, with these guys, if she would find him attractive, whether he would be different if he had another chance with her. As it is, standing here, he's not sure he knows what he thinks of himself, whether he even knows who the hell he is or where his life is going.

It is 2 a.m. Without alcohol to sustain him after the long

shift, Dan feels his eyelids droop. The dance floor is packed with people who all look like they're either on holiday or have just stepped off a plane from Ibiza.

'You'll be all right here for a bit?' Byrne asks, solicitous, one hand on Dan's arm. 'We leave in about half an hour. Just need to do a little business.'

'Sure, yeah. Course.'

Byrne and his sidekicks leave him at the bar. Dan assumes they're heading off to the gents for a bump, but even as the thought occurs to him, he sees Byrne on the dance floor with three women who appear to be absolutely captivated by him. As the beats pound, he leans in every so often to whisper something to one or other of them. Dan watches, transfixed.

Byrne attracts women like a magnet attracts iron filings.

A magnet, he thinks. How original, Dan, well done.

He smiles into his drink, feeling a bit mad now, a bit on edge. He's tired, wired after a double shift. He could have done so much more with the dead time. All the hours he's spent doing sod all, he could have done an MA by now. Anxiety grips him. Is this what comes with pretending to be someone you're not, this jittery feeling?

He raises the glass to his lips for another sip, side-eyeing his own biceps with more than a little satisfaction, liking the hint of tan. He needs to go easy. He told his mum he'd been out in the garden. She'd kill him if she knew the truth. But he's in much better shape than he was a couple of months ago. He's started eating better too, taking an interest in nutrition, a healthy diet, which basically is what his mum's been telling him since he was three. The improvements have come from Byrne; there's no way around it. Byrne wouldn't spend a shift scrolling through Instagram, eating out-of-date crisps for his dinner. He'd bring quinoa, avocados, seeds, be doing push-ups, creating content, making more of himself. He would have spent the time being a proactive force rather than a loser wiping down beer bottles in the shadows.

He looks up. He can't see Byrne any more. His chest tightens. But then he spots him. He appears to be dancing with the three women, hugging them as if they are old friends. This heartens Dan. Sometimes the way Byrne speaks about women is confusing, the terms he uses derogatory. But he always claims it's just banter and that really he cherishes them. There has been no mention of a partner and Dan has not dared to ask. Apparently, Byrne is respectful. He moved in quickly on these women, but they seem happy with the physical contact.

A jet of dry ice plumes onto the dance floor, obscuring the scene. But as the smoke disperses, Dan thinks he sees Byrne handing a card to one of the women, a business card maybe. She smiles and puts it into her shoulder bag. Byrne points to his cheek. Amazingly, the woman raises herself on tiptoes and kisses it.

What was that? Dan wonders. What did I just witness?

'Hi.'

He turns to see the woman who smiled at him earlier. She is quite short, not as pretty as he first thought, but her eyes are nice. A warm blue. And her hair is blonde and thick and wavy. He thinks of Byrne, the speed of him with those women.

'Hi,' he says. 'Can I buy you a drink?'

Her eyebrows rise. 'Wow. Don't you want to know my name first?'

Shit. Too fast. What would Byrne say now? Something sassy and cute. He'd pretend it was banter.

'How about I buy you a drink and *then* you tell me your name?' He laughs, to show he doesn't mean it, not really.

The woman laughs too. Thank God. He can't believe she's going for it, but she is. He points at her and hears himself say: 'Gin and tonic, am I right?'

She shakes her head. 'Rum and Coke. Morgan's.'

He nods with as much worldly understanding as he can muster. 'Stay right there.'

Feeling nothing short of *on fire*, he throws up his hand at the bar in the way he's seen Byrne do. By some miracle, the barman notices him immediately and takes his order. The girl next to him complains that Dan just jumped the queue. He apologises, hoping the woman waiting for him didn't see. When the barman puts the glass down and asks if he wants anything else, he says no. He can't afford this drink, let alone another for himself. But she doesn't need to know that. *Fake it till you make it, bro.* He apologises to the girl again and tells the barman she's next.

'One Morgan's and Coke,' he says and holds the drink out to the blonde woman, but when she reaches for it, he draws back his hand and attempts a teasing grin. 'We had a deal. Your name.'

'You said drink first, name second.'

'And I've got your drink. But you have to earn it.'

She laughs, though her laugh is less sure. 'What? So I have to do some weird task for my drink now?'

His face blazes. 'Er, no. I was just joking.' He hands her the drink, wishing he'd never offered. He has no idea how to do this.

'I'm Eliza,' she says.

'Cool. I'm Dan.'

'Dan the man,' she quips, eyeing his muscles while she pulls on the straw. She turns slightly from side to side, like a child at a dance class.

'Haven't seen you all night,' he says. 'Were you hiding?'

'No, just dancing.'

He asks her who she's here with. She tells him she's with her friends. He asks what she does. She tells him she's in marketing. He asks who she works for. She says he won't have heard of them. He says try me. She says she might. They laugh. It is boring and stressful and he wishes he could call a helicopter to get him out of here. Something like panic overtakes him. He reaches out and strokes her face, leans in for a kiss, just to stop the inane conversation.

She steps back. 'Er, the fuck are you doing?'

He throws up his hands. 'Sorry, I—'

'You what? Thought if you bought me a drink it was a done deal?' She shakes her head and he sees that she's hard. A hard girl who's used him to get a free drink. He doesn't like her. She pushes the empty glass into his hand.

'Goodbye,' she says. '*Creep.*'

TWENTY-FOUR
DAN

The day after

On the way back from the hospital, Dan tries calling Byrne, but he doesn't pick up. He thinks about trying Jay or Robbo, but he can't stand to hear their stupid voices. He's so done with those guys. Once he's had it out with Byrne and made him delete that photo, he'll pack his stuff and get back to Casey. Hopefully Mum will be there by then.

He holds up his hands and examines the grazes on his knuckles. An image flashes – himself, hitting Byrne in the face. Did he do that or is it just wishful thinking, a fantasy? He feels like he can remember it in his muscles, in his fists. And now Casey has been beaten up and is lying terrified in a hospital bed unable to remember what happened. The way she looked at him when he made his excuses to go was terrible. He felt like he was abandoning her, but he couldn't tell her why, could he? He should have looked after her better; now all he can do is put it right.

The Uber pulls through the gates of Heaven View. He thanks the driver, gets out and scans the now near-empty hillside, the scrubby staff bit barely visible. He remembers looking for Casey there last night but finding only that guy Spider. Come to think of it, he was at the bonfire last night too, lurking about, skinny fag dangling from his lips like a piece of straw, watching. Dan saw him with Casey a few times over the weekend, the two of them picking litter in their sad high-vis tabards.

Could Casey have gone back to Spider's tent last night? Or did he persuade her into that tent knowing it would be empty? Because he would know, wouldn't he? Could he have done this to her once they got inside? The more Dan thinks about it, the more it seems a bit too much of a coincidence that Spider found her, a good way of making sure any DNA or whatever they look for could be explained away by his Good Samaritan act...

He shakes his head. Nah. Casey doesn't go for crusties. Although he's not sure who she does go for, to be honest. She's only had one boyfriend, as far as he knows: Liam, who couldn't tie his own shoelaces and who used to jump three feet in the air if you said hello. Casey was fourteen when lockdown hit, and by the time things opened up again, her friends had gone from Haribos and dance routines to weed and blowjobs. By being the only one of her mates who kept to the rules, she got left behind. Maybe she's a bit naïve, more than she would have been if COVID hadn't happened.

There is one patrol car parked up by reception. The atmosphere is subdued, the site deathly quiet. He has to find Byrne. If Casey can't remember on her own, Dan will make sure to point the police in his direction. Show them the photo if necessary. He stops; downloads the photo from WhatsApp to his phone just in case Byrne tries to delete it. He passes the clubhouse, which is empty, closed up. Heading for the teepee, he realises it's possible Byrne and the guys have gone home, escaped in their pimped-up Capri, back to their Xboxes, their gyms, their crap senses of humour.

'We gonna be like kids in a sweetshop,' Byrne had said on

the way here, his strange London drawl taking over from his usual well-spoken voice. One hand gripped the steering wheel, the other pushed his enormous water bottle to his lips, the hourly consumption targets marked down the side. The water chugged, swished as he brought the hulking thing down. 'Man, oh man,' he added, shaking his head. 'Those chicks be sweet. Those cherries be *ripe*, and all we have to do is pick them.'

Robbo and Jay were – guess what? – laughing like hyenas. Dan laughed along with them. He actually laughed, on the outside at least, enough to convince. What a dick he has been. What an absolute moron. Mum would be so ashamed, but only as ashamed as he feels right now. He is hot, boiling hot with shame.

'So, if your dad ain't on the scene...' Byrne said. This was later, when they got to the six-man luxury yurt he was already referring to as Base Camp Alpha, one arm round Dan's shoulder, his tone confidential. 'You're the man of the house, yeah? That means your sister belongs to you, know what I'm saying? And your mum.'

'I look out for them,' Dan replied, fearing with a sinking feeling that this was not what Byrne meant, that his reply was for his own self-preservation, something he could later rely on in the court of his own mind. 'Casey's my kid sister. And my mum's just my mum, you know? They're... they're my family.'

Byrne sneered. 'But your family is yours, do you know what I'm saying? Your responsibility. Make sure you look after your sister this weekend, yeah? Keep an eye on her. I know what these chicks get up to on weekends like this, and you don't want her getting up to that stuff, man. You don't want your sister behaving like a cheap ho.'

A noise escapes him now, a kind of stifled heave. He pulls out his phone, the image of Casey half naked and clearly out of it branded onto his mind's eye. But still he looks at it – can't help himself. *Dan, bro, your sister is fit. Full picture tomorrow mofos*. His own message to Byrne: *Delete that photograph of my sister now or I'll fucking end you.* There's still no reply. Byrne's ghosting him, Dan guesses. Trying to scare him. But he has to get to him before he sends a full nude of Casey to those baboons. They will put it straight on the internet. They could ruin her life. He will not have his sister shamed like that. He will not let that photo be circulated. He will stand over Byrne and watch him delete it from the WhatsApp, from his phone, from his deleted folder. He will make him.

He studies the image. Case is clearly standing against a tree. There's a line of trees running the length of the site, pretty much. There are a few in staff camping and that little wood thing on the other side of the boundary. Was she drunk or spiked or did she take something? Did Byrne give her one of his pills? His gut churns. Byrne and his sodding pills. His powders. His cannabis vape. The early-evening psycho games of dib-dab back in the teepee: *Pick a hand, come on, you have to pick one*. Feeling like he had no choice, like it was some sort of test, Dan dabbed his finger in the left-hand baggie of powder and sucked, hiding his fear, his disgust at the hairspray taste. All for what? His own image reflected back at him in their stupid mirrored shades? Now, as if one memory has triggered another, he has a vision of himself lurching about in the orange bonfire glow, talking to randoms, grinding his teeth, loving everyone, then not loving anyone, then arguing with his sister, then hating Byrne, his friends, himself.

At the teepee, he stops dead. Details are filling the outline like watercolours. He did hit Byrne. He hit him with a force that astonished him. There was an argument. It must have been about Casey. So that must have been after the confrontation at the bonfire. How long after? After he drank cider and shots with a bunch of guys he didn't even know. He must've bumped into Byrne after that. Fought with him. Grazed his hand. It's possible Byrne headed straight for Casey then, furious, pockets full of pills and bent on teaching Dan a lesson by abusing his sister.

Is that what happened?

Shaking, Dan draws back the teepee door. Byrne's bunk is still immaculate. His white trainers still there. Jay and Robbo's gear is still a mess. They've not cleared out. They must be down at the beach. Dan makes his way back out of the field. At the top of the rise, he stops and closes his eyes. Sees Byrne, Byrne holding up little clear plastic bags: red pills, blue pills.

'Just like in *The Matrix*.' Stuffing the bags into his pockets. 'Because the Matrix is trying to control us all, and it's our job to stop that from happening, am I right, my brothers? Just slip one of these little sweeties in her drink and she's all yours.'

Dan, laughing nervously. Trying to keep it light, trying not to lose face. 'You're not serious? You don't... you don't give them drugs, do you?'

Byrne gave a wide yack-yack laugh, looking to the others, as if what Dan had said was hilarious, not because it was funny but because it was stupid. 'Oh my days, brother Dan!' He threw out his arms. 'I was being sarcastic!' Shaking his head, snatching back his own words, as if anyone who'd heard them couldn't possibly understand. 'I was using sarcasm for comedic effect. You know, humour?' He beat his chest with his fist. 'I don't need to spike a bitch. Have you seen me? Have you met me? They give it to me for free. And here, they're young and stupid. Fresh meat, and I'm the carnivore.'

The puerile guffaws of Robbo and Jay – Byrne's dumb chimps. Dan's own laughter making a monkey of him too.

'I hate you,' Dan whispers, too late, to no one. He should have punched Byrne's lights out there and then, told him he was a piece of shit. Except he didn't, did he? He punched him later. Later, when he was drunk enough to do it. And it's possible that right hook was what sent him to do what he did to Casey.

Fuelled by rage. Out for revenge. Out to damage Dan's property.

He takes out his phone and examines the photo. His sister doesn't look bruised.

So – what then? Byrne gave her one of his pills, or slipped one in her drink, and then took her photo.

He didn't sexually assault her.

Doesn't mean he didn't try to strangle her though, does it?

Dan finds himself at the bottom of the tarmac path. Straight ahead is the pathway to the beach. To the left is the gate to staff camping. Beyond that, the perimeter, the copse. Casey was photographed against a tree. Could he have taken her there?

He heads for the gate, slips past and goes sharp left down the track that leads along the other side of the tall hedge. He has seen a stream disappear near here down the edge of the fields. As he approaches the clump of trees, he sees the stream reappear, bubbling over rocks; he needs to jump across it to reach the other side. He finds the narrowest part and clears it in one easy stride. Continues, hesitating at the edge of... not a forest or a wood, no. Too small. He takes a few steps; checks back to remember his bearings. He takes another step, another.

'Anyone here?' The sound of his own voice makes him shiver, as if by calling out, he is acknowledging something bleak. Seal broken, he calls again and again – *Hello? Anyone here?* – taking slow steps deeper into the overhanging leaves, glancing behind him at intervals, pushing forward again. His breathing shallows. It is so secluded here. So silent. While the party was in full flow, no one would see or hear anything coming from here, no way. Some gut feeling tells him this is the place. This is where his sister was assaulted.

On the ground, he sees something white and blue, bright in the green ferns – an Adidas slider, just lying there, strange and familiar all at once. His heart quickens. That's Byrne's shoe; he's pretty sure.

'Hello?'

He takes a step, another. Something is rising inside him like water in a tank. And there is something else on the ground – further on, by one of the trees. A leg. Muscular, tanned. A man's leg. A man, lying on his back. Recognition claws at him. He knows those chino-style shorts, the washing-powder white of the T-shirt, though it is dirty now, muddy... or bloody, it is hard to tell in the dimness. Dan stops a few feet away, breath caught in his chest.

'Byrne?' he whispers.

The man doesn't stir. Another step. Is he sleeping? Unconscious? Dan's breath is vapour-thin. Sweat pricks on his top lip.

'Byrne? Mate? Is that you?'

He takes one step, then another; slow step by slow step until he is standing over his friend. He looks like he could be asleep. But there is a grey pallor under his usually smooth tanned skin. Black stubble shadows his chin. There is bruising under his left eye, the hint of blood crusted on the rim of his left nostril, a lacework of dried spit to the right of his mouth.

He looks so dead is the loudest thought in the clamour of Dan's mind. He makes himself take a deep breath and holds it in while he crouches, eyes screwed up, and reaches with trembling fingers for Byrne's neck. No sooner have his fingertips touched flesh than he recoils, staggering backwards, almost falling. Panting now, he presses his hands to his knees and spits on the scrappy grass. Byrne is as cold as stone.

There is no need to check. There will be no pulse. Byrne Sharp is dead.

PART II

TWENTY-FIVE
CASEY

Eleven days before

Casey reaches Heaven View just before three in the afternoon. Her rucksack is heavy, her back wet with sweat and she is still tired after finishing her last exam only yesterday morning. The others finish later today. In about an hour, in fact. She can picture them running out of the exam hall, shouting and hugging each other in the school yard, scribbling on each other's tops in permanent marker, heading, laughing, for the pub.

She sighs, takes off her hat and wipes her forehead with her arm. No point thinking about things you can't do. She had to get here a week early for training. That was the deal.

At reception, she introduces herself to a lady in a flowery sundress, who tells her to take a seat and picks up the phone.

'Candy,' she says into the receiver. Casey recognises the name of the site manager who offered her the job. 'I've got Casey Connor here.'

Casey waits, her leg jiggling about until the receptionist shoots her a look. Face flaming, she flattens her foot before standing up and wandering over to a large felt board pinned with hundreds of photographs. It's a collection of photos from Summer Camps past. After a minute or two, she finds Dan, grinning, arm round Rory. He looks fifteen or sixteen, thin, and so, so sweet. She can't believe he's coming back here at the age of twenty-three. Privately, she thinks it's low-key a bit lame.

From a door behind the desk, a woman emerges. Her light brown hair is pulled back into two short bunches, and she's not wearing much make-up. In long navy shorts and a white linen shirt tied in a knot at the waist, she's less put together than the receptionist but in a cool way. For an older person. She looks, like, thirty or so.

'Casey,' she says, holding out her hand and smiling widely. 'I'm Candy London. Welcome to Heaven View. You got here OK?'

'Yes, thank you. Train and bus.' Casey shakes Miss London's hand; wonders why grown-ups always ask if you got here OK when it's obvious you did. 'Bit sweaty.'

'Humid, isn't it? It's going to rain later, but next weekend's gonna be a scorcher, according to the forecast. I'm going to be nagging anyone not wearing a hat, and I've already told the bar staff to refill water bottles when asked. Don't want two hundred kids with heatstroke on my hands. Come on – I'll show you round.'

Casey follows her out into the site, which spreads down the sloping hillside towards the beach. When she sees the vast blue strip of sea in the distance, she takes a long, deep breath and feels herself settle a bit. She's here. She's made it.

'Wow,' she says.

'It's a big site,' Miss London says as they round the corner to a café bar fronted by a veranda with blue and red umbrellas over little tables. It's pretty for a campsite, nicer than Casey was expecting given the rumours she's heard of all the wild antics and bad behaviour. Behind the bar, a guy with a wispy goatee is watching a young girl make a coffee.

'This is the clubhouse. You'll be on bar duty and glass collecting,' Miss London says. 'Table service during the day, but only paninis and stuff. You've done table service before, haven't you?'

Casey nods. 'Sure, yeah. And I know how to make coffee. I think I said that in my interview?'

'You did. Fab.' Miss London nods towards wispy-beard guy. 'That's Joe. He's training right now so I'll introduce you later. You have one training shift and then a few quiet shifts to get you up to speed before next weekend. Don't worry, you'll soon find your feet. Everyone's super friendly. I only pick radiators.'

Casey frowns.

'People are either radiators or drains,' Miss London explains, 'and we can't have drains working at a holiday park, can we?' She smiles and beckons Casey to walk with her.

'Attached to the clubhouse,' she continues, sweeping her arm left to indicate a little shop, 'is the minimarket, where you can buy fruit and veg, pasta, noodles, et cetera. They have fresh doughnuts every morning; a van comes at around eight and sells croissants, sweets and stuff like that.'

Beyond the minimarket and further up the hill are about twenty large wooden huts.

'Chalets on the top field,' Miss London says, 'for those with cash to splash.' She gestures to a field directly ahead, filled with white yurts. 'Teepees, also for those on a more generous budget who want the camping experience without having to put up their own tents.' The path takes them right, then down past a large field with a sparse array of tents. 'This is general camping,' Miss London explains as they make their way towards the bottom of the site. 'Views aren't the best, but it's nearer the beach, so...' She shields her eyes from the sun, gesturing to a row of rectangular concrete blocks. 'Loos and showers, washing-up points and what have you.'

'Right.' It's like a class system, Casey thinks. It's the kind of thing Mum would say: the rich at the top, the working classes at the bottom.

'Still a few young families,' Miss London adds, 'and some oldies, but they'll be gone come next Thursday. By Friday morning, things are usually mental. A lot of kids. A lot of noise. A lot of litter. We'll see how much they've got left in them by Sunday night, eh?' She shoots Casey a wry glance. 'Don't peak too early, I say.'

Casey laughs. She likes Miss London. Judging by the calm vibes, it looks like she runs a tight ship, but she seems nice about it.

'Now, see those trees down there, where the river disappears?' Miss London is pointing towards the very bottom left of the site. 'You can just about see the smoke coming up over the tall hedge?'

Casey nods.

'That's the staff area. A lot of them have been coming here for years. It's pretty rough and ready, but there are solar-powered showers and compostable loos, so it's relatively civilised.'

The underclass, Casey tries not to think. Below the below.

'Plus,' Miss London carries on, oblivious, 'the staff actually pick up their litter, unlike your Gen Z peers.' She raises her eyebrows. 'You wait till they all leave on Monday morning. You'll be clearing up the tents they've left, clothes, you name it. Drives us mad, but we keep all the tents and donate them. Come on – I'll take you down so you can get settled.'

It takes about ten minutes to reach the very bottom of the hill. Running straight ahead is a sandy track, which disappears through the dunes. To the right is a small standpipe tap.

'That's the path down to the beach,' Miss London tells her. 'Tap to wash the sand off your toes and wherever else it's got to.' She chuckles.

To the left is a five-bar gate held closed by a length of tatty rope and bearing a sign saying *Staff Camping. Keep Out* above a skull and crossbones. Beyond are tyre tracks in the mud where the tarmac ends. Miss London lifts the rope and pushes the gate open. There is a thick hedge that acts as a kind of screen; to the left, the stream reappears, running alongside a clump of trees, tall and dense.

Music drifts towards them. It sounds like jazz. The smell of woodsmoke drifts.

'There's no fires or barbies on the site,' Miss London says. 'Just in the interests of keeping everyone safe. But these guys live here for the summer months, so they have their fire going the whole time to cook and keep warm. You'll get a staff meal every shift, and if you work late, there's always a few croissants and stuff about to go out of date, so you can help yourself. I prefer staff to eat any leftovers rather than throwing them away. We try and keep waste to a minimum, and whatever is left after that I have taken to a food bank in Weymouth.'

They round the hedge and a whole other campsite appears, a mix of tents and yurts, caravans and camper vans. Like dainty washing, bunting dips between some of the tents; coloured flags flap on the ends of long poles. This area feels different, more like a dwelling, a community going about their lives. The fire burns inside a huge rust-brown drum, above which stands a tall metal tripod, a rack making a shelf across it, a blackened kettle sitting on top. The soft flickering sound of the flames is soothing; the smoky smell brings back memories of camping holidays with Dan and Mum. Casey swallows a gulp of homesickness.

By the side of the fire, a woman with a thick white-blonde side-plait running over her right shoulder is nursing a tiny baby all but hidden by a muslin cloth. When the kettle spout blows out steam, she tucks the baby inside a papoose tied across her body and stands up. In one deft movement, she pushes her hand inside an oven glove, lifts the kettle from the stove and pours boiling water into a pan-shaped cup that looks like something from the Wild West.

'Ness,' Miss London calls out, lifting a hand in salute.

'Candy, my darlin',' the woman replies, stirring her drink and sitting back down, placing the cup on the grass and uncovering the baby once again.

'I've brought you a new charge. This is Casey Connor.'

Casey feels herself blush. Unsure where to look, she gives the woman – Ness – a wave and smiles. 'Hi.'

Ness attaches her baby back on the breast before looking up and smiling back. One of her teeth is gold. 'Pleased to meet you, Casey.'

'Can you guys show her what's what? I've got a call at four.' Miss London turns to Casey and rests a hand gently on her arm. 'Ness'll look after you, OK? We all call her Mama Bear, don't we, Ness?'

Ness is nodding, her smile lazy, maybe a bit ironic. Casey doesn't know whether to go over to her or stay where she is. Her rucksack weighs a ton. Should she take it off or what?

'I'll see you later,' Miss London says kindly. She meets Casey's eye. 'Don't look so frightened. None of us bite, and you've done hospitality before, so you'll be grand. It's not the Ritz; you just have to be friendly and halfway capable. When's your first shift?'

'Tomorrow at eight.'

'Great. I'll see you up at the clubhouse; you can make me your best cappuccino, OK? Any problems, ask Spider or Ness, and if they can't help, they'll call me.' She pulls a funny face. 'And if I can't help, God help us all.'

TWENTY-SIX

DAN

The day after

Dan uncurls himself slowly. He stares down at his hands, turning them over, examining the four dark scabs, glancing again at the bruising on Byrne's face. His right hand caused that damage. There is no denying it.

As if in confirmation, his memory shows him the image of himself punching Byrne in the face. And he feels all of it – the rush, the pain, the shock – and yet at the same time he is above, outside himself, hovering, other. A shiver passes through him. Byrne Sharp, who less than twenty-four hours ago was jeering at him, back when he was full of arrogance and life; this man who, for a few months, Dan believed had something to teach him. In the dappled shade of the trees, this dead body at his feet is all that's left. *Keep the fuck away from my sister*, Dan hears himself shout – himself, that other Dan, the one from last night. *Keep the fuck away from my sister. Just leave her alone.*

There are so many holes. But the holes are filling, and here comes Byrne into the void, face in shadow, smug, grinning, always with the grinning, throwing up his hands.

'Whoa, dude. Chill, yeah? We were only talking. Just chit-chatting, that's all. She's your bitch, man. Hands off your property, I get that. I respect that.'

The punch connected hard. He felt it all the way up his arm, the throbbing afterwards in his fist.

'Don't call my sister a bitch.' His voice was hoarse. White spray flew from his mouth. This body lying lifeless on the ground had taught him to punch like that. The irony of it. Oh God, the bloody irony.

Now, Dan closes his right hand into a fist and stares at it as if it belongs to someone else. Who even was he in that moment? Who has he been these last months? Who is he now? He can remember the cool of the night air fresh on his skin after the burning heat of the day, the tang of rage on his tongue, the white heat that flashed through him. He can feel the muscle memory of hitting out, the smacking sound, the crumpling collapse of his former friend onto the ground. The memory unrolls over and over, in slow motion and fast forward all at once, hitting and hitting, again and again and again. Byrne looking up at him, nose bloody, eyes black. The shock then. The shock, the shock, the shock.

People can die from a hard punch to the head. Didn't that prison documentary show that? Hasn't he been haunted by it ever since?

Byrne has died. Dan punched him and now he's dead. He backs away. Byrne is dead. He didn't mean to do that. He didn't mean to he didn't mean to he didn't mean to.

Staggering from the scene, it is all he can do not to burst into tears. His breath is shallow, his throat sore, his heart thumping wildly. *Don't call my sister a bitch.* How many times has he heard Byrne call other women that? Heard him and laughed along, like one of the boys, like a fool. And there he was, punching his friend's lights out for some sort of principle, the principle only becoming important when the words were applied to his own sister.

What a joke he is. What a loser. How did he ever get involved with these morons? And now he's the biggest moron of all, the biggest loser, maybe even a *murderer*. Like that guy on the documentary, who ruined his own life – for what?

Oh God, how he wishes he'd just gone with Rory and the lads and to hell with money worries and careers. Oh God, those punches connected so hard. Byrne lost his footing, thumped hard against the ground. Dan can still hear his cry of shock and pain. He had no time to break his fall.

What then?

Dan left him there. It wasn't Byrne who walked away – it was him. Didn't offer his hand, apologise, help him up. Didn't even stay to find out what damage he'd done. Just turned his back and walked off to the sound of Byrne's furious threats.

You're a dead man, Dan Connor. Fuck you and fuck your sister, bro. You wait. Just you fucking wait.

But where were they? It wasn't here, in the woods; it was somewhere near the tents, the beach party only a dull thump-thump in the distance. Byrne might have been disoriented, dazed by a hard blow to the face and by whatever he'd taken. He'd been hitting the coke, Dan knows that for sure, hitting it pretty hard. And pills – the reds and the blues and God knows what else. Must've ended up here in the woodland. Out of it and alone, he collapsed. No one to see him and say, *That guy needs a glass of water, a strong coffee*. No one to help him up and walk him around a bit, make sure he was OK. The cold came in. The night was cloudless. Cold enough for hypothermia? Dan doesn't think so, but he's not a doctor. Maybe in his confused state Byrne decided to have a rest, fell asleep and just... died.

You're a dead man, Dan Connor.

Threats in the dark. Later, Byrne sent that horrible photograph of Casey. Casey is lying beaten up and traumatised in hospital. Byrne attacked Casey to pay Dan back.

This is all his fault – all of it, the whole fucking mess.

Should he go back for Byrne's phone? Delete the photo? Protect his sister's reputation? He turns; takes a step back towards Byrne's body.

'No,' he whispers. There's no deleting it. Robbo and Jay will have it. Even if Dan deletes for everyone, they could have saved it. Besides, the woods are a crime scene now.

A crime scene. Shit. His fingerprints on Byrne's neck, his DNA all over his face, his blood on Byrne's face. Byrne's blood on his fists.

The cops can access stuff, can't they? Messages and stuff, even deleted ones. *Delete that photograph of my sister now or I'll fucking end you.*

That's literally a death threat.

'Shit.'

Threats dissipate in the dark. It was all about power play, a life lived like a game of *Call of Duty*. *We're all players, bro. All of us against the Matrix, man. It's kill or be killed out there. The blue pill or the red?* Byrne had been chatting Casey up all weekend. That was a power play, a mind game aimed at Dan. *I'm going to steal your property.* That's how Byrne would have seen it. And Dan retaliated as if... as if those rules were his. As if he owned his sister. Is that the truth of it? Is that why he beat up his so-called friend? To teach him a lesson? Had he been so brainwashed by then, or had the argument with Casey left him feeling so disgusted with himself he had to, in some warped way, fix it?

But who was he to fight his sister's battles? What kind of way was that to put things right?

TWENTY-SEVEN
CASEY

Eleven days before

'Sit yourself down, love.' Ness nods towards a camping chair propped up against a tree. 'Spider'll be here in a minute.'

'How come you call him Spider?' Casey lifts the chair and shakes it out, plants it beside Ness and sits down.

'His real name's Luke, but he goes by Spider, so who are we to argue? We are whoever we say we are here.'

Casey nods; wishes she could think of something wise to say back. This woman probably thinks she's an idiot. It's so embarrassing talking to grown-ups sometimes.

'We're a ramshackle bunch,' Ness says conversationally, smoothing the baby's head with the flat of her hand. 'But we look after each other. Spider's family.'

'Oh, right. Cool. What, so, like, is he your cousin or...?'

'Not biological. I mean family you choose. You can't choose who you're related to, that's for sure, but not all family's blood. Spider's been with us on and off since he was a kid.'

Casey tries for a knowing smile. 'Family's important. And friends can be family too.'

The baby breaks off from the breast. Casey turns away, feels herself blush yet again. When she looks back, Ness is cooing at her child, whose eyes are closed and whose lips are curled in a satisfied smile.

'They look off their heads, babies, when they're proper full,' Ness says fondly. 'Look like proper little drunks, they do.'

Casey doesn't know how to react; is grateful when Ness adds that the baby's name is Aura and that she would do anything for her, lie down on hot coals, you name it.

'Aura,' Casey repeats, like an idiot. 'That's such a cool name.'

'Ah,' says Ness, looking up. 'Here he is. Spider! We've got a new recruit for you.'

Casey follows her gaze to where a super-skinny guy is walking with purpose towards them. He is tall, legs like pipe cleaners in black jeans with rips at the knee, a vintage Cure T-shirt and big black lace-up army boots, which are caked in mud and scuffed at the toe. From his stripy beanie hat hang strands of blonde hair – not Viking blonde like Ness's; dirtier, as if he's combed it with muddy fingers, which, Casey thinks, he might well have.

'Hello, hello,' he says, grinning through yellowish teeth before sucking on a roll-up that looks like it's competing with his legs for skinniness. The tip glows. He exhales a cloud – the sweet, cloying whiff of weed.

'Hi,' Casey says, cursing herself for the little wave she really needs to stop doing when she meets people.

'Spider,' he says in a strangulated voice. A deep blue web has been inked all over his neck. It gives Casey the creeps. He offers her the joint. The tip is wet where his mouth has been. Gross.

'No thanks,' she says. 'Bit early for me. I'm Casey Connor.'

'Casey.' He raises his eyebrows but doesn't meet her eye, staring instead at her collarbone, which is quite weird and makes her feel self-conscious, like there's something there she doesn't know about. 'Is that KC or CC?'

'CC,' she replies.

'Casey Connor,' he says, as if to himself. 'CC. Copied in.'

The laugh that leaves Casey is as lame as the joke, if it even was a joke. What was it? More of a musing. She stores it for Dan, for later, for Mum. They love that stuff, love it when she imitates grumpy customers from work or characters she meets on the bus.

'Shall I show you where to build your little cloth house on the prairie?'

'What? Sorry, I mean... What?'

'Teepee. Yurt. Shelter. Lodgings. Your tent, madam.'

She stifles a giggle. 'Tent. Yeah. Great. Thanks.'

'Marvellousness. This way, if you please, my lady.' He turns away, raising a lolling hand to Ness, who dips her head, eyes closing like she's giving him a blessing.

Everyone here is mad, Casey thinks as she follows Spider, who walks with slow loping strides but whose pace is actually so fast Casey almost has to jog to keep up. He asks her questions the whole time – where she's from, how she got here, if she's been before, how her exams went.

'I presume you've just finished your A levels?' he says, turning to not quite look at her with narrow eyes that tell her he's just taken another toke.

'Yesterday actually.' She brushes her hand across her collarbone, but there is nothing there.

'And do you think you've made the grade? Or grades, as the case may be?'

'Erm. Not sure. Hope so.'

'I'm sure you have. Casey. On the case. Sharp as a blade, I'll wager. And where will your ivory tower find itself in this green and pleasant land?'

'My...' Oh my God, she can't wait to tell Dan about this guy.

It's like he needs a translator. It's actually hilarious, even if it's a bit creepy. 'You mean my uni? Where will it be? Erm, York. I mean, hopefully.'

He stops, his eyebrows rising like Gandalf. 'A very fine choice, if I may say so. Would've liked to have gone there myself. Collegiate. Steeped in history, some of it very dark indeed.' He widens his eyes, going for a spooky expression. Casey hopes she never has to bump into this guy at night.

'Right. So. So...' She knows that it's her turn to ask him something, but what?

'Dropped out myself,' Spider says, filling in.

'Oh. I'm sorry.'

'Bit of bother at the old alma mater.'

Casey frowns. 'I thought you said you didn't go to uni? Sorry, I'm a bit...'

He places his long, skinny fingers against his chest. 'The bountiful mother I'm referring to was my secondary education. But certain things came to pass, alas, as can happen sometimes in our country's finest boarding establishments. I absconded, you might say. Never made it to the heights of tertiary instruction.'

Casey wants to ask what happened – what were the *certain things* – but Spider is gesturing to a flat space in the grass. 'How big is your tent?'

Relieved that, for once, he has said something normal, she feels at last able to reply. 'Oh, it's, like, tiny. Here's easily big enough.'

'Have you brought security?'

'What?'

'A padlock? Not that you're likely to have anything stolen, not by us anyway. There's a couple of new faces since I last worked Summer Camp, but I'm sure no one will try and get in, not here.'

She feels herself flush. She never thought of someone

breaking into her tent. Of all the extra things her mum gave her, including the old Nokia she made her take to Reading in case her iPhone ran out of battery, she has no padlock for her tent zip.

'Don't worry.' He looks over towards a substantial khaki bell tent next door, decorated with rainbow bunting and a string of fairy lights. Outside, two sticks have been hammered into the ground, wellington boots placed upside down on them. There is a tripod too, also made of sticks and tied with twine, where a plastic washing-up bowl nestles, a cream enamel jug beside it, upside down on another planted stick. 'That's Mama Bear's abode,' he says. 'And mine is the white teepee over yonder.' He points to a skull-and-crossbones flag two tents away and turns to fix her with a deep peat-brown gaze. After avoiding her eyes the whole time, it feels like a laser beam. 'If you need anything,' he says, 'at any time, you let me know, OK? I mean anything at all. Information, help, anything. If I'm not hereabouts, find Ness, but come to me first, yeah? Ness is nursing and we're trying to make sure she gets her rest.'

Casey nods. This guy is *intense*. And his tent is nearer than she would like. Why would he mention people breaking into tents unless he'd thought about it?

'Do you want me to help you pitch?' He is already dropping tobacco and whatever else into a near-transparent rolling paper.

With a big *oof*, Casey shrugs off her rucksack, the air cooling the sweat that has soaked the back of her T-shirt. 'It's OK. My brother showed me how to put it up last weekend in the park. Well, he made me put it up while he watched, basically.'

'Wise man.' Spider smiles. 'Best way. It is upon doing that we learn.'

'Who said that?'

'Me. Just now.' He grins. God, his teeth are *terrible*. 'Once you've set up, find me and I'll get you sorted with some scranaroonski.'

'Some...?' Oh my God, she thinks. Literally though.

'Scran,' Spider almost clarifies. 'Comestibles. Nutritious fare. Food.'

'Food! Cool. Er, thanks.'

He salutes her. 'At your service, Miss Copied-In. See you at the fire pit in... How long will you need?'

She's not sure she wants to eat with this guy, but she doesn't want to be rude. 'Half an hour should do it,' she says. 'Probably less.'

'Tell you what.' He checks his watch, throwing out his hand and bending his arm like a character in a pantomime. 'Let's say rendezvous circa six in the post-meridian, give you some chillax time. Sound good? Down by the fire?'

'Er... six-ish. Great.' Casey watches him slow-stride down the hill on his long black-clad legs and smiles to herself. Six p.m. She's getting the hang of this dude already. But what was all that stuff about his school? Sounded like something bad went down. She wonders if something happened to him – or if he did something.

But what?

TWENTY-EIGHT
MELISSA

The day after

Casey's eyes drift over Melissa's shoulder. A moment later, she smiles and waves.

Melissa turns to see Dan at the reception desk of the ward. Deathly pale, black-eyed, shoulders hunched like a drug addict, he looks even worse than she feels.

'Won't be a tick,' she says, nerves fluttering.

'I'm right here if you want to go and talk to him,' Riley says, as if Melissa didn't know that, as if she wouldn't want to talk to her own son. It's like having a personal assistant you never asked for making suggestions you've already thought of.

'Thanks,' she says, her politeness by now varnish-thin, and goes. She passes a duty nurse, who apologises and explains that she can't allow any visitors at this time. Melissa tells her it's OK, she'll head out, before finding Dan skulking in the corridor with his arms wrapped around himself. She was going to tell him off for leaving Casey, but he looks so terribly fragile, she simply pulls him into her arms. They hold each other for a long time. She pretends not to notice that he's crying into her shoulder, that he smells stale, greasy, smoky.

'Nightmare,' he says when they break apart, wiping his eyes with his sleeve. He looks wrecked.

'Where were you?'

'I came before,' he says. 'I had to go back to the site.'

'Why?'

'I had to get my phone charger and some... stuff.' He looks away. Sniffs.

Melissa decides not to push it. He is an eggshell, hairline-cracked. 'OK.'

They sit side by side on two of the unprepossessing plastic chairs.

'I think Byrne did this,' he whispers.

Melissa makes herself breathe; slows herself down. 'Yes. Casey just remembered.'

He shakes his head. He is still crying, pretending not to. 'He was after Casey all weekend. But I didn't tell the cop that at the site. You know, before. I don't know why, and now, now I...'

Melissa checks over her shoulder. 'Don't upset yourself. It's OK. Everything'll be—'

'I was looking for her,' he blurts. 'Today. Before, I mean. She wasn't returning my calls and I was worried, and then I saw the police and...' He shakes his head; stares at the floor, the tips of his ears brightening. 'She was in the ambulance. I came here. The cop said she was being examined, so I waited. I... I did see her. But I had to get back because... because...'

'Dan. Love. Your sister woke up in a tent she didn't recognise. She was all but naked, and she'd been given Rohypnol. She's covered in bruises, and she's absolutely terrified. What was so urgent you had to leave her?' How she hates this, this not knowing how to act, what to say for the best, whether she's getting it right or making everything worse.

'Byrne sent this.' He sniffs and pulls his phone from his

jeans pocket. 'Before. But I only saw it when I got here. That's why I had to leave Casey. I went to tell him to delete it.'

Melissa takes the phone from him. At the sight of the naked shoulders and apparently intoxicated face of her beautiful daughter, she gasps.

'It's not her fault,' Dan whimpers.

'I know. I know that. But she wasn't sexually assaulted, and we have to hold on to that.'

Dan wipes at his eyes. 'But Byrne said he was going to send the whole photo.' More tears leak out.

Melissa glances around, to check no one is listening. She's about to tell him Casey has seen the photo, but—

'Maybe this is what he does,' Dan says. 'Takes photos and uses them... somewhere. Monetises them, I dunno.'

'Monetises? What do you mean?'

He shrugs. 'He talks... he talked a lot about making things pay, like, life stuff. I don't really know how he makes so much from what he does. I thought it came from these videos he makes, but I don't know.'

'Are you saying Byrne did this to your sister for *cash*?'

'I don't know. I know he took the photo, and I know he spikes girls. I thought it was a joke, but it's not. I think he does. And he was with Case earlier in the night. He was chatting her up, being all smooth, pretending to be nice. I warned him off her, but... I don't know what's going on.' Dan shrugs. He sniffs, draws the back of his hand over his nose and looks at her with pained eyes. There is something more. Melissa can feel it.

'Dan?' she says. 'What are you not telling me?'

His shoulders slump. 'I can't say it,' he whispers. 'It's too bad.'

Melissa checks the corridor again. There is still no one. Dan covers his face with his hands, and she sees then that the knuckles of his right hand are crusted with dark scabs. Dread stalks in. 'You can tell me anything, love. I'll love you no matter what – you know that.'

'He was in the woodland,' he half sobs.

'Who was?'

'Byrne. He was in the trees by the staff camping bit. I think that's where he took Casey. I think that's where he took the photo.'

'Right. But Casey wasn't found anywhere near there.' Melissa rubs her face. Her hands feel grimy. And now her face feels grimy. In fact, she feels grimy inside and out. This afternoon feels like a week ago. Last night, another lifetime.

'I hit him,' Dan says, the three words steeped in misery.

'What? When?' Melissa's chest tightens.

A swing door opens. A gurney trundles past, guided by two orderlies. The disinfectant smell hits her in a wave. It seems to take them an inordinately long time to make their way down the corridor and through the swinging double doors.

For a few seconds after the corridor empties, they wait; on the edge of what, she doesn't know.

'Last night,' Dan says eventually. 'I hit him a few times. I can't remember much about it. I was drunk. I was upset, so I... I drank some shots with some guys. And then I saw him. And he started chatting shit about Casey, and I just... I don't know. I just lost it. We were on the ground. I think I must've grazed my hand on the tarmac. I was trying to warn him off. He'd been flirting with Case all weekend and then he was saying things. He was way older than her, Mum. It was gross.'

'Right. Even so...'

Tears spill onto her son's cheeks. She takes in his newly worked-out physique, his white T-shirt, one of a whole stack she's found in the laundry these last few months. She'd thought this new friend of his was having a good influence on her son, getting him to take pride in himself, but now he's telling her he thumped him hard enough to be concerned about it. And at the same time, worryingly, he seems to be trying to justify it.

'I was so out of it,' he says, looking now more like a frightened little boy than a twenty-three-year-old man. 'Byrne's been teaching me how to fight, how to throw a punch. These guys are... I mean, they're grim, I know that now. I knew it. Deep down, I knew it. But... I got caught up in it. I was bored. It was their idea to come here. I think they like playing the big men, getting with girls.' He shakes his head. 'At first, he seemed so impressive. Byrne, you know? So successful. But the things he said, his ideas... I dunno, they seemed OK to begin with maybe, but then they just wormed their way into me, and it was only when I saw him with Casey that I realised... But I didn't mean to...'

Melissa's hair follicles rise. 'Didn't mean to what, love?'

But Dan has collapsed into tears, and if she pushes too hard, she knows he will close up.

'Hey.' She puts her arms around him, battling her own frustration. 'You won't be the first man who got into a fight, and you won't be the last. Why were you warning him off your sister? You can't have known about the photo by then.'

'Because he was, like, all respectful to girls' faces and then calling them bitches behind their backs. I thought it was just the way he spoke, just words, but it's not. It's not. Did you see the message? He promised to show us the rest of the photo later. I mean, what the hell?'

'It's disgusting. Of course it is.' *Why*, she wants to ask, *are you referring to Byrne in the past tense?*

Dan shakes his head. 'But the police. The police will see the photo.'

'Why is that such a big problem?' Anxiety blocks her throat. 'Dan? What is it? Why is the photo such a problem?'

'Because I replied that I'd kill him if he didn't delete it,' he hisses. 'But I found him. Just now, in the woodland. That's what I'm trying to tell you. He's dead, Mum. He's dead, and now I don't know what I've done.'

TWENTY-NINE
MELISSA

Two days after

Melissa stirs. For the first few seconds, she has no idea where she is. And then it hits her like a breeze block. Casey. Dan. Byrne Sharp. The whole damn mess. Her body flushes from toe to head, just as it did last night when Dan told her he'd hit Byrne, that he'd issued a death threat and now he was dead. Jesus, she'd thought, scarcely able to believe it. No, no, no, no, no.

'You didn't do anything, OK?' she said, pulling him into her arms, her heart beating so fast, she knew he would feel its rhythm thumping against him. 'Did you... did you report it?'

'No,' he sobbed. 'I came back here. I didn't know what to do.'

Holding him tight, she let him cry, her tired mind racing, trying to untangle the mess.

'Listen,' she said after a long moment. 'You just told me you didn't see that photo until after you got here, which was after you'd spoken to the cop at the site, yes? Someone will find Byrne, and when they do, they'll be able to ascertain his time of death, yes? And he'll have died way before you made that threat and way after you guys had your fight. So tomorrow, you come into the station with us, OK, and you tell them you have more information. And you show them the photo and you tell them when you saw it and say you haven't seen him since last night, OK? You're not to blame, love. Look at me.'

He raised his tear-streaked face to hers.

'You're not to blame,' she insisted. 'Whoever did that to him, it wasn't you.'

Dan broke down, his head falling into his hands. His shoulders shook and a wailing sound escaped him. Melissa glanced about, worried about someone seeing, reassuring herself that if anyone came by, they would think he was crying for his sister, which, in a way, he was. She told him it wasn't his fault, over and over, but it didn't seem like he believed her.

She can't blame him, she thinks now. She barely knows if she believed herself. She wonders if the police have found the body by now. Casey told them she remembered trees; it's possible they'll have searched and found much more than they were expecting.

Casey is still asleep, her bruises purpling on her neck. Sleep and time will heal her. But will she remember more when she wakes up? And is that worse or better?

On the chair, Riley is snoring softly, her hands clasped under her bosom, her head lolling slightly forward. Melissa tries not to make a sound while she stretches. Her eyes are gummy. Her neck feels like someone has welded it to her rocky shoulders, like her head will never again achieve independent movement.

Should she wake Casey? Try and talk to her while Riley is asleep? Should she tell her about Dan finding Byrne?

Another glance at PC Riley. Envy pricks at her. How is it even possible to sleep in that position? Melissa wonders if she herself has even slept at all. An hour maybe. Not much and not well, her mind revolving it all like a bloody washing machine.

The next twenty-four hours will be difficult. She has to tread carefully. Above all else, whatever happens, she has to protect her children.

Last night, she dropped Dan at the Premier Inn and left him with strict instructions not to say anything to anyone, to try and get some sleep and to call her in the morning. It was painful leaving him alone, but he needed rest, and she needed time to get her head around what he'd told her.

'We know Byrne did this to her,' he said in the car on the way to the hotel, close to tears, shaking his head. 'We know they were together where he died.'

'We don't know that actually.'

As if to offer proof, he held up that godawful photograph again. 'They must have been! Look at this! If I didn't kill him, maybe she did.'

'Don't say that,' she said after a moment, keeping her voice low. 'Do not say that, OK? You don't know anything. Nothing at all. We can't go round jumping to conclusions.'

'But he told me he was going to...'

'To what?' Outside the hotel, she stopped the car and turned off the engine. Silence pressed in, making everything louder somehow. 'To what, Dan? What was he planning to do to her?'

Her son shrugged, the tips of his ears glowing pink. 'Y'know. Have sex with her.'

'He told you that?'

'Sort of. After I hit him. Well, no, not exactly, but he called her a... a mean name.'

What was it about kids that made them think their parents were delicate flowers with no life experience? 'I'm not a child, love,' she said, voice firming. 'Just tell me what he called her.'

Dan looked like he wanted the ground to swallow him

whole. 'A ho,' he said, barely above a whisper, but she heard it loud and clear.

'What is he, a gardener?' She glanced about; lowered her voice to match his. 'Do you mean a whore? He called your sister a whore?'

Dan nodded, misery incarnate.

'Dear God,' she said. 'Smart young men calling young women whores. How did we get here?'

'I think it might be my fault,' he said.

'Your fault how? You don't call women that, do you? Do you?'

'God, no! Of course not.' He shook his head. 'I mean my fault he went after her. I think it was, like, revenge. For me hitting him.' He looked up at her, the beautiful brown eyes he'd inherited from his shit of a father imploring. She wanted so badly to take him into her arms, but shock had frozen her hands to the steering wheel.

'You don't know what happened,' she said eventually, ignoring the shake in her voice. 'And how can any of this be your fault? Casey was spiked, for God's sake. If he did this to her, it's for his own twisted reasons. It has nothing whatsoever to do with you.'

'Mum, you don't understand,' he whispered. 'You don't hit Byrne Sharp. You just don't. If he sent that photo later, it means he saw Casey after I hit him. And she's covered in bruises, and she's saying she can't remember, and Byrne had these pills...'

Melissa closed her eyes, heart pounding in her ears. 'When you give your statement tomorrow, don't say anything about Casey, OK? Don't tell them stuff you don't know. Just show them the photo and let them do their job. OK?'

'Do I tell them about the fight?'

'Yes. But play it down. Maybe... maybe say he went for you first, yeah? Just in case. You have a right to defend yourself. Say he hit you first. I mean, that's probably what happened anyway.

As you say, he must have found Casey after that, so he was obviously fine, but we don't know what happened next. You had a bit of a dust-up, that's all. It wasn't you, and it wasn't your sister. Don't go incriminating her, for God's sake.'

Damage limitation, she thinks now. She needs to do something. This is all her fault, after all.

THIRTY
MELISSA

Two days after

Casey is stirring, eyes swollen with sleep.

'Hey, love.' Melissa reaches for her hand and squeezes it. 'How're you feeling?'

Her daughter gives a watery smile; blinks her puffy violet eyelids.

'Scared,' she says, her voice hoarse.

'Don't be,' Melissa says. 'I'm here.' She stands to hold a glass of water to her daughter's lips; waits while she drinks a little, then nods that she's had enough. She sits down, is about to ask Casey if anything more has come back to her, but her daughter announces she needs to pee and moves her legs gingerly over the side of the bed.

Melissa watches her make her way to the loo like she's made of glass and feels herself fill with guilt. Casey should have been in that chalet with her friends. If only she, Melissa, hadn't been so bloody proud, none of this would have happened. But her knob of an ex-partner caught her on a bad day: defences down, hormones playing up, teetering at the rag-end of herself.

Excuses, excuses. And of course, it was only a few days after Casey had asked her about the chalet and Melissa was still a bit raw from that, still practising all manner of magical thinking, trying desperately to dream up a way of giving her daughter the two hundred and fifty pounds for the deposit. Most of the time, she manages to turn a blind eye to the Range Rovers, the Sweaty Betty leggings and the Bella Freud sweaters, but not that day. That day she was full of anger, she knows that now, but some days you just are, aren't you? Not much you can do about it except maybe have therapy. But who can afford therapy, especially therapy for being angry about not being able to afford obscene amounts of stuff?

She was coming home from Tesco. She'd walked to save the bus fare. The bag handles were cutting into her palms. She could feel menopausal sweat running down her back, her neck tight, shoulders promising pain for later.

A little ahead, on the high street near her flat, a car door opened and out he got like he was Jeremy bloody Clarkson, folding his sunglasses and slipping them into his blazer pocket as if he thought someone might be watching him from a window somewhere, admiring him. His thick silver-fox hair was pushed back. It reminded her of a Vidal Sassoon ad from the eighties. Even before she realised who it was, she hated him, just for driving a BMW, just for the way he folded his bloody Ray-Bans, just for how he dug out the gold credit card and slid it into the machine, not a thought for whether he was blocking the pavement. *He's so typical of people around here*, she was already thinking: the baseball-capped new mums in huge huddles with their gigantic jogging-friendly pushchairs, shouting their conversations, leaving old people struggling on walking sticks and people like her, laden with shopping, to somehow edge past or dive for the gutter.

And then she recognised him, and all the rage she was already feeling multiplied by a good hundred or two of whatever metric rage is measured in. And of course, she had to see him then, didn't she? Not when she'd just had a haircut, put on a nice dress or got herself a bit spruced up, no. Right then, laden with supermarket bags and looking like the wreck of the bloody *Hesperus*, that's when.

'Mel!' All chummy, one hand in a wave, her nickname on his lips like he had any kind of right to use it any more. His clothes were stiff. He looked square and old, and *Schadenfreude* shot through her like caffeine.

Red jeans, for fuck's sake.

'Rich,' she replied, since they were shortening. *Rich by name...* The worn-out thought made her feel even more exhausted, not to mention wishing her bags weren't full of yellow-labelled discount groceries, that she hadn't left this morning's dishes in the sink. Because of course he was going to want to *pop in*, wasn't he?

'Good to see you,' he said, an obsequious smile on his smug little mouth.

Her reply: narrowed eyes and a sarcastic grin.

'I was hoping to catch you actually.' He threw the ticket onto the dash, slammed the door shut and pressed the key fob. The car flashed. The expensive-sounding thunk of central locking.

'Here I am,' she said and heard the edge in her voice. 'I presume you've not driven in just for me.'

He raised his eyebrows. 'Why not? I was... Actually, I had a meeting in Twickenham, but I did want to see you about something. You look well.'

She bit back the pithy reply before it made it out of her mouth. Rich always was so full of shit; how had she ever found him attractive? And the worst of it was, he looked so like Dan, or Dan like him, and Dan was a peach of a man, no thanks to his father.

'You here to pay some maintenance?' she asked.

He had the decency to flinch but managed to turn it into a vague gesture towards the window of the third-floor flat she'd bought with her paltry share of the proceeds from the family home. 'Can we go up?'

'Is that absolutely necessary?' Her arms ached. But if she put down the bags, he'd think she was agreeing to some sort of conversation.

He spread his hands in front of his blazered chest. His palms are so pink, she thought. Like Spam.

'I come in peace,' he said, smiling. 'Please.' Had he had his teeth capped?

'The kids aren't in. Not that you're bothered.'

'That's not fair. We've been renovating, as you know, and they're busy with their own lives.'

'Dan's not busy. He's working late shifts at the pub, so he's free most days. As you know. He'd have loved to have seen you.'

'I'll text him. See if he wants to watch the football sometime.'

'In Wiltshire?'

Rich sighed. 'Here. Of course I meant here. Don't make this more difficult than it needs to be. I'll only be a few minutes, then I'll get out of your hair. I don't even need a cup of tea.'

'I didn't offer you one,' she quipped with petty grimness – or grim pettiness, she couldn't have said which – unlocking the door and praying to God Suzanne's cat hadn't peed in the stairwell again; she'd only just got rid of the rancid stink, and even now they needed an air freshener.

'You go ahead,' she said into the muggy lavender-with-a-hint-of-cat-spray-infused air. 'I need to check the post.'

What she needed was for him not to be looking at her arse all the way up the stairs.

'Do you want me to carry that?' he asked, glancing at the shopping.

'It's not heavy,' she lied.

With another weary sigh designed to let her know how difficult she was, he started up the stairs. She followed, focused on making herself breathe deeply but silently. His laboured breathing gave her a victorious feeling. One thing about walking everywhere was it kept her fit. By the time they got to the top, Rich's face was puce on its way to lilac, and he was panting like a St Bernard on twenty a day.

Inside, she told him to go on into the kitchen. That his big posh house in the country was about sixteen times bigger than the flat in which she was raising their children irked her, but it had irked her for years and she'd got better at swallowing it down. She still made him wait though, hanging up her raincoat with excessive care and changing out of her trainers into her slippers with the urgency of a snail.

'Right.' She found him in the kitchen, sitting at the table. He was squashed in, his belly bisected by the table's edge. He looked like a grown-up playing house with a child's toy furniture set. Small pleasures.

She pressed her back against the worktop.

'I come in peace,' he repeated. 'I'll get straight to it.'

'Do.'

'I heard on the grapevine that Casey's friends are hiring a chalet for this Summer Camp thing.'

'*What?*' She failed to conceal her shock. Damn. This would be a small win for him. 'How the hell have you heard that? I only heard it myself a couple of days ago.'

'Mags,' he said.

'Mags.' The shiny new wife.

'She's actually friends with one of the mums. Shirley, I think? Charlotte's mum. They went to school together. Her and Shirley, I mean. Not Charlotte, obviously, ha ha.' He cleared his throat. 'Anyway, Mags was on the phone to Shirley and...' With a rolling gesture of his hand, he trailed off.

Mags and Shirley, she thought. You really couldn't break

wind at one end of this town without someone hearing it at the other. She had nothing against either woman. Rich had met Mags after they'd split, and she was, miracle of miracles, a year older than him. If anything, Melissa wanted to call the poor woman and warn her what was in store once the novelty wore off. *Whatever you do*, she would say, *don't be a real person. Don't have flaws. Rich hates that.*

'Nice to know you keep tabs on your kids from afar,' she said eventually, hating how acid she sounded, how acid he made her, so acid she could feel herself corroding from the inside.

He closed his eyes; held them shut a moment before opening them again. 'Look, I'm sorry I moved, OK? I don't know how many times I have to say it. I know it's not been ideal.'

'Not been ideal?'

'Difficult then. Whatever word you want. Terrible. Horrible. But I couldn't have taken them with me, could I? They were settled here.'

Not true, but she ignored it. She would never, *ever* have let him take the kids.

'It's not exactly far to drive,' she said instead. 'But let's not do this. We've done it to death, and we are where we are. What do you want?'

'OK.' He stared down at his hands splayed on the table. His new wedding ring was already too tight, she noticed. 'But I do feel bad.'

'Why not carry on with the maintenance then?'

He looked up and frowned. 'Casey's eighteen now.'

'So, of course, all her needs are covered. We all know kids are completely independent at eighteen, after all.'

'All right. But she'll get the full maintenance loan for uni, won't she?'

'Which she'll spend half her life paying back.'

'Like most kids.' He waved his hand dismissively. Like he

always used to when they were together, whenever her feelings came into it. Fresh rage fired within her. She should never have let him into the flat. If she murdered him right here, right now, it would be a crime of passion. But the courts wouldn't see it that way.

'Say what you have to say,' she said quietly. 'And then you can go, OK?'

'You're going to like it, I swear, so hear me out.' He met her eye with what she knew he thought was boyish charm. How awful it was to know someone this well, to see through the perfect lawn of their once-adorable mannerisms to the earthworms writhing beneath.

'I heard about the chalet,' he began again. 'Mags said it was five hundred a head?'

She bit her lip, fighting the warning in her gut. He looked pleased with himself. That was never good.

'So.' The word lasted a while. He paused; she assumed for dramatic effect. 'I'd like to pay. The whole amount.' He smiled, a smile that said, *You weren't expecting that, were you?* That said, *I know. I'm a great guy.* That said, *No need to thank me; this is just who I am.*

Melissa waited until she felt calm enough to speak. It must've been a while because he said her name. Twice. Once with the full Melissa, the second time the more intimate Mel.

'Mel,' he said again. 'Are you going to say anything?'

'You want to pay for her chalet?' she managed.

'I can drop the money into her account today if you like.'

She pulled all the air she could find into her lungs; felt her chest swell with the hot gas of it.

'No,' she said. Nothing more came. She didn't feel capable of more.

'What do you mean, no?' He frowned deeply, as if what she'd said was ridiculous. 'Mags said she thought Casey couldn't pay the deposit.'

'Well, Mags heard wrong.' The half-lie slipped out, galvanised her. 'She hasn't paid it yet, that's all. We're paying it next week.'

'Right. Well, I could still pay it? The whole thing.' He said it as if he were lifting all her troubles from her, like so much dirty laundry.

'I don't want you to pay it,' she said, her calm tone frightening her a little.

'*What*? Why not?'

'Because I'm not having you waltzing off to Wiltshire to sip Chablis from crystal glasses in your country manor while I shop at three different supermarkets just so I can buy them shoes, to then swoop down in your cape and be the superhero. No. Just no. *I've* looked after them, *I've* taken care of their every need, emotional, physical, educational, you name it, so I'll be damned if I'm going to watch while you get to play the benefactor. Either help them properly or not at all. Do you get that? Please tell me you get that.'

He shook his head, his expression a mix of exasperation and incredulity. 'I think,' he said slowly, raising his forefinger, 'you're putting your ego above your children.'

'My ego? My *ego*? Oh my God.' She laughed mirthlessly. 'I've put nothing at all in front of *my* children. Ever. They've always come first, always. And they're your children too, by the way. Are you even aware of what you just said? But you're right. They are my children. D'you know why? Because I've been their parent, in every possible way. I've been both parents. So no, I don't want your charity donation, thank you. We can pay for the chalet ourselves. If you want to give them something, set up a savings account to help them through uni – although it's too late for Dan, isn't it? Dan who's working all the hours for minimum wage because he can't afford to go travelling with his friends. I assume you'd be giving him five hundred quid too? You can't give to one and not the other.'

But Rich was shaking his head, sighing, the faintest hint of amusement.

'Do something quiet and real,' she said as calmly as she could. 'Not this... this flashy gesture that's all about you. You can't buy them back, Rich. They've grown up. They're on to you.'

'Because you've poisoned them against me.'

'I haven't said a word against you. Not one. If your relationship with them is broken, you've done that all on your own.'

'I don't have to listen to this.' He stood, or tried to, stuck momentarily between table and chair, the chair having wedged itself against the fridge. Reddening, he unblocked himself and pulled briskly on the hem of his jacket. Under any other circumstances, it would've been funny. 'Thank you for reminding me why I left you,' he spat and strode out of the kitchen, then down the hall, his stream of expletives fading. A beat and the door slammed shut.

Once she was sure he'd gone, she followed in his footsteps, then on into the front room. Through the window, she stared down at the pavement below. Seconds later, his thick silver head appeared. She could see the fury in his body in the way he flung open the car door and got in. Another second and he closed it with a bang.

It was stuffy in the flat. She opened the sash to the familiar bustle of the high street. As she walked back to the kitchen to put away the shopping, the roar of his expensive engine reached her. She should've felt pleased, or proud, or victorious. But she didn't feel any of those things. In fact, she regretted every single word she'd just said.

In the kitchen, she put the groceries in the fridge and made tea and sat for fifteen minutes buzzing with shock. Shock at his presumption, but mostly at herself. What the hell did she just do? Did she really say no to five hundred pounds on her daughter's behalf? A grand, if she included Dan, not that that was on offer. She'd had no right to refuse that money. She'd known it the moment she said no. But a heady mix of rage and pride had got a grip of her in a way she hadn't been able to control.

And sitting here in the hospital in the aftermath of her disastrous decision and all that it has meant, she knows she should have phoned Rich and told him she'd changed her mind. She meant to, of course she did. Of course she would've taken his damn money – as long as Dan was going to get the same. Of course she would've swallowed down her resentment for the sake of the kids, let Rich be the hero if that's what he needed to appease his guilt.

But a few days later, Casey said she'd paid for the chalet and the urgency vanished. Still, Melissa meant to call Rich. Maybe persuade him to do like she'd suggested and set up a savings account in their children's names instead, think about putting a small amount in each month. But she didn't. She should have, but she didn't.

And now, here they are. Her daughter limping back from the hospital loo, her memory shot with trauma or drugs or both, her neck and arms blue-black leopard print, and all because she couldn't afford the chalet, which meant she felt she had to work at the site, which meant she ended up cut off, alone, prey to the likes of Byrne Sharp.

And Melissa can't even bring herself to tell her brave and beautiful daughter that she's the one who put her there.

THIRTY-ONE
CASEY

Three days before

The site empties on Thursday morning and starts filling up again late that same afternoon. Blue spreads through straggling streaks of white cloud, the temperature a very pleasant twenty-four degrees. From her vantage point at the clubhouse bar, Casey wipes down the counter and watches teenagers plod down the hillside, tortoise-like with their huge rucksacks, their bags bulging with cans and snacks. They must've all taken the same train, caught the bus together from the station, sharing jokes and excitement for the weekend to come. Immy and the guys won't be with them. They're not coming until tomorrow because the chalets are Friday to Friday. Plus, they're not on public transport; they're coming in the brand-new Seat 500 Immy got for her eighteenth.

Casey spots Olive and Ethan passing across the front of the veranda. She calls out hello and waves, but they're too busy chatting and don't hear. They look happy, like they really, genuinely like each other, and she feels a pang of something she can't quite identify. As they make their way down the hill, she sees they're headed for general camping, where her own group of friends refused to go. *Too posh to pitch* someone said; it might have been Miss London or Spider, but it could have been Mum or Dan. Mum makes no secret of the fact she can't stand Immy or Immy's mum. She says Immy's mum is the most competitive woman she's ever met and that whenever she's spoken to her for more than five seconds, she feels like she needs a shower.

At the thought of Mum, Casey feels another pang, this time much more recognisable. She misses her cooking, her hugs, even her endless philosophising. Maybe that's why she felt a bit sad seeing Olive and Ethan just now. It's all mixed up in her brain with the deep-down feeling that Mum is right about Immy, and that if she is, then that means Casey's teenage years have been wasted. Even Dan says Immy's a psycho, and with a bit of distance, Casey is coming to realise that if she'd been friends with Olive and Ethan these last few years, she would've been sipping cider from cans right now, pitching a tent in the main field and laughing at nothing. She doesn't mind having to work – it's not that. Spider and Ness and the other staff are all really nice, and she's loved the campfire vibes. But a whole summer without Mum feels too long, especially if she ends up going to York in September, and the reasons for her decision, which seemed so clear at the time, are now lost in a sort of fog.

She rinses the cloth and sets about giving the steamer nozzle a good clean. Lonely, maybe that's all she's feeling. Like she has no mates. In Year 9, when she changed schools after Mum and Dad split up, Immy showered her with attention, but lately Immy's friendship has felt like a contract Casey signed in a moment of weakness, and now, if she doesn't fulfil her job description, she'll get fired. Like the other week, when Immy wanted to go and see a film and Casey said she couldn't because she needed to revise, Immy sort of ignored her for a few days afterwards. When Casey asked what was wrong, she replied, 'Nothing, why?' As if it was all in Casey's head.

Her thoughts are making her feel sick. Immy's not a bad person, and she's not really the reason Casey's ended up here. But Mum's right – she is a bit spoilt.

'Copied-In,' a voice says. Spider. She smiles to herself. He's called her that stupid nickname since the first day and it's kind of grown on her. She suspects it's actually a shyness thing, all this not using the normal word for anything. Either that or he likes her in *that* way – he does seem to magically appear wherever she is a lot of the time. But she hopes it's not that.

'I was on the scrounge for one of your magnificent *piatti bianchi*,' he says when she turns around, grinning through his dirty teeth, which are kind of gross. It occurs to her she has no idea how old he is: anywhere between twenty-one and forty.

'Translation, please.'

'Flat whites. I suspect it means white plates actually, but never mind. Oat milk, if you please, miss.'

'Sure.' She turns away, rolling her eyes as she makes the drink. Spider is such a weirdo. But he has shown her where everything is, all the time-saving hacks, and he really pulls his weight. She just wishes he didn't keep popping out from behind trees and shower blocks as if he were spying on her.

'Now there's a sight I ain't seen for a while,' he remarks, nodding at the shambolic parade of kids. 'The incomers a-comin' in.'

'That's right,' she says, placing his coffee on the bar. 'How come you weren't here last year?'

'Last few years. Went me a-travellin'.' He stares into his flat white. 'Now that is one glorious mega Phil.'

'Glorious mega who now? Who's Phil?'

'Not who. M-E-G-A-P-H-Y-L-L. The humble fern.'

It takes another full second for Casey to realise he means the leaf shape she has made in the coffee foam. Megaphyll. Oh my God, what the actual...

'Thank you kindly.' Spider shakes out a sachet and slides

the sugar into the edge of his drink, stirring it in with painstaking care so as not to spoil the latte art. It is such a small thing, but it makes her heart squeeze. Maybe he's not weird, she thinks. Just sensitive. 'You watch. From now till Monday, our muddy boots won't touch the grass. What are your shifts again?'

Casey has noticed that once Spider relaxes, his speech normalises, and this makes her heart squeeze too, although why he wants to know what her shifts are is anyone's guess. 'Today till five,' she replies, 'then double tomorrow, late Saturday, then Sunday two till eight, which is decent.'

'You won't miss much. If memory serves, they don't light the fire till around six thirty. Your school chums here yet?'

At the mention of her friends, she feels herself blush. 'No, but I've seen a couple of people I know. My brother's arriving tomorrow.' She's unsure why she hasn't really talked about her actual group of friends to Spider; why, instinctively, she feels like she wants to keep him away from them. Or them away from him.

'You'll be able to party like it's 1999 once you knock off,' he says. 'Last time I worked here, it went on till dawn.' He takes out his tobacco and papers and begins to roll. 'And your brother is coming with some new *compañeros*, you said?'

She nods. 'I've not met them. He said they're a bit... I dunno how you'd say it. Straight? A bit yo-pro?'

'What in the name of long country walks is a yo-pro?'

'A young professional? Like, clean-cut, neat.' She refrains from mentioning their age because over twenties are not allowed into Summer Camp, and even though Spider probably wouldn't say anything, she doesn't want to get Dan and his mates barred.

Spider sips his coffee and stares into the middle distance. 'The young professional brigade,' he muses. 'Money magnets magnified into magnates. Cantaloupe smugglers, I'll wager.'

'Cantaloupe... what?' She narrows her eyes at him. 'You don't half talk in riddles.'

'Muscles, my dear. Biceps and triceps and what have you. I'm guessing they'll be of the worked-out variety. Gym bunnies. Yo-pro, as you say.'

God, he's exhausting. 'Nothing wrong with keeping fit,' she says.

'If you like that sort of thing.' He drains his coffee, foam leaving little white dots on his barely there moustache. She itches to wipe them off but doesn't want to give him the wrong idea. 'Not my cup of tea,' he adds, 'if you'll pardon my frankness. Speaking of which, that was an excellent flat white. Ten out of ten. See you later, KC and the Sunshine Band.'

'It's CC.' This time, she rolls her eyes openly.

But as he lopes away down the hill in his high-vis tabard, she feels uneasiness steal over her. There is something vulnerable about Spider, something a bit other-worldly. She wonders what happened back at his school, wonders what he was like, what his school was like. She's sure he said boarding school, which is weird because he looks nothing like she imagines a boarding school boy to look. It's so hard to know; he is placeless as well as ageless. He could be good or bad. He could be anything.

THIRTY-TWO
CASEY

Two days before

Casey is carrying a tray of paninis to one of the tables on the terrace when she hears her name shrieked into the sunny air.

'Caaaaaaaaseeeeeeeeeeeeeeey. Oh my Go-o-o-d!'

Immy is striding towards her, arms flung wide. She is wearing a string-bikini top and white cut-off micro-shorts, her long, toned, tanned legs dropping into perfectly scuffed black cowboy boots. Matty and Charlotte follow behind like hand-maidens. It is a little after three.

'Hi,' Casey says and hears the coolness in her voice.

'Nice threads,' Immy says, her palm tracing a figure-of-eight in front of Casey's Heaven View staff T-shirt. She giggles into her hand, throwing a glance at Matty and Charlotte. 'Check out the T, guys.'

'You can buy them in the site shop,' Casey deadpans. 'I can try and get you all a discount.'

Matty and Charlotte titter, whether with her or at her it's hard to tell. Matty is standing with his feet crossed, twirling a lock of his long dark-auburn hair, which has fallen from his ponytail. His undercut is freshly shaved, and he's wearing three glittering cross studs in each ear. He's handsome in a fine-boned English-rose way, his chin Lego-brick square and his slim physique accentuated by a tiny cream linen waistcoat and matching super-wide-legged trousers. From a thin leather strap round his neck dangles a silver skull of what might be a goat.

'He-ey,' he says and waves with the ends of his fingers.

Charlotte just about manages a *hey*. She can't help being beautiful, Casey thinks. But with beautiful people, shyness comes off as arrogance. Or maybe it's actual arrogance. She doesn't really know Charlotte well enough to know, since Immy keeps her closely guarded.

'Gabby's coming tomorrow now,' Immy says randomly. 'Think she wanted to come in her own car.'

'Cool.' Casey nods towards the tray she's carrying and moves past them. 'Be right back.'

By the time she returns, the three of them are settled at Table 16.

'So, like, when do you get off work?' Immy asks, unwrapping a packet of Vogue cigarettes and looking about her. She yawns, crossing her infinite legs. How are they tanned? Casey thinks. When?

'Not until nine or maybe ten.'

Immy's mouth drops in disgust. 'Oh my God, isn't that, like, slave labour?'

'Well, I get paid, so I don't think so.' Casey makes herself smile. 'Do you guys want a coffee or whatever?'

'Oh my God, yeah,' Immy says. 'We're literally parched, and my blood sugar is under*ground*. Can we get iced coffees?' Her blue eyes twinkle.

'Sure.'

'Cool. Do you guys like hazelnut iced lattes?' She turns to the others. 'You've gotta try them – they're insane. Can we get, like, three hazelnut iced lattes?'

'Sure.'

Casey leaves them and goes to prepare their drinks. She hadn't been looking forward to seeing them, and now they're here it's worse than she thought it would be. It could be to do with how quickly they got Immy's mate Gabriella to fill Casey's place in the chalet, though she is trying hard not to think like that. She's embarrassed having to wait tables in front of them, even though that goes against pretty much her whole upbringing. Hopefully Dan and his friends will get here soon. Maybe she can hang out with them later instead.

She takes the coffees over and places them in front of her friends. Immy gives a machine-gun handclap, but when Casey holds out the card reader, none of them meet her eye.

'It's, like, thirteen fifty?'

Immy looks at her with something like horror. 'Oh no,' she says. 'Do we have to pay? Sorry, I thought...' She shrugs, smiling cutely.

Casey feels herself blush. 'Er, I'm not... I can't really... I mean, I'd get fired. Sorry.'

'It's *fine*.' With obvious annoyance, Immy digs in her bag before throwing it to the ground. 'Matt? Matty, darling. My phone's dead. Can you get these and I'll pay you back?'

Once they've gone, Casey clears their empty glasses and wonders if Immy *will* pay Matty back. From her own experience, she doubts it. Immy is great at forgetting her debit card, and her Apple Pay never seems to work either.

As she watches the trio disappear left into the chalet field at the top of the rise, it dawns on her that she is only here because of them – not at Summer Camp but *here*, working at this damn bar, when she could be chilling in the sunshine. She has missed all the end-of-term parties because of them, left her mum behind to face the entire summer alone because of them... all for this. And what even is *this* anyway? Getting to hang out with three people she's not sure she really likes any more. Except she won't even be hanging out with them, will she? She'll be working. If she'd just been brave enough to come on her own, she could've hung out with Olive and Ethan and those guys. They would have been chill about it.

Feeling a bit hot and panicky, she grabs the cloth and gives the entire bar a good clean, scratching off dry, congealed drops of whatever-the-hell with her thumbnail. Why is she so crap? How is this her life? Why didn't she make better friends when she first changed schools instead of letting herself be seduced by Immy and her fake sympathy?

'Hi there.'

A tall guy in mirrored gold-rimmed police shades, six-pack stacked in a tight white T-shirt, is standing at the bar. His black hair is slicked back, the sides shaved close, and he has a diamanté earring in his left ear. Everything about him screams *player*.

'Can I help you?' she asks, unable to completely stifle the smirk.

He points at her, and kind of frowns and smiles at the same time. 'Casey, right? Casey Connor?'

'You read my name badge. You can read. Congratulations.'

The guy leans back and laughs. Like, really laughs, as if he's surprised. His teeth are white and even. God, they're so, so white. He grips the edge of the bar, like he has to hang on because he's laughing so much. His forearms are tanned, and his biceps are so... Her mind offers up a thousand dancing cartoon cantaloupes.

'I hadn't seen the badge, I swear.' He grins. It's a mischievous grin, full of warmth and conspiracy, like they're friends, not the strangers they actually are. 'I'm a friend of Dan's. I must've seen a picture of you on his phone.' He throws up his hands. 'Full disclosure, I did see a picture. He's very proud of you, you know. I can see why.'

Casey battles not to feel a flush of pleasure tinged with embarrassment. Smooth, she thinks. No wonder his skin is so clear; the zits must just slide off. Does he think she can't tell when she's being flattered? But then the penny drops. This is the guy from the self-defence channel: Stay Sharper with Byrne Sharp.

'Dan would never tell *me* that,' she says, returning the grin without acknowledging that she recognises him. What is she, flirting now? 'Actually, that's not true. Dan's top.'

'He is indeed.' Byrne Sharp thumps his fist to his bulging chest. 'Dan's a real stand-up guy.'

A beat passes, the two of them smiling like idiots at one another, until he laughs again, shakes his head.

'So did you guys just get here,' she says, 'or...'

'Just arrived.' He gestures vaguely towards the teepee field, one down from the chalets. 'I drove, so I'm letting them sort things out while I have a well-earned cortado.' His eyes return to hers. At least she assumes they do behind the sunglasses. 'If that's OK?'

Literally no one has ordered a cortado since she's been here. It's her favourite coffee. But she's not about to tell Byrne Sharp that.

'Good choice' is as far as she's prepared to go. She can't tell where he's looking, whether he's checking her out or what. If he is, at least he's not being creepy about it.

'You didn't say what your name was,' she adds when she places the cortado in front of him, and yes, now she's flirting, she definitely is, even though he is so not her type, apart from his nice manners maybe. Oh, and the sense of humour.

'Sorry,' he says. 'I should've introduced myself. Great-looking coffee by the way. A good life skill to have.'

'Are you taking the piss?' He still hasn't said his name. It's like he's trying to divert her attention. Or maybe he knows she knows.

'Not at all,' he says, and laughter escapes him yet again, as if joy is always there near the surface of him, but at the same time, she can't tell if he's being sarcastic. 'Believe me, I've tried to do the whole fern-in-the-foam thing and it always comes out looking like... well, I can't say, not in polite company anyway.' He laughs once more but at himself, kind of self-deprecating. 'I'm Byrne anyway,' he adds at last. 'Byrne Sharp.'

THIRTY-THREE
CASEY

Two days before

Casey knocks off shift a little after ten. Her back aches; her little toes feel like she's got blisters from her trainers. The bar is still really busy, stiflingly hot despite the whole of the front windows having been folded back to let in the cool evening air.

She moves through the crowd, searching for her friends, but there's no sign of them. If they were here, she'd know. Immy carries a kind of electric charge. She crackles, her frequency somehow drawing others to her. Casey doesn't recognise anyone in here; she can't even spot the nerds from her school who were outside the shower block doing Jägerbombs earlier and thinking they were hardcore.

She gives up. They're probably hanging out at their chalet, staying chill before the big weekend. As she walks down the hill towards staff camping, she texts Immy:

Hey. Just finished. Where are you guys?

The text waits. The phone signal is so crap on the hillside; it's better right at the top. After a moment, she sees it's delivered.

She passes general camping, scanning the tents, hoping to spot Olive and Ethan, but there is no sign of them either. She wonders if Liam is here. Immy said he told her he wasn't coming, which is kind of pass-agg and a bit pathetic. Just because they went out, it's not like they can't speak to one another ever again. Maybe it's good he's not here. She's so lonely there's a danger she'd get with him just because she knows she can, and that wouldn't be fair.

Down towards the dunes, kids are grouped outside tents, iPhones hooked up to speakers, drinking, vaping, laughing. She feels a pang of something, that feeling again like she's an outsider looking in. When Dan got back from Summer Camp years ago, he looked wrecked and he was scrawny, like he'd lost weight in just a few days. He hadn't slept *at all*, he told her with pride. *Oh my God, it was mental, I can't even...* He slept for a week afterwards.

Dan wasn't an outsider, she thinks. He fitted in.

Fighting a downer, she reaches the bottom of the site. Where is everyone? Where is Dan? Where is that guy Byrne? He was kind of easy to talk to. A laugh. Light in the darkness she's been fighting all day.

The crash of waves on sand reaches her, the gurgling roar of the water being sucked back into itself. When the tide is high, you can hear the sea from this bit of the site. A reward for it being the dampest part with the most waterlogged ground. There have been a couple of mornings when she's gone into the dell next to staff camping, just to sit alone, and the mist was hovering over the ground and the blades of grass were pricked with dew and the low, throaty sound of the ocean flooded her with a sense of how small she was and how huge the world. It felt like she was more alive than she had ever been. Not that she'd ever tell Immy and those guys. She would tell Dan. And Mum of course. There are only a few people you can share the mad stuff with, the stuff you wonder if anyone else feels until you dare to tell someone and then that someone says, yes, I get that, I feel that too. And then you feel less mad. Less alone too.

With no one to hang out with and no real clue what else to do, she makes her way over the grassy hump and down the track to the beach. Maybe Dan and his friends are there. Maybe Immy, Charlotte, Matty and Gabriella are too. Maybe there's no phone reception on the beach and that's why Immy hasn't replied.

The track over the dunes is dark. The further away from the site she goes, the darker it gets, until she can barely see her own hands. She digs her iPhone from her back pocket and uses the torch to find her way along. It is proper spooky. Her heart beats faster and faster, and she's aware of her own breathing.

Just when she decides to turn back, the sharp grass gives way to soft sand, buttery in the half moonlight. More kids are here, silhouetted against the sky, more spindly music from iPhones, the fruity drift of vape smoke, the stickier, earthier sweetness of weed. Some of them are sitting around portable barbecues, their faces softly lit. They're not allowed barbecues. But there's no way she's going to tell kids her own age what they can and can't do; it would be so cringe. Spider says he often pretends not to notice things. Says he's not paid enough to get into a fight.

She wanders towards the groups, eyes flitting everywhere for any sign of her friends. No one she recognises. A brief glance at her phone – no reply from Immy. There are no new messages at all on the Heaven View WhatsApp group. Weird.

She yawns. Decides in that moment to go to bed. She'll catch them tomorrow. Failing that, Sunday night. Sunday night's the real party. And she doesn't care if they've not replied, not really. She almost doesn't care.

Back on the campsite, the tents are a hotchpotch of fabric shapes spreading up the hill, the neon strip of the clubhouse at the top a beacon. She can't stop yawning. Her eyes feel gritty.

Her belly growls. She remembers the falafel wrap she took with her at the end of the shift and searches her bag.

'Shit,' she whispers to herself, finding the foil split, yoghurt sauce leaked all over her bucket hat.

Hungrily, she eats, using her hat as a kind of plate. From staff camping, the smell of woodsmoke is like a homing signal. On the far side of the hedge, the fire pit throws flickering orange light. She can see Spider talking to Ness, his thin, funny face animated, their two heads bent together. It occurs to her that she doesn't know who baby Aura's father is. It's possible she'll never know; it's not like she's going to come out and ask, and anyway, it's none of her beeswax.

'We've got hot chocolate in the pan,' Ness says as Casey approaches, already half standing. Aura is no more than a swaddled lump against her body.

'I'll get it. Don't get up.' Casey takes the last bite of falafel and shoves the screwed-up foil into her bag along with the yoghurty hat. One thing she's really noticed since she's been here is how no one ever drops litter in staff camping, and by contrast, how much people her age throw on the ground. It's shocking, even though she remembers it from the Reading festival a couple of years ago. Maybe their mums didn't drum it into them from birth not to drop trash. Spider said loads of them will leave their pop-up tents behind, which is also just like it was at Reading, even though they're all supposedly into the environment.

By the time she reaches the pan, Spider is already out of his seat and pouring thick hot chocolate into a wonky pottery mug.

'Here you go, Copied-In,' he says, the nickname by now sounding more like Coppadin. 'You've earned this, I'll wager.'

'I have,' she says, suppressing a smile and flopping on the camping chair next to him.

'Anything to report from the battlefield?'

She smiles; blows on her hot chocolate. 'All quiet on the Western Front.'

Ness laughs. 'You're too young to be using that reference.'

'I don't know where it's from,' Casey replies. 'Just something my mum says.'

'I suspect even your mum's too young,' Spider says. '*Im Westen nichts Neues*. Literally *Nothing New in the West*. It's a German novel from' – he closes one eye and raises his straggly beard to the sky – 'the late twenties, I think. About how war ruins young men, or alternatively, how it brings out men's true nature. Depends what you believe about men, I suppose.'

'Right,' Casey says. 'Here's me thinking I was just telling you there's nothing doing on the site.'

Ness laughs. 'No such thing as an offhand remark with Spidey around. You should know that by now.'

'I do.'

They fall into good-humoured conversation. Casey sips at her hot chocolate, feeling the tiredness drain through her. They chat about nothing much – the punters, the imminent heatwave, things that need doing tomorrow.

The hot chocolate isn't like it is at home. It's thicker and has something else in it, maybe cinnamon or nutmeg, but it's delicious and she drinks it gratefully, and as the night darkens and the campsite grows quiet and there's still no word from Immy or the others, a warm feeling comes over her, so strong and deep that from one moment to the next it genuinely no longer matters if she hears from them or not. Funny, she felt so alone earlier. Now, here, with these relative strangers, she could close her eyes and happily drift away, knowing that even if she was flat-out asleep, someone would probably carry her to her tent and make sure she was OK. What was it Ness said that first day? Something about family. *I'm already lucky with my family*, Casey thinks. *I just need to learn to choose friends that feel like family.*

Another epiphany jolts her from the gorgeous drifting:
Immy and those guys do not feel like family.

No, they are not the family she has chosen. They are not people who make her feel like this.

They are not her friends.

Her eyelids are growing heavy. The soothing burble of Ness and Spider talking is rocking her to sleep. Everything is OK, she thinks. Everything is going to be OK.

THIRTY-FOUR
DAN

Two days after

At the police station, there's no sign of Mum and Casey, and his heart quickens. Mum said they were on their way. They should be here by now. Should he wait outside, or go in and give his name, ask to make a statement? He can't think straight. Hasn't slept at all. Will they have found Byrne's body? Maybe. But it's not a murder investigation until they do; it's just an assault. They won't have had teams of cops scouring the site. Byrne is probably still there. His dead body. His corpse.

Dan shivers. When he shows them the photo, they'll see Casey against a tree. And they'll go and look in the trees. And then they'll find him. He takes a deep breath. They'll find him. *Just show them the photo*, Mum said, *and let them do their job*. That's all he has to do. Show them the photo. And then they'll find the body.

If he waits out here, he might look suspicious or like he's scared. It's just a statement. That's what the cop said on the phone. Just a formal statement. He's here to show them the photograph. He didn't get it until after he spoke to the SOCO, so it's fine.

Inside, nerves still jangling, he gives his name to the duty officer, who tells him to take a seat, someone will be out to see him in a minute. He sits on one of the plastic chairs in the foyer. Five minutes pass. Ten. Fifteen. Still no sign of Mum and Case. His knee jackhammers. He makes himself plant his foot flat on the linoleum floor. It smells of some sort of cleaning product in here, a fake lemony smell.

'Daniel Connor,' comes a woman's voice. A soft Dorset accent.

Dan's stomach flips over. He glances up to see a hawk-like woman at the doorway to the interior of the station, dressed in a short-sleeved white blouse and grey skirt. She looks at him intently, as if he's an animal in a zoo, hiding at the back of a cage, and she's trying to figure out if he's in there. His stomach tightens. One last glance towards the doorway. No Mum and no Casey.

Just do it, Dan. All you have to do is show them the photo.

He brushes imaginary dust off his shorts and stands up. Smooths out his new white T, still in its square creases. He coughs into his hand and makes his way, head down, towards the woman. Knows he should look up, but she is too intimidating, and now the fear strikes him that she can read his mind, that she can see his every thought, his every recent memory, everything he's done.

'Mr Connor?' she says.

'Yes,' he replies, making himself meet her eye if only for a second. 'Dan.'

'I'm Detective Inspector Chambers. Come with me.'

Detective Inspector? He'd been expecting some jobsworth PC in uniform, not a detective. Nerves flare in his gut. What does this mean? Surely they don't bring out the big guns for an assault that wasn't even sexual? Does it mean anything, or is she just on duty?

But it is too late to do anything other than follow her down a corridor into an interview room, which looks like the ones he's seen on television: soulless, a cheap table with two plastic chairs on each side.

At the door, he hesitates. 'Do I need, like, a lawyer?'

'This is just a statement,' she replies, sitting down. 'We're interviewing everyone who was at the site. You're not a suspect at this stage, but you're related to the victim so—'

'At this stage?'

'Come in,' she says flatly, gesturing towards a chair. 'Take a seat.'

His mouth dries. He hesitates another second before going into the room and sitting down in the indicated chair. The seat is hard and cool beneath him. Every surface in the room is hard.

'Nasty grazes on your knuckles there,' she says.

Heat flames in his face. 'Uh. Yeah. Bit drunk last night. I mean Sunday night.'

She raises her eyebrows as if to say, *Go on*.

'Fell over,' he adds. A laugh chokes in his throat. Did Mum say to tell them about the fight with Byrne or not? He can't remember. The detective is not laughing. The detective is nodding. Panic flushes through him. But she doesn't know he had a fight with Byrne. She can't know about that. No one knows about that except Mum.

'So, Mr Connor... Can I call you Dan?' When he nods, she goes on. 'We've asked you to come in today to give a written witness statement regarding events at Heaven View between Sunday evening and Monday afternoon relating specifically to the attack on your sister, Casey. However, I need to inform you that there's been a significant development.'

Dan swallows.

'Last night, at approximately eleven forty-five, the body of a young male was found in woodland adjacent to the staff camping quarters.'

The air leaves him. His body curls, as if from the force of a blow. Byrne has been found. He has been found. Dan brings the air back into his lungs, knows he should speak, but what the hell should he say? What would be the normal thing to say if he didn't know anything? He can't look at the detective. Knows he must, must look at her.

'Sorry,' he says, forcing himself to glance up but letting his gaze drop back to the tabletop almost immediately. 'Sorry, that's a shock. A body. You mean, like, someone dead? Do you... do you know who it is?'

The detective – Chambers – shifts in her chair. 'The victim has been identified as Byrne Martin. Though you might know him as Byrne Sharp.'

'Byrne? Oh my God.' He covers his mouth with his hand, panting for breath now. 'Wait, what? Was he using a fake name?'

'Not exactly. Sharp was his public persona, I believe.'

Nausea rises. Shock and panic are close, he thinks. Some things he doesn't have to fake. 'Sorry. I feel sick, sorry. He... I know him. He was a... a friend.' But Sharp wasn't his real name. Who the hell was he?

'I'm sorry for your loss. It must be a terrible shock.'

'Yeah. It is. Sorry. I mean, thanks. So how did he... how did he die?'

'That's what we're trying to find out. But for now we're just going to run through the timeline and you're going to tell me whatever you can remember in as much detail as you can, OK?'

'OK.' He nods. Should he show them the photograph now? Or later?

'In a moment, I'll start the recording, and you can give your name and your relationship to the victims. Once we've finished recording, the statement will be typed up for you to sign. Does that sound OK?'

'OK.'

Chambers starts the recording and nods for him to proceed.

'My name is Daniel Connor,' he says, his voice collapsing. He clears his throat. 'I'm the brother of Casey Connor and a friend of Byrne Sharp.'

'Thank you.' The detective leans forward in her chair. 'Yesterday you arrived at the tent where your sister was found shortly after the ambulance departed.'

'It was leaving, yes. I saw it go, but I didn't know my sister was in it at that point.'

'And you told the SOCO you'd been looking for Casey since midday, is that right?'

'I had, yes. Maybe a little later. From when I woke up.'

'And you' – she glances at her notes – 'first became aware something had happened to her when you spoke to her colleague at the scene?'

'That's right. Spider told me what was going on.'

His throat tickles. He coughs into his hand; worries that he's coughed too many times, that it looks suspicious. He wants to ask for a glass of water but can't. He doesn't know how to. It's all he can do to breathe. He takes another deep breath in, wonders if the woman hears the shake when he exhales, what she would read into it if she did – nerves or guilt?

'Can you tell me why you were so keen to find your sister?'

'I was worried about her. We'd had an argument the night before and I'd texted her a few times asking her to tell me she was OK. She hadn't replied. I knew it could be that she was still angry with me, or her phone had died, but I was worried because we don't really argue. Not like that.'

'What do you mean by "not like that"?'

'Like, we don't really fall out. I stormed off. We were both drunk. Well, I was. It got a bit out of hand, I suppose.' Out of hand? What the hell did he say that for?

Chambers nods, her expression unnervingly neutral. 'And what was this argument about?'

'I can't really remember,' he says, hearing how weak that sounds, how obvious it is he's lying. 'I mean, I was being a bit... overprotective, I guess,' he adds. Shit. He's immediately contradicted himself, what an idiot. 'She told me to back off, basically.' He closes his eyes briefly. He has given an answer. But in his attempt to put some distance between himself and the argument, the argument and Byrne, he has effectively circled back to it, to him.

'She's your kid sister, is that right?'

'Yes.'

'My understanding is she was working at the site. Can you tell me why you felt the need to be protective? Who you were protecting her from?'

Shit. Another shaky sigh leaves him. 'I could see she'd had a few drinks.'

'She was drunk? I thought *you* were drunk.'

'Not drunk drunk. Just... you know, like she'd had a drink. I was worried about her, that's all. But she's eighteen and she didn't like that. She told me she wished I hadn't come to Summer Camp.'

'Were you protecting her from anyone specific?'

'Just... you know. Lads. In general.' He feels himself blush. Lame, he thinks. Lame, lame, lame.

'OK. So you fell out. Did you look for her later that night?'

'I think so. I can't really remember. I can remember sort of walking about. I was pretty out of it. Sorry.'

'But the next day you were looking for her.'

'She hadn't replied to my texts. My phone was dead, but when it charged up, I saw she hadn't replied. I called her but she didn't answer, and I knew she should be awake because she had a shift.'

'So you wandered round the site looking for her.'

'Yeah. I went to the bar where she was meant to be working. And then I went down to the beach. When I came back up, I saw the ambulance.' His heart thumps. 'Her mate – her colleague – told me Casey had been found in a tent. Spider. Don't know his real name, sorry. The guy with the web tattoo on his neck?'

'Great. Just for the timeline, you woke up in your own tent at around midday and went looking for her then?'

The heat in his face intensifies. 'Maybe later. Maybe, like, one? Yeah, I think it was after one.'

'You said you saw that she hadn't replied to your texts. Did you see anything else on your phone at that point? Any other messages that would give you cause for concern?'

His scalp prickles. 'Yes,' he says. 'I mean, no, not then. I was planning to come in anyway because there was a message on WhatsApp, but I didn't see it until I was at the hospital. It was a... it was a photo of Case. It was from Byrne.'

'Can I see the photo?'

Heart pounding, he takes out his phone and shows Chambers the photograph.

'For the tape,' she says, 'can you describe what we're looking at?' She doesn't seem shocked. It's like she's already seen it.

He clears his throat. 'It's a WhatsApp message from Byrne Sharp. It's a photograph of my sister. He'd been flirting with her earlier. Earlier that night and over the weekend.'

'Can you describe the photograph?'

'She... er, my sister looks out of it. Like, drunk. Her eyes are closed, and she looks like she's not wearing anything. She looks like she's by a tree.'

'And the caption reads?'

He swallows. 'The caption reads, "Dan, bro, your sister is fit. Full picture tomorrow mofos."'

'Thank you. And can you read your reply? I mean your direct reply to Mr Sharp.'

'OK.' He finds his message. When he reads it, his voice trembles. '"Delete that photograph of my sister now or I'll fucking end you."'

THIRTY-FIVE
CASEY

The day before

Casey wakes up early. She knows it's early even before she checks her phone because it is so, so quiet, the kind of quiet you only get when you're camping, away from the noise of a town. She unzips the tent and pokes her nose out. The air is cool, but even now she can feel the promise of heat from the low vanilla sun.

She wriggles out of her sleeping bag, grabs her wash gear and takes a chilly shower over at the makeshift cubicles. Shivering, she towels herself dry, the shivering turning to a kind of hysterical giggling, her teeth chattering like those wind-up fake teeth she got one year in her Christmas stocking. Still trembling, she wraps her towel around her and, hoping she doesn't bump into anyone, makes a dash for her tent. The cool air on her damp skin almost takes her breath away, and again, the urge to giggle comes to her. As she half skips over the bumpy ground, flip-flops flicking dew onto her toes, it is all she can do not to shriek.

'Alive,' she whispers to herself, giggling then at how mad she sounds. 'Alive, alive-oh.'

'Coppadin.'

She startles, yelps. Spider is sitting on his little tripod stool outside his tent, long legs bent at the knees like a black grasshopper's. He is staring at her, smoking a roll-up and nursing a tin cup of black coffee.

'Sorry,' he says through a vanishing cloud of smoke. 'Didn't mean to startle you, miss.'

Instinctively, she grabs the top of her towel. 'Spider...' she begins. 'What are you doing up?'

'I like to watch the sunrise,' he says simply. Like, in actual plain English.

'Do you... do you do it every day?' Her fingers tighten. Her towel is so short. She can feel her nakedness under it, the insecure covering of it. There is no one else awake. No one can see them.

His weedy fag glows. 'I do indeed,' he says, the words forming their own little puffs of grey cloud. 'Quite often watch the night too.'

She nods, unsure what to say. More than anything, she wants to go and get dressed, but something in Spider's face makes her hesitate. It's not the creepy fact of him seeing her in just her towel; it's his eyes. They're red, as if he's been crying.

'Are you OK?'

He raises his eyebrows. 'Of course. Never better.'

Casey takes a step, then stops. *Ask twice*, comes her mother's voice. *Ask twice if you're not sure someone's OK.*

'Are you sure?' she asks. 'You don't seem like yourself.'

He meets her eye, and she swears his are too shiny for someone who's supposed to be fine.

'Urgh,' he says, more of a noise than a word, and kicks the toe of his boot against a tuft of grass. 'Saw someone I used to know last night, that's all. Bit of a collywobbler, but I'm fine. Just enjoying an early-morning coffee and a smoke before the oncoming rigours of the day.' He pinches at his teeth, pulls out a strand of tobacco. For the first time, she wonders if he's gay, straight or what.

'Who was it?' she asks. 'The person you saw, I mean.'

But he waves his hand. 'No one. A no one from my schooldays specifically.'

The alma mater. The trouble he left behind. 'Did they... did they say something to upset you, or... I dunno, threaten you?'

He shakes his head, the ghost of a smile flickering at the corner of his thin lips. 'Oh, they didn't see me. Wouldn't have recognised me if they had. I'm a spirit of the shadows. A wood nymph. A skinny wizard.'

'Skinny wizard!' She laughs a little. 'What are you like? Well, at least you sound more like yourself now. If you're sure you're OK...'

'I'm sure.' He gives a watery smile. 'Thank you though. Thank you for checking in. You're a kind one, Coppadin.'

After coffee and yesterday's leftover croissants with some of Ness's home-made plum jam, Casey makes her way up the hill. At the top, she messages the group WhatsApp.

Hey, guys. I'm at the clubhouse. Where u?

She's about to send one to Dan when she sees him on the veranda with two men she doesn't recognise and one she does. Mr Cortado. Mr Mirrored Shades. Mr Muscle. Mr Muscle! Ha! He is so not her type. So why has her face gone all hot?

'Dan,' she calls out, striding towards him, flushing with relief at seeing one person she knows, flushing with something else too at the sight of a guy she absolutely does not fancy. No way. Just no. 'Dan! Danny! He-ey!'

'Case!' A grin breaks across his face. He looks tired, like he had a big one last night, but also so happy to see her, her eyes water. It's weird seeing him this far from home.

'Hey.'

They hug.

'Let me introduce you to the boys,' Dan says when they break apart. 'This is Robbo.' He gestures to a stout guy with blonde hair, a quite badly sunburnt face and arms, and a gross moustache that makes him look like a pervert. 'This is Jay.' Jay is a bit taller, with a brown mullet and a silver hoop through the top of his ear. He also has a moustache, which lines his top lip like a hairy slug.

'And that's Byrne,' she interjects, glancing over and smiling politely.

Byrne presses his hand to his chest. 'You remembered me.'

'Of course I do. I don't have Alzheimer's.'

At this, Dan's three new friends crease up. Surprised, almost shocked, she finds herself laughing along. She glances at Dan, who is also laughing, though not as much as Robbo and Jay. Byrne, meanwhile, has already got himself under control.

'Touché,' he says. With another gracious smile, he bows his head a fraction in acknowledgement.

'Ah, that's right,' she replies. 'Aren't you a fencer? That's a fencing term, isn't it?'

Byrne Sharp could not look more surprised if she'd told him she knew where he lived.

'Astute,' he says, his bottom lip pushing up against the top, nodding slowly in what looks like appreciation of her incredible intellect.

'I think a lot of people know where touché comes from,' she says.

He raises his forefinger. 'You overestimate people,' he says. 'Most have no idea where that term originates.' He half stands, his chair scraping across the stone slabs of the veranda. 'Let me get you a coffee. Cortado?'

The way he smiles at her makes her feel like laughing and telling him where to go all at once. But if they're doing banter, she's in.

'Astute yourself,' she says. 'There. I'm parrying.' There's no need to admit she's watched his fencing videos with Dan; let him think she just knows this stuff.

'Excellent riposte.' He shakes his head and claps. 'I'm going to disengage before this bout draws blood.'

The guy is witty, she'll give him that, and it's nice of him to buy her a coffee. She can't remember telling him cortado was her go-to, but he must have guessed. An educated guess, she thinks. She said it was a good choice. Really, she should tell him she gets her coffee for free, but despite him obviously thinking quite highly of himself, she's not about embarrassing people, and besides, he's gone.

She joins the others at the table. Dan digs her in the arm. When she meets his eye, she reads his question as clearly as if he had asked it out loud: *What the hell?*

She frowns, mouths, *What?*

THIRTY-SIX

DAN

The day before

Byrne starts flirting with Casey the moment she reaches the table. Like, he doesn't even wait till she's sat down. Dan's stomach tightens. This was not what he was expecting. Byrne's got all the moves, moves Dan realises he doesn't want him to use on his sister. Casey's cool. There's no way she would go for a guy like Byrne, is there? But she's giggling, throwing back banter like they're in some sort of cheesy romcom. He can see her being drawn towards him, like he's mesmerising her or something.

Byrne rides off on his charger then to get Casey a coffee she's perfectly capable of getting herself. Dan glares at her. But she only glares back and asks him, *What?* Like *What's wrong?* Like she doesn't know.

She knows.

Dan sits out the next few minutes of shanter from Robbo and Jay and lets his sister handle them, which she does the way a zookeeper handles animals at feeding time.

'So do the staff all sleep together in, like, one big tent?'

Robbo asks, glancing at Jay for backup, an expression Dan can only describe as stupid on his stupid face.

'Yeah, we do,' Casey says. 'All in this one big sleeping bag. When one of us rolls over, we all have to roll over.'

The boys laugh a bit, but the laugh is quiet, like it's had the air punched out of it.

'We have one solar-powered shower between us too,' Casey goes on. 'It's more eco and it's so much easier to pass the soap.'

'More eco.' Jay grins like an idiot, completely at a loss.

'Good for rubbing each other's backs too.' Casey smirks as she watches the two men-children blush, one hundred per cent the winner.

Byrne comes back with the coffee of gallantry.

'I asked them to put a heart on it,' he says, placing it in front of her like it's a diamond ring, while Robbo and Jay chorus, *Whoa, dude.*

Casey tips the flat of her hand to her brow and appears to be checking Byrne out. Dan won't lie – the guy could be a model. His biceps are offensively perfect, his thigh muscles are actually square, and he doesn't have one single spot on his perfect skin. But Casey hates posers, doesn't she? She's done nothing but roast Dan for weeks on account of how he's filling out his T-shirts lately, using more skincare products than her, calling him a player, a ladies' man. Which is not true. He's just trying to change, to make something of himself. Byrne was supposed to be helping him do that.

'They put a heart on everyone's,' she says. 'Although I'm a fern girl myself.'

Hearts? Ferns? What the hell? And whatever that smile is they're exchanging, Dan doesn't like it.

'Have you two met before?' he asks.

'We have,' Byrne says. Dan wonders why he hasn't mentioned it. 'This amazing woman made me the best cortado I've had in my life yesterday. And I've had a lot of cortados.'

Again he directs his Cheshire Cat grin to Casey, who returns it.

Dan frowns. He knows that grin, knows the softening warmth of it. What the hell is going on?

'Thanks,' Casey says. 'I owe you a coffee.'

Byrne throws up his hands. 'My gift,' he says. 'From me to you.'

Dan feels like he's having some sort of fever dream. And as in so many dreams, he can see himself more clearly. He can see himself months ago, on the receiving end of that grin, that night in the pub. He can see himself leaning on the bar, drinking in Byrne's life advice, then on the balcony at Byrne's flat, hanging on the promise of a place in the business, the promise of success.

This is what Byrne does. Makes people feel seen, special. Offers them something. Takes control.

'Oh my God, get a room, guys,' Jay says and sniggers.

'What the hell?' Dan says, almost out of his chair.

'Chill.' Casey pushes her hand down on his arm, as if to restrain him, looking at him as if he's actually mental.

'What?' he asks her. 'He's making insinuations. It's gross.'

'I can handle it,' she says. 'I'm a big girl.'

'Show some respect, yeah?' Byrne says to Jay. 'You're embarrassing yourself, brother.'

Jay slumps down in his chair, crestfallen.

'We going to the beach or what?' Robbo says. 'It's boiling. I'm gonna catch me some rays.'

'What, so you can look even more like a lobster?' Jay says, and the two start pretending to beat each other up.

'Why don't you boys go on down there?' Byrne relaxes in his chair, clearly not intending to go anywhere. Dan's stomach churns. 'It's a beautiful day and the chicks will be out.'

Dan's mouth fills with bitter saliva. Chicks? Is he from the fifties? Can Casey even hear this dude?

'What about you?' Jay asks Byrne. 'You coming?'

'I'm not your mum,' Byrne scoffs. 'If you want to go, go. I'll be down later. Dan, why don't you go too?' He grins. 'Save me a space, yeah? We'll get a banana boat when I get there.'

Through the camouflage of his sunglasses, Byrne's expression is unreadable. But his ability to put himself in charge is seamless: the warm smile, the affectionate inclusion, the promise. What he's actually doing is telling Dan to piss off while simultaneously putting him in a position where to refuse will seem like he's making a big deal out of Byrne talking to his sister. If Dan refuses to go, he will look like a weirdo.

'Mate.' Robbo is looming over him, blocking the sun. 'You coming?'

Dan turns to Casey, who is sipping her tiny coffee. 'Shall I wait for you?'

She looks up at him and raises her glass. 'Just gonna finish this. I'll be right down.'

THIRTY-SEVEN
CASEY

The day before

Casey watches her brother and the two idiots disappear towards the teepee field. She can tell just by the set of Dan's shoulders that he's pissed off, and she feels a stab of resentment. Why is he here anyway? When he told her he was coming, she thought he'd have her back, but it's like he thinks he's the boss of her or something.

'How's the coffee?' Byrne asks.

'It's nice,' she replies flatly. 'Thanks again.'

'Oh, I didn't mean it like that. I wasn't asking for thanks; I was just making conversation. Are you going to go to the beach?'

She feels bad now. It's not his fault she's in a mood. She shakes her head. 'Probably not. I start at two.'

'When do you finish?'

She hesitates. Wonders where this is going. 'It's two till ten,' she says. 'But it'll probably go on till midnight.'

'Ten hours,' he says and whistles. 'You've got some stamina.'

The way he says it is like he's admiring her. She thought he was angling to see her later, but no, he was just making conversation, and he's not looking down on her for having to work. In fact, he's not even asked her *why* she's having to work. She feels herself blush but steels herself. He's not her type. But at the same time, at least he has some brain cells, and it's not like she's figured out what her type is. Even Mum said that's part of what being young is about, trying different things. Sometimes opposites attract.

'Have you known those guys long?' she asks, nodding towards their backs as they make their way down the rise.

He nods. 'They're bozos, but they're all right really.' He laughs. 'How come you're working here?'

Ah. He has asked. She sighs. 'I'd have thought that was obvious.'

He sits back in his chair and throws up his hands. 'Sorry. None of my business.'

'It's fine.' She shrugs.

'It's not. It's not fine. I'm sorry. Really. I admire you having a summer job. It's very cool.'

She looks at him. It's hard to see what he's thinking when he wears his sunglasses all the time, but his jaw shows no sign of amusement. Maybe he has something wrong with his eyes, like a sun sensitivity thing. Great teeth though. Must have had a good dentist growing up.

'Don't worry about it,' she says, meaning it.

'I admire you,' he says again.

'Why? You don't know me.'

'I know you're clever. Dan said you're predicted A stars across the board and you're going to York University. Anyway, I can tell you're clever because you're as sharp as a tack. Witty. I love funny women. Funny people, I should say.' He laughs. 'But no, you're really sharp.'

'Like you.'

'Me?'

'That's your name, isn't it? Sharp?'

He laughs. 'Oh, I see. Very good. Like I said, you're quick.'

'You're no slouch yourself. Dan says you're an athlete.'

He gives a bashful smile. 'I was.'

She doesn't mention his dizziness thing or whatever it was. If he wants to tell her about that, he will. 'I watched some of your self-defence videos on YouTube,' she says. 'Dan showed me.'

'Pays to know how to take care of yourself.'

'And does it? Pay? To teach people that stuff, I mean.'

Another smile. She can't tell if it's shy or modest, or just him pretending to be shy or modest. 'I do OK.'

'Dan says you're a businessman. It sounds very grand.'

He almost laughs; rubs his chin with his hand. His nails are clean, white-tipped. 'I'm good at monetising.' He looks away, towards the sea.

The day is getting hotter. Casey wishes she'd worn her bucket hat, but it was still wet from where she washed the yoghurt sauce off it. That was stupid. It would have dried by now.

Byrne is standing up. 'I'd better join the others,' he says. 'Can't trust Robbo and Jay on their own. One will have buried the other in the sand by now and forgotten the tide's coming in.'

It's a joke, but one that, like a lot of jokes, contains a seed of truth.

'Sure,' she says and smiles. 'Catch you later.'

He gives a barely perceptible bow. 'I sincerely hope so. Have a good shift. You make the best cortados. Don't take any shit.'

'Oh, I won't.'

He grins. And then he's gone. She watches him as she watched the others, heading not down towards the beach but upwards towards the teepees, she presumes to pick up his stuff. His shoulders are a thing of beauty, so wide and so powerful, his back a perfect V. She has a flashing thought of him changing into his swimming shorts in the dusky light of the tent. Heat climbs her neck, her face.

What the hell is wrong with her? He's a player, a smooth operator. But then what does she know about guys like that really? Who is she to say what they're like or not like? It occurs to her now that not once did he try to compliment her on her appearance, or capitalise on having bought her a coffee or the fact that the two of them found themselves alone just now. He was all in with the flattery, yes, but the compliments were about her as a person; he wasn't all, like, oh you have beautiful eyes or anything like that, and he didn't invade her space or pin her down to an arrangement later. No. He just bought her a coffee, which was generous, chatted to her for a bit and then left her alone. The fact that he's here in his twenties is a bit of a red flag, but then her brother's here too, isn't he? And her brother is a top guy. The best. She feels bad about freezing him out just now, but he was being a bit of a dick. She'll try and find him later and smooth things over.

Maybe he'll be with Byrne.

THIRTY-EIGHT

DAN

Two days after

Chambers barely twitches. Mum said he had nothing to worry about, but he knew this would happen, knew the police would check his phone. But it isn't his phone they've checked; it's Byrne's. He should have shown Chambers the photo straight away because now it looks like he was hiding something. And it doesn't matter, it's all the same, because it all leads to him and Casey. Casey was with Byrne. Byrne did something horrible to Casey. Dan threatened to kill him. And now he's dead. They'll think Dan killed him in a rage and left him there to rot. His body fills with hot dread.

'So Byrne Sharp had been flirting with your sister for what sounds like most of the weekend. How did you feel about that?'

'I wasn't angry about that. I was angry with him. Obviously. Sending a photo like that. That's... It's abuse. If she got with him, well, she's eighteen. It's her choice. But then he goes and takes a naked picture of her and threatens to send the full shot to the guys.' His hands close into fists. 'The message implied there were more where that came from sort of thing. When I said I'd end him, I didn't mean I was going to kill him. Obviously! I just wanted to stop him sending any more photographs. I wanted to stop it going on the internet. It would've ruined Casey's life.'

Chambers says nothing. On Dan's wristwatch, the second hand stutters on.

'Let's go back to Sunday. Can you tell me a little bit more about where you were and what you were doing from early evening through to whenever you went to bed?'

'Sure.' He swallows. 'I was with the guys.' Seeing the detective's eyes narrow and understanding she wants him to elaborate, he adds. 'Robbo, Jay and... and Byrne.'

'And these are the same young men as on the WhatsApp group called Boiz, B-O-I-Z, the same men to whom Mr Sharp sent the photograph, is that correct?'

He nods. 'Yes.'

'And that would be Robert Baker and Jacob Crossley?'

He shrugs. 'I only knew them as Robbo and Jay.'

'What's your relationship with these men?'

'They came into the pub where I work a few months ago. We played pool. We went back to Byrne's flat to play Xbox. Went clubbing once. They invited me to come to Summer Camp. My mates are all away at the moment, so I thought, may as well.'

'Which pub is that?'

'The Coach and Horses. On the riverside in Twickenham.' He wants to ask what the hell that has to do with anything but keeps his mouth shut.

'So. These men befriended you. Would that be accurate?'

'I suppose. We weren't close exactly. Byrne was giving me a bit of... I suppose you'd call it life coaching.' He sighs. Life coaching, advice, kindness. Byrne Sharp was going to take away his problems. He was going to show him how to be a man. But in expecting Byrne to fix things, he's not been a man, has he? He's been a boy.

'He was giving you life advice,' Chambers prompts. 'That sounds helpful. Kind of him.'

To his horror, his eyes prick. He stares down at the table; waits until the blurry wood veneer reclarifies. 'No.'

'No?'

'Wait.' He holds up his hands. 'Sorry, I... Yes, I thought he was kind. I admired the way he looked after himself, you know, like he didn't drink very much and he kept himself in amazing shape, and so at first I thought, OK, he's not someone I'd be friends with under normal circumstances, but he seems like a good guy, and it's not like I really had anyone else to hang out with. He invited me to things. He said he'd show me how to be better at, you know, life stuff. Like money and health and whatever. But then when we got to camp...' It's hard to continue. He can't untangle himself from what Byrne Sharp turned out to be, can't erase the stain of it, the embarrassment.

'But then?'

'Like on the way here, he started coming out with other stuff. Like calling women bitches. I mean, he did that a few times before, but then he'd say he was only joking, or that he was being sarcastic, and I'd think, it's only words, you know? Or he'd say something about how men should take care of women, and I was down with that. I live with my mum and my sister, so of course I want to look after them, of course I do. I dream about buying Mum a house one day, taking all her worries away from her, and that's sort of what I thought he meant. But he didn't. When we got here, I realised he didn't mean that.'

'What did he mean?'

'He meant... I think he meant women belong to men. Like, we should pay for everything, but it's transactional. Like a business deal or something. You pay and in return you get to say what they can and can't do, if they can go out, who with, all that stuff. I mean, I didn't realise he meant it like that until we got here. He was quite intimidating, so it was hard to challenge him, but if I did, if I asked him what he meant, he'd get... I dunno. Slippery. Jokes. Sarcasm. You never knew if he actually meant it, if he was actually serious. And it was all mixed up because he had this self-defence channel for women. And I thought that was cool. I suppose... I suppose I wanted to believe the self-defence video was what he was really about. I wanted to believe he was a good guy underneath.'

'Are you aware of any other of Byrne Sharp's channels?'

'You mean the lifestyle and the fitness ones?'

She shakes her head. The women in the club, he thinks. The business card.

'We're investigating Mr Sharp's background and business affairs. It's... interesting.'

Chambers pauses. Dan wants to ask her what *business affairs* means but can't seem to find the words. Another silence settles.

'Let's go back to Sunday evening,' Chambers says after a moment. 'You were with Byrne and the others. Were you all getting along?'

'I guess. I mean, Robbo and Jay are always scrapping, but I think they're tight – I think that's part of their friendship. The way they joke around is very... strong. Harsh, even, but it's just what they do. And they hero-worship Byrne. Worshipped, I should say. God.' He shakes his head.

'And would you describe Byrne as your friend at this point? Or had the scales fallen from your eyes, as it were?'

'Sunday evening? If I'm honest, I'd have to say no. I mean, yes, the scales had fallen or whatever by then. Maybe a bit before we went to Heaven View. But I got caught up in the momentum... Does that make sense?'

She nods, and he feels himself settle just a little. 'It does.'

'In the end, I didn't really know what he thought about

anything. It was all smoke and mirrors – like his mirrored sunglasses; you can't see through them. He had these pills – red and blue. Like in *The Matrix*, he said. He said we should slip them in girls' drinks... but when I said *What?*, he acted like I was stupid and said there was no way he'd do that. But I was beginning to think he threw out all these jokes so he could hide the truth in them. The truth of his intentions. And then... and then when he started hitting on Casey, I just suddenly felt really uncomfortable.'

THIRTY-NINE
CASEY

The day before

At 9.20 p.m., forty minutes before the end of her shift, Immy finally replies to the WhatsApp message Casey sent this morning.

Hey, babes. We're heading up to the clubhouse in like 5 r u there?

Casey frowns at the phone. Pockets it. If they can't be bothered replying for a whole day, she can't be bothered telling them where she is. Besides, she doesn't want them to come here. She's on glass collection and it's the worst, and will be even worse than the worst with her so-called friends watching her, sneering as she tries to balance fifty glasses in one hand. Already tonight, three lads on three separate occasions have tried to topple the tower from her arms. What is it they think is funny? They're not even glass; they're hard plastic, dishwasher-proof, recyclable. If they fall, they won't even make an exciting crashing sound or smash into a million glittering pieces or do anything dramatic at all; they'll just bounce around. Literally, what's the point – is it just to humiliate her? It must be. How pathetic.

She puts the fresh pile of empties on the counter and goes out onto the veranda. It's heaving, clouds of vape smoke filling the air, the chatter a roar in the night. It's still warm, warm enough that the girls are dressed in slinky little clubbing tops, some in tiny shorts, some in miniskirts, some in long floaty numbers. They're laughing, shouting into one another's ears, playfully pushing and pulling at each other, loose with alcohol and whatever else. She moves past them, looking for empties. She'd love to be out here in her little top chatting with her friends, whoever they are. She could meet new people. Everyone here talks to everyone.

She sees Spider coming across from the main pathway. As always, popping up nearby as if he's stalking her or something. From the way he's walking, he looks tired, his high-vis jacket wide across his skinny middle, his trademark roll-up dangling from his mouth. At intervals, the smallest dot of orange pulses and glows.

'Hey,' someone says from behind her, an aggressive sound, male.

She turns. A nerdy lad who can barely keep his eyes open is swaying in front of her. His lips are wet, his forehead slick with sweat. His T-shirt looks like it's had something thrown at it.

'Everything OK?' she asks.

'Can you bring us some shotsss?' One finger hovers at her, as if trying to pinpoint where she is.

She laughs it off. 'I think you've had enough, mate, don't you? And it's not waitress service.'

'It is during th'day,' he says with belligerent authority and staggers forward, his finger in her face, still waving about.

Casey takes a step back. 'You're so right,' she says, humouring him but allowing herself a lacing of sarcasm she doubts he'll spot. 'But no waitress service at night, yeah?'

Behind him, his friends are laughing. Whether at him or at her, she's not sure. Her face heats. Really, she is so done with this tonight. Who do these entitled pricks think they are? On Thursday, when she was out picking litter, a lad just like this one told her she'd missed an empty can. She almost told him to shove it up his arse but had to content herself with a withering stare. It's so-o-o boring. Spoilt schoolboys with no manners are really not her vibe at all, especially not drunk ones. Dan is never like this when he's had too many. Neither is Rory. Neither is Liam. They're always sweet, even when they're drunk as skunks.

She is about to turn away – ignoring being the best policy and all that – when the lad lunges at her, his meaty paw gripping her shoulder.

'If I give you twenny quid, will you bring us some shotsss?'

She shakes him off. 'Er, still no.'

'Thirty?'

She sighs and shakes her head at him. 'I wouldn't bring you shots if my life depended on it, and if you touch me again, I'll have you thrown off the site, OK?'

'Whoa!' He staggers backwards, throwing up his hands. 'Calm down! Juzta suggessstion.'

Calm down. Because that always works. Her free hand closes into a fist. It is almost scary, the violence she can feel coursing thought her. Exhilarating too, the certainty that if she hit him hard, he would go down like a sack of spuds. She takes a breath. Straightens out her fingers, her spine, lifting her head as high as it will go. Not to be prissy or anything, but she would love to get this guy and his mates thrown out just to make a point. How she would love to watch them trooping out through the main gate, bent under their rucksacks, muttering at the unfairness of it all.

She looks around to see if Joe, the duty manager, is anywhere about. Maybe he can bar them from the clubhouse; that would be something.

Byrne Sharp is standing in the shadows on the far side of

the veranda. He is watching her. She almost startles. He is not wearing his sunglasses. His eyes are small, beady, his gaze shrunk to pinpricks. His slick of black hair shines under the lights. His eyebrows rise. He points at her and mouths: *You OK?*

She nods, gives him the thumbs up.

'Fordy quid,' the drunk boy is saying, swaying about. 'Come on. Jusst four shotsss of tequila. You must need the money if you work here. What are you, local? You a local girl? Kiss?' His eyes close. He puckers up.

Casey brings the cloth from her apron, the one she's used to wipe up fag ash, beer and God knows what else.

'Here,' she says. 'You've got something on your nose.'

His eyes open.

She pushes the cloth into his dumb, leering face and rubs it as hard as she can. 'There,' she says. 'Got it. Have a good night.'

She throws a glance over at Byrne. He is clapping. She walks away, a thrill passing through her.

'That was epic.' Byrne Sharp is standing beside the table on the veranda where Casey is sitting with her free pint of cider, her reward for staying an hour late. It is after eleven. Her legs and back ache, and her eyes are itchy. She saw him approach out of the corner of her eye a few seconds ago, but only now that he's spoken does she look up at him, as if he has surprised her. The table and floor are sticky with dried drink. Byrne is wearing a loose cream linen shirt with one too many buttons undone. The deep V at his neck shows a tanned, hairless chest. She wonders if he's waxed it or if he's naturally smooth. The flashing image of herself putting her hand to that V, the tips of her fingers sliding inside the shirt, causes her face to glow hot.

'What was epic?' she asks, knowing exactly what he's referring to.

'The way you dealt with that loser.'

She tips back her head; scrutinises him. 'I don't believe in splitting the world into winners and losers. It's an offensive binary.'

His eyebrows shoot up. He blinks rapidly, over and over, like someone's flicked water in his face.

'An offensive binary,' he repeats, doing that thing he does – the push of the bottom lip up against the top – and nodding, an expression that says *touché* without him having to say a word. His head cocks to one side now. 'I'm going to have to think about that. I'm really going to have to think about that.' He laughs, and she finds herself laughing with him. 'All I meant was,' he continues, 'the way you handled him was very impressive. And by loser, I mean I guess I'm not a fan of drunk posh boys hassling women.'

'Fair,' she says. 'I'm not a big fan myself, to be honest. But thanks for not rushing to my defence.'

'Oh,' he says. 'I'm sorry. I would have—'

'I'm not being sarcastic. I mean it. Like you said, I was handling it and I didn't need you to help. But it was cool that you let me know you'd have come in if I'd wanted you to.'

His brow knits. 'Great. I'm glad I got it... right.'

She laughs. 'I'm not a schoolteacher. I'm just saying, I appreciated you not undermining my ability to deal with some drunk knob who would have fallen over if I'd flicked him on the forehead and who probably won't remember any of it in the morning.'

'The trouble with that much alcohol is it makes you behave like an asshole.'

'Very American,' she teases. 'Asshole,' she adds, in an American accent.

'You know what I mean.' He smiles, but it is a shy smile, like he's enjoying being teased.

'Potato, potah-to,' she says. 'Tomay-to, tomato.'

'Let's call the whole thing off.' He smiles again; she returns it. 'I also happen to think that if you're an *arsehole* drunk, maybe, just maybe, that's who you really are.'

Now it is Casey who raises her eyebrows, who pushes her bottom lip against the top while giving a slow nod of consideration. 'I'm going to have to think about that. I'm really going to have to think about that.'

He laughs, his wide, generous laugh, which makes her giggle a bit. She likes men who laugh, especially ones who laugh at her jokes, although she worries that's big-headed. It shouldn't be a big deal for a guy to laugh at a girl's jokes, but it can feel like that sometimes.

'Where are your mates?' she asks. 'Where's Dan?'

'They're down at the beach,' he says. He pauses before gesturing to the free chair. 'Do you mind if I sit down?'

'Not at all. Sorry, I should've said. Most of the guys I know wouldn't wait to be invited, LOL.' She lifts her glass briefly. 'I'm just going to drink this, then I'm going to bed.' At the mention of the word *bed*, she feels her blush deepen. She'd need to grab a shower if anything were to— *Casey! Stop!*

'You're not going to party? I have something that will pep you up.' He raises his eyebrows a little.

'Like what? MD?'

'Bit of everything.'

It's shocking, especially after him going all Judge Judy on how much that guy had drunk.

'I'm fine, thanks,' she says simply. If he pushes it, that is a red flag.

'Wise,' he says. 'A good girl.'

She frowns at him; feels a second shot of unease. 'Not sure what you mean by that. Good girls, bad girls. You love your binaries, don't you? I'm just tired, that's all. I've bust a gut to get here, and I'm going to make sure I enjoy the big one tomorrow night.' She smiles at him, to show she's not angry. 'Ask me again tomorrow.'

He gives a slow nod. 'I will.'

They talk for a while longer. Casey sips her cider, a little on guard for any more dodgy statements, but no more come. He asks her all about herself, which is nice, a nice change. As the minutes turn into half an hour, her nerves rise again. Will he expect to come back to her tent? Will he offer to walk her back, then push his luck? She's never slept with anyone casually – only Liam, and that was in a long relationship and was the first time for them both. She kind of wants to, is curious, but the thought is a bit scary at the same time. He would know what he was doing, at least. All this she thinks, only half listening while he talks about meeting Dan, saying nice things, how Dan needs to find his confidence, how he really wants to help him with that. She feels herself soften towards him. He has a really nice mouth, his beady eyes kind of intense, less like dark holes now she's used to them, his tanned hands so clean around his half of lime and soda. He is the opposite of that drunk guy, she thinks. Sober and considerate, interesting, interested. As for his body or physique or whatever, he's low-key a god.

But could she trust him?

'Anyway,' he says, breaking her train of thought, 'it's late.' He stands to go, and she feels disappointment seep through her. 'I'm going to go to the beach. If you're headed back to staff camping, we could walk down together?'

This is it, she thinks. This is the play. But it would be nice not to have to be alone for once. Would she get fired if he came back to her tent?

'Sure,' she hears herself say, apprehension tingling on her skin.

But as they walk down the rise in the beautiful starry night, he does not take her hand or lay any cheesy lines on her. He says he wishes he'd gone to university, that being rich is great but he admires anyone with an education, that he might apply as a mature student, pay the fees as he goes once his business starts running itself. And at the standpipe tap at the end of the sand pathway through the dunes, he says only that he'll see her, he hopes, at the bonfire party if not before.

'For a cortado,' she says, raising her hand to wave. 'I'll make you one on the house.'

'That's very kind,' he says, touching the ends of his fingers to the ends of hers in a way that makes her want to step forward and put her hand on the back of his neck.

'Goodnight then,' he says, withdrawing his hand and turning away.

She watches him disappear into the dunes, the grass tips lit softly by the moon, his white shirt billowing behind him as he walks.

'Night,' she whispers. But he doesn't hear.

FORTY

DAN

Two days after

Dan is not sure how they got here, but he's beginning to think he should have a solicitor present after all. He's not a suspect, he reminds himself. He's not under arrest. This is a witness statement. He just has to tell the truth. Most of the truth. But he's beginning to wish he'd reported Byrne's body immediately. He thinks that might have been a mistake.

'So,' Chambers says. 'Mr Sharp was flirting with your sister in front of you. How did that make you feel?'

'Erm. Well, I didn't like it. I mean, she can handle guys. She's pretty feisty. But Byrne's... he's a lot older than her. Was, sorry. And he was acting all gallant and stuff, getting her coffee and joking, but with vibes. Even the others noticed. I didn't want her to be fooled by him, but she seemed to be enjoying the attention.'

'It must have been unsettling have him target your sister. The sexist language, knowing he had sedatives.'

'It was, but at the same time I wasn't sure they weren't just for his own use. I mean, he didn't drink but he was pretty into his Class As. And as I said, he does these self-defence videos, and there was all the stuff about looking after women, so it wasn't like I was *scared* for her.'

'Did Casey watch those videos?'

He shrugs. 'A couple. We tried a couple of them. Like, just for laughs.'

'Just for laughs.' She watches him, her gaze unwavering. 'But you practised the moves?'

'Well, yeah. But that's good, isn't it? For girls to know a few moves.' He stops; feels himself redden. What has he said? What the hell has he just said? Byrne is dead. And here he is telling a copper his sister knew how to handle herself in a physical fight? Fuck.

'So, Mr Sharp was keen on your sister?'

'Casey's pretty and clever and funny. Guys go for her, you know? I just didn't think she'd be his type, that's all. I thought he'd go for someone more...' How to say it? Glamorous? Tarty? He can't say that. Everything he even thinks sounds sexist and wrong. 'You know, high heels, make-up and that. Casey barely wears any make-up.'

'And did Byrne continue to pursue your sister?'

'Yes. I mean, I saw them talking on Sunday night. By the bonfire.'

'Why didn't you say this to the SOCO? Sorry, the officer you spoke to yesterday?'

'I didn't know about Byrne then. I didn't know it was relevant. My sister had been taken away in an ambulance, and I just said I'd been looking for her and I hadn't seen her, but I... I didn't know he was dead. Maybe I should've said more, but all I could think about was getting to the hospital.'

'OK.' She nods twice, slowly.

His neck heats. The heat climbs. The Byrne thing is getting bigger; he can feel it like a creeping black shadow.

'So your sister and Byrne were becoming acquainted. Were they being physical with one another?'

'I don't know.'

'How would you describe them? When you saw them together?

'They were just, you know, chatting but like flirty chatting.'

'And you warned her off him at that point?'

'He went away. This was at the bonfire. I mean, he knew he was out of order without me saying anything. Except he wasn't, not really. But he was by his own code, if that makes sense. Like, by his code, Casey was my property and I was his mate, so in theory he shouldn't have been moving in.' He glances up, frustration blooming at the impassive wall of Chambers' face. 'I'm not saying I believe that. I'm just trying to explain. Anyway, then we had words, me and Case.'

'Do *you* see it as your job to protect your sister?'

'Yeah. I mean, no, not as in the property sense. But from men like him, yeah. He wasn't showing her his true colours. I was worried she was falling for it.'

'But she didn't want your protection.'

'That's right. She said she could look after herself.' His eyes prick. 'So I left her alone.'

'And after that?'

'After that, I just hung out.' Should he mention the fight?

'And you stayed at the bonfire all night?'

'I can't remember. I had a lot to drink. There were some guys giving out shots. I had some. I put a couple in a can of cider someone gave me. I suppose I was drinking because I was pissed off with Byrne. And Byrne doesn't like drinking, so I... I drank.' Hearing how pathetic that sounds, he drops his forehead into his hand.

Chambers remains perfectly still. 'So you can't remember anything more until the next day, when you woke up.'

He decides not to mention the fight. 'That's right. Byrne wasn't in his bed when I woke. Sorry, just remembered that.'

Chambers sits up. She must be able to see how red he is. His face is burning.

'Byrne wasn't in the tent when you woke up?'

'That's right. So when I saw the photo, I put two and two together.' No matter which way the conversation goes, he seems always to be edging towards incriminating his sister or himself.

'And you saw the photograph while you were in the hospital. Did you return to the campsite?'

'Yes. I went back to find Byrne. I wanted to make sure he deleted the photo. I hoped Casey would never have to see it.'

'And did you find him?'

He shakes his head, blood thrumming in his ears. 'No. I mean, I looked all over but I didn't find him. So I went back to the hospital. Mum was there by then. She'd booked a room in a hotel, so she told me to go there and come in and tell you about the photo in the morning.'

'Mr Connor. Dan. Sorry to keep dragging you back to Sunday evening, but you say you can't remember anything after your argument with Casey.' She pauses. Dan waits, stomach rolling. She looks up, right at him. 'I have two witnesses who saw you fighting with Mr Sharp on Sunday night. Around ten thirty. You were near the staff camping area, on the path towards the bottom of general camping. They said you threw several punches and that you were shouting at him. Quite dramatic, I'm sure you'll agree. Not easily forgettable. Are you sure you can't remember that?'

Dan flushes hot from toes to head. 'Er, no.'

'How did you really come to hurt your hands, Dan?'

'I...' He looks at them; turns them over. 'I can't remember.'

'Yet earlier, you said you fell over. It seems to me there's a lot you can't remember. Your sister can't remember anything either. And I'm faced with telling a young man's mother that her son is dead, a young man who seems to have been involved with your sister, about whom you are very protective.'

'What? Casey's got nothing to do with this.'

'With what?'

'Byrne... being dead. His death.'

'You seem very certain. Are you sure you're not being protective right now?'

'No, I—'

'Because from what I'm hearing, I think you and your sister very much do have something to do with Byrne Sharp's death. I don't think you fell over. I think you got those grazes when you punched Byrne Sharp repeatedly in the head.'

'I punched him in the face. Not in the head, not like that.'

'So you *do* remember what happened? Funny, you said you didn't. But now you do.'

Dan feels the swell of tears on the rim of his eyes. Horribly, pathetically, he wants his mum.

'I'm sorry,' he says. 'I'm so sorry.'

'You've told me you looked everywhere for your sister yesterday morning. You said you looked everywhere for Byrne Sharp in the late afternoon, but that, alas, you didn't find him.'

Dan cannot speak. There is something else coming, something about to land, and he knows what it is. But it is too late to dodge out of the way. It's coming straight for him.

'Mr Connor,' Chambers says again. 'We have a witness who watched you go into the woods adjacent to staff camping. You didn't go straight back into general camping; you went into the... well, I'd hardly call it the woods, more a clump of trees. She said that about ten minutes later, you emerged looking very distressed. That you ran away like the devil was after you. Can you tell me why that was?'

'I was desperate to find Byrne. I had to stop him...' The tears break; roll down his cheeks. He pushes them away, but more follow. He can't look at Detective Chambers. He can't.

'Mr Connor,' she says. 'Dan. Talk to me. I can't help you if you don't tell me the truth.'

Silence falls. It waits, there in the grim, hard room.

'I'm sorry,' he whispers. 'I should have reported it.'

FORTY-ONE
CASEY

That night

The site is deserted, the clubhouse closed now for the party. As she passes in front of the veranda, she can see a plume of grey smoking rising from beyond the dunes, smell bonfires on the air. Above, a sliver of moon hovers, wan in a sky only now beginning to darken, too pale yet for the stars to show themselves. It is still so warm, breezeless, almost like being abroad.

Which is perfect, she thinks as she half runs down to staff camping. Excitement fills her. She's been saving her new top for tonight and was worried it would be too chilly. It's super skimpy, but she's feeling confident enough to wear it and know she looks good in it. One week at this place has made her feel fit and toned and tanned, the unanticipated benefit of having worked hard in the sunshine.

She can't wait to get to the beach. But she's not going without a freshen-up after her shift. She has a perfume sample in a little cardboard wallet that Mum got free with a magazine. She put it in her bedside table and saved it to bring with her.

She doesn't know if it's any good, but it's by Dior, so how bad can it be, right?

The campsite shower is freezing, but it wakes her up. Even her eyes feel refreshed. Outside her tent, she applies make-up under the failing light – not too much, just a cat lick of black on her eyelids, mascara, some tinted lip balm and a little shimmer at her temples. Her hair is still wet, but it will dry wavy; she pushes at it, pleased at how nice it looks down after being tied up pretty much since she got here. It never goes this thick usually. Must be the salt in the air.

There's no full-length mirror, but she's tried the silver halterneck on back at home, knotting it so that it falls in exactly the right way. Her maxi skirt is a bit hippyish, but it contrasts with the top and it looks cool. She angles her compact mirror, trying to get an overall impression of herself. There's no way to tell, but when she tried the whole outfit back at home, her mum teared up and told her she looked incredible, so she's feeling pretty good.

A movement in her peripheral vision catches her eye. It's Spider, there again, walking towards her from his tent.

'You're looking completely beautiful,' he says, as if he's stating a fact.

She smiles, disarmed, and glances around to see if anyone's about. 'Thank you.'

He stops a little distance away and nods. 'Seriously. You look Hollywood terrific. Now go and have a bloody good time.'

She feels herself blush. 'Aren't you going to come?' She knows he won't and that she doesn't want him to. It's not that she doesn't like him, but he wouldn't really fit in with kids her age. And Byrne and his idiot sidekicks, Immy and those guys, she instinctively knows, would ask her what she's doing with him or freeze him out. The thought confuses her. If she were a good person, she wouldn't care about any of that; she would just tell him to come along and sod what anyone else thinks.

He raises a hand. 'I'm going to stay and keep Ness company,' he says. '*In loco parentis.*'

She frowns. 'What does that mean?'

'It means Aura's father abandoned the nest before the egg even hatched, so I try and fill in where I can. Ness and me go back a long way. Like I said, we look after each other.'

'Are you... are you, like, together?'

He shakes his head. 'Friends. Which is no small thing. Sometimes, it's the bigger thing.' He smiles, a little mysteriously. The pause that follows is awkward. Casey can hear the music, the whoop and roar of her peers, but she doesn't want to be rude.

'Is Cinderella going to this ball then?' Spider asks. 'Or is she going to stand here all evening among the cinders?'

Casey laughs. 'I'm going, I'm going.'

She makes to go but stops. Turns back to Spider. He isn't going to follow her to the party. He's going to give her space and hang out here with Ness. She breaches the two strides between them. Holding out her arms for a hug, she waits.

'Not if you don't want to,' she adds, but he leans into her, allowing her to hug him. He is brittle, hesitant, but after a moment, his arms close around her and he holds her for a few seconds, careful not to let his chest touch hers, the two of them an A like a stepladder. He is so skinny, his arms like thin branches. He smells of smoke and patchouli. She breathes him in.

'Thanks for everything,' she says when they break apart. 'For looking after me and everything. You're a good guy.'

'Try me best,' he replies with an embarrassed chuckle. Still, he looks preoccupied, as if he has something on his mind.

'Bye then,' she says, raising her hand.

'Have a good time. And watch yourself. Don't drink anything unless you've seen what's gone in it. Avoid pills and powders. Don't go into the woods with any strange men.'

It's her turn to laugh. 'As if,' she says. 'Don't worry. I can look after myself.'

FORTY-TWO
CASEY

That night

Casey checks her phone. No messages from Immy or the others on the Summer Camp WhatsApp group. Paranoia stalks in. Either Immy, Charlotte, Matty and Gabriella have been without a signal all weekend – or they have set up another WhatsApp group without her.

They must have set up another group. Are they even her friends any more? Or is it a case of those who can't chalet can't party?

She walks over the darkening dunes, the low feeling she's had on and off all weekend stodgy in her gut. Homesickness too, sudden and deep, and for one horrible moment she fears she might start crying, here in the dark on her own. Somehow she has ended up on the outside of everything, fingers pressed to the glass. She has moved heaven and earth to be with her friends, but now, on the night of the party, the whole reason for being here, she could not be more alone. All day she's been so excited about tonight. If she's honest, she's been thinking of Byrne, of spiky exchanges over a few beers, how it would feel to dance with him, pressed close against his hard chest, his huge arms around her waist. How different that would be from Liam; how easy Byrne makes things compared to Liam and all his over-thinking and hesitation.

The beach opens up before her. To the right, the huge bonfire reaches into the navy sky, the stars glittering studs above it. Straight ahead, the sea laps and crashes on the sand. There must be over a hundred kids here, maybe two hundred. The ra-ra of them all talking at once. Music pumps into the air from two massive speakers at the far side of the fire, lights flashing and swirling, lasers darting and stuttering. At the top of the dune, she stops, hit again by that sour feeling. Even the rough grass seems to whisper: *Everyone belongs here but you. Everyone else is with friends. The party has already started and you are too late.*

Timing's all wrong, she thinks. Story of her life. She left town too early and missed the end-of-exams celebrations back home; she has arrived too late to be part of this, whatever this is.

She taps out a text.

Hey guys. I'm at the beach. Where are you?

She sends it realising she holds no hope of an answer. How depressing. How depressing that this is her friendship situation. Most likely they won't hear their phones, but the fact is, even if any of them get the message, they won't bother to reply. Surveying the scene, it occurs to her with crystal clarity that her friends have moved on. It's not just paranoia. Some silent understanding has crept in, so incrementally it is impossible now to identify a before and an after. It wasn't when she told them she couldn't be part of the chalet. It was before that. Something to do with sticking to the rules during COVID while they met up in big gangs in the park, with missed nights out and clothes she doesn't own or cigarettes she refused to smoke. The reasons are vague, but one thing is utterly certain: Casey is not part of that gang any more.

Which leaves her where exactly? Standing on a sand dune half wishing she could turn back and sit around the fire pit with Ness and Spider and drink thick hot chocolate and listen to their stories.

Friends, Spider said before. *Which is no small thing. Sometimes, it's the bigger thing.*

Friendship *is* big. It's the solid floor you stand on. It is something she no longer has. She has nowhere to stand.

Despite the plague of dark thoughts, she forces herself to walk towards the party. She half slides down the dunes, sand breaching her Havaianas, until she gives up and takes them off. The sand is cool now the evening is here. The fire is raging. She can feel the heat on her face even metres away. She puts her flip-flops back on and pushes through the groups of kids talking and vaping and smoking and drinking to where others are dancing to the music. No sign of Immy and the rest. No sign of Dan. The music is soulful – Michael Kiwanuka. Later, it will be hardcore drum and bass – Charli XCX, Bicep and stuff, and then everyone will go mad. Usually she would be right there, lost in it, but tonight she's just not feeling it.

At the near side of the dancers she sees Byrne Sharp looking on, can in hand, his shirt neon white in the dark, the skin of his neck darker still against its brightness. His sunglasses are pushed back on his slick of black hair, giving him the look of a Premier League footballer with a hairband. She moves so that she can see him better. He is swaying from side to side, the hint of a smile on his lips. On his chest, a gold necklace catches a roaming light. Dan isn't with him. Neither are Robbo and Jay.

She checks her phone. No reply. She could either spend the night looking for her so-called friends, or she could go and talk to Byrne, ease herself into the party vibe. At least Byrne won't make her feel crap. Plus, he might have a spare can of something, maybe a dab.

'Hey,' she says.

Even in the dark, she sees his face light up at the sight of her.

'Wow,' he says, leaning back. 'You look amazing.'

She feels herself blush, glad the daylight is long gone. 'Thanks. You look good too.'

He clamps a hand to his chest and gives a little bow.

Cheesy, she thinks. This guy is so cheesy. But cheese is nice, isn't it? Cheese tastes good.

'Where are the others?'

He looks towards the makeshift dance floor. 'They're in there somewhere.'

'Don't you dance?'

'Ah. Not really. I prefer to talk. Or read. Always have.'

'I would've thought you'd be super coordinated with all the fencing?'

He laughs. 'You'd think. I suppose I am. Maybe I need someone to dance with.'

'Touché.'

He throws up his hands. 'No more fencing terms, please!'

She laughs and feels courage rush through her. 'Come on,' she says. 'Dance with me.'

They push into the crowd. He doesn't move too badly for a boy. A man, she reminds herself. A real man. She cups her hand to her mouth and shouts above the music, 'How come you guys come here? You're so much older than everyone else.'

He bends towards her to reply, his breath warm on her ear. 'We're not that old! But we've been coming for a couple of years now. It's just tradition. You do something twice and it becomes tradition. But this'll be the last one. You're right – we're getting a bit too old. Nothing lasts forever.' He straightens up; meets her eye with what looks like a meaningful glance, though she's not sure what the meaning is.

She breaks his gaze, searching now for Dan. The track fades, chased by Tame Impala. Everyone cheers. When she returns her eyes to Byrne's, he is watching her and smiles. He holds out his can. She takes a sip.

'Is this lager?'

He nods, bending again to speak into her ear. 'Non-alcoholic.'

She raises her eyebrows. 'It tastes weird.'

'I'm used to it.'

'Don't you like to let go?' Barely has the question left her lips when she regrets it. It sounds like a line. Maybe it is.

'I do like to let go. Just not with alcohol.' He grins, and her insides fold.

He is so not her type, she thinks.

But how can she know what her type is if she's only tried one?

FORTY-THREE

MELISSA

Two days after

'I'm scared,' Casey says, her voice small.

'Don't be,' Melissa says, helping her out of the police car outside the station. 'Just... tell them what you remember.'

'I already have.'

Melissa scrutinises her but sees nothing. 'Anything else?'

'What? You're acting like you don't believe me.'

'Of course I believe you.' Melissa glances at Riley, who is hovering like a... like a hovering thing, like a hovering thing with ears. She puts her arm around her daughter and tells herself to calm down. 'You've told them who did this, that's the main thing.' *And who did this is dead*, she doesn't add. The poor girl will freak, and if she freaks, who knows what she'll say.

'Sorry.'

'Don't be. You've done nothing wrong. Come on. Sooner we get in there, sooner it's over and I can take you home.'

The reception area of the police station is all hard surfaces and scary posters fraught with warnings. At the desk, a duty sergeant stares into a computer screen. Riley tells him who they are and why they're here.

'Is my son here?' Melissa asks. 'Dan Connor. We're supposed to be meeting him.'

'Your son has gone through,' the duty sergeant says blankly. 'He's talking to DI Chambers.'

Melissa tries not to react, though her throat all but closes. She never got to tell him the police already have the photograph. She was hoping to catch him somehow, get out of earshot of Big Ears Riley. It doesn't matter, she tells herself. It shouldn't matter. If he shows it to them without being asked to, all will be well. They can't possibly know he found the body and didn't report it.

They go to sit on the plastic chairs. Through the main door strolls a boy of about Casey's age, brown hair shaved at the sides, leaving only a tufty strip, what Melissa would call a relaxed Mohican. He glances at Casey then looks away, as if he's been caught staring. He is wearing shorts and those awful poolside sandals that are so fashionable with kids these days. Even more awful are the sports socks pulled up so high they look like they're held up by invisible suspenders.

From her daughter's thigh, vibrations pass to her own.

'Casey,' she says softly, placing her hand on her leg to stop it from jiggling.

'Sorry.' Casey is staring at the guy's sandals as if they're a bomb. She is shaking.

'Casey? Love? Are you OK?'

'Erm... I'm just...'

Melissa follows the line of her gaze. It's the sandals. She's definitely staring at the sandals – sliders, she thinks the kids call them. 'It's OK,' she soothes. 'Just... flatten your foot. Jiggling about will make you more stressed, not less.'

Casey flattens her foot. She takes Melissa's hand and holds it. At the contact, Melissa feels herself fill with nerves. She cannot distinguish between her own and her daughter's fear. They are bound together, the skin between them porous. It reminds her of the earliest years, when Dan and Casey felt like her own limbs, watching them toddle into preschool a painful severance that left her bereft and somehow aimless. Motherhood is a road she has travelled as best she can, aware always of the fight between letting her kids make their own mistakes and build resilience, and keeping every hair on their heads from the smallest threat of harm. But right now, the road feels like it's at an end. Once her daughter is called through, she will have to wait here as if at some invisible school gate, every second an hour, every hour the longest day. Quite simply, she cannot do any more. Casey will be on her own.

She glances about her, at the door leading into the interior of the station. No sign of Dan yet. Hopefully after this they can all go home together, or at the very least, stay in the Premier Inn on cool clean sheets and an actual proper bed.

Feeling suddenly soupy with tiredness, she pulls out her phone and texts Sarah.

All OK. Just giving statements. Hopefully back tomorrow, maybe even later tonight. Xx

Thank God for Sarah, her backup, the nearest thing she has to a partner despite her being married and having kids of her own. The kindest of the school mums, the funniest, and utterly loyal. If she has a fault, it is that her generosity is sometimes excessive, a little suffocating, something Melissa has had to fend off as gently as she can. The near-constant invitations to Sunday lunch in the early days, the annual invitation to Christmas dinner, even to join them on holiday in Majorca – until Sarah must have realised Melissa was quite happy on her own with her kids, camping in Dorset or taking day trips when money was tight, which it has always been. Sarah has spare keys to Melissa's flat and her car. But with typical sensitivity, she made Melissa take hers too. She has always made sure never to let their financial disparity be an issue, and this, perhaps, is her biggest kindness.

The station is empty apart from the three of them sitting in the heavy silence: Melissa, Casey and the tenacious PC Belinda Riley. The lad in the pool sliders has gone, thank God, his every step followed by Casey's intense gaze.

In the car, Belinda told them they need a formal statement from Dan because he's connected to the victim. Melissa watched her for clues. Did she know there were two victims and that one of them was dead? If she did, she hid it well. Melissa wonders if the body's been found. It's not a given. As far as the police are concerned, this could still be at most a case of a group of boys spiking and sexually assaulting girls. If someone found the body between last night and today, that will have changed.

'I'm scared,' Casey whispers again.

Me too, Melissa thinks and squeezes her hand. 'Try not to think about it.'

'But that's the thing,' Casey whispers. 'I think... I think—'

The door opens. Detective Chambers pushes through, cool and fresh-looking despite the heat of the day.

'Good morning,' she says, striding over. 'If you'd like to come with me.'

Casey's hand slips from hers. That separation, a limb being torn from her. Her baby, her blood, her fabulous girl. Casey turns. Her eyes are rimmed with tears.

'If you could come too,' Chambers says, nodding gravely to Melissa. 'And you, PC Riley.'

Surprised and unsurprised all at once, Melissa follows her into the interior. This must be it. They're going to tell them Byrne Sharp has been found. Everything feels spongy, dreamlike. In an interview room, they sit on four chairs around a table: the detective and Riley on one side, herself and Casey on the other. There is so much she wants to say but cannot, is not sure whether words would even form.

'I just wanted to bring you somewhere a little more private,' Detective Chambers says. 'There's been a major development. Late last night, the body of Byrne Sharp was found in woodland adjacent to the staff camping area of Heaven View.'

'Oh my God,' Melissa replies.

Casey is making a weird high-pitched humming noise, her leg shaking violently under the table.

'And I'm afraid I have to inform you,' Chambers goes on, 'that your son, Daniel, has confessed to his murder.'

FORTY-FOUR
CASEY

That night

When Byrne circles his arms around her waist, Casey pretends she hasn't noticed. They continue talking, her skin tingling, little pulses racing up and down her legs.

'So how do you let go?' Byrne asks.

Casey shrugs. 'I run.'

'You run? Anything else? Gym?'

She laughs. 'I can't afford the gym.'

He looks downcast. 'I'm sorry, that was tactless.'

'It's OK. People who have money make assumptions. My friends do it all the time.'

'In what way?'

'Just in the things they suggest. Like, for them, going for a cheeky Nando's is nothing. Their parents give them a twenty without even thinking about it. Their lives are subsidised and they don't realise. And they claim they're skint *all the time.*' She laughs, but at the same time she's kicking herself. How have they got on to this? It's heavy and she wants light. Byrne is supposed to be light. Light entertainment to pick her up after being dumped by her so-called friends.

'It's not a big deal,' she says. 'I always pay my way, and if I can't, I just say I'll meet them later. It's fine.'

'If you were mine, I'd pay for everything. I'd get you a gym membership. I'd get you a car.'

She laughs. 'Don't be ridiculous. I'm fine. I don't want anyone paying for me.'

'You're stoical,' he says.

'Stoical? What does that mean?'

He laughs, and she feels relief drain through her. They are back to being light.

'It means you handle things without a fuss. Like, if you had toothache, you'd probably pop a few painkillers and tell everyone you were OK.'

'Sounds like my mum. She's stoical.'

'That's where you get it from then. Your brother's like that too. I don't know how he works in that dead pub night after night, but he does, he shows up, and I admire that. It's what made me go back, made me extend the hand of friendship.'

'*Extend the hand of friendship?*' she teases and pushes against his chest playfully. It is like pushing a rock.

'You know what I mean.'

She can't tell in the dark, but from his expression she'd guess he was blushing.

'I'm thinking of bringing him into the business,' he says. 'Not yet. He's not ready yet. But soon.'

'What, like, the self-defence videos?'

He shakes his head. 'Another strand. The most lucrative strand. He'd make an excellent scout, once we've sorted his wardrobe and got him a decent haircut.'

Before she can reply that there's nothing wrong with her brother, that he's lovely as he is, a shout reaches them. Her name, cried out through the crowd.

'Casey!'

She turns to see Dan. He's right there, face like thunder. As if she's given him an electric shock, Byrne releases her, throws up his palms and takes a step back.

'Hey, bro,' he says, looking from her to her brother. 'Catcha later, yeah.'

'Safe,' Dan mumbles. 'No worries.'

The two bump fists. Byrne backs away. Without a word to Casey, no apology, no nothing, he turns and pushes through the crowd. What the hell was that? Some boy code? What is she, chopped liver? She is about to say as much when—

'The fuck?' Dan grabs her arm, his grip tight. The shock of it sends her pulse racing. This is not Dan. And yet it is.

'*What?*' she shouts into his face.

'What are you doing with him? He's way too old for you. He's twenty-six. And he's not nice, all right? He's not a nice guy.'

'Why are you friends with him then?' She shakes his hand off. 'If he's not a nice guy? You can't tell me who to talk to. What are you even doing here anyway? It's like you're spying on me. Honest to God. You're such a loser.'

She walks off, tears pricking, mind flailing. What just happened? The way Dan grabbed her arm. The way Byrne backed away from her at the sight of him, as if she were something he'd stolen, something you needed permission to touch, to borrow, to have. She storms away from the beach, smarting, furious, confused. Maybe Dan's just drunk. Maybe he's taken something. Yes, maybe that. Something that's made him weird, although, thinking about it, he's been a bit weird all weekend. And Byrne, so into her one minute, then brushing her off the next – like she's nothing.

She checks her phone. No word from Immy or anyone. Her battery's on fifteen per cent. Shit. Could this night get any worse?

But then, through a gap in the crowd, she sees Immy and Charlotte dancing to Dua Lipa. Her anger dissolves. They're just in the moment; it's totally fair they're not checking their phones. Two lads she doesn't recognise are dancing with them, the strong vibes obvious even from a distance. It makes her miss Liam. It's not that she still loves him. She's over him, totally, but right now it would be so good just to have someone to be with, someone nice who would put his arm around her shoulders and let her share whatever he's drinking, share her night, stay in her tent and hold her.

'Immy,' she says.

The two girls scream their greeting and pull her into a hug.

'Oh my GOD,' Immy cries. 'You're here! So cool.' She crouches and pulls something from her bag. 'Here,' she says, handing up a can of mojito. 'This was Gabby's, but she's gone back to the chalet with Matty. Have you even had a drink?' She opens the can and sucks the fizz that foams out. A moment later, she's rubbing her forefinger and thumb over the opening. 'A few cheeky sprinkles to get the party started. You're playing catch-up, yay!'

Casey takes the can and drinks. Drinks some more. Raising her eyes to Immy, she says: 'Thanks, babe. I needed this. Oh my God, I so needed this.'

The cocktail in a can helps, but Casey can't shake off the fight with Dan or the way Byrne just dropped her like a shitty stone. Dan grabbing her arm like that, shouting at her like she was a naughty child; it's impossible, surreal. Byrne, all charm, making her feel like the only person on the beach, only to throw up his hands the moment Dan appeared.

The more it circles in her mind, the more impossible it becomes.

Immy and Charlotte and the two boys are moving closer,

touching one another's arms, whispering into one another's ears, laughing like lunatics at jokes she knows won't be funny. The idea that they might all start getting with one another in front of her becomes a real possibility. Except it isn't because there's no way she's sticking around for that. She wonders if the evening, the evening for which she's given up so much, could get any worse.

She claps Immy on the back and shouts into her ear.

'I'm gonna find Dan,' she says, doubting very much Immy can hear her. 'I'll be back in a bit.'

'OK, babe!' Immy's eyes are sparkling. Casey could have told her she was going to walk into the sea and never come back and she would have given the same answer.

They hug. At least with a shiny new boy on the horizon, Immy isn't giving her a hard time for going off.

Casey pushes through the bodies and the gossiping groups. The fire is raging. It seems to warm the whole beach, light half the sky. People are dancing where they stand, their movements looser, the beats getting faster, the roar of voices louder. She pushes on. She has to find Dan, sort things out. She won't feel right until she's seen him, and she has to do something to save the night from total ruin.

The dunes are pitch-black, but there is light from the party, and she can see iPhone torches bobbing up ahead. People are coming and going from the site, grabbing more drinks from their tents instead of paying for expensive beers from the beach bar. The air is cooler, much cooler, away from the fire. She passes a couple of faces she recognises but only vaguely. Olive and Ethan and their crew will be somewhere on the beach, she supposes. If she sees Dan, she will make him talk to her. If she sees Byrne, she will give him a fat piece of her mind.

She arrives at the cold-water tap and looks up at the site, lit up, all but empty. Darkness plumes between where she's standing and the big gate to staff camping. She stays where she is, dithering. After a moment, she moves towards staff camping.

Out of the thick dark, a white T-shirt floats like a ghost. At first, she thinks it's Byrne and her heart quickens, but he is too short, his posture not right, and as he clarifies out of the darkness, she sees it is Robbo. He is grinning at her in a way she doesn't like at all.

'Casey,' he says, not stopping until he's right up in her space. 'You look hot.' He brushes his hand up her arm, and she shivers with disgust.

'Robbo,' she replies and takes a step back.

He steps closer. She steps back; feels the ramshackle fence that separates the site from the dunes at her back.

'Casey,' he says again, gurning. His eyes are spinning tops.

'Listen, Robbo,' she says shifting sideways. 'I'm actually—'

'Actually, actually,' he mimics. 'What are you actually?' And then he's on her, his tongue pushing between her lips, thick and wet and strong. She shoves him, hard, but a second later he's up in her face again. She tries to remember the self-defence video, but nothing comes. His mouth is on her cheek, her ear, his hands pushing against her shoulders. He won't budge. His strength is terrifying. He is pinning her to the fence, his meaty hand closing around her throat.

'Robbo!' someone shouts – a man's voice. 'Get off her. Get off her right now.'

Robbo's grip loosens. He steps back; wipes his mouth with the back of his hand. Nausea rolls in Casey's stomach. She drops her hands to her knees, panting.

Byrne appears, walking a little stiffly.

'I'm OK,' she tries to say, but she's fighting for breath. 'I was handling it.'

Anger fires. She'll be damned if she'll let Byrne Sharp be the hero of the hour. But as he gets closer, she sees he has a bloody nose and that his left eye looks swollen.

'What the hell?' He is shoving at Robbo's shoulder over and over, sending him staggering backwards as Casey tries to regulate her breathing. 'What the fuck, bro?'

'We were just messing,' Robbo says, still with that idiot gurning grin on his stupid fat face. 'She was cool with it.'

'I was not cool with it,' she shouts, standing up straight. 'I'm going to call the police.'

'Robbo,' Byrne says, his voice stern. 'Go back to the teepee, yeah? Sleep it off, man. You're wrecked. Go. Now. I don't want to see you till tomorrow.'

'Fuck's sake,' Robbo mutters, but, incredibly, he does as he's told, shaking his head, slumping away and up the hillside like a castigated dog.

Casey stares after him, amazed.

'Casey,' Byrne says. 'Did he hurt you?'

'Your eye!' She rushes towards him. 'Oh my God, what the hell happened?'

FORTY-FIVE
CASEY

Two days after

'No!' Casey's fingers dig into her head. The interview room blurs.

'Love?' Mum is squeezing her hand, but she shakes it away and flings herself out of the chair. It falls back, lands with a crash. 'The sliders,' she whimpers. 'The guy in the foyer. Oh God, oh my God.' She feels like she's going to explode. It's all falling in on her. That night. Byrne. Everything.

'Love? Just take a beat, love.' Her mum's voice. Far away. Casey can't look at her. She can't look at her.

'Casey.' DI Chambers stands up. Her arms rise, her hands pink. 'Sit down, Casey. Please sit down.'

She can't sit down. She can't – all she can see is Byrne's white slider on the forest floor. His leg, carved like wood. The tree. The bark against her back. The leaves in the... not moonlight. Not moonlight, no, no, no. It was the security light. The security light was shining through the leaves from the watchtower...

'Casey.' She hears DI Chambers as if from another room. 'I

know this is difficult, but I have to ask you to sit down and remain calm.'

'That doesn't mean he did it,' Mum is saying, and she too sounds like she's not in the same room. 'It doesn't mean he did it. He can't have. There could be any number of reasons why he'd say that. Dan would never...'

They're both talking at once. Talking at once in another room. Casey holds on to her head. She just needs to... she just needs... she just...

'Mrs Connor. If I could also ask you to stay calm. We've arrested your son because if someone confesses, it's procedure. But we're still awaiting forensics as to the cause of death. We are still very much gathering the facts, so I would ask you to be patient, but we're going to have to keep him here for the time being.'

'You don't understand.' Casey's heart feels like it's beating in her throat. She brings her fists down on the tabletop: *bang*. 'He didn't do it. Dan didn't do it.'

'Casey?' Mum is looking at her, panic in her eyes. Casey meets her gaze. Her head spins. She knows Mum's trying to tell her not to say anything stupid, but she can't let her brother go down, she cannot.

'It's OK, Mum,' she sobs.

'Casey,' her mother warns her. 'Just take a moment, OK? You're in shock, love.'

'No, Mum,' she hears herself say. 'This isn't right. It wasn't Dan. I know it wasn't because... it's all come back. That guy's sliders. I remember Byrne's sliders. I remember it all. Dan didn't kill him. I *know* he didn't. Because I did.'

FORTY-SIX
CASEY

That night

Byrne touches his fingertips to his forehead. 'I'm fine. Don't worry, I'm fine.'

She grabs his upper arm – solid and round as a cannonball. 'You're not fine. You're hurt. Who did this to you?'

He glances up at her; seems to scrutinise her for a moment, as if unsure whether to tell her. 'I think...' He takes a deep breath before continuing. 'I *think* I might have got on the wrong side of your brother.' He holds up his can of lager and offers her a lopsided smile.

'What?' Casey takes a step back. '*Dan* did this? Are you *sure?*'

He nods, his expression apologetic, and takes a swig. 'I don't think he liked me talking to you.'

'*What?* Oh my God, what is wrong with him? Who the hell does he think he is? I'll kill him.'

'He's just looking out for you, that's all.' He offers her the can again. She takes it, takes a swig and hands it back.

'I can look out for myself! I don't need him fighting my... Oh my God, I'm so sorry.' She moves towards him again, raising her hand to his face. He flinches away but catches her hand in his. For a second, she thinks he might kiss it, but he lowers it slowly and keeps hold.

'Don't be sorry,' he says softly. 'It's me who should be sorry.' He has still not let go of her hand. She tries not to notice, but the same electricity courses through her, like before. He is so sure, so confident. It's scary. It's exciting.

'I shouldn't have walked off like that,' he says, the merest pulse of a squeeze around her fingers. 'But your brother had warned me off, and I didn't want you to be embarrassed by him making some big scene, so I removed myself. Of course, as soon as I got some distance away, I realised how it might look, like I'd just dropped you and run instead of defending you.' He meets her eyes, his own full of panic. 'Not that you need to be defended! You know what I mean. I'm making a mess of this. I came straight back, but you'd gone, and I just thought, I'm done, you know? You were the only interesting thing about the party, and there was no one else I wanted to talk to. So I came back up to the site. I figured I'd get an early night, start fresh in the morning, head home early. But I bumped into your brother. We had... words.'

'I can't believe he hit you.' She shakes her head, tears threatening.

'Don't worry about it. Stags clashing antlers, that's all it is.' He laughs. 'Hey, do you want to go for a walk, find somewhere so we can talk? I'm feeling a bit shaky. Bit wired, you know? Do you know somewhere quiet?'

'Sure. Of course. You poor thing.'

She takes his arm and leans into the solidity of him. It reminds her of the XL bully dogs that have been in the news recently. Not a scrap of fat, solid muscle power, violent if not properly trained.

'Let me take you to this place I found,' she says. 'It's not open to the public. We have to go into staff camping, but only for a few steps, then there's this cute little stream and, like, a dell. It's really chill there.'

'Sounds good.'

Together, they walk towards the five-bar gate with the skull and crossbones. He offers her the can again, but she tells him no thanks, she doesn't really like it. She asks him if he needs water, or food, or anything at all, but he says no, he's fine, a lot better for seeing her, that he feels calmer just for talking to her. He shivers, and she leans into him, lending him warmth and strength.

'It's just through here,' she says when they reach the gate, unhooking from him; cool air lands in the crook of her arm.

She holds the gate. He walks through, still moving tentatively. She shuts it and holds out her hand. He takes it, letting her lead. A trickling sound reaches them. A moment later, the stream appears, the cool rush of it, the dancing flashes of light on water.

'That's beautiful,' he says.

'I wish I could say it was moonlight,' she says. 'But it's the security tower.' She motions above them, and he smiles.

'You know secret stuff,' he says.

'I am full of secrets.' She giggles.

'Are you?' His fingers tug on hers. When she stops to see why he's stopped, he steps forward and kisses her on the mouth.

A thrill passes through her – at his courage. And it's a good kiss, a really good kiss.

He pulls back, his intense eyes searching hers. 'Was that OK?'

She nods. 'But you're not my type, you know. So don't be getting ideas.'

He laughs. 'You're not mine either, but you've got something about you. You've got something...'

She squeezes his hand. 'I'll show you the bit of the stream where you can cross – come on.'

'A magical mystery tour,' he says. 'Like it.'

At the narrow section, no more than half a metre wide, she lets go of his hand and jumps over. 'Can you jump OK?'

'He only hit my face, you know,' Byrne drawls, striding over without needing to jump, his movements suddenly surer, no sign of pain. 'Everything else about me is in perfect working order.'

He grins, and she catches the implication, which makes her blush red hot. Liam would never have come out with a line like that. It's silly, risky, and she finds herself on the edge of a giggle. Kids her age are so serious. Byrne's full of fun. She turns away to hide her smile, glad of the leaves breaking up the light, leaving them both in the quiet semi-darkness of the dell.

On the other side of the stream, they hold hands again and step forward, side by side now in the more open space. The air smells different here – fresher, greener, like dew on grass.

'I don't go too far in,' she says, 'but it's peaceful here, isn't it? It's like a secret bit that no one knows about. When I'm on shift, there's, like, so many people, all asking me for stuff, but here there's just me. It's calm.'

'It is.' He pulls her to him and kisses her again, and again she is hyper-aware of the tight, contained strength of him. He pushes her gently against the thick trunk of a tree, the bark rough and cool against the bare skin of her back. He runs his hands down her sides, up, brushing over her breasts. Her heart races. He's so sure, but this is fast, a little too fast. Her top is so flimsy, a thin shield between his hands and—

She breaks off. Tries to bring her own hands up to push against his chest, but he seems to take that as a cue to grab them, to lower his mouth to her neck. He is holding her by the wrists now, her arms tight at her sides. The physical sensation alone is lovely, but she can't stop the quiver of panic beneath. He's holding her fast. She can't move.

He lets go then and moves his hands to her waist, her hips, tracing the outline of her in a way that makes her feel like a goddess. This is better. As he plants baby kisses on her neck, she tries to relax into it. But again her brain races forward, splitting her in two, half senses, half worry. He slides his fingers under her top, round her waist, dips them into the waistband of her skirt.

'Wait,' she says, pushing at his arms.

But it is like trying to move a chest of drawers. He's not looking at her. He's too close. He reaches round her neck. She feels a sharp tug on the straps of her halter top. The knot comes undone quickly, too quickly. The top falls. All that's keeping her breasts covered is his body, pressed hard against her own. Her heart quickens. He moves back. The top drops and gathers at her waist. She gasps. Her blood pulses in her ears. He steps forward, cups her breasts with his hands, thumb glancing over her nipples. He's kissing her neck again but harder now, pressing himself between her legs, forcing them apart, pushing her roughly against the scratchy bark of the tree. The skin on her back snags. He pins her there, lowers his head and takes her nipple in his mouth.

'Wait,' she manages, shoving as hard as she can at his shoulders. 'Just slow down, OK?'

He stands back. She grapples with her top. He is so much taller than her, so much bigger, and the thought of the XL bully returns. Those dogs kill, she thinks. Byrne Sharp could kill her.

'I thought you wanted this,' he says, frowning with a petulance that scares her. She notices his eyes then, jumpy and kind of crazy.

'I do,' she says carefully. 'But let's go easy, OK? Let's check in with one another, make sure we're both into it?' She takes his hand. She has no idea what she's doing. It feels like she's woken up and all she knows is that she no longer wants him, and she needs to get out of here and back to the site as quickly and as safely as she can.

'These woods are a bit creepy actually,' she says. 'I think they're creeping me out. We could go back to my tent?'

That way they'll have to go past the fire pit. Hopefully Ness and Spider will still be up and she can run to them.

He smiles, but his eyes are as black as a shark's. He takes a baggie out of his pocket and shakes it in front of her face. Inside are little round pills, brownish in the patchy light from above. 'You're probably a bit straight. One of these'll help you relax, I promise.' He takes a pill from the packet and moves forward like a shadow. She feels herself once again pinned back against the tree. 'Open wide. Come on. It'll help, I promise.'

She clamps her mouth shut and turns her head away, frightened now, frightened and sick at herself. Stupid. She has been so stupid. Her brother tried to warn her, but she didn't—

'OK,' he says, the pressure of him releasing a little. 'If you won't do a pill, let me take a photo of you.'

When she turns to look at him, he is returning the pills to his pocket and pulling out his phone. He holds it up. 'Drop your arms.'

'What the hell? No!'

'Come on. You're beautiful. Just for me.'

'Fuck off.' She turns her head away, closing her eyes. She tries to keep one arm over her breasts and pulls at the straps of her top with the other. She stays like that a second, arms crossed, trying to figure out how to get the halter back in place without leaving herself vulnerable to another attack. 'You don't get to take a photo just because you want to,' she says and hears the tears in her voice. 'Why are you being like this?' She reaches with both hands to tie the straps behind her head. To her relief, he lets her.

'What, so you're a prude now?' He is still holding up the

phone. For all she knows, he could be filming her right now for some sick purpose later; to make a joke of her maybe, for his gibbon sidekicks. 'What did you even wear that for if this isn't what you wanted?' His voice is cold. 'A flimsy top, no bra. What were you hoping to gain?'

'Gain? What? What are you talking about?'

'You're half naked. Come on. You know what you're doing. You wanted this – you brought me here for this. All I'm doing is giving you what you wanted, and now you don't want it all of a sudden?'

She tries to knock the phone from his hand, but his grip is too tight. 'I said no. Have you heard of consent?'

'Bullshit. Stop playing games. You gave your consent when you brought me here. What am I supposed to do, keep checking every five seconds? Pretty unromantic, don't you think? This OK? That OK? Like a fucking pussy? Is that what you want?'

She turns to go, to run, but then somehow his massive hand is around her neck. Shock takes the breath from her. His stranglehold presses against her windpipe. The tree bark breaks the skin on her back. She cries out in pain. Her head starts to throb. The self-defence video, she thinks. Flat of the forearm. Oxygen. Six seconds until... She can't think, can't...

She pushes against his arm. It doesn't move, not one millimetre, but he loosens his grip, enough for her to draw in as much air as she can. Then his hand clamps once again around her neck. He shoves her hard against the tree, and she feels her head crack against it. He's choking her. She can't breathe. She shoves frantically at his arm, trying to release the stranglehold. What did she rehearse with Dan? There's nothing, nothing at all in her mind. Panic has stolen it from her. She pulls and pushes, trying to free her throat, but he's too strong. Her head spins. Why isn't it working? She can't breathe, can't shout for help, can't do anything at all. Her vision clouds. He's going to kill her. He's killing her.

Squat down. Squat down! That's what she hasn't done. Squat down, feet apart, punch the flat of his arm, then elbow to the face. With every last bit of strength, she drops low and punches his arm away. Gasping, she brings up her elbow, hard. He reels, staggers backwards, clutching his eye. She can't remember what comes next. All she can do is suck in air and blow it out again, over and over.

She drops her hands to her knees, panting, wheezing, gasping. She should run. Run, she tells herself. Fucking run. She glances up. Byrne is swaying, seems to be seeing stars. She needs to get away. She needs to leg it.

The flat of his hand comes to his chest. She coughs, gasps, coughs again, breathes as best she can, trying to stand up straight, but she's too dizzy, her legs boneless. Byrne is still listing in a kind of slow circle. He brings his hands over his ears and closes his eyes. With a roar, she lifts herself and kicks him hard between his legs, then falls back, landing hard. He collapses backwards like he's been shot. His head hits the ground with a sickening thump.

The dull beat of distant music. The white security light broken by the trees. The whispering of the leaves. The moss soft and cool on the palms of her hands. Her ragged breath. Her entire body shaking.

She crawls over to where Byrne is lying still, dead still, his head resting on a fat curling tree root.

Snivelling, she pulls herself to her knees. He looks like he's out cold. She leans over, presses two fingers to his neck. Shakes him by the shoulder, calls his name once, twice, three times. No response.

'Oh my God,' she whispers, over and over.

He's dead. Byrne Sharp is dead.

FORTY-SEVEN
CASEY

Two days after

DI Chambers and a more junior-looking cop arrange themselves on the chairs opposite. The duty solicitor sits next to her. The interview room is airless. Chambers gets up, opens a window and sits down again before pressing record on the machine and making the introductions for the benefit of the tape.

Casey barely hears. Her whole body feels numb, her sense of herself in this room only tenuous. The bad thing was there all along, buried somewhere. She could feel it, but now she can see it. She knows it. The whole nightmare has surfaced in all its terrifying details, and one thing is clear: protecting her family is all she has left. Dan cannot go to prison for her. Mum can't help her now. The thought makes her want to cry forever. She's not a murderer. She didn't do it on purpose. She just has to hope they will see that.

'Casey. Earlier, you claimed to have killed Byrne Sharp. Firstly, and for the record, we need to inform you that the deceased's name is in fact Byrne Martin. Do you want to take us through how you came to take Mr Martin's life?'

'Byrne Martin.' She nods, processing the name change. Sharp must have been a pseudonym for his YouTube account. More catchy than Martin, she guesses. More masculine. A cutting edge.

She takes a deep breath. And begins. 'Byrne and I had been chatting on and off over the weekend...'

Slowly, she tells them, stopping to clarify when Chambers interrupts with questions – *What time was this? Where were you at this point? Why would your brother claim to have killed Mr Martin?*

'My brother and Byrne had a fight a few minutes before I saw Byrne again. My brother isn't violent, not at all. I think that was probably his first physical fight in his whole life. Maybe he was shocked at himself. Maybe he thought he'd killed him. But that's not how Byrne died. As I said, when I saw him again, he looked like he'd been in a scrap, but that was all. That was definitely after the fight because I was with him then until... well, until he died.'

She tells them how, in her sympathy for Byrne, she forgave him for his rudeness earlier in the evening, how he gave a perfectly plausible explanation for why he did that, how he gave her a drink from his can of lager, explaining away the weird taste by telling her it was alcohol-free.

What took place in the woods is harder to explain. She asks for a glass of water. Chambers has to stop the tape while the PC goes to fetch it. The water is in a glass that looks unwashed. When she sips it, it is lukewarm, as if he couldn't be bothered to run the tap.

Composing herself once more, she places the smeary glass on the hard tabletop and tries to recall the exact sequence of events. How Byrne accused her of leading him on, how he...

Tears well. 'I was so frightened,' she says. 'I just did what he said. He undid my top. All I could think about was how to stay alive. I know now that he took a photograph of me like that, against the tree. I asked him not to, but he just did it. And then he tried to strangle me.' She takes another sip of the tepid water. 'I thought he was going to kill me. I don't know if he even wanted sex or if it was just about overpowering me. Humiliating me. I'd said no to him. He was so different to how he'd been all weekend; the whole gentleman thing was gone and now he was trying to... And now I'm thinking it's ironic because he does these self-defence videos, and me and Dan had a go at some of them. When he was choking me, I tried to remember them. And with Dan I remember saying, but how does anyone get away? You know, after? These things take you so far, but even if you get a second to escape, if they come after you, they're still faster, aren't they? I mean, that's what we're dealing with, isn't it? Men can still kill you, whatever you try to do. And I never said I wanted it. I swear, I never...

She starts to cry, great sobs that feel like they're coming from the deepest part of her. She'll never stop, she thinks. She will never stop crying, not just about what happened to her but about what happens to women at the hands of men like this, men who put everything back centuries, who ruin everything for women and for men and even for themselves. Because how can any of this be enjoyable to anyone? How can this be what anyone wants?

'Take your time,' Chambers says softly.

She nods, sniffs. Someone slides a tissue across the table. She blows her nose, nods again.

'I don't know when I remembered the move, but I sort of dropped down then smacked his arm away.' She mimes it, then brings up her elbow. 'And then I elbowed him in the face like that. I didn't even think it would work. But then he sort of staggered back. I didn't think I'd hit him that hard. I knew I should run, but I couldn't breathe and I couldn't seem to send the message to my legs, like I couldn't work out how to get away. And then he put his hands over his ears and I saw my chance. I just sort of kicked out. I kicked him in the... between his legs. I just wanted to escape. But he dropped. He just, like, collapsed. I heard a bump. I think he might have hit his head because when I felt for a pulse, I could see his head was resting on a tree root. I couldn't see any blood, but it was quite dark, it was about midnight, maybe a bit before, maybe half eleven, and I couldn't find his pulse, but I don't really know how to take someone's pulse so I wasn't sure, and then I just... I just panicked and ran back to my tent.

'I took out my phone to call for help. I knew Byrne was in a bad way, and I knew I had to call an ambulance. But my phone was dead, and Spider and those guys weren't there, so I ran out into the main site to try and borrow a phone. But there was no one about, and I think by then the drugs must have started to kick in because I felt sick and dizzy. I can remember a load of tents. I knew one of them was empty, and I must have found it.'

She looks up. 'And that's it. That's it. I remembered bits and pieces, but when you said about Byrne, I just saw his slider on the grass in the dark and I knew he was dead. Like, somewhere inside me. And then you said my brother had confessed, and I just thought no, no, that's not what happened, and it all came back like a... like an avalanche, and I knew it was me. I'm so sorry. I'm not a murderer. I didn't mean to kill him; it was an accident.'

She bursts into tears. It is all so hopeless. Whatever she does or says, the truth is, Byrne Martin didn't sexually assault her, and she killed him. Her life is over. Her vision blurs. Tears drop from her chin onto the table. She blinks; makes herself look up.

'Can I... can I see my mum?'

FORTY-EIGHT
MELISSA

Two days after

This is unbearable. Every second tolls, every minute stretches so long it is hard to believe time hasn't come to a standstill, that out there in the world, people are spending hours lost in a task or watching a movie or chatting over coffee, not remotely conscious of the minutes, the seconds, the split seconds that make up the seconds.

Melissa sips the tea given to her five minutes ago by a cop who looks about twelve. It is in a chipped black mug with *Police Do It in Patrol Cars* in white font on the side. She hates drinking out of dark mugs. You never know if they're clean, and they make the tea look weird.

'I just don't understand why she would say she killed him,' she says to Riley. 'Why would she say that? How can a slip of a girl kill a bloke in his prime?'

The cop gives her a sad smile. 'Let's wait and see. She'll give a statement and they'll take it from there. Let's try and stay positive.'

'Right. I'll keep my chin up, shall I? And meanwhile both my kids have been arrested for murder.'

Riley's face falls, but Melissa doesn't care. Stay positive? How can she stay positive when the whole situation is... She has no words for what it is.

'Bruises all over her neck and a nasty graze on the back of her head,' she says, more for herself than anyone else. 'What are they going to charge her with – assault? If she lashed out and he... I don't know, fell over, that's hardly her fault, is it? It's ridiculous. Absolutely ridiculous.'

Riley does not reply. They sit in a rather stony silence. Seconds crawl. Minutes slouch. Melissa's stomach rumbles over her looping thoughts. What is Casey telling them? It is unbearable not to be able to sit by her side.

The door opens. Chambers steps through, her face grim but unreadable. She walks in that confident way she has. Unhesitating.

'Mrs Connor.' She sits down; glances about her briefly before returning her eyes to Melissa's.

She looks tired, Melissa thinks. Her skin has a greyish tinge. She's probably worked through the night.

'We've taken statements from both your children. They've both been placed under arrest.'

'Wait. No. Don't you need proof? Can't you see they're just trying to protect each other? They're very close. Surely you can't think—'

'Mrs Connor. I'm going to have to ask you to calm down, OK? I know this is hard to hear, but it's procedure. We're processing them now, and they'll be given bail.'

'How much will that cost?'

'Nothing. We don't—'

'Well, what are you charging them with then?'

'We're not charging them at this time. They'll be released, but they may not leave the country and they may not see one another while on bail until further notice. Is that clear? It is absolutely imperative you adhere to the rules or I'll be obliged to keep them here.'

Melissa nods. 'OK. I get it. I'll keep them apart.'

'We've got their belongings here. I need to keep their phones, but strictly no phone calls on any other devices. No texts. We can check these things.'

'OK. Understood.'

Chambers inhales audibly. 'Once we're in possession of the full facts, we'll be in touch. I'd strongly recommend you don't talk to the press.'

'Good Lord, there's no chance of that.'

'Is there anywhere your son can stay? We can drive him there.'

'Er, yes. Sure. I can call my friend. But he was nowhere near, and my daughter was just defending herself surely? She's covered in bruises. Surely you can match them... forensically or something? It's obvious Byrne attacked her.'

For the first time behind the animal alertness, Melissa sees what looks like kindness flit across the detective's face as she stares for a brief second out towards the entrance.

'It doesn't do to speculate,' she says eventually, her eyes returning to Melissa's in silent communication. *Trust me*, Melissa reads there. Or maybe it's what she wants to read there.

'I know it's difficult,' she adds, 'but let's try and be patient and see what transpires, OK? We have to follow procedure.'

'Can I collect their things?'

'As I said, their possessions have been seized at this time. Call your friend, Mrs Connor. Don't tell her anything other than to say they've been arrested. We really need to keep the press out of this until we've contacted the deceased's next of kin. We'll process Dan and Casey, and you can take your daughter home.'

. . .

Chambers disappears back into the bowels of the police station. Melissa calls Sarah, who picks up, thank God. They have exchanged texts, but there has been no time or space to call.

'Hey.' Sarah sounds breathless.

'Are you OK?'

'Just going for a run. Needed a break. How's it going?'

Melissa's eyes fill. 'Not good. They've both been arrested.'

'*What?* What the hell for?'

'I can't say.'

'Oh my God.' Sarah's voice catches. 'Oh my God, Mel. But isn't Casey a victim? And what the hell has Dan done?'

'It's complicated. Listen, I'll tell you everything when I can.'

'What can I do?'

'Well, actually, there is something...'

Sarah agrees before Melissa has even asked the question. Dan and her son Rory have been pals almost since the day Melissa moved her family to the area.

'Rory's room's free obviously,' Sarah says. 'And without him here, it's actually clean and tidy. I'd love to have Dan around the place.'

'Thanks, mate. I'm not sure how long he'll have to stay, but make sure he pulls his weight. He's house-trained.'

'I know that! Last time I saw him, he made Keralan curry for us all. I said to Rory, I said, so boys *can* cook, can they?' She laughs, but it's hollow, and Melissa knows her friend is trying to find a speck of brightness in the murk.

'He should be there by this evening,' she says. 'The police are driving him. And he can't contact Casey, OK? No contact at all.'

'Understood.'

'Even if he asks nicely to borrow your phone, say no, OK?'

'Sure. Hang in there. Text me with anything. I won't say a word. To anyone.'

'Thanks, love.'

She rings off; offers a brief conciliatory smile to Riley. 'Is it OK if I ring Heaven View? I just wanted to thank the manager and ask her to thank the staff.' The pretext sounds as lame as it is. She's so desperate to know what's going on behind the scenes, what the police have evidence-wise. But what is she expecting? That Candy London will brief her on the forensics?

'I don't see why not,' Riley says. 'As long as you don't say anything.' Of course. She'll be listening in.

Melissa calls the campsite. When she explains who she is, she is put through immediately to the manager.

'Candy London speaking. Is that Casey's mum?'

'It is, yes. Melissa. Hi.'

'Melissa. Oh my God, how is she?'

'She's... you know. She's pretty shaken up.'

'What are they saying?'

'They're not really saying anything. I think they need to gather all the evidence before they do anything else. I'm sure they've told you the same.'

'They have. I'm so sorry this happened on my watch.'

'It's not your fault. You can't keep an eye on all of them all of the time.'

'I know, but I've never heard of anything like this happening here until this year. I mean, you hear about spiking, assault, but it's always such a nice crowd.'

'It happens though, unfortunately. It happens.'

'Jesus,' Candy says, sounding chastened. 'What's happening to our young men?'

Melissa's blood stills. 'Hang on. You said until this year.'

'Well, yes. We've never had any reports of sexual assault before.'

'How do you... I mean, how do you know that's what it was?'

Candy stutters. 'I... I just meant... I mean, I'm speculating, I suppose. Only there was another complaint. Apparently this bloke – the dead guy – and a couple of his friends were hassling girls all weekend. I heard this Sharp character had tried to choke a girl while they were being... you know, intimate, in her tent. Tried to get her to take something but she refused, so he got heavy with her, said he'd taken a photo of her and if she told anyone he'd put it online. A couple of her friends heard the commotion and intervened, and he said it was just foreplay, though what kind of foreplay that is, I don't know. Poor girl was so freaked out she went home. That was Friday, but I only heard about it yesterday. The girl didn't report it, didn't tell me or anyone, otherwise I would have done something. Didn't even pack up her tent. I wish I'd known; I would have—'

'Have you told the police?'

'I told them last night. Turns out her tent was the one Casey...'

'The one she was found in?'

'Yeah.'

'And had he... did he, you know...?'

'No, thank God. But he did threaten to kill the girl and her friends if they reported him. Told them no one believes women anyway. Told them they couldn't prove anything.'

Melissa reels. 'Oh my God. That's so much more...' She stops herself. It is so much more than the police have told her, but this is not the reason she's given Riley for the call. 'Listen,' she says. 'I just wanted to say thanks and to ask you to pass on my thanks to Spider and all the staff who helped the police with their enquiries.'

'Will do. Will you let me know when you hear anything? We loved having Casey here. She's a proper good worker and a lovely girl. Ness and the gang loved her. I wish they'd told me she hadn't turned up for her shift; I would've known something wasn't right immediately. She's such a responsible young woman. If you ask me, it sounds like he tried it on one too many times and some girl thumped him and ran. But that's not murder. We have a right to defend ourselves after all, don't we?'

'We do,' Melissa says. 'We certainly do.'

And then, her baby. There in the doorway, looking thin, groggy, eyes red-rimmed, black-shadowed. A uniformed female police officer ushers her through. Within the brutal context of what they are doing to her children, everyone is so kind. It is impossible to know how to feel anything other than a kind of floating state of confusion, as if everything is happening beneath her to a stranger in an unknown place. A bird's-eye view. Herself, her family, on CCTV.

Melissa stands, legs trembling. She wants to rush towards her girl and fold her into her arms. She knows this is what she needs, what they need, but it is too big; it is all too big, and she can't move.

Casey bursts into tears and rushes towards her. 'Mum.'

Melissa holds out her arms. Her daughter falls into them; dissolves into sobs, face pressed into her shoulder.

'Hey,' she says, rubbing her back. 'It's all going to be OK.'

A promise made by every mother at one time or another, the one promise no mother can keep.

But this is all they have right now. Empty promises and one another.

PART III

FORTY-NINE
MELISSA

Two days after

Melissa opens the door to the flat. After only two days, a closed-up, fusty smell assails her. Usually, its source – the patch of damp on the bathroom wall – would be enough to stress her out, but tonight it is the equivalent of aromatherapy. The essential oil of their safe haven. At least for now.

'Home,' she says, stepping inside.

Casey shuffles in behind her. Melissa tries not to read too much into how diminished she looks, how cowed and cracked, like she might disintegrate at any moment. She has slept the whole way here. Melissa too would have slept had she not had to drive, a Starbucks grabbed from the service station all that kept her from falling asleep at the wheel. Now she's home, she could sleep for a week.

'Can I grab a shower?' Casey asks. Her voice is so quiet Melissa almost doesn't hear.

'Sure,' she replies. 'Shall I make us some eggy bread?'

Casey's brow creases. Her shoulders rise a fraction, then drop. 'Actually, yeah. That's a shout.'

'Off you go then. I didn't stop the timer, so there should be plenty of hot water. Don't forget to open the window.'

Casey trudges to the bathroom, still in the clothes Melissa brought to the hospital. She looks saggy, beaten in more ways than one.

'Throw your dirty washing out,' Melissa calls. A second later, the bathroom door opens and a crumpled pile of laundry lands on the hall carpet. Casey will want to wash every bit of herself, Melissa knows. She will want to scrub her skin raw. She will wonder if she will ever be clean again.

She picks up her daughter's discarded clothes and goes into the kitchen. For the first time in what feels like weeks, she is alone, finally, just her and her thoughts. The last God-knows-how-many hours hunch over her – a looming shadow she will never shake.

She pulls out a chair and sits down a moment, Casey's things bundled on her lap. Quite absently, she brings the clothes to her face and breathes in. Her daughter. This baby, this child, this young woman. This being whose every cell she loves with every cell of her own. Something collapses through her, slides down the inside of her, down, down to her toes, ushering in a bone-deep exhaustion. Her head lolls forward. It feels as if it's filled with lead. How does this end? she thinks. How does this end?

Her phone buzzes. Sarah.

Hey. You on way back?

Just this second home, she replies. *Too tired to talk. Thanks again for Dan. He shouldn't be too long.* She is about to add more detail but cannot think how to start or how to stop. *Can't call but will keep in text*, she finishes; adds a heart emoji.

Let me know if you need any shopping, Sarah replies.

Thanks, babes. Love you x

Sarah sends three hearts.

· · ·

Finally, at supper, Melissa manages to ask Casey about her police statement. Haltingly, her daughter takes her through it word for word. When she's finished, she reaches over the table and takes Melissa's hand.

'Do you blame me?' Melissa asks after a long moment, unable to stop the tears from falling.

Casey shakes her head. 'Of course not.'

'You're so brave. I'm so proud of you.'

After supper, Casey goes into the living room to watch TV. Finding herself alone, Melissa knows with a sinking feeling that she should call Rich.

'Come on,' she mutters to herself. 'Let's get this over with.'

He picks up quickly. 'Mel?'

'Hi,' she says, her voice breaking. 'I need to talk to you.'

She tells him, simply and without anger or blame. What's happened is bigger than any of the grievances she harbours towards him. It must be the same for him too because he is, for once, sympathetic, understanding, chastened. He asks how he can help, if she wants him to come over.

'It's OK,' she says. 'But thanks. I'll call you as soon as we hear anything more.'

'Thank you,' he says. 'And thank you for calling me. Look after yourselves.'

'We will. You too.'

'Anything you need, OK? Anything.'

'Thank you. Thanks, Rich.'

After the call, she emails work to tell them she'll be taking the rest of the week off due to a family emergency before finally having her own long, hot shower. She washes her hair, then every part of herself, twice, with far too much soap, and lets the water drum on her head until it starts to cool. Once out, she makes herself pause. Stop a second. Moisturise your legs. Clean your teeth. Floss.

After that, wrapped in her towel and sitting on the loo seat, she closes her eyes and makes herself stay perfectly still. Slowly, she begins to count to ten. The room is steamy even with the window open. After seven seconds, she gets up. She's too hot. She's far too hot. She's combusting.

In the living room, she finds Casey, the miracle of her, safe and pink-clean and home, at least for tonight. The bitter absence of Dan then. Dan, who should be with them. Her son, her poor boy, who must be so afraid. She can't call Sarah. Chambers didn't say she couldn't talk to her, not specifically, but she did say they have ways of checking if the kids have been in touch. If Melissa calls Sarah, Chambers could accuse her of putting Dan on the phone to Casey.

No, it's too risky.

A message buzzes in. From Sarah. *Dan's here. He's grabbing a shower. I'll look after him.*

You're the best, Melissa replies.

She stares at her friend's message, feeling a rush of deep love. Longing too, for her boy, her frightened young man. She has a flashing memory of holding his hand and staring into his eyes, long ago, when he had to have stitches in his forehead after he fell and split the skin on the edge of a step. She held his hand and talked and talked to him. He kept his gaze on her throughout, not making a sound. Afterwards, the doctor said she'd never seen such a brave little soldier. He *is* her brave little soldier. His life hasn't gone so well these last couple of years, and he has suffered. Watching him slide into low energy, she tried her best with pep talks and favourite foods and suggestions of long walks at weekends, to no avail. Then lately, he seemed to perk up, started getting up in the morning, exercising, eating healthy foods. She gave him such a row for using half a week's groceries in a smoothie, but at least it wasn't tobacco in his pockets – or hash. This friend he's met is a good influence, she thought.

How wrong she was.

. . .

Together, without either of them uttering a word, she and Casey move the coffee table to the side of the sofa, fold out the sofa bed and get in. They are dressed in what passes for pyjamas in this house: Casey in soft old cotton tracksuit bottoms and a vest, Melissa in an ancient sundress she downgraded to nightwear after someone put a cigarette hole in it at a party years ago.

'It's like Christmas Day,' Casey says, grabbing her mug from the coffee table. 'Well, not, I suppose.'

'Do you want to talk some more?'

She shakes her head. 'Let's not. It only makes me feel sick.' Her eyes fill. 'I wish Dan was here.'

'So do I, love.'

It is too hot for the duvet. Casey jumps up and opens a window, letting in cool air, the arrhythmic sigh of traffic. Fumes too, Melissa thinks, but ah well. Her daughter climbs back onto the bed and cuddles in close. Her legs are tanned, toned from walking everywhere, from the tens of thousands of steps she has taken picking litter up and down that sloped campsite. Her child is not a child any more. Neither of her children are. Their adulthood has been forced upon them – too quickly, a violation. Grow up, Melissa used to say to her ex.

Why? she thinks now. What's so great about growing up?

FIFTY

CASEY

Three days after

Casey's first waking thought is of her brother. It's so weird he's not in the next room. She can't believe she can't knock on his door and go and chat to him, even for five minutes. There is so much she wants to tell him and, no doubt, stuff he wants to tell her too. She saw the grazes on his knuckles; knows he thinks he dealt Byrne a fatal blow. But will he think she confessed to save him? Or maybe he knows she did it. Maybe that's why he confessed – to save her.

Oh God, if only she was allowed to talk to him, find out what he told the police.

In the kitchen, Mum is drinking coffee and staring out of the open back window, where pigeons shit casually in the shade of their neighbour's overhanging roof. She is in her nightie. The sight of her freckled shoulders makes Casey want to cry. Over the aroma of coffee, the smell of cigarettes drifts.

'Sandra's smoking again,' her mum says, reading her mind. 'I quite like the smell actually. Reminds me of my youth.'

When Casey smiles, her mouth feels strange.

'Coffee in the pot,' her mum says. 'Did you sleep?'

'A bit.' She pours some coffee into her favourite mug. 'I wish I could talk to Dan.'

'I know. So do I. But we can't risk a phone call. They'll know.'

'This waiting.' She frowns, reaching into the fridge for milk and splashing a drop into her coffee. 'We could both be in a cell, I suppose. I can't believe they've let us come home.'

'You're hardly armed and dangerous. Not a flight risk either.'

'LOL,' Casey says, nowhere near laughing out loud. 'When they said they'd need our passports, they couldn't believe it when I said I didn't have one.'

Mum smiles sadly. 'Not exactly jet-setters, are we?'

'I didn't mean that.'

'I know you didn't, love.'

Casey sips her coffee. It has had time to cool and is just right. She wonders if Mum will go for what she's about to ask. 'Mu-um?'

'Uh-oh. What?'

'I was thinking. I know I'm not allowed to call Dan, but if you called Sarah on your phone—'

'No.' Mum puts her mug down and shakes her head. 'Don't even think about it. Promise me. You can't have any contact with your brother. It's a condition of your bail. Serious face, Casey. Look at me.'

Casey meets her mother's stern expression. 'OK.'

'OK?'

'But if I went to Immy's—'

'Casey! I don't want to talk about it, OK? I know I sound paranoid, but walls have ears.'

She sighs. 'It's so hard. I just wonder if he confessed to protect me. It's so not fair that he's under arrest too. I can't bear it.'

'We have to be patient, love.' Mum is looking out of the window. In the late-morning light, her eyes shine with tears. 'We have to get used to the fact that this thing might not go as we want. I'll see if Sarah knows any lawyers. Maybe someone can give us an idea of what to expect. But try and think about something else, eh? You'll drive yourself mad.'

'How can I think about anything else? Mum! How?' Casey starts to cry. 'Sorry. I didn't mean to shout.'

'It's OK.'

'I just wish I'd called the police straight away.'

'Well, that's not what happened, so there's no point torturing yourself with it. We are where we are.'

'And where we are is in the shit.' She sounds bitter and cross with her mum, the one person who always has her back.

Part of her is.

Later, Mum insists on joining her for a long walk. Neither of them believe she needs air; both of them know she's making damn sure Casey doesn't sneak off and see Dan.

When they get home, there's a massive bunch of flowers in the porch. Mum picks them up. A moment later, she passes them to Casey.

'They're for you,' she says.

'What?' She takes the flowers. They are beautiful – purples and blues and sage-coloured leaves. A small white envelope with her name on it is lodged between the blooms. She plucks it out, handing the bunch back to Mum. The little card inside has a picture of a rose.

To my darling girl, she reads. *Thinking of you. Love, Dad.*

She looks up at her mum, who's biting her lip, face etched with anxiety. 'They're from Dad. Did you tell him?'

With an apologetic smile, Mum gives the bouquet back. 'I had to, love.'

'That's OK,' Casey says. 'I suppose he is my dad.'

They share a smile before going up to the flat. Upstairs, she arranges the flowers in the water jug. They are beautiful. They must have cost a fortune. Half of her wants to throw them out of the window, but she keeps the thought to herself.

'He wanted to come and see you,' Mum says, as if reading her mind. 'But I said we'd be in touch once we hear anything.'

Casey nods. 'OK. Sure.'

Leaving her mum in the kitchen, she takes her second shower of the day. She knows she'll never wash Byrne off, but she can't stop scrubbing herself. Her skin is already sore. When she puts on moisturiser, the perfume in it stings. And still she cannot wipe his face from her mind, cannot erase the sight of him lying there, just lying there, the crashing certainty that her life as she knew it was over.

In her room, she tries to read but is too antsy. With no phone to scroll through and all her studies finished, she genuinely can't think how to pass the time. She can't go for a run because her legs ache after the walk and she just feels totally exhausted. Why can't the police ring and tell them that's it – they're going to charge her? They can't charge Dan. They just can't. But then Mum said Dan and Byrne had a fight. Forensics will find traces of Dan on Byrne Sharp's body – blood or fibres maybe.

After some persuading, Mum lets her log into the old iPad Sarah gave her on condition she doesn't take it to her room or do anything stupid like access her email. BBC News hasn't got anything about Byrne's death, but she googles Weymouth local news and finds the headline: *Two Assaulted and One Dead in Teen Summer Party Tragedy*.

She shouldn't read it. She shouldn't.

She reads it.

> A man believed to be in his twenties has been found dead in woodland adjacent to Heaven View campsite just hours after a teenage girl was discovered unconscious and injured in a tent.

That's not exactly right, she thinks.

> The deceased, who has not yet been named, had been attending the end-of-exams party at the campsite along with three other men. All four were over the age limit for the Summer Camp event, which is held every year for school leavers.
>
> The assault victim, an 18-year-old female, was found by campsite worker Luke Chapman.
>
> 'She was disorientated and afraid,' said Mr Chapman. 'An ambulance was summoned, and the good people of our emergency services took it from there.'

There is no mistaking that this is Spider. Casey smiles to herself. Why couldn't he just say they called 999? Her eyes prick then. He made no mention of her being almost naked. A gentleman to the last. He was always looking out for her. She feels bad for ever thinking he was creepy.

'You sure you want to be reading that?' her mum says, placing another cup of decaf tea in front of her.

'It's fine. I'm fine.'

She waits for Mum to leave the kitchen before pulling up Instagram. She's not a big Instagrammer, but there's nothing else to do and she can't settle. There's a post from Immy – of course there is. In fact, there are several, all of her, Charlotte, Gabriella and Matty pulling fun but attractive expressions and holding up a variety of cocktails in a variety of outfits. The most recent post is a rare photograph of something other than herself – a view of the sunset as seen from the beach, with the caption:

Can't believe what happened here. Heart goes out to my best friend Casey Connor. Love you, babe. #metoo #notallmen #endviolenceagainstwomen

Casey wonders if Immy has even tried to call her. She knows where she lives, could have put a letter or even a card through the door instead of naming her on Instagram for the press to find. But no. Her post is such attention-seeking BS.

'Not all men,' she whispers, rereading the hashtags just to wind herself up. 'How about not all snakes, Immy? You still wouldn't want to be left alone in a room full of them if they told you one was poisonous, would you?'

She scrolls. Dan has posted. She frowns. Dan never posts on social media, always says his life is too boring. But he has. Today he has. He must have used Sarah or Rory's laptop. That's a lot of trouble to go to. Unless...

It's a clip of a band called Romany Trail singing 'Was it You?'. The caption reads: *Feeling these words today..Look after each other, people.*

'What?' she whispers. What even is that band? The caption is so cheesy, so humourless, so not her brother. But then she remembers hearing him on the phone a week or so before she went to Weymouth.

'Yo,' he said, his voice suddenly deep. 'Yeah... yeah. Safe. Calm.'

She had been primed and ready to roast him when he got off the phone, but he disappeared into his room, and by the time he came out, Casey was studying. She'd found it hilarious, him using words like *safe* and *calm*, like he was a drug dealer or a gangster. But now, in the light of all that's happened, it sounds sinister. He was talking to Byrne – she knows that. Byrne was grooming him. Is that what that was? Can someone groom someone if they're only a couple of years older?

She plays the clip again. Swipes. The second photo is a screenshot of lyrics.

> *Was it you? Tell me, tell me, tell me.*
> *When I was low.*
> *Was it you, was it you, was it you?*
> *Tell me, baby, I gotta know.*

Her skin tingles. This is not a post; this is a message. A message for her.

'Oh my God,' she whispers, hand closing over her mouth.

Her brother has found a way to communicate with her. He is asking her if she killed Byrne Sharp.

FIFTY-ONE
DAN

Three days after

Dan scrolls through Instagram for the fifth time. Downstairs, he can hear Sarah and her husband talking, though he can't hear what they're saying. It's so weird being here without Rory, and he remembers how bittersweet it always was seeing how well Rory's parents got on. He feels bad about using Rory's laptop, but not bad enough not to. He checks Insta again. He has forty likes, five comments.

None are from Casey.

Good. Hopefully she's got the sense not to comment or tag him in anything. But it could mean she's not seen it. Or not understood.

Three checks later, he goes to her profile. Wait, she *has* posted, two minutes ago: a video clip. Madonna. He swipes. There are no lyrics.

He plays the clip, knows before Madonna has sung one word that the song is 'Live to Tell'. The caption reads: *Lying low after a tough few days. Thanks to everyone for beautiful messages of support.* A regiment of red heart emojis.

'Case,' he mutters. 'Fuck's sake.' What the hell? He tries to recall the lyrics. Googles. Understands. She's playing it less obvious than him, but the message is clear. She has a secret and she will tell him once they get out of this mess. He has no doubt this is what she means, no doubt at all.

She knows exactly what really happened to Byrne Sharp.

FIFTY-TWO
CASEY

Three days after

A gentle knock on the bathroom door. Her mother's voice.

'Case? Casey, love? Do you want to watch a movie?'

In the thick steam, Casey looks down at her legs – bright red, her arms a traffic light of fading bruises and pink skin. At least she doesn't have to look at her mottled grey neck; the mirror is completely opaque.

'Casey? You OK, love?'

'Just a minute.' She closes her eyes. Mum won't let her out of her sight. She doesn't know if she wants to watch a movie or if she wants to be alone. She feels like scratching her skin off. She feels like pouring bleach into her mind so she can white out that bastard and his empty black eyes. She feels like sitting on the wet bathroom floor and crying until she has no tears left.

She opens the door. Steam plumes out into the hallway, shrouding her mother.

'The window, love!'

'Soz. I forgot.'

'Never mind. Do you fancy a movie?'

'I'm fine.'

Neither of them move. Slowly the fog dissipates. Mum's expression is almost unbearable. They are both suffering. Her own pain she can take, but not Mum's.

'Really,' she says, reaching for her mother's hand. 'I'm fine.'

'You're going to make your skin sore,' Mum says.

'I know.'

'Can you manage a film, do you think?'

Casey nods. 'Can we watch a kids' film?'

'Sure. I'll make cold hot chocolate.' Mum heads towards the kitchen.

'Cold chocolate.'

She stops. 'Huh?'

'Cold chocolate. It can't be cold hot chocolate. It's just cold.'

Mum rolls her eyes, but she's smiling. 'Sure. Sure thing.'

In her room, Casey puts on a clean Vaccines T-shirt and a clean pair of the boxers she wears for bed. She combs the knots out of her hair and glances at Instagram. Dan hasn't tagged her. Of course he hasn't; that would be mental. She goes to his profile and sees he's posted again. Another song clip. This time it's 'Run' by Hairshirt. She plays it but knows the lyrics already.

> *Cops on my tail*
> *On bail, I need to run*
> *I need to run, run, run, run, run, run, run.*
> *I deserve all I get*
> *It was dark, I am young, it went to my head*
> *I saw red, I hit out, and now I'm on the run, run,*
>   *run, run, run, run, run.*
> *I'm on the run, run, run, run, run, run, run.*

She's never taken any notice of the words, kind of sung them without hearing them, never thought about what they mean, but now, with a hot, slick feeling that spreads over her skin, she understands that they are Dan's own 'Bohemian Rhapsody'. He thinks he killed a man and now he has to run away. Surely that's not what he means? He didn't kill Byrne Sharp! And if he runs, he'll look guilty. Is he telling her he's going to go fugitive? Is that what the message is? She has to stop him.

Her heart tightens at a flash of memory: Byrne clutching his head. Then dropping, as if he'd been shot. Her own confusion, knowing that the elbow blow didn't land, not like that, not enough to do that. Was it a delayed reaction, she wonders, to something Dan did? Surely not. Mum is always going on about that, about how they need police coming into schools to tell young lads never to kick or punch someone in the head, that it can be fatal. But if he saw red, like the song says; if forensics find blood from her brother's hands on Byrne's head...

Oh Dan, she thinks for the first time. What did you do?

'Casey?' Her mum's flip-flops slap down the hallway.

'One sec!'

She needs a reply – and quick. Dan posted this an hour ago, is probably sitting there biting his nails. But she can't think of anything that will tell him it wasn't him. That it was her. That it was both of them maybe.

She googles: *It wasn't you it was me lyrics*.

A second later, she is staring at a bunch of clips, the top one an exact match, some random woman called Buzzy Starling, a piano in one of those fake black-and-white films. Who the hell is she? She clicks. The camera pans out. A love song: slow, soulful, full of remorse. From the eighties, she thinks. Or maybe nineties. The woman is black and has puffed sleeves on her dress. She sways as she sings, low and velvety:

> *It wasn't you. It was me.*
> *It wasn't you who broke my heart.*
> *But I knew you would, sooner or later*
> *So I did it myself anyway.*

I didn't care. I did it anyway.
It wasn't you, baby. It was me.

She pauses it. It's enough. It's about something else, but Dan will understand. She googles: *Don't go lyrics.*

Another old song. A band called Yazoo. It's up-tempo, a thin eighties synth, tragic pretentious video: some woman in a white fur coat and a trilby, some bloke with a shaved head and a flat length of blonde hair at the front like a big tongue. Gross. The woman gets out of a car and sashays into a big mansion; the guy is in the hall playing the synth. In other circumstances, she and Dan would be laughing their heads off, but it's kind of iconic too; it's kind of bonkers.

Don't go! the woman shouts.

The message is too on the nose. It's too dangerous. But fuck it. She has to stop Dan from doing a bunk. She doesn't even want to think about what will happen to him if he does.

She posts two clips, the caption one word: *Mood.* Then she closes Insta and deletes the search.

In the living room, Mum has already unfolded the sofa bed. She has put squirty cream and choc chips on the cold chocolate and is holding it out, her expression that of a hopeful kid, trying to make everything better when she can't.

Casey's eyes fill. 'Thanks, Mum.'

'*Harry Potter and the Philosopher's Stone* OK? The OG?'

'Perfect.'

Casey snuggles in; tries not to think that this might be one of the last times she gets to cuddle her mum for a very long time. They have talked over and over about what happened that night, but for their own sanity, they have agreed to stop. Nor do they discuss the possibility that Casey will go to prison. Mum flat-out refuses, says it won't come to that. The inside of a cell flashes – some mean-faced woman with a razor blade. Casey shivers.

She watches the movie without taking it in. Halfway through, when Mum pops to the loo, she rushes to the kitchen and checks Instagram. Dan has posted another track. Mad. He is so mad. He's going to get himself, get them both, locked up. But when she sees what the song is, tears prick. 'I Love You' by Fontaines D.C. She touches her fingertips to the screen and whispers: 'I love you too, bro.'

FIFTY-THREE
CASEY

Five days after

Casey is towelling her hair in her bedroom. On her desk are thirty or so cards wishing her well, wishing her luck, telling her they're thinking about her. A really nice card from Olive saying *Let's go out and get drunk soon*. Immy has sent a massive bunch of flowers with the message *Thinking of you, babe*. She's called too, on Mum's phone, but Casey isn't ready to talk to her. Or anyone.

Mum's phone rings. She's taken it off silent and put the volume up to the top so they won't miss a call from the police. Her footsteps thunder down the hall in the direction of the kitchen. The phone is still ringing. More footsteps, the ringtone coming closer. A knock, Casey's bedroom door opens. Mum's face, set with worry.

'It's a Dorset number,' she says.

Casey's heart quickens. She checks her watch: a little after four in the afternoon. 'You'd better answer it.'

Mum's face is tight, her eyes full of fear. It's as if they both know this is the last moment before their old life ends. She slides her thumb over the screen and puts the phone to her ear. 'Hello? Yes, speaking. Wait a second. I'm here with Casey. Can I put you on speaker? Thanks. Wait a second.' She fiddles with the phone, drops it.

Casey picks it up, puts it on speaker and lays it on the bedside table. 'Hi,' she says, 'this is Casey. Sorry, we dropped the phone. You're on speaker.'

'OK. This is DI Chambers. Can you both hear me?'

'Yes,' they say. Casey thinks she can hear cars in the background.

'OK, I'm calling because there's been a significant development.'

Casey's legs almost give way. She sits down on the bed. Mum sits beside her, their legs touching.

'Will you be home in the next hour or so?'

'Yes,' Mum says when Casey doesn't reply.

'OK. We're on our way. Should be with you before six.'

Mum lifts the phone and speaks into it. 'OK.'

'Oh, and can you get your son to come to the house? I have to go, but I'll see you in a short while.' The detective rings off.

'Here?' Mum says. 'What does she want? Why didn't I ask her? Why couldn't she just tell us? A significant development? For God's sake, what does she mean?'

They are both staring at the phone. A moment later, they are staring at each other.

'Do you think they've found something?' Mum asks, her eyes wild with fear.

'I don't know.' Casey bursts into tears. 'But if they need Dan here, it means they're going to charge both of us. Why would they need him otherwise? They're going to charge us, Mum. They're going to take us away and put us in prison.'

'No, they're not.' Mum pulls her in and holds her tight. 'If it comes to that, we tell them everything.'

FIFTY-FOUR
MELISSA

Five days after

Melissa's phone gives a loud beep, making her jump. This is why she normally has it on silent; she's a nervous wreck, but she can't afford to miss a call from Chambers. There are two texts displaying, one from Sarah asking her how things are going, and one from the detective. *Should be with you in 15 minutes. Can we park outside the property?*

Melissa thumbs a reply. *You need a parking pass, so if you text when you get here, I'll run down with one.*

She presses send; checks to makes sure it's delivered. Surreal and prosaic all at once, she thinks. In what could be the last conversation she has with her daughter in the free world of their lives, she asks, 'Do you think I should tell Detective Chambers we're above the bookie's?'

Her daughter frowns. 'Not much of a detective if she can't figure out where we live, is she?'

They laugh. Casey wells up. Melissa reaches out and takes her hand. They have put the sofa bed back to its daytime couch and are sitting side by side, staring at the phone as if it's the oracle.

'Where the hell is Dan?' Melissa says. 'It's been nearly three quarters of an hour! How long does it take to walk over from Sarah's, for God's sake?'

'He'll be here,' Casey replies, looking anything but convinced.

Unable to sit, Melissa leaves her daughter watching an umpteenth Harry Potter. In the kitchen, she cleans the surfaces for the eleventh time, questions circling endlessly, maddeningly. Why couldn't Chambers just tell them what she had to tell them over the phone? Put them out of their misery? She knows why. The only possible answer is that she's coming here to charge Dan or Casey for the murder of Byrne Sharp.

Why else come in person? But then if she's charging one of them, why ask for them both to be here?

Casey appears, pale as a ghost despite her tan.

'Do you want a cup of tea?' Melissa asks.

Casey shakes her head.

'*Cold* chocolate?'

'I'm fine. I can't...'

'I know. Me neither.'

The smile they share is unbearable.

'It'll be OK,' Melissa says. 'I promise.'

The intercom buzzes, startling them both. Casey's face drains of what little colour it had. The bruises on her neck are yellowing now; her face is tinged green.

'This is it, I guess,' she says.

Melissa's feet are momentarily frozen to the spot. 'I should go down.'

Tears roll down her daughter's face. She nods. Melissa hugs her tightly. They stay like that, the only sound the cooing of the pigeons outside the window.

'My precious girl,' she whispers. 'My precious, beautiful girl.'

A last kiss on her daughter's shampoo-scented hair and she leaves her. The stairwell is dark, no windows to light it and a bust bulb on their floor. She rounds the final flight, the light from the doorway seeping in now. Her flip-flops slap on the tiles of the communal hallway. Junk leaflets pile on the ragged welcome mat. She's not sure, but she thinks she can still smell cat pee. Through the window, the silhouette of DI Chambers. The woman who has come to take her children away from her.

FIFTY-FIVE
MELISSA

Five days after

As they climb the stairs, the only sound is the tap-tap-tap of DI Chambers' footsteps behind her. The other officer, a young man who Chambers introduced but whose name Melissa didn't catch, is outside, scratching the date and time onto a parking slip. They reach the third floor. Melissa inhales deeply before pushing the door open. From below comes the brisk, athletic tread of the young cop running up the stairwell.

'Come in,' she says.

'Thank you,' Chamber replies.

'Would you like tea or coffee?'

'We're fine, thank you. We grabbed a takeout en route.'

The young cop appears at the door, a little flushed and trying not to pant. Melissa gestures for him to come inside. She is aware of how dark and small their hallway is, the fact that she doesn't have a driveway where they could have parked, how many flights of stairs they've had to climb.

In the living room, Casey is standing at the open window, her back to the sill. The sun is low, making a yellow outline of her head, casting her face in shadow. The room smells of the pizza they didn't eat. It feels wrong to do this in a room that smells of pizza.

'Please sit down,' Melissa says, indicating the sofa, hoping they don't feel the springs of the bed beneath.

The bucket chair she picked up in a charity shop a couple of years ago is the only other available seat. She never intended anyone to sit in it, least of all her; it was just meant to make the room look more homely. The shop assistant told her it was an *accent*. Even the thrift stores round here have ideas. She squeezes herself into it.

'Is your son here?' Chambers glances about as if Dan might materialise from the wall.

Melissa shakes her head. 'Sarah texted to say he was on his way, but...' But that was over an hour ago, she doesn't add. For a ten-minute walk.

'Can you call her again?'

'Sure.' Melissa calls Sarah, but she doesn't pick up. She drops her phone to her lap. Dan, she thinks. For God's sake. 'No answer,' she says. 'I'm sure he won't be long.'

She cannot look at Casey. Knows without seeing her daughter's face that she will be worried sick about Dan. It occurs to her that he might have done something rash, run away or... or what?

Chambers clears her throat. 'I was hoping to speak to you all together, but I guess if he's on his way...'

'So I'm allowed to see my brother now?' Casey asks, her voice ragged.

Chambers nods and clasps her hands. 'As I said on the phone, there's been a significant development.'

Melissa bites her thumbnail clean off. She picks it from her teeth, presses it between her thumb and forefinger. Pushes her hands between her knees. Makes herself breathe.

'We've had the forensics back from the body of Mr Sharp.

His name was actually Byrne Martin, as I told you at the station, Casey. He grew up in Scotland and attended a rather famous boarding school called Rainforth. I don't know if you know it. It's in Northumberland.'

Melissa shakes her head, mirroring her daughter.

A key rattles in the lock. A moment later, Dan calls out.

'Mum? Case?'

Oh, thank *God*.

'We're in here.' Melissa hears the note of hysteria in her voice. She tries to free herself from the chair, but she's wedged in. But her son is already at the door, eyes round as he takes in the two police officers on the sofa, his sister gripping the window ledge.

'Hi,' he says, an expression of bewilderment sinking into something darker. A sheen of sweat on his brow. 'Sorry I'm late. I didn't realise you'd be here so soon. I went for a walk.'

'DI Chambers was just telling us there's been a development,' Melissa manages, nerves utterly shredded. 'Come in, love. Just come in and listen.'

Dan almost tiptoes into the room. He and Casey exchange a glance readable only to them. What was that? Melissa wonders. Dan sits down on the floor. He crosses his legs and coughs into his hand, interlinks his fingers and rests them on his lap. Casey leaves the windowsill and goes to sit next to him. She folds her legs and positions her arms exactly like his.

They look like children.

Chambers waits a beat.

'As I was saying to your mum and sister,' she says, fixing Dan with her shrewd stare, 'there have been some significant developments concerning Mr Martin's death. By the way, we became aware of the name change through your colleague Luke Chapman.'

'Luke... Do you mean Spider?' Casey's mouth drops open.

Chambers nods. 'Mr Chapman had recognised Mr Martin earlier in the weekend. They attended the same school.'

'Oh my God.' Casey colours slightly and whispers, 'The alma mater.'

'As you know,' Chambers goes on, mostly addressing Casey, 'there was no evidence of a sexual assault. But we found saliva traces on your neck that matched Mr Martin's DNA.'

She pauses a moment, perhaps to let that sink in. Melissa feels sick. Why can't this woman just cut to the chase?

Chambers shifts in her seat, moving carefully, as if consciously slowing herself down. 'Now. As to the scene. Casey, we found blood traces matching yours on the bark of the tree adjacent to Mr Martin's body. We also found partial prints matching your flip-flops. With little nicks and gravel indentations, shoe soles can develop their own kind of fingerprint, if you like. Several silver micro-sequins were discovered in the grass near the same tree.'

'From my top,' Casey says.

'Yes. We believe so. But we can't find the top or the skirt you said you were wearing. Have you any recollection, any idea where they might be?'

Casey shakes her head. She does not look at Chambers, or at Dan, or at Melissa. At the mention of Casey's missing clothes, the pit in Melissa's stomach tightens. Shit, she thinks. This is bad.

'I must have stripped off when I ran away,' Casey says, keeping her eyes steadfastly on Chambers' face. 'Maybe someone took them, packed them up with their own stuff by mistake, or nicked them?'

'It's certainly possible. Nothing was found in the bonfire or the fire pit, the rubbish bins, the stream or any of the grounds. Nothing's washed up from the sea. No one has come forward. There were too many footprints going over to the beach to track, but I suppose it's possible you threw them in the sea or, as you say, dropped them somewhere on the site and someone took them.' DI Chambers leans forward. 'But it's all pretty consistent with what you told us.'

'OK.' Casey gives a solemn nod; Melissa stifles a sigh.

'As for the deceased.' Chambers uncrosses and recrosses her legs and turns her attention to Dan. 'Daniel,' she says. 'Some of the blood found on the victim's face matched the sample you provided at the station.'

Melissa can't look at her son. Can't look anywhere.

'Fibres found under Mr Martin's fingernails matched those of a T-shirt identical to the ones in your rucksack. Fruit of the Loom, I believe. They were among items we seized from your teepee. A match was also made between partial footprints found at the scene and your training shoes. This would fit with you finding the victim late afternoon, early evening on the Monday.'

Dan swallows. He eyes the detective with an expression so hangdog Melissa gets a glimpse of what he might look like when he's old. Her stomach folds. She braces herself for what is surely coming. When it does, she will need to intervene. There is no way she'll let them take her son or her daughter to prison.

'There were several other sets of prints,' Chambers goes on. 'But we gather this area of woodland is often used for... getting away from the crowd, so they were inconclusive.' She pauses. 'Now. I've come here in person because I wanted to speak to you all face to face before this makes it into the public arena. We have cause of death.'

Melissa holds her breath. Blood thrums in her ears. An accident. Please God, say it was an accident.

'Once we had Mr Martin's correct name, we contacted his mother and retrieved his medical notes from his childhood GP. Mr Martin suffered repeated labyrinthitis infections as a teenager, which caused episodes of vomiting and fainting and left him with recurring balance issues. I believe it's something to do with damage to the inner ear, but don't quote me on that. The balance issue can be exacerbated by stress. It was interesting talking with Mrs Martin. Her son sent her money every month, apparently, and was a great help to her after his father died. But I got the sense their relationship was strained. She said he reacted very badly to the infections, particularly when he had to forgo competitive fencing.' She glances at Dan. 'You might know he was a keen fencer?'

Dan nods. 'The YouTube channel.'

She returns the nod. 'He had several. I probably shouldn't tell you this, but the bulk of his income came not from the channels you saw but from a webcam business. He sold women, basically. Access to private broadcasts.'

'What, like, porn?' Dan blushes.

'Depends on your definition,' Chambers replies. 'He picked women up in clubs and promised them money, and indeed, they did earn money, though perhaps not as much as Mr Martin and his associates. We think he seduced these women, then took compromising photos and films and used them to blackmail his victims into working for him.'

'The photograph,' says Casey.

'Monetising,' Dan adds.

Chambers gives a brief, almost bitter little smile. 'Monetising, indeed. His business partners' – the term is laced with disdain – 'were very keen on that word. Coercion is the word I'd use. There's a whole other investigation under way. Mr Baker and Mr Crossley are helping us with our enquiries.'

Dan's blush deepens. 'Robbo and Jay,' he says, as if to himself, shaking his head and looking as nauseous as Melissa feels.

'But getting back to the cause of death.' Chambers refocuses on Casey. 'The working theory, based on your description of him holding his hands to his ears before he collapsed, is that he suffered an attack of either tinnitus or dizziness and, quite simply, fainted.'

'And hit his head,' Casey says, the merest note of hope in her tone. 'That's how he died? From hitting his head?'

'He did hit his head on a tree root,' Chambers says. 'Your ability to defend yourself might have stressed him enough to bring on an attack of vertigo and cause him to collapse; the tree root might have left him concussed; but neither the attack nor the fall was enough to kill him.'

Casey frowns. 'So how did he die?'

'The bloods taken from Mr Martin showed a cocktail of cocaine, MDMA and high levels of sildenafil. The sildenafil caused a heart attack, which is our cause of death.'

'What?' Casey's mouth is a perfect O. 'Sil... what?'

'Sildenafil. More commonly known as Viagra.'

'*Viagra?*' Dan's mouth drops open, a mirror of Casey's, of Melissa's own.

'We retrieved two baggies of pills from the pockets of Mr Martin's shorts,' Chambers says. 'One contained small red pills, which were found to be flunitrazepam. Flunitrazepam – or Rohypnol, as you guys know it – was also discovered in the can of zero-alcohol lager found adjacent to the deceased.' She turns to Casey. 'We believe this to be the can you said you shared with Mr Martin. My guess is, he pretended to drink from it and offered it to you.'

'Oh my God.' Casey pales. She is blinking hard. 'It tasted funny. But I don't drink non-alcoholic beer so I didn't... I can't... I can't take it all in.'

'So hang on,' Melissa interjects, unable to wait any longer. 'Are my children still under arrest or not?'

'No is the short answer.' Chambers turns to face her, her wide eyes lighter now, her brow clear. The room seems to fill with air. 'That's why I came. I wanted to tell you in person. There's simply no case. Your son had a minor skirmish with the deceased earlier that evening.' She turns back to Dan. 'A punch to the head can be deadly; you were right about that. But you struck him in the face, enough to cause a nosebleed and a bit of a black eye, that's all. You should have reported the body immediately, and that's a chargeable offence. But you were no doubt upset about your sister and weren't thinking straight.'

'Er...' Dan shakes his head.

'What I'm saying, Daniel, is that I'm not going there, OK? I could have you for failure to report a death, but, frankly, I don't need the paperwork, and I think you've been through enough. But do me a favour and if you ever find another one, get in touch, yes?'

Dan covers his face with his hands and exhales in one long, shuddering sigh. Melissa's eyes fill, but still she doesn't feel quite able to breathe.

Chambers turns to Casey. 'You pushed your attacker away in order to escape. Which you have every right to do. Under the circumstances, I doubt we'll be pressing charges for assault.'

A smile then, no more than a flash. Melissa is unclear whether there's been a joke.

Whatever. It's irrelevant. No one is laughing. No one is crying. No one is speaking. The information is still falling, dust motes glittering in the sun.

'So we're actually... free?' Dan asks.

Chambers nods, her smile surer this time, the smile of someone engaged in one of the nicer parts of her job. 'You've made your statements. There won't be a trial, at least not for murder. There's no one to prosecute, not for this crime anyway. Mr Martin killed himself. By accident, yes, but by his own hand. Without giving too much away, he accessed a great deal of pornography. Often those who view this kind of material need a stronger and stronger hit. The real world becomes... not enough. It's not unreasonable to hypothesise that he needed more and more... help to perform, as it were, in that real world. Hence the Viagra.'

'And violence,' Casey says. 'He needed violence.'

'All of which is found in more extreme forms of Mr Martin's chosen viewing material.' Chambers' smile is wider now. Warm. Humorous even. 'Ultimately,' she adds, 'the deceased died of excess.'

FIFTY-SIX
MELISSA

Five days after

The cops are standing to leave. The kids are hauling themselves off the floor. They are shaking their heads and... oh, their sweet, sweet smiles are spreading across their beautiful faces. Words are flying about. Chambers is promising to update them over the coming days and weeks, to return their belongings, to keep in touch. Melissa should get up, she knows. She should squeeze herself out of this too-small chair and say goodbye and thank you, thank you so much for giving my children back.

Casey is showing the cops out, her face streaked with tears. But they are tears of relief, and Melissa's own cheeks are wet. Relief. Oh God, the relief. She raises a hand to the cops. It is all she can manage. She should speak. She should say something. She should stand up. But her brain won't connect to her mouth or her feet. She clasps her hands and bows her head in a kind of prayer as the voices fade into the hallway. *Thank you. Thank you so much. Thanks again. Look after yourselves.*

The door opens. Someone laughs. The door closes: *click*.

Traffic noise from the street brushes the silence: eternal comings and goings, gear changes, the song of electric buses, chatter from the pub opposite. Melissa looks up. Through her blurry vision, her kids are outlined in the door frame. They are holding on to one another. One of them is moaning softly.

'Hey,' she calls. 'Can someone help me out of this chair?'

Laughing, Dan and Casey cross the room and pull the chair from her behind. Her legs are shaking. She holds out her arms and then they are three, huddled together, weeping for happiness, for relief, for the most awful ordeal of their lives being over.

'I can't believe it,' Casey whispers. 'He literally died from...'

'Hoisted by his own petard,' Melissa says. 'I think that's the phrase you're looking for.'

'What does that mean?' Dan says.

'I have no idea.'

They burst into more laughter, laughter caught up with tears, with emotions too complicated to name.

'I can't believe it.' The colour has returned to her daughter's face. It is the most like herself she has looked in days.

'It's a miracle,' Melissa says. 'But we still need to talk.'

'About Kevin?' Dan says.

'We need to talk about Byrne,' Casey deadpans, and the two of them collapse into delirious laughter. Gallows humour. Survivors' hysteria. It's all they can do. Until they can calm down.

Minutes later, Melissa composes herself. She wishes she didn't have to say what she has to say. But there's no way out of it. She wishes she could hang on to this moment a little longer, but Dan needs to know now. She reaches for her daughter's hand and squeezes it. Casey stops laughing; meets her eye. *Do we have to?* the look says. Melissa nods: *Yes, we do.*

'Come on,' she says softly. 'Let's do it now, then it's done.'

'Do what?' Dan says, face falling.

Melissa inhales, exhales, feels herself to be on some sort of edge. She takes another breath, reaching for his hand. Holding both her children's hands in hers, she meets her son's gaze.

'Let's sit down,' she says. 'We need to tell you the truth about what happened on Sunday night.'

FIFTY-SEVEN
CASEY

That night

Casey runs from the wood, heart pounding, searching for Spider. He'll know what to do.

She glances at the fire pit. Night bricks are keeping the fire alive till the morning. But there is no telltale glow of a cigarette end, no one sitting in the shadows. She checks her watch. It's a little after 11.30 p.m. Spider and the others must be on late shift or gone to bed. Ness will have turned in early with the baby. For God's sake, Spider's always around, always popping up, and now, just when she needs him, he's nowhere.

She needs to call the police. Tell them it was an accident.

Breath ragged, heart still hammering, she runs to her tent. There, she takes her phone from her bag. It's dead. Shit. She should have charged it before heading back out, but she was too desperate to join the fun. She finds her mobile charger, a feeling of dread gathering. She meant to recharge that yesterday, but...

Dead.

'Shit,' she half sobs into her hand. What is she going to do?

The Nokia! The stupid old pay-as-you-go Mum made her bring.

Take this, just in case. You know what iPhones are like.

Casey had protested – *Mum! You're being mental! I'm eighteen now and—*

I know. I know that, but it's just for emergencies.

Casey packed it to keep the peace, just as she had when she went to Reading two years ago. She didn't need it then, but now she dives for her rucksack, pulling everything out, finding it finally in the hidden zipped pocket at the back of the main compartment. She switches it on. It lights up. Mum said she'd put her number in it. Sure enough, there is only one contact: *Mum*.

She calls, hears her own fretful groaning, so small, so high and quiet, like an animal trapped but too weak to howl. The phone rings and rings and rings.

Just as she's about to give up, her mother answers, a groggy, 'Casey?'

Casey bursts into tears. 'Oh my God, Mum, something horrible's happened. I was with this guy. He tried to... he... I pushed him off me, but he fell and hit his head, and I think... I think I've killed him. Mum, I think he's... I mean, he is. He's dead.' She subsides into uncontrollable sobs.

After a long moment, she becomes aware that her mum isn't saying anything. She stops crying, confused. 'Mum?'

A second, two, passes before her mother speaks. When she does, her voice is so slow, so grave, it shakes Casey into silence. 'Listen to me,' she says. 'Listen hard, OK? Go to your tent and stay there. I'm getting in the car. I'm coming. I'll call you. I'll call you on this number when I'm near and you can meet me at the site entrance. It'll be two and a half hours, give or take. Don't let anyone see you. No one, do you hear me? If I'm not there, wait. If you have to call me, use the Nokia.'

'Wait, what?'

'Just do what I say. I'm hanging up now. I'm on my way.'

'Mum?' Casey says, but the line is dead.

She stares at the phone, bewildered. Mum didn't say call the police. Maybe she forgot. Or maybe she thinks Casey shouldn't call the police. If she thought she should call the police, she would have said that, wouldn't she? Oh my God, maybe Mum thinks she'll be done for murder. She makes herself breathe. Mum said stay in the tent. She said to wait two and a half hours then go to the entrance.

The next two and a half hours are the longest of her life. She curls up on her sleeping bag, crying, fretting, thoughts looping, torturing her. She's killed someone. Mum didn't say call the police because she knows Casey will go to prison. Oh my God, this is a nightmare. Her life is over. Everything she's worked for, everything she was looking forward to is gone. Should she go back and check? He might just be unconscious. Stay in the tent, Mum said. That's right, the right advice. If she goes back and Byrne is still alive, he'll kill her. Mum was weird down the phone. It was like she was on standby, lying awake, waiting for the call.

At ten to two, the little black phone rings in the tight curl of her fingers.

'Hello?'

'I'm fifteen minutes away. Meet me at the entrance. Don't let anyone see you. Are you wearing the same clothes?'

Casey nods. 'Yeah.'

'OK. Bring the Nokia and your iPhone.'

The line dies.

Snivelling with fear, Casey pulls her black hoodie over her silver top and crawls out onto the cool grass. The staff area is silent save for soft snores coming from one of the camper vans. She creeps down to the fire pit. She can hear the throb of music coming from the beach. In an hour or two, it will start getting light. It's already not quite black. She curses the white glare from the security tower.

Why didn't Mum tell her to call the police? Has she already called them?

Flip-flops in her hand, she half runs, eyes on stalks, senses on red alert. From general camping comes the low burble of chatter, the occasional shout or laugh. Fuzzy silhouettes sit about, plumes of cigarette and vape smoke. She tightens her hood, sticks to the line of trees on the far side of the path. She cannot be seen, Mum said. She should have called the police. She has already committed a terrible crime by leaving Byrne in the woods, but what else could she have done? Her heart pounds. She's killed a man and the world has no idea. It's just carrying on as if nothing has happened. A cluster of friends sit near the path, cans at their feet, tinny melodies straining from little speakers. They don't hear her. They don't see her. They don't know what she's done.

The clubhouse is closed, windows black panels, chairs tipped against the veranda tables in case of rain.

At the site entrance, only darkness and silence, not one car, not one set of headlamps to light the dark. She sits on the narrow grass bank, hugging her knees, shivering. After ten minutes or so, lights haze on the road. She turns her face to the hedge, hood pulled over her face. A car passes. It is a little after quarter past two. The sky is dark navy. Another set of headlamps, but again the car passes. She peeps from her hoodie. It's not Mum's car.

But a little way ahead, the vehicle slows, two wheels mounting the bank. It stops. The red tail lights die. The driver's-side door opens. Casey's heart pounds fit to burst. A woman gets out, black hoodie, just like her own, hood up. Black jeans. The woman turns.

Mum.

Casey stands up shakily and walks towards her. Why is she not in her own car? Wait, is that Sarah's car?

Seeing her, Mum breaks into a run. And then Casey is in her arms, sobbing. 'He—'

'You don't need to say it, love. I know. I know what he did.' Mum pulls back, holds her at arm's length. 'There'll be time to talk later, but for now, we have to focus, OK? Are those the clothes and shoes you were wearing?'

Casey nods.

'Good.' Her mum pockets the car keys, glancing about, face set in determination. 'Show me.'

Together, they jog down the rise, keeping to the trees. The site is quieter even than a few minutes ago, only the diehards still at the beach. At the bottom, a straggly group of six or seven kids appears, coming over the dunes. Casey pulls at her mother's sleeve. But she has seen them and the two of them turn and crouch against the five-bar gate in perfect synchronisation. The group passes in a storm of drunken banter, laughter too loud, too easy. They hunch trembling in the shadows. Casey wonders if Mum can hear her heart battering.

The group fades away up the rise.

After a beat, Casey tugs her mum's sleeve.

'Over here,' she whispers, leading the way along the stream. A short distance along, they jump over. Casey's footsteps slow in the thickening trees. Byrne isn't here. He's got up and gone, furious, embarrassed. He won't get away with this. She will report him for sexual assault. She will go to Miss London first thing and get her to expel him and his stupid friends for being over the age limit.

Another step and she stops dead, hand flying to her mouth. Byrne's white Adidas slider lies against the dark green floor.

'Here,' she whispers, feeling Mum close by.

His leg then, pale brown, carved with muscle, smooth like a piece of wood. He has not moved. He has not moved one centimetre. And in that moment, she knows with unshakeable certainty that he is dead and that she has killed him. An accident. A terrible, terrible accident.

But who else will see it that way?

'Oh God.' A metre from the body, she falls to her knees.

'No time,' Mum whispers, eyes flitting back and forth, as if she's downloading it all like some sort of AI. Casey has never seen her like this. 'Right,' she says after a moment, before, incredibly, surreally, pulling on a pair of the disposable gloves she wears when she chops chillis. But Casey has no time to wonder how the hell her mother could have thought of that because she is already indicating the iPhone on the ground. 'That his?'

Casey nods.

'Right, here's what we're going to do.'

FIFTY-EIGHT
MELISSA

That night

Melissa takes in the scene, throat all but closed, sweat prickling at her hairline despite the chill of the night. The boy is lying on his back, head almost touching the base of a wide tree. Fallen, hit his head. That's what it looks like. Not Casey's fault, not her fault at all, but they are where they are. And she couldn't have known where they were until she got here and saw for herself.

There's one shoe on his bare foot, one lying nearby as if he has thrown it there. His arms are out, slightly away from his sides, his palms up, as if he'd simply decided to lie down and meditate under a tree.

'I can't...' Casey whispers, face deathly pale inside her black hood.

Melissa holds up the flat of her hand. 'Stay there, baby.'

Steeling herself, she creeps towards the boy. She can hear the trickling rush of the stream, feel the soft press of her old trainers on the mossy ground. She will have to get rid of them, she thinks. Everything she's wearing. Everything Casey's wearing. The fear-induced focus is fading, the automatic pilot switching to manual, ushering in fear: she is wrong; she is making things worse; she has already made things worse; she cannot save her daughter from prison. She will go to prison herself. Casey is all but convicted of murder, Melissa now an accessory.

But when Casey called, blurting out through tears what had happened, she couldn't think past the fact that her daughter was alone, that she had been sexually assaulted and that she, Melissa, had been expecting this since the moment she waved her daughter goodbye. Not only since then. Since she went to Reading two years ago, since she started going out with her friends until late, since she insisted on walking home from hockey practice in the dark. Yes, that call was something she has planned for, planned exactly what she would do.

She should have told Casey to call the police. But she was on a mission, blind with love and terror, unstoppable. She felt herself fill with the wanton abandon of giving herself over to adrenaline, to her own wild, battering heart. Grabbing Sarah's car keys from the kitchen drawer, she succumbed to the inexorable chain of events some tiger version of herself had set in motion both minutes and years before. But now, in the dark woodland, hindsight is already whispering to her that she should've called the police herself and explained the situation. If Casey called her on what she has privately called the bat phone, it means her iPhone ran out of charge. She could have told the police that, and that she had told her daughter to stay in her tent until they got there. But a little under three hours ago, that clarity of thought was not available to her. All she knew was that a boy, this dead boy in front of her, tried to do something she cannot even name in her own thoughts to her baby girl, and that her baby girl's retaliation had resulted in disaster.

Her daughter needed her. The rest was noise.

Standing over the boy, she sees he is more of a young man, and that his eyes are open. He looks stupefied, his mouth a dark void, his eyes glassy. This is the glassy stare of the drunk and the dead, she thinks. She presses her fingers to his neck. Nothing, not a flicker of pulse. He is dead. She stands up. In seconds, she takes it all in against the thump of blood in her ears. A can of lager a little beyond, an iPhone, one leg of his shorts wrinkled up to show a thick, muscular thigh, his bright white shirt muddied, pulled to one side by the fall, a thin gold necklace on a tanned, hairless chest. His black hair is slicked back, the sides of his head close-shaved. He is quite beautiful, she thinks. A fallen angel. A god.

How the hell did he become a boy who violates girls?

She steps over him and picks up the phone, her hands already sweating in the gloves she grabbed from under the kitchen sink – a last-second brainwave. The phone is some latest model; she can tell by the size. It will be facial recognition, she thinks, not a thumbprint, not an old passcode like her own. Swallowing back terror and disgust, she holds the phone over his face. A split second later, his complexion glows white. She yelps. A corpse, a waking corpse. But it's the phone, of course it is. The light from the phone. God, this is gruesome. She's out of her depth. She should call the police. She should call them right now. Even now, it is not too late. She can call them and explain that she fucked up, that she panicked, that she's just a mum. She can explain: they were forced into this mess by this man. They were too scared to act rationally.

But the thoughts that circled all the way here loop around again and are joined by new information, the words Casey couldn't quite say as they crept down towards the woodland minutes ago. *Mum, he didn't actually, you know... I pushed him before he...*

The terrible irony of it all is that her daughter has not been sexually assaulted, not in any way that will stand up in court. And she has killed this man. They have only her word for what happened. She has a few bruises, yes, but so what? Murder or manslaughter, either way she could end up in prison.

Carefully, Melissa carries the phone over to Casey, whose arms are now wrapped tight around herself. She is crying doggedly, tears streaking down her face.

'We can't do this,' she says, dropping her arms, hands shaking as if to dry them. 'We need to call the police.'

Melissa grabs her daughter's wrist and fixes her with a stare. Her daughter's dark eyes are wide, full of terror. 'Listen to me. If you say he was going to sexually assault you, it's your word against a murder scene. Were you talking to him earlier in the evening?'

Casey nods.

'People will have seen you together. You came here with him of your own accord. There's no evidence of sexual assault. Darling, I'm sorry, but the police won't believe you. You'll go to prison, maybe not for murder, but they could still put you away. And it will ruin your life. Why should he get to do that? Why should he take away your life just because you tried to defend yourself? Just... trust me and do what I say, OK? You have to trust me.'

Chastened, Casey nods. She pulls down her hood; wipes the back of her hand across her nose.

Melissa suppresses a cry, closing her eyes momentarily. Her daughter's neck is covered in bruises, blue-black even in the dappled light from the security tower, which glints on the straps of her beautiful silver halter-neck top. How delighted she was when it arrived from ASOS, how thrilled with how good she looked in it, oblivious to the chill that had passed through Melissa even as she said the words *Wow! You look incredible*.

That should be OK, shouldn't it? To look incredible? At eighteen?

And now look at her, battered and traumatised and facing

jail for what? For looking *nice*? For wanting to do what all teenagers, all humans, are programmed to want to do?

Her daughter gasps.

'What?' Melissa says, hand flying to her chest.

'Mum,' she whispers. 'I think he took a photo of me.'

'He did?'

'I think so. Maybe we could send it to one of his friends? It could be, like, evidence?'

Melissa nods. 'OK. That could work. How would I find a photo? Tell me what to do. Don't touch the phone.'

Under Casey's instruction, Melissa accesses the camera roll. The last photo causes her eyes to fill with tears.

'He did, love,' she says, pulling up the photo: her daughter, mouth open, arms crossed over her naked chest, eyes half closed. She swipes the photo to one side, then to the other. There is only one. The others are of some beefcake lads gurning idiotically and holding up cans of Guinness.

Wait.

One of those lads is...

'Dan,' she whispers. 'Dear God.' She glances at Casey. 'Does your brother know about this?'

She shakes her head. 'He knew Byrne liked me. He tried to warn me off him. We had a row. A bad row.' She bursts into tears. 'I thought he was being a dick, but he... he knew. He knew what Byrne was really like.'

'Wait. Is this Dan's friend from the pub?'

'Yes. Byrne Sharp.'

'Right.' Melissa reels. What the hell has happened here? Her son, friends with a predator. With a *rapist*? 'It's OK,' she says, even though it's nowhere near OK. 'We have a photo at least.' She shows Casey the image.

'Oh my God,' Casey sobs. 'He said he hadn't taken one, but he had.'

'You look smashed,' Melissa says.

'I was closing my eyes because I didn't want him to take a photo. It just looks like I'm out of it.'

'No, but that's good.' An idea is forming. 'If you look like he spiked you or something, that's good. We can send this to his friends and it'll count as proof of intent.'

Casey nods. Sniffs. 'And does that mean they'll believe me?'

'I don't know. But he's dead. Forensics will probably lead to you. So if we can get ahead of that... maybe we can think of a story.'

'No.' Casey closes her eyes. 'I've just... We can't. The police will establish time of death. They'll know the message was sent after he died. Way after. It's been hours. Oh God. It's hopeless. It's completely hopeless. I should've called them.' She pushes her hands over her face and bursts into fresh sobs.

Melissa's heart feels like it's going to leave her chest. She crouches in front of her daughter. 'Hey,' she soothes. 'Come on. This is not your fault.'

'I was only trying to get him off me.'

'I know that. I know that, love.'

'Why won't the police believe me?'

'They might. But they might not. We're here now. We are where we are.'

'What are we going to do, Mum? What are we going to do?'

FIFTY-NINE
MELISSA

That night

Her daughter is staring at her, willing her to have the answers. It's unbearable. Melissa studies the phone a moment, her daughter's sobs intermittent from the forest floor. It feels like they've been here hours, but the clock on the phone tells her it's only been a few minutes.

'Right.' Her mind is whirring. Byrne. Dan's new friend from the pub. This dead man is... was her son's friend. He seduced her daughter, brought her here, then turned. As men can. What to do? What to do, what to do, what to do?

'Do you think he could've already sent this?' Casey reaches for the phone, but Melissa swerves out of her way.

'Don't touch it. Just tell me what to do.'

Casey tells her how to pull up WhatsApp. The phone is tricky; the apps fly from under her thumb. But she gets there. Finds the latest thread, the last message on that thread. 'Dear God.' She shows the message to her daughter. 'Bastard.'

On a group chat called Boiz, Byrne has sent the photograph

of her daughter with the caption: *Dan, bro, your sister is fit. Full picture tomorrow mofos.*

'What on earth...'

But the high, keening sound of her daughter's steady weeping breaks her out of her horror.

'They'll put it online,' Casey weeps. 'It'll be all over school. All my friends will see it.'

'We won't let that happen,' Melissa says. 'Jesus, who *are* these people? Is this what young men do now?' *Your sister*, she thinks. *Your sister is fit*. With a hot feeling of dread, she checks the group members, knowing already who she will find. And there he is. 'Dan,' she whispers. 'Jesus, son.'

'I think Dan thought they were OK, but when he got here, he realised what they were like. Honestly, Mum, Dan's not like those boys. He would never—'

'Well, that's for another time. For now, let's try and focus on the fact that this Byrne has done our job for us. Come on. Let's get out of here.'

Melissa walks back to the body. She crouches down, attempts to slide the phone into the lad's pocket. But the pocket has something else in it and the phone won't go in. She places it next to the body as if it has fallen there and reaches into the pocket, draws out a clear plastic bag of small pills and turns to her daughter.

'Are these the pills he tried to get you to take?'

Casey has walked nearer and is waiting a little distance away. She squints at the bag and nods. 'Yeah, that's them.'

'Bastard,' Melissa mutters. If he weren't already dead, she'd kill him herself with her bare hands.

She empties four pills into her palm. As she stands up, bones aching like she's been kicked, the can of lager on the ground catches her eye. 'Wait.'

She drops two of the pills into the can, swirls it around and replaces it on the ground. Throat all but closed, she replaces the baggie in the boy's pocket as best she can.

'Right,' she says again. 'We really need to move.'

They run, jump the stream and creep down the bank to the gate, where they stop, breathing heavily.

'What now?' Casey asks, eyes like saucers.

But despite the fact that Melissa had three hours to nail this plan down on the way here, none of it is what she was expecting and now she's floundering. *You think I always know what to do*, she wants to say. *But I don't. I just don't. I have literally no idea what I'm doing.*

'Mum?'

'Let me think.' The sky is beginning to lighten – only just, but still, Melissa feels like she might be sick. 'Can you go back to your tent without being seen?'

'Maybe. No one in staff gets up till six or seven.'

Melissa thinks. Is that the best option? The main site is silent. There, no one will be awake for a long while. From somewhere behind them, the low beat of distant music.

'The party's still going,' Casey says. 'It'll finish at, like, dawn.'

Melissa checks her watch. It is half past three. Most people are on the beach. The sun will start to come up in half an hour or so. If the teenagers don't go to bed till dawn, they'll be dead to the world until this afternoon. An idea forms.

'Case,' she says. 'Could you crash in someone else's tent?'

'I guess.'

'OK. I'm thinking that when whoever it is gets back to their tent, they'll discover you and all you have to do is say you can't remember anything.'

Her daughter looks at her like she's lost her mind.

'It's all I've got,' Melissa says helplessly. 'You say you can't remember. It'll be stronger if you're not in your own tent. The police will find that photograph on Byrne's phone. They'll interview you and you'll tell them you remember sharing the can of lager, and then... nothing. You're covered in bruises. They'll think he fell and hit his head. They'll match his head injury to the tree root. Yes! That's it.'

Casey bites her nail. Normally Melissa would tell her off, but this is not normally, not any more. 'There's a pop-up that's been empty since Friday. Someone's either left or got with... is sleeping in someone else's tent.'

'Good. We need to go there.'

Melissa follows Casey through the tents, eyes on stalks for any kids not at the party. The ground is a bomb site of cans, clothes, trainers, God knows what else. Casey stops in front of a small pale green tent. 'It's this one.'

'Get inside,' Melissa whispers. 'Sorry. Please. Just do it.'

Casey wriggles into the tent. Melissa lies on the ground and peers through the opening. There is nothing in the tent, nothing at all. Her daughter is sitting up, her head touching the top of the dome, looking at her intently.

'OK,' she begins, barely thinking now, caught in the red alert of the next seconds and minutes, knowing she has to get out of here fast. She holds out the two remaining pills. 'Do you know what these are?'

Casey nods. 'They're probably roofies. Rohypnol.'

'And that's a sedative, yes?'

'Some lads slip them in girls' drinks.'

'Jesus.' Melissa takes a breath, searching for the words to wrap around the only idea she has. Can she ask her daughter to do this? Can she?

'OK,' she says. 'Once I've gone, you're going to wait a while, an hour or two. Then you're going to take one of these pills, OK?' Even as the words leave her, she can barely believe what she's suggesting. 'It'll just make you drowsy or send you to sleep.

When you wake up, go and find help. OK? Go and find help and say you can remember going to the woods with Byrne, that he came on to you and you can't remember anything after that. You woke up in this tent and you've no idea how you got there. OK? Someone will call the police. They'll do the rest. Give me your clothes. I'll dispose of them and the Nokia. Keep your iPhone. It ran out of battery, so that'll check out. Keep your pants on.'

'Mum! I can't go looking for help in just my pants!'

'OK, OK. I'll find something. You can put it on and say you must have found it but you can't remember. Does that work? When the police check you out, they'll find traces of sedative in your blood. They'll assume you've been spiked. You got away before it kicked in. The less you say the better.'

'I guess.' Casey bursts into tears. 'Don't go. Please.'

Melissa fights not to cry. 'I have to, my love. I have to leave now before anyone wakes up. I have to get home, and I have to go to work. Everything has to be normal. No one can know I was here. You can do this. You're one of the strongest people I know. And you're not going to prison for his crimes. OK, love?'

Her daughter nods, but there are tears streaming down her face, and as she starts to peel off her clothes, it is all Melissa can do not to cry out at the sight of the black bruises up her arms, superficial markings of deeper damage to be dealt with later.

While Casey carries on undressing, Melissa runs lightly back through the war zone. There are clothes everywhere, but nothing that looks wearable. Her heart beats hard and fast. She can't leave her daughter naked in a tent. There's a disposable barbecue on the ground, a huddle of camping chairs around it. On the back of one, a dark-coloured fleece.

'Oh, thank God,' she whispers, almost weeping when she grabs it and discovers it is dry. She races back to her daughter, who is shivering and weeping, arms locked around herself.

'Here.' She hands Casey the fleece and takes her clothes.

'Just do exactly what I said. You don't remember anything, nothing at all, after going into the woods. They'll take you to hospital. They might want to examine you. Just agree to everything. You have nothing to hide, OK? They'll make the link, but let them come up with the theory. You've done nothing wrong, my love. Nothing. We'll get through this. I love you.'

SIXTY

DAN

Five days after

Dan stares at his mum and Casey, blood pulsing in his head. The two of them stare back, waiting for him to speak. They rigged a crime scene. His mother and his sister rigged a fucking crime scene. It's... it's...

'*Why?*' he asks eventually.

'In hindsight,' Mum says, 'it was a stupid thing to do. But if we hadn't, I don't see how—'

Dan feels anger bubbling up inside him. 'But it was... What the hell were you thinking? You could *both* have gone to prison!'

Mum can't meet his eye. 'There's no record of me being there,' she says. 'You heard the detective – the footprints were too jumbled to read. Besides, I threw my trainers away. I threw them away with the clothes and the Nokia. There's no CCTV on the lane—'

'How did you know? Seriously, Mum.'

'I took Sarah's car.'

'Oh, so Sarah could've gone down for it?'

'Of course not! She was home with Alex. They're not going to check every car that came down the M3. And anyway, why are we talking about this? It's over. We just wanted you to know because we're family. We don't have secrets.' Mum has started to cry, and now he feels bad. 'I didn't know Casey would genuinely not remember a thing. I didn't know you'd hit Byrne or that you'd discover him and not report it. I didn't realise we wouldn't be able to talk to one another. But I would never have let either of you go to prison. If they'd charged either of you, I was going to tell them the truth. Of course I was.'

Dan plunges his face into his hands. 'Jesus.'

Beside him, his mother sniffs. Guilt leaks into him. She's not the only one who has been stupid. He has done things he never thought he'd do. Ever. He fell for Byrne Sharp and all his lifestyle bullshit, ignored the toxic heart of it because he had nothing else. Byrne Sharp has made them all stupid. He has made them all victims.

'I'm sorry,' he says. 'I'm just trying to get my head round it, that's all.' He turns to glance at his sister and sees that she's crying too. 'Sorry, Case.'

His sister's eyes are so intense, he takes refuge once again in his hands.

'It was an accident,' she says, her voice thick. 'I thought I'd killed him. We both did. And the police don't always believe victims of...'

'You think you know what you're going to do if something like this happens,' Mum says, so quietly he barely hears her. 'God knows, I've planned it a million times in my head, but...'

'I thought I'd hit him too hard,' Dan says. 'I thought I'd killed him. You let me think it was me.' But even as he says this, he knows it's not true. His mum told him it wasn't him; it was his own paranoia that did for him, his own failure to report the body that tied him in guilty knots. At the hospital, it was too risky to talk. And once they were separated, there was no way Casey or Mum could have told him the truth.

'I didn't know the police would split us up,' Mum says. 'I didn't know that Riley woman would be stuck to us like bloody Velcro.'

'I called her a barnacle.' Despite it all, a smile twitches at his lips. 'I did hit him hard. I hit him so hard I hurt my hand. And then Casey. We'd practised those self-defence moves. I thought maybe we'd *both*—'

'Dan,' Mum says. He feels her hand warm on his back. 'It's over, love.'

'I can't believe I let him influence me like that,' he says, near to tears himself now. 'But he was so... and I just felt like such a los—'

'You're not a loser,' Casey interrupts, almost aggressively. 'People who see the world like that are dicks. And anyway, he's the loser, not you. I know he's dead, so I probably shouldn't say it, but he was horrible. I wish the Byrne Sharps of this world weren't able to brainwash boys like they do with their toxic bullshit.'

'It's not all boys,' he says, hearing how frail it sounds.

'I never said it was. But the trouble is, how do we know the nice guy isn't suddenly going to switch to the bad guy? How do we ever let ourselves go? How do we ever feel safe?'

Sadness fills him. 'I'm sorry it's like that. Sometimes I think we should bring back all that gentleman bullshit. At least that's better than this.'

'I think we could all be gentlemen,' Mum says. 'Gentlepeople. To one another, to everyone, all the time. Non-gendered chivalry for all.'

'I'm sorry we argued,' Casey says, ignoring Mum's bonkers manifesto. Her arm snakes around Dan's shoulders. 'I should've listened to you.'

'No, I was being a dick. I was trying to be Dad or whatever. Trust me, I get how annoying that was.'

'If you were being like Dad,' Casey says quietly, 'you wouldn't have been there at all.'

SIXTY-ONE
MELISSA

Two months later

Melissa is in Sarah's huge glossy kitchen. It's a late-summer day, the sun mellow and still warm through the sliding patio doors. The aroma of coffee fills the air as Sarah works her magic on the slick chrome Gaggia.

Dan has gone to hang out at the open-air pool with Rory, who is back from his travels. Casey has gone into London with a new pal called Olive, with whom she celebrated her A-level results. Olive is off to York Uni too, and if pressed, Melissa would admit to having listened outside Casey's bedroom door to the two of them making excited plans together. Casey's bruises are gone. She's stopped taking ten showers a day. But the sound of her giggling again has been the sweetest sign of her daughter's recovery. Sometimes they talk about what happened, but mostly these days they don't. *I won't let him define me* is Casey's warrior cry. *My kids are strong* is Melissa's. Casey has even managed to wangle Dan a job at the café where she's working for the summer. Dan likes that he's never bored and that he has actual customers to chat to. Casey likes the free hazelnut iced latte she's allowed at the end of each shift.

Speaking of which, right now Sarah is placing a latte before her on the marble breakfast bar.

'Sorry it looks more like a knob than a fern,' she says. 'My latte art isn't quite up to standard, although you look like you need it too much to care.'

'A knob or a coffee?'

'Both maybe.'

'Thanks a bunch.'

They laugh.

'I meant you're a fragile beauty this morning,' Sarah says. 'Catherine Deneuve with a hangover.'

She turns back to the machine. A whir as it grinds a fresh set of beans, a long groan as thick chocolate-coloured espresso trickles from twin jets, a roar as the steamer rod froths bog-standard semi-skimmed milk into the lofty heights of micro-foam.

'Remember when Nescafé was sophistication itself?' Sarah asks, sitting opposite Melissa on a high bar stool.

'A Nescafé and a Silk Cut and we thought we were Joan Collins, didn't we?'

They laugh. Melissa takes in the airy room, its leather corner sofa, the pristine paintwork, the chic, quirky art on the walls. It is a treat to come to Sarah's, a place she is always welcome, where someone always looks after her. Sarah is that someone, has been for years. There's a lovely smell in here too, beneath the coffee, something like vanilla or sugar or caramel, Melissa's not sure. Some expensive scented candle probably.

'So,' Sarah says, giving her a look. 'Funny thing I've been meaning to ask you. Funny two things actually.'

'Oh?' Melissa sips her coffee; tries to hold Sarah's gaze but fails.

'Don't tell me if you don't want to, OK?'

'Sounds ominous.' Melissa's gut flips.

'So I can never remember where I've parked,' Sarah begins. Melissa's stomach clenches. 'But the week after Casey was... assaulted...' She frowns into her coffee. 'It was weird because when I came to use the car, I had a sense it'd been moved. And when I started the engine, the petrol tank was fuller than it'd been the last time I'd driven it. I know I'm menopausal, but that's weird, isn't it?'

'Maybe you forgot you filled it up?'

'And my name's Tallulah Cherry.' Sarah stares right at her. Melissa can feel the heat of her blue eyes. Her best friend, this woman who has been solid and good and kind, who has never wavered.

'Hey,' Sarah says, her voice full of apology. 'I'm sorry, I didn't mean to... I don't mind you borrowing the car, you know that. It's not about that. Forget I said anything. I just thought, a bit of time's passed now and I... Look, forget it.'

Melissa feels her eyes fill.

'I did borrow it,' she says. 'I should've told you. I'm sorry.'

'Hey.' Sarah reaches for her hand and holds it. 'Forget it. Seriously. I only brought it up because it's funny. You didn't need to fill it up, you div.'

'Casey called me,' Melissa almost interrupts, the need to share overwhelming her now. If she's going to tell anyone, it will be Sarah, only Sarah. 'That night,' she says. 'She called me in a state.'

'Casey called you on the Sunday? Oh my God. I thought she was unconscious?'

Melissa meets her friend's gaze. Neither of them speak.

'Oh my God,' Sarah says again slowly. 'You drove to Dorset? I thought... No, hang on. You took your car.'

'I took my car on the Monday. On Sunday night, I took yours.'

Sarah is, for once, dumbstruck.

'I didn't want the police to trace my number plate,' Melissa says after a moment. 'If it came to that. I had it all planned, you see. Case had a cheap pay-as-you-go phone for emergencies. I bought it for her when she went to Reading.'

Sarah nods. 'I remember, yeah.'

'I made her take it with her to Summer Camp. She thought I was nuts, but you know what kids are like. They never charge their phones, so you give them a charger and they never charge that either.' Melissa laughs mirthlessly and sips her coffee. 'I put my number in the contacts. Except it wasn't my iPhone; it was the number for an old Nokia I had kicking about. I call it my bat phone, but I suppose they call them burner phones now, don't they?'

'They do if they're drug dealers.' Sarah looks aghast.

'I just thought, if I ever had to go to her, you know? If I needed to not be traced or my iPhone didn't have enough charge. I... I was paranoid. I'm sorry I took your car.'

'You know you don't need to apologise. For emergencies, we said, and if that's not an emergency, then I don't know what is. For God's sake, I can't believe you did all that on your own. And don't tell me anything else if you don't want to. I shouldn't have mentioned it.'

'You've every right to mention it. I didn't tell you because I didn't know how. And I didn't want to make you feel compromised in any way.'

Sarah waves her hand. 'If you want to lighten the load, then tell me. It might help. But honestly, you don't owe me an explanation. If one morning you found me sleeping on your couch, you wouldn't mind, would you?'

'Well, it might be weird given that's where I sleep.'

Sarah sighs. 'Bad example.'

They share a smile.

'But thank you,' Melissa says after a moment. Inhales, then exhales a long, shaky breath. And tells her friend the whole messed-up rest of it.

By the time she's finished, they are on their second latte. Decaf.

'Wow,' Sarah says. 'Jesus.'

Melissa braces herself for what comes next, what she has known would come next if and when she decided to tell her friend the truth.

'I don't think I'd have reacted so quickly,' Sarah says. 'I don't think I could have. And you had it all so meticulously planned out.'

'I'd rehearsed it.'

'*What?*'

Melissa sighs. 'Sometimes I think I've been rehearsing it since the day she was born. Every time she goes out, every time she has to get the bus home. Every day really. I'd lie awake at night and rehearse what I'd do if... I'd go through every scenario I could think of. Little variations. Of course, nothing bad happened at Reading. Nothing bad has happened on any of her nights out apart from the odd catcall. And actually, when something did happen, what I'd imagined was worse, in the end. And what happened was worse than I'd imagined, in a whole different way. I never thought about a death. So in a strange way, when Casey called, I was expecting some version of what I'd already envisaged. I knew before I answered, not just because she was calling my old phone, but because I knew' – she taps her chest – 'in here. Isn't that terrible?'

Looking up and seeing no judgement in her friend's eyes, she goes on, unable to stop now she's started. 'It was like I was reading from a script. Something off the TV where the woman is a school secretary but she's also an undercover agent, you know? I'd always planned to take your car. From the moment we swapped keys. I'd imagined leaving my iPhone in your house so I could claim I'd been with you, but in the end, I just left it at mine.'

'Whoa.' Sarah shakes her head in what looks like wonder.

'I knew they wouldn't believe her if she went off with some lad and things took a turn. At least, I worried they wouldn't. And when I got there and she told me he hadn't actually… well, you know he hadn't… I just thought, she'll go down for this. She'll go to prison. That's all I could think about. And I couldn't let that happen. So we did what we did, and I thought, if push comes to shove, I'll say it was me. I almost did. When they both got arrested, I almost did. Thank God I didn't. Thank God. It was wrong, I know that, but I just… I'm a mum, you know? I'm her mum.'

For a moment, neither of them speaks, until Sarah asks: 'Is this what it's like being the mother of a girl?'

'It is for me. I don't know how we got here. But it seems worse now than when we were young. You've got kids in clubs threatening gang rape, girls being stabbed, porn on tap, boys who want women who look like blow-up dolls, girls shaving off all their body hair so they look pre-pubescent – well, like the women in the porn, I suppose. This guy, this Byrne guy, tried to choke her. Choking's big apparently. Did I tell you that?'

'You did.'

'He was rich because he was coercing women, not because he was teaching them self-defence. Imagine using that for your cover. I don't know. I don't know where it begins and ends, and it's terrifying. It's totally terrifying. I've always tried to talk to Dan about the internet, about pornography, sex, about all of it. And Rory's a lovely kid, isn't he? And your Alex is a lovely man. I know loads of lovely, kind, gentle men.'

'They're good lads,' Sarah says. 'And yes, there are fabulous men in the world. It's terrible for them too. I think it's pretty terrifying for young men, in a different way.'

'It is. The world's telling them they're not good enough. They can't get jobs, can't afford houses. And these internet preachers are out there telling them that women are to be bullied and choked and raped, and that's frightening, isn't it?

No wonder I'm paranoid.' Melissa can't stop the tears now. 'I'm sorry,' she says. 'I think it's the relief. I wanted to tell you, I did. I just didn't know how.'

'Oh, my darling.' Sarah slides off her stool and comes around the bar to pull her into a hug. 'Try not to upset yourself. She's safe. It's over. It's over now. Let's close the door on it, eh?'

They stay like that a moment.

'You had it all prepared,' she says, almost wistfully. She kisses Melissa on the head, but the silence thickens until it is heavy, sticky, loaded. 'It happened to you,' she whispers quietly into Melissa's hair. 'It happened to you, didn't it?'

And there it is, the question. It feels like an open door. It feels like all she has to do is step inside. And Sarah's house is always warm and safe. There is always someone to look after her here.

'It did,' she says. 'A long time ago now.'

SIXTY-TWO
SPIDER

That night

Spider was picking litter when he saw him. Byrne Martin. Large as life. And immediately came the familiar sensation: his insides a burning lift, cables cut, plummeting through the length of him. Body ablaze with old terror.

He backed behind a tree, watched the superior sneer he remembered so well, the same preening energy, even the same coterie of chimps loping in his wake. Byrne Martin. Here, at a kids' summer camp. Here, where he could be king, no doubt. Once a bully...

Spider found himself short of breath. He leaned forward, hand pressed against his chest. Rested the litter picker against the tree a second, pushing his palms against his knees. It was disappointing to find himself filled with fear like this after so long. How long had Byrne Martin been coming here? Must've only been the last two or three years or Spider would've seen him before. But what could Martin do to him now? He wouldn't even recognise him. Wouldn't even see him. But he didn't need to. For Spider, it was enough that he was here, enough to spark the memories he had tried to lay away for so long: his head in the toilet bowl full of piss, his rucksack being thrown around the classroom, the football pushed from the crook of his arm as he walked the school corridor, passed between Martin and his friends while he, Luke Chapman as he was then, had not the sense to leave them to their game and had instead run about, arms up and grasping uselessly, pleading and whining for them to please give him back his ball. He stopped playing after that.

He'd thought it was gone for good, but turns out humiliation was a piece of grit in his soul. Funny, when a person has reduced you to the thinnest scrap, when they've taken everything you thought was OK about yourself and made it seem pathetic and laughable, when you've had to pack your bag and escape in the dark of night, just to get somewhere you were sure you'd never have to see them again, when you've done all that, you think in time you'll rebuild yourself. You think in time you'll recover.

And he did, to a degree. He rebuilt his life, a new version of Luke Chapman, a new name. Spiders spin webs, and he spun his, even if that meant disappointing the old parents, rejecting them and all the dreams they had for their young Luke – football star, doctor, maybe even a surgeon one day – turning his back and pretty much running away to join the circus. Maybe he wouldn't do that if he had his time again. But that's what he did. *Tempus fugit.* Time flies, indeed it does, but it doesn't go back.

And there he was, in the world he found or the world that found him. *Hey diddly dee, a traveller's life for me.* Ness, baby Aura, the tribe who welcomed him in, let him eat with them, work with them, smoke with them. Friends who became family, though he wrote cards to his mum and dad once a month, called in when he could, tried not to see the sadness in their eyes. He wanted to tell them don't worry, that he'd found a safe haven, happiness, even if it felt fragile sometimes.

The years passed. Time healed. And like that, one day, he was whole again. Ink on his skin. Dirt under his fingernails. Woodsmoke in his hair. A life lived under the radar. But he was fine and dandy. This he told himself.

But then out of the blue: him. A bully boy become man, a fighting cock whose bulging muscles and bright clothes shouted that same superiority. Rainforth fencing captain, destined for Olympic glory, but here instead, in a campsite closed to all but teenagers. There should have been some shallow satisfaction for old Spider as he saw Byrne Martin striding down the path with his henchmen, trying to chat up teenagers, but he was too busy with the notion that the only reason he'd stayed calm all these years was, yes, a functioning addiction to roll-up cigarettes lined with a little something for the nerves, but mainly because he just hadn't been unlucky enough to see that particular person in a very long time. And now he had. And look at him, shaking behind a tree, sweating, failing even to breathe.

He tried to warn her. Casey. CC. Copied-In. A good kid, the best. Kind, hard-working, a thinker. But he was too opaque, as usual. She didn't catch the drift of his drift. Because didn't he then see her chatting to that monster, right outside the gate. *Run*, he wanted to shout. Leopards are not known for changing their spots, and he could see, just by the tilt of the man's head, the fakery in his charms, the tinkle of her laughter, that she was falling for him. He remembered the local woman who came to the school to complain that her daughter had been taken advantage of by Rainforth boys. A big assembly on it, they had. Headmaster in a right old lather. Detention for everyone unless the culprit came forward. Spider knew it was Martin and his monkeys, everyone did. But nothing ever stuck to greasy frauds like him, the sneering pricks that pick on those weaker than themselves just for fun.

And when he took CC's hand and led her into the woodland, Spider followed. He had to. He dug out his pocket knife and tracked them into the dell. Once more he hid behind a tree, but this time he wasn't shaking. He was ready, listening out for the scuffle that inevitably came, the cries of protest, the sickening thud. Fearing the worst, he stepped out from his cover, knife aloft, but then she came streaking past in a blur of silver, crying uncontrollably, panic electric in her slipstream. Too fast for him to stop her. She was out of there like a whippet. He didn't know what to do. Go after her or find Martin. Martin, who had not followed her out. Martin, who was waiting in the trees.

Spider decided: confront him, finally.

Further into the trees, there he was, lying on the ground. Spider crept closer, not daring to put the knife away while he took in the scene. Martin was moaning, groggy. A can of lager on the ground by his side. One of those big old idiot iPhones too, as if it had been knocked out of his hand. He gave an incoherent shout. Spider nearly jumped out of his skin.

And then he was standing over his former nemesis. One swift kick in the head and he could've finished him forever. The world would be better without him, of that he had no doubt.

But no. Not right to take a life, is it? Even one like this. A quick search offered up a packet of pills in his shorts pocket. And boy, did it all fall into place then. It all falls into place in the end. That girl he saw leaving on Friday, tears streaking down her face, the rumours spreading like the proverbial wildfire in her wake: someone had roofied her drink; she'd woken up not knowing what had happened to her; she'd been raped; she hadn't; she'd been beaten; she'd been threatened; he'd filmed her; he'd taken her photo; he'd tried to blackmail her. Different versions of the same old-as-time story. A bully using his strength over someone smaller. A brute. Rohypnol, was it, the pills in that little clear plastic bag? Some kind of sedative for sure.

So that was his game. Him and his sycophantic orang-utans.

Sedating women. Overpowering them for fun, as if they were less than human, less than animal, nothing.

Spider's eyes flicked then to the abandoned can, back to the pills, back to the can. From his back pocket, he dug out a pair of the hygiene gloves he used when he cleaned the toilet block. Pulled them on with a snap. He emptied out three or four of the little pills from the baggie, blue in the patchy light.

Another groan from the monster, a failed attempt to sit up.

'Bastard,' Spider muttered, still standing over him. 'Reckon you can sleep a bit longer. That way you can't go bothering anyone else tonight. Let's see how you like waking up not knowing how you got here or what you've done or had done to you.'

He reached over and grabbed the can. Martin held his head and groaned again.

'It's OK, mate,' Spider said, soothing 'You've hit your head, but you're OK. Here. Couple of paracetamols.'

With the gentle care of a nurse, he lifted Martin's head; dropped the pills onto his big pink tongue. *Wash them down with the lager, that's right, me dear. Drink up.* He coughed a bit, but the drugs sailed down like sweets. 'That's it. Something to help you sleep. You'll feel better in the morning.'

He laid Martin's head gently back down on the tree root. Replaced the baggie in his shorts pocket. Positioned the can exactly where it had been. Alcohol-free. Funny choice. But it'd be something to do with perfection, wouldn't it? He was always in the school gym pumping iron, even back then. All the better to beat up lesser physical specimens. And, of course, to impress the girls.

Spider stood back. His old school bully looked so peaceful there on the log, like butter wouldn't melt. Pretty soon, the drugs would work their magic. In the morning, Spider would be looking to see the fear in his eyes. Maybe he'd let Miss London know there were over-age men here who should be expelled as a matter of urgency. Yes, he'd do that.

'Good night, monster,' he whispered and blew a sarcastic kiss. 'Sweet dreams.'

Back at the staff camping, he threw the gloves into the embers of the fire pit; watched them flail and dance into blackened strips. Wondered if he should check on CC. But he could see the light on in her tent and didn't want to scare her. She'd had a close shave this night. She'd learn from it, he hoped, and vowed to watch over her at least for the rest of the summer.

But for now, she could sleep. For now, at least, she was safe.

A LETTER FROM S. E. LYNES

Dear Reader,

Thank you so much for reading this book. If you've read my others, welcome back! If this is your first, hello! If you'd like to be the first to hear about my new releases, you can sign up to my newsletter using the link below. Your email address will never be shared, and you can unsubscribe at any time.

www.bookouture.com/se-lynes

I've wanted to address the topic of toxic masculinity for a while now but couldn't quite find the right story. And my job, as I see it, is not to write opinion pieces or provide answers but to explore the things that trouble me and that I think trouble others through characters and drama. Finally, a situation came to me: a young girl who wakes up in an abandoned tent at some sort of youth gathering with no idea how she got there; a mother who gets the call every mother dreads. As I built the idea up and found she had a brother, I felt the narrative become suddenly more complex and got that tingly feeling all authors get when they know the idea has legs. I knew this story would allow me to dig into this complex issue within the framework of a psychological suspense novel while hopefully keeping my readers turning the pages.

When *Adolescence* appeared on our screens recently, I had

handed in my first draft and was fascinated to see how that TV drama dealt with this topic. The programme took a very different approach, exploring the story of a barely teenage boy who has been radicalised by the online manosphere and how other elements in his life conspired to make him vulnerable to its messaging. It was brilliant and chilling and provoked real reaction and possibly even change.

In *Every Mother's Nightmare*, toxic masculinity is made flesh in Byrne Sharp and his cronies, the victims of its fallout a teenage girl, a young man and their mother. The internet has the power to walk into our lives just as Byrne Sharp walks into Dan's. It presents a curated facade every bit as glamorous as a living person who hides their true motivations from view. From bumper-sticker philosophies, nutrition and beauty tips to must-have fashions and lifestyle advice, the internet appears to have all the answers. And Byrne appears to have all the answers for Dan.

The internet and smartphones are of course never far away. Casey constantly checks her WhatsApp and feels left out and deflated; Dan scrolls through Instagram and feels even more inadequate as he struggles to start his life post-uni. Without a private income or financial help from his parents, or contacts or any kind of male mentor figure in his life, it is hard for him to figure out how to get out of his dead-end minimum-wage job. As such, he is vulnerable to toxic messaging in the form of Byrne Sharp. In my research, I found that at first internet gurus seem very positive, promoting fitness, pride in oneself, the willingness to be proactive and work hard for success. From there it goes downhill, but by then its followers are often in too deep to turn back.

For Casey, Byrne represents a breath of fresh air, someone wiser and more confident than the boys her age, but his laid-back approach and interest in her as a person are revealed to be nothing more than the moves of a manipulator whose motivations are deeply transactional.

Meanwhile, faced with almost sole responsibility for navigating the complicated waters of parenting young adults, Melissa battles not to be overprotective, not to fall into bitter resentment, not to fail her kids, all the while harbouring the deepest fears and escape-room-style plans of a survivor of sexual violence. There is perhaps something in the fact that she resorts to old, pre-smartphone technologies in order to come to her daughter's rescue.

I hope you enjoyed reading about Melissa, Dan and Casey. For me, they are good people who do stupid things for valid reasons but who ultimately come through it a little wiser. There was I think a terrible irony in the fact that Casey was never sexually assaulted, that she and Melissa felt more vulnerable, not less, in the face of a violence that was somehow not enough. When Byrne takes a photo without consent, when he rushes her and tries to choke her, it is not the first time in just a few days that she has been treated badly but the third – the verbal abuse in the bar, the attack by Robbo and then finally by Byrne. Maybe there's a question here – what is too much? At what point do we have a right to be taken seriously and to defend ourselves?

Enough already. I for one am glad Melissa and her kids escaped criminal conviction, and I wish them all the best!

If you enjoyed the book, I'd be over the moon if you left me a review on Amazon or Goodreads. If you recommended it to your friends, bought it as a gift or suggested it for your book club, even better! Reviews, word-of-mouth recommendations and of course copies sold really help authors to keep writing. And if you want to contact me on Instagram or Facebook, I'd be delighted to hear from you and answer any questions you might have for me. My links are on the next page.

Thanks again. By the time you read this, I'll be writing the next one and thinking of you and about how I can make you keep turning the pages!

Affectionately yours,

Susie

                   facebook.com/Lynesauthor
                   instagram.com/selynesauthor

BOOK CLUB QUESTIONS

1. How relatable is the title? In terms of what parents of young adult women worry about, is sexual violence the top of the list?
2. Melissa's paranoia is founded on her own historic experience of sexual violence and is what makes her prepare so meticulously for the worst. Are women more or less safe now than they used to be, in your opinion, and why do you think that is?
3. Dan is often confused about whether or not Byrne's use of sexist language matches his real views. How much do words matter? In making certain terms unacceptable, do we encourage people to think about the implications of those terms and change points of view?
4. How do we tackle the growing problem of the manosphere and its influence on young boys?
5. Were you surprised by the final reveal, and what do you think about Melissa's choice?
6. Who do you think is ultimately to blame for Byrne's death?

ACKNOWLEDGEMENTS

First thanks, as ever, go to my editor, Ruth Tross, who is one huge reason I enjoy what I do and don't melt into a puddle of angst. Thank you as always for your wisdom, kindness and readiness to thrash things out, and for your little notes in the margins, which always keep me going in the long editing hours when my Fitbit has started to wonder if I've died. Thanks, again as ever, to my agent, Veronique Baxter, the third point of stability in this power throuple and much-appreciated enthusiast when it comes to the literary output of S.E. Lynes.

Thanks to all the team at Bookouture. Thanks for keeping me from looking like a twit to my amazing copy-editor, Jane Selley, and proofreader, Laura Kincaid.

Thanks to every single one of my readers and bloggers, who have become too numerous to name but who know who they are. Thank you for your support over so many books. I actually can't believe you are still with me when there are so many fabulous authors and books to choose from. A huge shout-out to the Facebook book clubs who provide forums for reviews, discussions and spaces for readers to communicate with writers and vice versa. I appreciate you all so much.

Thank you to my author colleagues and friends who offer constant friendship and support, often over WhatsApp and occasionally IRL. The friendships that have come through being published are the most wonderful and unexpected consequence of sitting alone in a room inventing people and events for a living.

Thanks to my other half, Paul, who keeps me grounded with chat about how our heating system is working and how long it took to put the bins out. Thanks to my kids, who make me proud every day and without whom I could not have written this book. Thanks to my dad, for reading only my books and never straying to a single other author – LOL. And finally thanks as always to my first reader and loyal fan, Mum.

PUBLISHING TEAM

Turning a manuscript into a book requires the efforts of many people. The publishing team at Bookouture would like to acknowledge everyone who contributed to this publication.

Audio
Alba Proko
Sinead O'Connor
Melissa Tran

Commercial
Lauren Morrissette
Hannah Richmond
Imogen Allport

Contracts
Peta Nightingale

Cover design
Aaron Munday

Data and analysis
Mark Alder
Mohamed Bussuri

Editorial
Ruth Tross
Sinead O'Connor

Copyeditor
Jane Selley

Proofreader
Laura Kincaid

Marketing
Alex Crow
Melanie Price
Occy Carr
Cíara Rosney
Martyna Młynarska

Operations and distribution
Marina Valles
Stephanie Straub
Joe Morris

Production
Hannah Snetsinger
Mandy Kullar
Nadia Michael
Ria Clare

Publicity
Kim Nash
Noelle Holten
Jess Readett
Sarah Hardy

RAISING READERS
Books Build Bright Futures

Dear Reader,

We'd love your attention for one more page to tell you about the crisis in children's reading, and what we can all do.

Studies have shown that reading for fun is the **single biggest predictor of a child's future success** – more than family circumstance, parents' educational background or income. It improves academic results, mental health, wealth, communication skills, and ambition.

The number of children reading for fun is in rapid decline. Young people have a lot of competition for their time, and a worryingly high number do not have a single book at home.

Our business works extensively with schools, libraries and literacy charities, but here are some ways we can all raise more readers:

- Reading to children for just 10 minutes a day makes a difference
- Don't give up if children aren't regular readers – there will be books for them!

- Visit bookshops and libraries to get recommendations
- Encourage them to listen to audiobooks
- Support school libraries
- Give books as gifts

Thank you for reading: there's a lot more information about how to encourage children to read on our website.

www.JoinRaisingReaders.com